The Longest Drought Ever

The Longest Drought Ever

Keith L. Bell

Library of Congress Control Number: 2015918385
ISBN: Hardcover   978-1-5035-8900-1
                 Softcover   978-1-5035-8899-8
                 eBook   978-1-5035-8898-1

Printed in the United States of America by BookMasters, Inc
Ashland OH
January 2015

Rev. date: 12/04/2015

To order additional copies of this book, contact:
Xlibris
1-888-795-4274
www.Xlibris.com
Orders@Xlibris.com
720590

"If I Could"

If I could do anything in the world once, just one time, I would probably take a trip to Europe to visit Romania or to Italy to check out the old Roman Empire of Rome. Yeah, that sounds like royalty. But there must be something more superior than visiting Europe and Italy right? So . . .

If I could do anything in the world once, just one time, I would probably kick it with the president of the United States of America or instead of landing on the moon I'll land on the sun. But I couldn't do that because I'll burn to death before I got there so I'll shoot for the stars and become star struck, literally. Now that's extraordinary! But still, there must be something even more extravagant than that, so . . .

If I could do anything in the world once, just one time, I would probably climb the highest mountain ever or scuba dive to the deepest part of the sea to see what's really down there or pass through the Bermuda Circle to see what's really on the other side. Now that's adventurous! But still there must be something more promising, so . . .

If I could do anything in the world once, just one time, I would probably end all poverty and feed every hungry stomach in the world. Or I would probably rewind the hands of time and go back a million years to when God first created the Heavens and Earth and help Him bring the universe into existences. Yeah now that's promising and probably what I'll do!!

But nothing I said in this poem was definite. Everything had **"probably"** in front of it. So if I could **"definitely"** do anything in this world once, just one time, I would bring my mother back. If it was only for a day, an hour, a minute I would bring my mother back. If it was only to hug, hold and kiss her I would bring my mother back. If it was to only say the things that was left unsaid or to do the things that was left undone I would bring my mother back. Yeah that's exactly what I'll do. "If I could" I'll bring my mother back . . .

—Keith L. Bell

Prologue

What's up, world? I'm Keon Campbell better known as Kilo to the streets of the underworld in Youngstown, Ohio. I grew up fatherless just like 85 percent of the other black kids that grow up in the hood. And without a father figure teaching me how to take on responsibilities and be a man, I turned to the streets unknowingly for guidance. At thirteen my "boyhood" journey began tearing the hood up with my three closest friends: Slim, Fresh, and Quick. My nigga Slim government name Issac Cook is what we (hood niggas) like to call a trill ass nigga. He kind of put you in the mind of the late New Orleans rapper Soulja Slim. My nigga is way past loyal. Some people think he got his name trying to impersonate the rapper but actually got his name because of his height and weight. Slim stands five feet nine inches and weighs 165 pounds, fresh out the shower soaking wet with bricks around his ankles. And just like me, he grew up fatherless.

Now my nigga Fresh, born Marshawn Morgan, is a real flashy flamboyant ass nigga. A real live wire that loves to be the center of attention anytime we go out. Fresh's gift from God, as he says, "is to attract the baddest bitches created." And he has no problem doing just that with his thugged-out, pretty-boy looks. Fresh stands about five feet seven inches and weighs 190 pounds straight muscle. Thanks to his fitness trainer, Fresh could easily pass for an NFL running back. I can hear my nigga now: "Dreads hanging, a mouth full of gold, and a bankroll that won't fold it ain't a bitch I can't mold." It's self-explanatory how Fresh got his name.

Then it's Lorenzo "Quick" Edwards. Quick got his name from his swiftness in the game. He was always ahead of everybody else out the clique. Even when we were in school, he'll finish his work before everybody then sits back and sends text messages on his phone while everybody else works. Some people think that my nigga has been here before through reincarnation, but I say that my nigga is just one of a kind. Quick loved the hustle. He loved waking up in the morning to hit the streets to get his grind on. "Ain't nothing betta to do" if you asked him. Quick stands about the same height as Fresh with a little less weight and muscle and rocks his hair in dreadlocks like mine and Fresh's. Come to think of it, everybody in the click got dreads besides Slim who kept his haircut into a low fade. My niggas and I stuck together like conjoined twins. When one moved, we all moved; once one shined, we all shined; and when one beefed, we all beefed. We share an unbreakable bond that came from looking out for one another. We did everything together from wearing one another's clothes to fucking one another's hoes. Shit, we even slept in the same bed when we spent the night over one another's house. My niggas and I used to go $2 and $3 on a $5 dollar blunt then give the weed man four of those dollars and use the other one to buy two cigarillos. We would make two lil bitty-ass blunts out the one blunt we bought and sit upstairs in Slim's room, get high playing the video game and cracking jokes on one another, laughing until our stomachs hurt. My nigga Slim's momma was super cool, so she didn't mind us smoking in her house as long as we weren't out getting into trouble. Smoking weed started off as just a weekend and before-and-after-school thing but eventually turned into an all-day every-day "before after and in the middle of school" thing. It seemed like all we did was smoke weed and chase after every girl from around the way that looked like something. Out of the four of us, I know that we made every girl that had a name and was pretty one of our girlfriend with Fresh lead in numbers with the most girlfriends of course. We did this for two years straight until one day, while we were in one of our smoke sessions, Quick said out of nowhere, "Have ya'll thought 'bout how much money Big Ed makin' off this shit that we are constantly smokin'?" "Ion kno how much he making, but I know that nigga showl is shinin'," Fresh said, picturing himself rocking the type of ice Big Ed rocked and driving the type of cars Big Ed drove. Slim blew out a cloud of smoke from the pull he just took from the blunt and said, "That's a good question. I was thinking the same thing a week or so ago." Then the room fell silent. The only noise being heard was John Madden announcing something about the Pittsburgh Steelers and the Tennessee Titans matching up on the game. "What you think he makin', Kilo?" Quick asked, grabbing the blunt from Slim, taking a long drag, staring Kilo in the eyes while waiting on a reply. One to always think a few seconds before he spoke, Kilo gathered his thoughts then said, "I haven't really put much thought into how much Big Ed makin' and could really care less because I love to smoke this shit." "So you mean to tell me that you haven't thought 'bout makin' money instead of smokin' it?" Quick asked, shocked by Kilo's response. "Come on now, Quick, you should know me betta than that," Kilo said. "I'm just saying cuz. Hearing that got me confused," Quick said followed by a "Me too" from both Slim and Fresh. Kilo chuckled a little, getting the blunt from Quick. Before taking a hit from the blunt, Kilo said, "Don't be confused, my niggas. I'm just stating facts. I love smokin' weed and ain't tryna sell it." Kilo then took a long hard pull from the blunt and held the smoke in for a second before exhaling it. Quick, Slim, and Fresh just looked on, all thinking the same thing: *This nigga tripping!* "But you know," Kilo said, getting everybody's attention, "I have been thinking 'bout how much money Heavy D and Lil Jimmy been gettin' sellin' crack." The words were like a breath of fresh air to Slim, Fresh, and Quick because for a minute Kilo had them second-guessing him. But hearing the names Lil Jimmy and Heavy D surprised them more because those two names alone practically ran the entire drug trade in the state of Ohio. And there ain't no telling how many other states they ran. Lil Jimmy's and Heavy D's names should be swapped around to Heavy Jimmy and Lil D because Heavy D is nowhere near heavy weight-wise. I think he put Heavy in front of D because of his heaviness in the dope game. Lil Jimmy, on the other hand, I'm guessing kept his childhood nickname because I know that he's every bit of 385 pounds easy. But anyways, this was the conversation that changed our lives forever.

Chapter 1- The Beginning

"Damn my nigga you been doing a whole lot of thinkin' then 'cus them niggas pockets are deeper than Shan's momma pussy," Fresh said, causing everybody to laugh, thinking about Shan, the neighborhood freak, and her momma who got nine kids by eight different niggas. "Yea, I guess that is a lot of thinkin' then, ain't it? But seriously, tho, my niggas, them niggas gettin' real paper. I mean they run shit 'round here. They might be the ones supplying Big Ed and his team. Who knows?" Kilo said, thinking about how he wanted in on the drug trade in his hometown. "Man, it ain't no tellin' what Heavy D and Lil Jimmy would do if they found out that we tryin' to interfere with their cash flow. That's why I asked 'bout Big Ed because everybody knows his reputation 'round here. Besides, why would we jump straight into the fast lane of sellin' crack when we know nothing about it?" Quick asked Kilo. "Yea, I see yo point, Quick, and I know you see mine with the money differences. I mean why sell weed and cop a Nissan when we can sell crack and cop a Benz truck?" Kilo replied, ready to go all in. Taking another pull from the blunt that was halfway gone, Kilo handed it to Fresh. "I feel where both of ya'll are comin' from, but ain't nobody thought about how we gone get our hands on enuff product to even make a profit. Look at us now. We're barely gettin' enuff money to buy these lil dime bags we've been buying," Slim said. "And besides, that ain't nobody in here over fifteen, so who gone take us serious if we step to them talkin' 'bout 'A, my nigga we tryna get down and make this money,'" Slim finished. "Yea, you right, Slim. But I was thinkin' that if we came at Big Ed from the right angle, then he might put us on with a few ounces or sumthing," Quick said. The room fell silent again with everyone lost in their own thoughts. "Pass the controller, my nigga. You lost," Kilo told Fresh after beating him 35–28 with the Steelers. "I had next," Slim said, grabbing the controller from Fresh.

"The only reason I lost is because I got shining on my mind. Nigga, you know you can't beat me," Fresh told Kilo, thinking about how many more girls he was going to be able to fuck once the money started pouring in. "Just did. Now sit back make yoself useful and roll that other blunt up, nigga," Kilo said, laughing. "Man, how 'bout we say fuck it and just rob that nigga Big Ed ourselves? His bitch ass ain't gone do shit but make a bunch of threats tryin' to scare us," Fresh said, splitting a cigarillo with his nails. "Shit, we could, but why rob him when we can slide up under him and get him to front us until we're able to buy our own? That way, we won't have to worry about no unwanted problems or makin' a bad name for ourselves," Quick said. "I feel ya. But what if that nigga don't want to deal with us, then what?" Fresh asked. "Hopefully, we won't have to deal with no 'what-ifs.' But if we do, then we'll deal with that accordingly and rob his bitch ass blind," Kilo butted in, not really feeling the thought of wasting his time selling weed but knew he didn't know a thing about selling crack, Kilo decided to go along with the plan until he found more out about dealing with crack. "So when we gone step to Big Ed?" Slim asked. "We need to holla at that nigga right now. Shit, I'm tryna hit the mall and ball. ASAP!" Fresh said, getting excited thinking about upgrading his wardrobe. "I think we should holla at him tomorrow after school while we pickin' up our regular smoke sack," Quick said. "But this time, it'll only be me and Kilo going," Quick added. "Aite bet," Slim and Fresh said, almost in the same second. After they finished smoking their last blunt, it was like Ms. Cook read their minds. "Issac!" Ms. Cook yelled up the stairs. "Mam!" Slim yelled through the door. "I just finished making chilidogs if ya'll are hungry. I'll be back in a few. I'm going over to Peaches's house for a little while." Peaches is Ms. Cook's gossiping buddy. They will sit for hours catching each other up on the latest news that happened around the way. "Okay, Momma, we will be down there in a second to eat." "Okay. Issac, call my cell if you need me for anything. Love you," Ms. Cook said, leaving out the door. Turning around after shutting the door back, Slim couldn't help but laugh at the way Quick, Fresh, and Kilo were lined up behind him, looking like some hungry-ass dogs. "Man, ion know what the fucks so funny. Nigga, I'm starvin'! And we all kno how yo momma be throwin' down in the kitchen so get the fuck out the way, fool," Quick said, damn near knocking Slim over trying to get out the door with Kilo and Fresh on his heels. "Yeah, fa real, my nigga, moms can cook her ass off," Kilo added. "I know. That's why once my bread get right, I'ma open up a restaurant for her." After everybody filled their stomachs and played another round of Madden, it was close to eight o'clock, and a curfew was enforced for every child in the hood by the parents. They say at night the most crimes occur, but I think that's just to get us in the house so we can get ready for school because in my hood the killing and drug dealing don't stop. It's 24/7 365 days a year around here. "I'm 'bout to get up outta here. I'll catch ya'll niggas in the mornin' on the way to school," Kilo said, getting off the bed, and headed out the door. "Yea, me too," Quick said then asked Fresh if he was leaving. "Yeah, I'm 'bout to bounce to, but I'm stoppin' by Mikayla's house to get my birthday present," Fresh said, moving his hands up and down like he was getting some head. "Nigga, yo birthday ain't 'til next month. What you mean birthday present?" Quick questioned, already knowing what Fresh meant. "I know when my birthday is, fool, but she don't. I told her it was this month so I don't have to deal with her next month. You know I gotta squeeze all my bitches in one way or another," Fresh said, causing everybody to laugh. "You a fool, Fresh. But I hope you wrappin' yo shit up, nigga," Slim said seriously. "You betta kno it" was all Fresh said before heading out the door. The next day at school seemed like it was dragging by for them, especially for Quick who was probably the most anxious of them all about negotiating with Big Ed about putting himself and his boys on. Sitting in his fourth-period math class, not listening to a word the teacher was saying, too busy trying to get his thoughts together, Quick didn't hear Maria Sanchez, a pretty lil Spanish chick, asking him if he did his homework while flirting the whole time. But one thing Quick did hear was the bell ring signaling that class was over and school was out. Walking down the hallway, Quick made his way toward the lockers where he, Kilo, Fresh, and Slim had one right beside another. And just like usual, they were already there kicking the shit. "What's up, my nigga? You ready to handle this bizniz?" Kilo asked Quick, giving him some dap. "I've been ready since last night, fool. It seem like all my classes was twice as long today," Quick said, dapping Kilo back. "What up, Fresh, Slim?" "Same ol shit, just a different day," Fresh said. "Yeah, but hopefully, today will be the start of a new one for us. If you know what I mean," Slim said. "Dig that, my nigga," Quick said back. On the way home, Kilo and Quick discussed how they were going to get Big Ed to put them on. Quick told Kilo he should do the most talking since he was more persuasive than he was. "Aite cool. Just back me up when I need you to," Kilo said. As they were about to take their usual route to Big Ed's spot, they told Slim and Fresh to wait for them over Slim's house until they were done. While walking up the block halfway to Big Ed's spot, Quick and Kilo spotted Shan and her best friend Ebony sitting on Shan's porch. Shan lived two houses down from Big Ed's weed spot. "Hey, Kilo," Shan said in the most seductive voice she could muster. If one didn't know Shan they would probably think that she was a dime and girlfriend material. Shan stands about five feet five inches tall with hazel-brown eyes, beautiful brown skin, and long black hair. Shan was a year older than Kilo but could have easily passed for nineteen the way her curves formed her body. Kilo being Kilo didn't respond verbally to Shan; instead, he gave her the head nod. Walking up the few steps to Big Ed's front door, Quick knocked on the door. *Knock, knock, knock.* No response. So he waited another ten seconds and knocked again. "I know this nigga ain't gone nowhere because his Infiniti Q45 parked in the driveway," Quick said right before hearing the long metal bar slide across the racks on the inside of the door and the locks being unlatched. "What's up, lil niggas? Where ya'll other running buddies at?" Big Ed asked after Rico secured the door back. Rico is Big Ed's left-hand man, a.k.a. his hit man, and is known around town for his murder game. Rico was one of those niggas with no heart or feelings but got unquestionable loyalty to Big Ed. I think that's only because the money is good. You can't trust niggas like Rico. "Them niggas stayed after school to watch the basketball game," Kilo said, letting the lie roll smoothly off his tongue. "After me and Quick get our smoke sack, we headed right back up there. You know, high school games is where all the bitches be." "You right 'bout that one, Kilo. But I ain't been to school in so long all I 'member is every day was like a fashion show. Nah mean?" Big Ed said, remembering how he used to pull up at school in his '72 Cutlass sitting on twenties. "I kind of miss pullin' up at school gettin' all the attention from both niggas and bitches. Niggas hatin' me and the bitches wishin' they could date me," Big

Ed said, sitting back. "I bet them niggas was hating on you riding like that cuz niggas hate me and my niggas and we ain't got shit but what our momma buy us. So I know they hated you pullin up shinin' like that," Quick said, stroking Big Ed's ego. "In this crazy world we livin' in today, you ain't gota have shit and they will still hate on you. But what ya'll lil niggas smokin' on today, same thing?" Big Ed asked. "Yea, let us get a sack of that good shit," Kilo said, referring to "good shit" as the potent sacks of marijuana Big Ed was known to have. "We also came to discuss a lil bizniz too," Kilo said. "Bizniz? Shit what kind of bizniz ya'll lil niggas tryna discuss?" Big Ed said, grabbing a freshly rolled blunt out the ashtray that was sitting on the table. "Look, I ain't gone cut no corners or bend no blocks with you. Me and my niggas tryna come up. So we figured—" "Hold up right there," Big Ed said, cutting Kilo off mid sentence then took a pull from the blunt, coughing a little. "Everything that look good about this game from the outside ain't always what it seem. All the money, cars, clothes, and hoes could cost a nigga his life tryna come up. Nah mean? Ain't nothin' sweet about this shit," Big Ed said then thought about how it was back in the day. "See the game done changed. It ain't how it used to be where getting money to provide for ya family was the main objective. Now days it's a lot of niggas that can't get out here and get their own, so they robbin' and killin' to get." Big Ed said, taking another pull from the blunt. "Then you got these niggas that can't hold their tongue and do their time that got the game all fucked up too." "We undastand all that but—" Quick tried to say something but was cut off also. "But what, huh? What make ya'll lil niggas think I'ma be ya'll come up anyway?" Big Ed asked. "How old are ya'll—sixteen?" "Come on now, Big Ed, you know just as well as I know that age is just a number in this game. It's all about determination and dedication," Kilo replied. "Dedication and determination, huh? You right 'bout that. But you still haven't told me why I should put ya'll on." "It'll be another opportunity," Quick added. "Opportunity?" Big Ed said the word real concisely. "Who wouldn't love the opportunity to make more money? I mean you are an opportunist, aren't you?" Quick continued, trying to get the ball in their court. And right before Big Ed could get a word out, Kilo spoke, "Think about how much money you missin' from the high school kids and all the other kids that stay around here that are too scared to knock on your door to buy some weed. So puttin' us on will give you the opportunity to lock down that end of the game as well," Kilo said, watching Big Ed's facial expression lighting up like he was considering what Kilo just said. The three went back and forth, neither one letting up on trying to get their point across. Finally, after about thirty minutes of debating, Big Ed finally broke, "Aite so ya'll think all can handle a pound?" Knowing that a pound could cost anywhere from $750 to a thousand dollars, but coming from a nigga like Big Ed, it could be cheaper. Kilo said, "Yea, we can handle that. But what's the ticket?" "I need like a rack a piece fo them thangs. I got some killa mid in," Big Ed said, sizing Kilo and Quick up to see where their head was, knowing that he could let a pound go for $700 and still make a $400 profit. "A rack? Damn! Why you tryna tax us? We tryna eat not starve," Quick shot back. "This shit ain't grown in the backyard or on trees, lil nigga. This shit shipped straight from the land," Big Ed said. "I feel ya. But damn a rack? I know you can drop the price a lil, especially since them thangs are comin' from Cali," Quick said. "So what am I s'pose to do? Give them to ya'll for what I'm gettin' them for?" "Nawl, I ain't sayin' that." "Well, look 950 is the best I can do," Big Ed said, seeing how far Quick would go. "You didn't take nothin' but $50 off. What's that s'pose to help?" Kilo asked with a little irritation in this voice. "Aite $900 is the lowest I'm goin'. Take it or leave it," Big Ed said, checking the time on his cell phone. "Aite, we'll take—" Quick was about to say but was stopped by Kilo. "Eight hundred dollars a pound since it's us who will be doin' all the footwork and takin' a lil heat off you at the same time," Kilo said, looking Big Ed dead in the eyes. Lighting the blunt back up that went out from too much talking and not enough puffing, Big Ed gave in to $800 a pound all because of the hearts the lil niggas had for even stepping to him the way they did. Besides, he wasn't losing on $800 a pound. He was still winning and knew that if anything happened to them and he had to take a lost what was $800 to a boss. "Aite, eight hunnit it is. Rico, grab a pound out the back for these lil niggas," Big Ed told Rico who hadn't said a single word since Kilo and Slim entered the house. "Let us get a pair of those scales you got right there 'cause we showl gone need them," Kilo said, pointing to the table where three sets of scales were. Big Ed grabbed a pair of the scales then handed them to Kilo along with the blunt that he was smoking. Kilo took a hit from the blunt and started coughing immediately. "Damn! What's this straight THC rolled up?" Kilo asked, still coughing holding his chest. "That right there is some of Cali's best. Call it Snoop Dogg," Big Ed said, laughing. Kilo took another hit then passed the blunt to Quick who took a hit from the blunt and started coughing so hard it sounded like he was going to throw his lungs up. "Damn, this shit strong," Quick said. Rico walked back into the room and dropped the pound of weed on the table then sat back down on the couch beside Big Ed. Big Ed grabbed the pound off the table and tossed it to Kilo then told them to remember that just because they were kids didn't mean that the streets would treat them like kids. "Ya'll put ya'll self in men shoes, so that's how ya'll will be treated. I'm givin' ya'll two weeks. After that, I'ma be expectin' my money." "We ain't worried 'bout how the streets gone treat us. We can handle our own. And as far as your money, we will get that to you as soon as we get it," Kilo said, sticking the pound of weed and the scales inside his backpack. While Rico was unlocking the door for Kilo and Quick to leave, Big Ed's final words were "Two weeks." Everything felt different walking out of Big Ed's spot back to Slim's. Heading up the block, lost in their own thoughts, they were brought out of them by a female's voice. "Damn, it took ya'll long enuff in there. I thought he was holdin' ya'll hostage or sumthang," Shan said, walking toward them with Ebony right behind her. "Nawl, we was handlin' our biz. And in case ya'll ain't heard, me and my niggas got the weed for sell now," Kilo said, hoping to score his first customers. "So anytime ya'll tryna get ya'll smoke on, holla at us." "Okay, well, tomorrow my momma 'pose to give me some money, so I'll buy a sack from ya'll then," Shan said. "Yea, me too," Ebony said, speaking for the first time, looking Quick in the eyes. "Aite, catch us at school then. And tell the rest of your homegurls the bizniz," Quick said. "I will but what ya'll funa do now? Me and Ebony bored and was hoping we could have some 'fun' with you and Kilo," Shan said, putting emphasis on the word *fun*. "Me and my mans got a few moves we're about to make. We really ain't got no fun time. Matter fact, we gota go meet Slim and Fresh so we'll catch yal at school tomorrow," Quick said, walking off. After walking a few blocks and stopping at the corner store to buy some sandwich bags, they made it to Slim's house but not before stopping some of the other neighborhood kids that smoked weed to let them know that they were holding now. Sitting on the porch, waiting on Kilo and Quick, Slim and Fresh started to become impatient and worried until they saw the two come walking down the street with a new aura about themselves. Heads high, chest up, and a grin on their face told it all. It confirmed everything. "What's up, my niggas? "Slim said, giving dap to Quick and Kilo as they walked up. "The sky 'cause that's the limit now that we got Big Ed behind us," Quick boasted. "I knew he came through. I could tell by the way ya'll was walking down the street with ya chest all out and shit," said Fresh. "Yea, we good. It's time to break this shit down and get rid of it now. We got two weeks to move it," said Quick. "Two weeks? How much did he front us, a pound?" Fresh said, taking a guess at how much and getting it right. "Yea, how you know, my nigga?" Kilo questioned. "Shit, I was playing. But the nigga put that much weed in our hands?" "A pound is like an ounce to a nigga like Big Ed. He want $800 back. After we break it down, we'll all get a QP [a quarter pound], which is four ounces. We can easily make $100 off each ounce. That's $1,600 dollars when we're finish. We give him $800 of the sixteen and we got $800 to split. That's $200 apiece," Quick said, breaking down the calculation evenly so they all had the same amount of weed and see the same amount of profit. "Let's go upstairs Slim to weigh everything up," Kilo said wondering how long it was going to take them to sell the weed. Upstairs in Slim's room being the amateurs they were at weighing and bagging up, it took them close to three hours to break the pound down into ounces and then into nickel and dime bags. After everything was broken down and bagged up, they began to divide the sacks. Taking $300 worth of dime bags and $100 worth of nickel bags each they then sat around trying to come up with a plan to sell it. "How about we split up in pairs? Me and Kilo take care of the whole bottom walk of the school, and you and Fresh take care of the top. That way we can cover the entire perimeter of the school," Slim said. "That's not a bad idea. Matter fact, it's a good one. To get our clientele up we could all take five nickel bags out our sacks and just pass them out to let muthafuckers know we got it," Kilo said. "Yea, that's cool. We will still profit $175 apiece after passing the free sacks out," Quick said, feeling good about everything. "Seeing all this weed got me ready to smoke. Where that sack ya'll was 'pose to get?" Fresh said. "It was so much being discussed I forgot all about buyin' our smoke sack. But we got our own weed now we can roll up out of," Kilo replied. After smoking and playing the game for hours, they decided that instead of taking all the weed to school, they would each take ten dime bags and ten nickel bags to school. That way, they wouldn't risk getting caught with all their product. The next day at school was unbelievable for them. Before lunchtime all the weed was sold. Most of their customers got the word that they were holding from Shan who was one of the ones that got a free sack they passed out. "A yo, Kilo, let me buy one of them dime sacks from ya my nigga," A kid named Benjamen said, walking up to Kilo after school. "I ain't got no more on me right now, but I'm about to pick some mo up. You want me to bring it to you on the block?" Kilo said, stopping to conduct business with Benjamen. "I'm headed to the center. You think you can bring it by there?" asked Benjamen. "Yea, I got you homie." "Aite, cool. You might wanna bring some extra 'cause ain't no tellin' who tryna get their smoke on, on this good Friday," Benjamen said, walking toward the bike rack to get his mongoose bike he rode to school every day. Once at Slim's house, they added the money up, which totaled $600 dollars, not including the three extra sacks Kilo got rid of at the center. "Damn, my niggas we made $600 at school. Think about how much more money we can make if we hang out at the center for a while," Quick said, thinking about how fast they would be able to pay Big Ed his money and get another pound. "Shit, we might make enuff money today to pay Big Ed his money and get another pound from him to make more money," Kilo said, taking the thoughts right out of Quick's mind and putting them into words. "I was just thinking the same thing. You know, the faster we sell it, the more we'll get, which means the more money we'll make, right?" Quick said. "Well, let's all grab another ten dime bags and ten nickel bags and go get this money," Slim added. "Man, if we keep moving at this rate, I'll be able to get the new Jordan's every time they come out," Fresh said looking down at his Air Max 95's that his momma bought two months ago. "Before we leave, I'm gone stash the money we made at school in this shoebox and push it under yo bed Slim," Kilo said putting the $600 dollars in the box. "Aite." As they walked down the block they cut through a cut to get to the next street where all the action went down and the first thing they saw was a big dice game going on. Walking by the dice game Slim heard Mannie, a dope boy from around the way yell at Mall, another one of the neighborhood dope boys, to pass the blunt. "Damn, nigga, what you gone do, babysit the blunt all day or pass the muthafuckers?" Feeling like he could get a sale here, Slim said, "Me and my niggas got plenty of that shit ya'll blowin' if you tryna purchase." Mannie looked up at Slim for a second before replying. "Fa real, what that shit looking like? Light or dark? 'Cause we don't smoke that dark shit 'round here, lil nigga." Pulling out a few sacks showing them to Mannie, Slim said, "I feel like you just cussed me out asking it is light or dark? Come on my nigga, I know what the hood love to smoke, so Ima keep the best mid around." Taking a sack and smelling it, Mannie said, "Yea, this is some cool, lil mid. What yo quarter ounce go fo?" By this time, the dice game was on pause and the attention was on Slim. "I ain't got none bagged up. Just dime and nickel bags but its $25 a quarter," Slim said, remembering the "It's $25 a quarter" line from Big Ed's phone conversation with a customer while they were at his spot one day. "That's what's up. Let me get two of them sacks then lil nigga," Mannie said, peeling off a $20 bill handing it to Slim. "Sell me two of them sacks too lil homie," Mall said. "I might as well get me something to smoke the way ya'll niggas be acting over this small-ass shit. Let me get a sack of that" One of the other niggas shooting dice said. Leaving the dice game making it to the center Kilo, Quick, Fresh, and Slim sat around kicking it with the other kids that was shooting basketball, playing Ping-Pong, shooting pool, or just hanging around playing cool trying to get with some of girls that were there. Seeing Mikayla and Kimberly some girls from school coming toward them, Kilo elbowed Fresh in the side then tilted his head in the direction in which they were coming from. "Hey Fresh, what you doing at the center? You ain't neva," Mikayla said, walking up on Fresh. "I ain't doing too much, just hangin' tryna get some of this weed off. Why? What's up?" Fresh said, admiring Mikayla's frame and her almond-colored skin. Mikayla wasn't a freak like Shan and Ebony. She was one of those girls that "tried" to be hood but really live in the suburbs with *both* parents. "Just hanging, huh? Well, how did you like yo birthday present?" Mikayla said, licking her lips. "I didn't like it. I loved it. We need to do that more often not just on special days," Fresh said, remembering how good Mikayla's lips felt wrapped around him. "Oh, we can but my girl Kim is tryna buy a sack and word on the street is ya'll are the ones to see," Mikayla said, hoping that Fresh really liked her birthday present and wasn't just saying he did since that was her first time giving head. "We're just tryna get ours like everybody else," Fresh said, pulling out a dime bag and handing it to Kimberly. Kimberly paid for the sack and she and Mikayla were on their way. "Word sure do spread in the hood. Did ya'll hear her say 'Word on the streets is we're the ones to see'?" asked Kilo. "Yea, I heard her. Pretty soon, we'll be selling weed to every weed head around here," Quick said. "The more people we serve, the more money we make. And the more money we make, the fresher I stay," Fresh said, wiping himself off. "We all know where yo money going," Quick said, causing everybody to chuckle. "A yo, Kilo, I heard ya'll got that fire bud for sale," A kid named Dre said, walking into the game room. "Yea, we got that killa. You tryna smoke?" Replied Kilo. "Hell yea! What them sacks looking like? I hope they fat." After selling Dre a sack and a few other kids some weed Quick thought it might be better to leave the center and hit the block to sell some more weed. "Aite bet. We ain't gota worry about Mannie and them because they don't sell weed. They all sell dope," Kilo said. They left the center and headed back to the block which was the same way they left it. Only difference was the dice game seemed to have drawn more attention. After selling a few more sacks on the block, they all decided that since it was getting dark they should go back to Slim's house and count the money before curfew hit. After counting the money and smoking a blunt they parted ways leaving a little over $700 in the shoebox under Slim's bed with plans on waking up early to make the rest of the money to pay Big Ed. The next day around noon Kilo and Quick were knocking on Big Ed's door ready to re-up. Once inside, Quick spoke first, "Look Big Ed, we seem to have a problem on our hands." "Well, ya'll lil niggas better put ya heads together and become the problem solver because I don't solve problems," said Big Ed, wondering why in the hell did he front them the weed in the first place. "Us running out of weed is the only problem we have. And I'm sure you can solve that problem, can't you?" Kilo said, pulling the $800 dollars from his pants pocket. "I just gave ya'll the weed Thursday. It's Saturday now and ya'll mean to tell me it's gone?" Big Ed said, not believing his ears. "Yea, we ran through that. We need another one to keep it coming," Quick said, taking the money out of Kilo's hand and counting out $800 flat. Big Ed smiled and told Rico to grab them another pound out the back. "If ya'll keep this up the pickup may become bigger and the price might drop to $700 apiece." "We ready whenever you ready," Kilo said, grabbing the pound from Rico and stuffing it in his Nike bag he brought with him. "I'ma see how the next couple runs go first. Ya'll might just be having beginner's luck," Big Ed said to Kilo and Quick before they were out the door. And that was our first time actually hustling but it sure wasn't our last. Big Ed was seeing us two or three times a week for months before he finally decided that we could handle more than a pound at a time. Once he realized that we were ready for it, he started fronting us five of them thangs. We'll run through that in a week and be right back for more. As time passed and our names became known in the hood, our clientele grew and we eventually began to sell everything from a blunt of weed to an ounce. By the time we were seventeen, we were getting twenty pounds a week from Big Ed. Five pounds apiece every week. Big Ed dropped the price to $500 a pound and every re-up I was making close to $2,000 dollars profit. I fell in love seeing my money stack. So to see it grow even more, I began to buy five pounds myself along with the five pounds Big Ed was fronting. Quick and Slim did the same, but Fresh said he was cool with the five pounds being fronted to him, and as long as he can maintain and continue to hit the mall and keep a bankroll the size of a toilet paper roll, he was straight. For some reason, I wasn't satisfied with the money I was making. I knew that I could make twice as much money selling dope than weed. So one day walking from the center I stopped Norman, the neighborhood crackhead and asked him, "What do an ounce of cocaine go for around here?" "I don't buy my dope from Mannie and them. Their prices are too high, and the dope ain't worth shit. I get my dope from Fonzi. You're probably too young to remember him. He's been 'round since the seventies. He just doesn't deal with everybody. He's a *real* OG in the game," Norman said, wondering why Kilo was asking about cocaine prices. "I thought you and yo boys sell weed." "We do, but if I put a limit to what I sell then I'll be putting a limit to the money I make. Get me?" Kilo asked. "Yea, I see yo point but I really can't do much for you. All I can do is tell Fonzi about you and if he wants to deal with you, he'll reach out and touch you," Norman said, eager to tell Fonzi the news hoping that he'll give him a free hit. "Do that for me then, Norman. Here's something for your trouble," Kilo said, pulling out a knot of money and gave Norman a $20 dollar bill. Norman snatched the money and had it tucked in his pocket before Kilo had a chance to put his money back in his pocket. Norman was a crackhead who had been around the hood since the hood been the hood, so he knew everybody and their momma. Probably their mommas' momma too. "The next time I see Fonzi, I'll be sure to tell him about you. Thanks for the money and tell Ms. Campbell I asked about her," Norman said, walking away. "Man, why did you just give Norman junkie ass $20?" Fresh asked. "Because I know he'll take and spend it with Fonzi and tell him about me," Kilo said, smiling. "You serious 'bout selling dope ain't you?" Slim asked. "It's an opportunity to make more money, so why not?" Kilo replied. For the next couple days all Kilo did was gain any info he could on selling dope. None of it was really being useful because in the dope game you have to actually be in the grind to figure out the grind. It took Norman damn near two weeks to get back at Kilo and when he did, he still didn't have the information Kilo was hoping to hear. "Fonzi told me to tell you that he'll get up with you. He didn't really say when, just said he would," Norman told Kilo. "Check this out. I ain't gone sit 'round waiting on a nigga I ain't never heard of yet alone seen. So I'm gone holla at Mannie and get straight. I'm gone need you to cook it for me. Can you cook?" Kilo asked Norman. "I'm one of the best 'round here, youngin'. You betta ask somebody 'bout Norman." I took to the streets like a pro, making more money than I've ever made. I was hustling with a strategy that had to be passed down through my genes. Once I learned how to cut and cook the dope myself, it was over. After seeing me elevate to being the man, my niggas eventually joined me. And the rest was history—until the drought hit.

Chapter 2- Two Years Later

"Man, it's hot as hell out here," Fresh said, leaning against Slim's '75 Chevrolet Caprice sitting on twenty-eight-inch Forgiatos and a candy-coated burnt-orange paint job. "Too hot for TV. It's just the beginning of May and feel like the middle of July out this bitch," Slim said, dressed in a wife beater, a pair of off-white Coogi shorts, a new pair of white Chuck Taylors, a ten-row diamond bracelet on his wrist, and a diamond chain around his neck. "I'm fina hop in this bitch and bend some blocks. You rollin'?" Slim asked Fresh. "I think I'ma do a lil shinning myself and pull my drop out the storage. Follow me there and well bend some blocks together," Fresh said, walking toward his Ram truck, getting in. "Dig that my nigga," Slim said, hopping in his '75 Caprice. Pulling into the storage units Fresh pulled out his smoke-gray '73 Impala sitting on twenty-six-inch smoke-gray Ashanti's trimmed in blue. Unlike Slim, Fresh put close to forty grand into his car. Most of it went toward the rims, paint, and interior. Slim put close to the same thing into his drop but put $15,000 under the hood alone. "It's 'bout time to add a few mo inches to that thang, ain't it, Fresh?" "Nawl, I'ma keep this '73 as is. I like the way the frame squat on 'em sixes," Fresh said, letting the storage door down and locking it back. "Let's hit the car wash so I can clean this thang. Then we can tear the streets up." After Fresh got his car washed they rode down damn near every street in Youngstown, getting mad love from the females and envious stares from half the niggas. But Slim and Fresh weren't worried about the niggas hating because they knew that hate came with shining. And the way they were coming up in the game, they already knew the haters would come. They also knew that since they were young that somebody would try them so they prepared themselves for any type of unwanted attention. By the time Fresh and Slim finished tearing up the streets in their whips, the block was in full swing when they pulled back up. Summer time was the best time in Youngstown. It seemed like everybody and their momma came out to enjoy the weather or to show off an outfit or whatever it is they just bought. Majority of the bitches in the hood be in the smallest shit they can find and it's always a dice game, card game, dominos, or something going on. Then you got the badass kids throwing water balloons at the cars passing by, a big grill going in the field with hot dogs and hamburgers for whoever that was hungry thanks to the dope boys in the hood, which was probably Kilo and his click. To top everything off, you still got the sells coming to cop and the hustlers out supplying them. As they parked and hopped out their whips, everybody showed Slim and Fresh love when they got out. The little kids running up asking for $5s and $10s instead of dollars and the females asking for hugs or to bust a block in their cars. "Ya'll could have let a nigga know ya'll was bringing them toys out today. I would have pulled out my box of Fruit Loops," Quick said, talking about his box Caprice that had a flip flop paint job sitting on thirties. "Shit, I didn't even know. I pulled up on the block in my truck and seen Slim sitting in his drop talking on the phone," Fresh said, scanning the block with his eyes. "It's pretty out here. Why not pull out that piece of fruit?" Slim said, pointing at his whip. "It's live out this bitch. I ain't seen the block this live in a second. What's all this about, Quick?" Fresh asked. "Shan's momma Rita is having a birthday party for one of her nine kids," Quick said. "Which one is the question?" Slim asked, chuckling. "Ion know. Let's go find Rita and ask," Fresh said. After speaking to damn near everybody out there and passing out over a hundred and fifty dollars in $5 dollar bills to the kids, they still couldn't find Rita. "Where yo mama at Lil Timmy?" Quick asked Rita's lil boy as he was running by. "Ino know her was . . . uhhh . . . over there," Lil Timmy said, pointing toward the grill. "Which one of ya'll birthday today?" Slim asked. "It's my birthday. I turn six. Where my present?" Lil Timmy said, sticking his hand out knowing that he was about to get some money from Fresh, Quick, and Slim. "You turned six, huh?" "Yep." They each pulled out a bankroll and gave Lil Timmy a $20 dollar bill. "Happy birthday, lil nigga," Fresh said to Lil Timmy's back. Lil Timmy ran off as soon as the money hit his hands without saying thank you or anything. Walking past the grill and heading toward the cut where most of the niggas were standing around talking shit, they spotted Rita coming their way. "What's up, boys?" Rita said, strutting up on them. Rita may have nine kids, but if you didn't know it then ain't no way in the world you would be able to tell. Rita stood about five feet six inches and weighed 145 pounds with dark skin, short hair, brown eyes, and a body some of the women her age wish they had. Rita got an ass like Serena Williams and acted like she's still twenty-five instead of thirty-five. "Same ol' shit ain't nothing changed but Lil Timmy age," Fresh said, lusting openly at how fat Rita's pussy was in the tights she was wearing. "Lil Timmy? Lil Timmy age don't change till the end of October. The twenty-eighth to be exact," Rita said, peeping Fresh looking at her pussy print. Watching him look, she shifted her weight to one leg to make her ass wiggle a little bit. *I bet that get his dick hard,* Rita thought. "That lil nigga gone be one hellava con artist then. He told us today was his birthday and got us all out of $20," Quick said, laughing at how fast lil Timmy lied. "I'm gone kill that lil heffa. I done told them about lying. I'ma get ya'll money back. Matta fact, where his lil—" Rita said before Fresh cut her off. "Nawl, we straight. Shit that lil nigga just getting his hustle on." "Lying ain't hustling. There are two types of people I can't stand, and that's a liar and a snitch. Really three because I can't stand a man with a lil dick," Rita said, being real blunt looking at Fresh in the eyes. "Well, you'll love me because I ain't neither one of those," Fresh said, giving Rita the same eye contact. "I hope not," Rita said, walking off making her ass bounce. "I'ma fuck the shit outta Rita thick ass, watch," Fresh said. "For what to have a Lil Fresh runnin' 'round here?" Slim said, laughing. "Shid, I know them tubes tied by now. Anyways, where Kilo ass at? I ain't seen him all day," Fresh said. "I talked to that nigga right before I bumped into ya'll. He said he was on his way to Susan's to get his hair retwisted," Quick said. "It's about time for me to get my shit done too. I wonder who Susan got after Kilo," Fresh said, pulling out his cell phone to call Susan. Monday-Saturday Susan's Hair Salon be jumping. Susan's was where most of the people from the hood who are established go get their hair done. If you were seen getting your hair done at Susan's, the media "assumed" that you had money all because of the prices at the salon. "Susan's Hair Salon. This is Susan. How may I help you?" "What's up, Susan? Dis Fresh. How many people you got in front of me? I'm looking like a real Haitian by the head." Laughing at Fresh, Susan said, "Let me see. I'm doing Kilo now. I got one, two, three more people after him. I could get you in probably a little later or first thing in the morning. But of course, you can always come and wait on one of the other stylists." "I'll wait on you. Get me first thing in the morning," Fresh told Susan. "How about nine? Is nine o'clock okay?" "I'll be there." Hanging up the phone, Fresh said, "Man, Susan probably make mo' money doing hair than we do selling dope. Her shop stay packed." "Ours do too. I'm 'bout to swing by the Chicken Shack to grab a bite to eat. Ya'll hungry?" Quick asked. "Nawl, I'm straight. I'm 'bout to pick this chick up I met the other day. She talkin' 'bout she wanna get to know me," Fresh said, grinning. "If she only knew. What's her name? I hope it's not Mikayla you talkin' 'bout," Quick said. "Her name Olivia. She stay on the west side. A bad lil broad too. The bitch look mixed with something but claim to be fully niggerious. Ya'll gone see her one day," Fresh said, walking towards his whip. "What's up, Slim? You up for some chicken?" "I gota run by the spot to drop off some more work and pick that bread up. You know how that go," Slim said, almost forgetting that Benjamen, their homeboy from school, called earlier and said that he and Cutt were ready to re-up. "Benjamen called earlier. I damn near forgot about them over at the Fish Tank." The Fish Tank was a name Kilo gave the spot after buying it to remember that only half of bricks and bricks get sold from there. "Since nothing but bricks get sold from here, we gone call it the Fish Tank. Bricks come in squares, and those squares are fish scales," Kilo said and put Benjamen and Cutt in there to work the spot. "Aite. Hit me when you through then, and we'll meet up and smoke something," Quick said, walking toward his Dodge Charger. "A Quick, switch whips with me for 'bout a hour so I can go handle this bizniz," Slim yelled before Quick got in his car. "You ain't said nothin' but a word, my nigga. We can switch for the day if you want to," Quick said, heading back toward Slim, dangling his keys in the air. "We can do that. Ain't nothin' in there I need to know about, is it?" Slim asked, switching keys with Quick. "Uhh . . . It's a Glock 40 in the armrest that you might need handling yo bizniz." "Nawl, I'm good. But you gone need it ridin' on them eights like that. I keep my burner on me like my nuts," Slim said, lifting up his shirt showing a baby .380. They pulled off the block and headed in different directions. Quick pulled up at the Chicken Shack banging "Welcome To My Hood" repeating Plies verse over and over "I'll never buy a Phantom 28's can't fit, they say I'm fed bound they call me high risk, a full-blooded goon lames make me sick, you getting' three or four birds where I'm from they call ya rich." Slim, on the other hand pulled up to the Fish Tank with the radio on mute lost in his own thoughts. Everything was exactly like it always was at the Fish Tank when Slim walked in. "What's good, my nigga?" Slim greeted Benjamen with some dap. "Same ol shit, just a different toilet. Ain't nothin' changed," Benjamen said. "True. Where Cutt at?" Slim asked, letting his eyes roam around the living room. "He went to get us something to eat. Sellin' dope and countin' money is like exercising. It leave a nigga hungry," Benjamen said, grabbing a duffel bag stuffed with one hundred and twenty-five thousand in it that he and Cutt made from the five bricks Slim dropped off two days ago. "It's all there." "I believe ya. Ima hit you as soon as this is counted and let you know where to pick up the other five up," Slim said headed toward the door with the duffel bag full of cash in hand. Meanwhile at Susan's Hair Salon sitting under the hair dryer dressed in a white V-neck, some Black Label cargo shorts, some all-white shell toes, and a 24-carat gold-diamond-studded medallion hanging from his neck, Kilo was starting to become annoyed with all the girlish gossip that being in a woman's domain brought. A hair salon, unlike a barber shop's small talk, is mainly about the best-looking male superstar, who's fucking who in the industry, and what nigga got what in the hood. So if you're trying to get the 411 on a nigga, take a trip to your nearest salon. *I wonder if me and my niggas' names ever come up in hair salons,* Kilo thought. And just as soon as the thought came, it was answered by a big booty hood rat named Cookie. "I kno' ya'll done heard of Fresh," Kilo heard Cookie say. "Girl, who don't know that fine-ass nigga?" Some chick with a towel wrapped around her head said. "Gurl, dat nigga gota sex drive outa dis world. And he don't mind breakin' a sista off some of that money he got," Cookie said, popping her lips. "I heard him and his niggas got shit on lock around here too," Kilo heard another female say. *What a coincidence. I wonder if anybody in here besides Susan knows who I am,* Kilo thought to himself. It was like Cookie could read Kilo's mind because her next words were "I heard da same thing. They say he got a cuzzin' that I've been tryin' to catch a glimpse of. But don't nobody kno' what he look like. Just know his name." "Girl, who you talkin' 'bout? Quick?" Towel head said. Hearing the conversation between the girls got Kilo's full attention. But instead of acting interested, Kilo unclipped his cell phone from his waist and started texting his girlfriend Kenya. "Un-Un, girl, his name Kilo. It should be Mr. Hard to Find 'cus I swear that's what he is," Cookie said, setting the magazine down and walking toward a hairstylist named Tammy. Looking up from his cell phone, Kilo caught eyes with Susan and gently shook his head no, silently telling Susan not to expose him to the lady wolves in the salon. "Girl, I've done heard that name somewhere," Towel head said sitting in the booth right next to Cookie. Kilo got up from under the dryer and pointed to his hair, signaling Susan to pull the clips off his head so he could bounce. As the last clip was pulled from his hair, Kilo stood up to pay Susan. Hearing the doorbell chime, alerting an entrance or an exit, Kilo looked up and caught eyes with the most gorgeous female he'd seen in a while. *Damn, lil momma giving my Kenya a run for her money,* Kilo thought peeling $300 bills off his bankroll, handing it to Susan. "The extra is for not blazing me. I'll see you in another two weeks." "Thanks for the money. But you know I'll never give your identity to none of these high-maintenance hoochies that come through here," Susan said, smiling. "Yea, I know, and I show'll appreciate that. But who is lil mama that just came through the door wearing that white-and-silver cache outfit?" Kilo wanted to know. "Oh, that's Lisa's daughter. They live on the east side of town where the upper class live. You mighta heard of her daddy Jeffery Dosson or JD. He used to run with Fonzi back in the day until he got caught up on a murder charge and did fifteen years before giving it back," Susan said, admiring her handiwork on Kilo's head. "Shit, ain't no way I know her daddy. I was four when he went in. But in another place and better timing, Ima get to know her," Kilo said, wishing that Cookie and them weren't on the prowl, trying to find out who he was. "What's her name by the way?" "Harmony." Leaving the salon making eye contact with Harmony, Kilo winked then blew her a kiss letting her know that he was attracted to what he saw. Just as soon as he was out the door Harmony walked up and asked Susan, "Who's he? I've never seen him before." Crossing the street to his black-and-yellow supercharged Yamaha 1100, Kilo felt his phone vibrating. Recognizing the number, Kilo answered "What's good, my nigga?

How ya living?" "Aw, man, you know it's BET and MTV how I'm living ya feel me? But the fishes ran outta fish food," Slim said, pulling out of the Fish Tank driveway using the codes only he and Kilo knew. "Aite, meet me at my crib and we'll go to pets' mart together," Kilo said before disconnecting the call. Sliding on his helmet that matched his bike, Kilo didn't feel or see the pair of eyes watching him from Susan's Hair Salon window. Zipping off the street and heading toward the interstate, Kilo jumped on and weaved in and out of traffic and was pulling in his apartment complex on the lower north side of town fifteen minutes later. "Kenya!" Kilo yelled, standing in their living room. "I'm in the bedroom baby," Kenya yelled back. He opened the bedroom door and seeing Kenya standing in front of the full-length mirror hanging on the wall in her panties and bra, fixing her hair, aroused Kilo instantly. Kenya was what we like to call a bad bitch that has beauty and brains. With her honey-colored skin, she kind of put you in mind of Lauren London, only a tad bit darker. Kenya stood there, combing her natural jet-black hair that hung past her shoulders, in her panties and bra, knowing that she had Kilo in a trance. Turning to look at Kilo staring, Kenya said, "You see something you like, Mr. Campbell?" Then did her best top-model walk with her hands on her hips toward Kilo. "Come on, boo, you know that I lose all control when I see you in some sexy-ass shit like that," Kilo said, watching Keya sashay her way toward him. "Oh . . . is that right?" Kenya said, grabbing Kilo's dick through his cargo shorts then licked her lips. "Well, how about you lose control inside of all this wetness you've caused?" Kenya said then grabbed Kilos hand and slid it down her panties to let him see just how wet she was. "Shit girl, Ion know who I love more you or her," Kilo said, inserting two fingers inside Kenya. "It wouldn't matter who you loved most because were the same person. Now bend us over and fuck the shit out of us, Keon," Kenya said, wiggling out of her panties, then climbed on the bed in a doggy-style position, exposing her full vagina. "Damn, girl, you don't play no games do" Was all Kilo got out before feeling his phone go off on his hip. "Shit, I almost forgot that I told Slim to meet me at the house." "What!" Kenya said more as a statement instead of a question. "We gotta go handle some bizniz but shit he'll be aite for a while. At least, let me get a quickie," Kilo said, his dick as hard as a rock. "I thinks not, Keon. I'm not in the mood to let you get yours and not me. I'm in the mood to go for hours," Kenya said and got up to go get herself some clean panties and another bra and headed for the shower. "Well, we'll finish this tonight," Kilo said, buckling his belt back up, then answered the phone, "Speak." "I'm out front nigga." "Aite, come on up," Kilo said, walking toward the bathroom door. "A, Kenya, have some clothes on when you come out. Me and Slim will be in the living room." He opened the door for Slim, and the two sat on Kilo's all-white leather sofa and counted the money from the Fish Tank and the money that came from another one of Kilo's spot called the Juice Box. The Juice Box got its name because only ounces got sold there. "I think I'ma buy a money machine to count this bread next time. This shit make a nigga hand's cramp up," Kilo said, thumbing through a fistful of hundred-dollar bills. "Counting out $300,000 will cause a nigga to sweat. I got half matter fact buy two of them, and I'ma give you yo bread back for one," Slim said separating the $50s from the $20s. Thirty minutes later, they were so caught up counting and putting rubber bands on the money that they didn't notice Kenya behind them. "I'll be back in about an hour or so Keon. I gota run by Susan's to get some highlights added to my hair. And I told your momma I'll come over today." "Okay, boo. I might be gone when you get back. Did you say you were going by Susan's?" Kilo asked, thinking about the gossip that went on in there. "Yes. Tammy just gone add some highlights. Why? Is there a problem?" "I was at Susan's earlier, and the gossip that goes on in there will get a nigga indicted on a federal charge. All they do is sit 'round, talking about who's doing what. So don't ever mention nothing I do in there or to *nobody* for that matter," Kilo said, putting emphasis on the word *nobody*. He looked at Kenya in the eyes to let her know he wasn't joking. "Keon, do you think that I'll be dumb enough to do such?" Kenya said, mad at Keon for even saying something like that. "Nawl, boo, I don't and I apologize for even saying it. You look good in that blue-and-yellow Bebe outfit too." "Thanks, baby. And I guess you can't speak, Slim? It's cool. Ima tell my girl Ivonne not to call yo ass nomo." "You know it ain't nothing like that, Ken. I was just waiting till ya'll finished ya'll conversation. And yo homegirl don't ever call a nigga anyways. She always talking about she's been busy," Slim said putting a rubber band around a stack of fifties. "I can vouch for her on that busy part because she is studying law, trying to become a lawyer. She hardly ever calls me," Kenya said, walking in the kitchen. "Is ya'll thirsty?" "Nawl, I'm good, boo." "Yea, grab me a bottled water please. And how is yo schooling going?" Slim asked. "It's getting harder now that I graduate in July. But let me get out of here before I miss my appointment," Kenya said then asked Kilo for some money. Kilo gave Kenya $300 dollars out his pocket and she was on her way. "Man, I see why you're so crazy about Kenya. She's drop-dead gorgeous and she got yo back 100 percent," Slim said, holding a fistful of twenties. "Yea, I guess you could say that now but I wonder what she'll do when the rough times get thick," Kilo said. Kilo and Kenya had been fooling around since Kilo was seventeen. Back when he was selling weed for Big Ed. Kenya, being two years older than Kilo was more experienced at sex and put that pussy on him and had him whipped ever since. At least, that's what she thought. "Never trust a big booty and a pretty smile," Fresh once told him. But Kenya was different. He felt totally attached to her mentally way before he had her physically. Kilo learned everything about Kenya. Flaws and all. "All nigga you know she's yo Bonnie," Slim said. "Yea, I know but fuck all that. Let's get this shit counted so we can re-up," Kilo said. Then out of nowhere a thought of Harmony slipped into his mind. "A Slim, you know a chick name Harmony?" "Harmony? Harmony . . ." Slim repeated, searching his memory bank. "Nawl, Ion think so. Why?" "I seen her earlier at Susan's and for some reason she just jumped into my thoughts." "She must look like something after seeing all this money in front of you and yo old lady leave out not even ten minutes ago," Slim said, banding another stack of twenties. "She was something I've never seen before. Like a Gabriele Union mixed with a little Ashanti or something," Kilo said, still mesmerized. "Damn, that bitch was supermodel bad then, huh? You might wonna ask Fresh about her. You know that nigga fucking everything," Slim said. "Yea, I know it was some hoes at the salon with his name in their mouth. Ima check on that but finish banding the rest of them twenties while I call this nigga and see if he's ready for us," Kilo said, dialing some numbers on his phone. The phone rang four times before it was answered on the other end. "Yo," the voice said. "I'm tryna go fishing and catch me twelve basses. What's good?" Kilo said, using the codes *go fishing* and *catch me twelve*, meaning reeing up on that fish-scale dope and buying twelve bricks. "Meet me at the lake," The voice said then hung up. "Everything's a go on that end. What we looking like over here?" Kilo asked. "Everything's everything," Slim said putting a rubber band on the last stack of twenties then took $252,000 out the $300,000 and stuffed it back into the duffle bag he brought in. Kilo then took the $48,000 that was left and split it in half, giving Slim $24,000 thousand and sliding his share under the couch to put up later. "You ready?" Kilo questioned. "Yea, just let me grab a grocery bag to put my money in right quick." Headed out the door locking it behind them Kilo patted his hip to make sure his Glock 40 was still there. "You got that thang on you, don't ya?" Kilo asked Slim who were a few steps ahead of him, making sure the coast was clear. "Better know it. Ion leave home without it." Walking down the stairs and out the door, Kilo saw Quick's Dodge Charger parked next to his Dodge Magnum. "What ya'll do, switch cars?" "Yea, I had my donk out today and didn't feel like driving way across town to get low," Slim said, walking to the trunk of the Charger and put his share of the $48,000 inside it then slammed it shut. Kilo's Magnum matched his Yamaha but instead of the Magnum being yellow and black everywhere, it was jet black with jet black tint on the windows and a yellow hemi sign. But once you opened the door, it looked like a bucket of mustard was poured inside. Kilo's favorite football team being the Pittsburgh Steelers, he did everything in black and yellow. He even dyed two of his dreads yellow. It took Kilo twenty minutes flat to get to the lake to meet the connect. "You ain't got that new Boosie mixtape in here?" "Yea, it should be in the CD case on the backseat," Kilo said. "Man, you 'pose to have that in the deck you tripping," Slim said, swopping CDs putting Boosie in. "I been listening to that old 50 *Get Rich or Die Tryin'*. That's when that nigga was hungry like I am now," Kilo said, lowering the volume on the stereo to make a call. "I'm three minutes out be looking for me," Kilo spoke into the phone. Pulling up in front of a two-story house with an iron gate around it, Kilo had to be let in by two Ray Lewis lookalike security guards. Hopping out the car, grabbing the duffel bag off the backseat Kilo told Slim not to forget to leave his burner in the car. Climbing the small set of stairs to the front porch, Kilo knocked on the door. The door was answered by another security guard. "What up, Big Blu?" Kilo said to the guard at the door. "Same

ol shit, fool. What's good?" Blue replied. "You know what I came fo,"
Kilo said, stepping into the house. "What up, Slim?" Blu said, locking
the door behind Slim. "Ya'll know where that nigga at. Shit ya'll been
here more times than me. I ain't gotta walk ya'll down there," Blu
told Kilo and Slim, slacking on his job. Walking down the hall then
down a few steps into a den, Lil Jimmy sat in a La-Z-Boy chair,
smoking a blunt. After Kilo stopped selling weed for Big Ed, he
began to buy his dope from Mannie, getting an ounce at a time. He
eventually started running through the twenty-eight grams so fast
that Mannie started having trouble supplying to him. Norman, the
neighborhood junkie, told him, "Kilo, you'll come out cheaper buying
a half brick or the whole thing because Mannie cutting yo head
selling you singles." Kilo stepped to Mannie the next day. "What's
the ticket on the whole thang? I'm tired of calling yo phone four to
five times a day buying singles. I rather just buy enuff at once." Kilo
said. "I'on got it like that. I'll have to call my peoples and find out the
price." "Well, call them now and tell them I'm tryna get straight," Lil
Jimmy called to meet Kilo in person because he always heard of Kilo
but never seen him. And the rest was history. "If it ain't Mr. Thousand
Grams himself and his right-hand man Slim. How's everything
looking on yawls end of the stick?" Lil Jimmy asked. "Everything's
sunny right now. We ain't got no complaints. Nah mean?" Kilo said,
speaking for himself and Slim. "Yea, I know. Tell me 'bout it. Look,
don't tell Heavy I told ya'll but the prices are 'pose to drop to like
18.5 or 19. Somewhere around there. We just waiting to see if shit
blow over right with these damn Colombians." "I was wondering
when they was gone drop. I mean they ain't bad but I'm buying ten
or more two or three times a month," Kilo said. "We'll find out in
due time. Just give me a couple mo weeks and I'ma get back to ya'll
on that one. Let's take care of bizniz tho," Lil Jimmy said, grabbing
a Gucci duffel bag from under the table and taking out twelve neatly
wrapped bricks and placing them on top of the table. Kilo unzipped
the duffel sitting beside his foot, then looked up at Lil Jimmy and
said, "It's all there. Where you want it?" "Um . . . I tell you what, just
leave it in that bag and I'ma put these back in this duffel and we'll
just swop bags." "That's what's up. I'll call when we're ready to re-up
again," Kilo said, grabbing the Gucci duffel bag off the table and
headed toward the door. "Aite bet. Ya'll niggas be careful out there,"

Lil Jimmy said, firing his blunt back up. "Where's Heavy at by the way?" Slim spoke his first words since entering the house. "Heavy shot off to Vegas this morning to the casino. He tryna get reservations to rent it out for his birthday next month. I know ya'll gone come through and show love, right?" "You better know it. That'll be an early birthday present for my nigga Quick. His birthday is nine days after Heavy's," Slim said, remembering the dates. "Damn, Quick's birthday is next month. June 20, ain't it?" Kilo said. "Yeap, he'll be twenty too. So going to Vegas gone kill it," Slim said. Back inside Kilo's apartment, Slim sat at the kitchen table taking 125 grams out each brick while Kilo cut the brick with a liquid additive called pro scent. After Kilo cut the dope with the pro scent, he'll mix it then compress the bricks back together with a small hijack compressor. After this process was over, the dope would still be 85 percent raw and they would have a free brick and a half after cutting the dope. "I showl hope that meeting go right with them Colombians and the price drop on these muthafuckers," Slim said as his cell phone rang. "Man, I hope you didn't fall for that 'the prices 'pose to drop' line. I read straight pass that bullshit. He just said that to keep us shopping with them," Kilo said, rewrapping the last brick. "Now look who decides to call a nigga. Ivonne's busy ass. Too bad, she'll have to wait now because I'm busy. But you think that Lil Jimmy was talking out the side of his neck about these prices dropping?" Slim asked. "How long have we been shopping with these niggas? Have the price dropped yet? Aite then. Game recognizes game. Remember that, nigga," Kilo told Slim. "I see yo point. Let me call Benjamen right quick to tell this nigga where to meet me at," Slim said, dialing Benjamen's number. "I'm tryna find a new plug anyway," Kilo said, walking out the kitchen to get his money from under the couch to put up. "Meet me at the waffle house in ten minutes," Slim told Benjamen then hung up the phone. After taking care of business with Benjamen and making a few stops, Slim decided to call Ivonne back, but the phone just rang until the voicemail picked up, "Hi, you've reached me at my voicemail. Sorry I couldn't get to your call, but if you will leave me your name and number, I'll gladly return your call." *Beep.* Slim hung up and said to himself, *At least she can't say I didn't call back.* Then his phone rang. "Hello." "Sorry I missed your call, Slim. I was on the other line talking with my mother," Ivonne said, sitting Indian style in the middle of her living room with law books and school work in front of her. "No need to explain. It's yo world. I'm just a squirrel," Slim said. "Tryna get a nut, huh?" Ivonne said back laughing showing her sense of humor. "I'll wait a lifetime if I have to for that nut. But what you been up to Ms. Busybody?" asked Slim. "Oh, you know just the usual work, school, and studying. I've been thinking about changing my major. Studying law can become very overwhelming at times." "Nawl, don't give up that easy baby girl. It can't be that hard. Besides, we need more beautiful black sisters working inside the system helping the black brothas out that seem to keep getting hung," Slim said, pulling in front of his momma's house to change cars. *Ion see why so many people like these damn Chargers,* Slim thought. "Yeah, I know it's just at times it feel like this isn't for me. Like the only reason I'm doing this is because the state gave my brother a life sentence for something he didn't do. Somebody just said he did it. And I want to get him out," Ivonne said, thinking three years back when the police came and took her brother away. "Since I've known you, I always thought you had the ambition and drive to do whatever you put your mind to and learning the ends and outs of the law is something that you'll just have to put yo mind to and stick with it," Slim told Ivonne stepping out Quick's Charger. "But it's just so hard." "That's life, boo. Besides, it wouldn't feel like a real achievement if it was easy. How about I take you out to eat to get your mind off things for a lil while?" Slim questioned, leaning against the Charger watching four little girls play hopscotch on the sidewalk. "I don't know Slim, I really need to—" "I'm not taking no for an answer. I'll be over there in one hour. That should give you plenty of time to get ready," Slim said, cutting Ivonne off. "Excuse me then mister. I guess I have no choice. But don't you be trying to get a nut, you squirrel." Ivonne said before hanging up and rushing into the bathroom to take a shower. "Isaac, boy, I thought that was you leaning on that car. What you doing out here and how many damn vehicles do you possibly need to ride around in?" Ms. Cook said from the doorway. "What's up, Ma? I was just catching some of this good weather talking on the phone to my lady friend," Slim said, kissing his momma on the cheek. "Uh-huh, but what you trying to do open your own car lot. What's this, car number five?" "Nawl Ma, that ain't my car. That's Quick's. We switched whips for the day. And I only have three cars. Don't forget I gave Tia that Impala she's driving for a graduation present. Where is Tia at anyway?" Slim asked about his sister who was a year younger than he was. "You just missed her. She's gone to the mall or somewhere with her friends. Since you gave her that car, she can't sit still it's like she got ants in her pants," Ms. Cook said, looking at the children play on the sidewalk remembering how Tia and her friends used to do the same thing. "Have she found out what college she wants to go to yet?" "She still haven't made her mind up. But she was saying something about Tennessee State University, Florida State and something else. I can't remember." "She's tryna shoot South, ain't she? At least she gota head on her shoulders and ain't out here like some of these other young girls." Slim sat and talked to his mother a little while longer before getting a "wrong number" call and realized he had twenty-five minutes to pick Ivonne up. "Ma, what you tryna do make me late for my date? I came by to change cars not talk about history." "I'm pretty sure she's fast and will wait a lifetime on you. There's nothing wrong with spending time with your mother every now and then. I barely see you as it is," Ms. Cook said. "Come on Ma, you know you're my favorite lady," Slim said, kissing Ms. Cook on the cheek. "Don't forget that either," Slim said, walking toward his Yukon. Halfway to Ivonne's house Slim decided to swing by Big Ed's spot to grab a sack of purp to smoke after his meal with Ivonne. Pulling in front of Ivonne's house eight minutes late, Slim dialed her number. "I'm out front. Come on out," Slim said after Ivonne picked up. "Well, it's about time. I thought you forgot about me as long as you took," Ivonne said, trying to act mad but was actually excited about getting out the house with Slim. "How could I forget about someone as fine as you? Quit playing and come on out and remind me just how pretty you are." "I'm sure you have a lot more females chasing you that's ten times prettier than me. Don't be trying to run that on me." Wearing a tan Banana Republic skirt with light-blue stitching and a tan and light-blue Banana Republic vest with the shoes to match, Ivonne stepped out the house looking real sophisticated with her long black hair pulled tightly into a ponytail that touched her back. And the nonprescription glasses she wore gave her that innocence schoolgirl look. "Damn," Slim said out loud watching Ivonne walk toward his truck. Being a gentleman, Slim got out and opened the door for

Ivonne and helped her in. "Nice truck," Ivonne said once Slim got back in. "Thanks, but riding with a beautiful black queen like Ms. Ivonne on the passenger side makes the value of this truck rise. You know that, right?" Slim said, causing Ivonne to smile showing her perfectly white Colgate teeth. "Was that a compliment or one of your many lines you use on every female that gets to ride with you?" Ivonne questioned, liking Slim's sense of humor. "Neither. It's the truth and for the record I do not have a lot of females around and in my bizniz. That's how most niggas get jammed up. Females love to talk and gossip." "So why you got me around? I'm studying law let's not forget. What makes you think I want turn you in?" Ivonne said, wondering what made her so special. "That's a good question Vonne, and the truth to it is I don't know. I mean . . . you're different. It's something about you I like and feel attached to. Besides, there is two sides to the law and the side you're studying is the side that help not hurt niggas like me," Slim said, enjoying Ivonne's presence already. "Yea, I hear ya talking but can we please go get something to eat now? I'm starving." "Is there anything inparticular you wanna eat, Ms. Why Do You Trust Me?" "Yes, there is actually, Mr. There's Something about You I Like. I've got a taste for some of Applebee's finest chicken and fruit pasta if that's okay with you." "You can have whatever you like, boo," Slim said, pulling off. Inside the restaurant the two ate and made mostly small talk finding out that they had a lot in common. Slim and Ivonne sat and enjoyed each other's company even after the food was gone and dessert was served. Learning that Ivonne grew up without her father around made Slim feel even more attracted to Ivonne. Slim wanted Ivonne to be his girl so that he can be the one to provide, protect, and love her. "Damn, that was deep boo. Looking in from the outside, I would have never guessed that someone as fine and self-driven as you been through so much in life," Slim told Ivonne after she shared with him how her family was ripped apart when she was younger. "Going through all that made me stronger. It made me want more out of life and not be like my mother who was with my daddy only because of the money he had. The day those stickup kids took my daddy life is the same day I found mine. I just wish it didn't have to come to my daddy losing his life for me to open my eyes," Ivonne said with tears in her eyes. "It's okay baby, I know how you feel. But God took your daddy for a reason. He's in a better place now looking down smiling proud of his princess," Slim said, wrapping his arms around Ivonne pulling her close so that her head could rest on his shoulders. The rest of the time, Slim spent lightening the mood. Leaving Applebee's, Slim helped Ivonne into the truck, got in, and said "I hope you don't mind, but I gotta put one in the air after that meal." "Nope, I don't mind under one condition." "And what's that?" "Let me drive while you smoke." "Shit, that ain't a condition. That's a privilege. You should have been said something. Ain't nothing like riding shotgun smokin' purple with Mary J. Blige lil sista behind the wheel," Slim said, hopping out the truck, getting into the passenger seat. "Hope you didn't mind me climbing over the seat." Ivonne said adjusting the mirrors. "It's all good boo. I just hope you don't mind chauffeuring me around," Slim said, breaking down a cigarillo and stuffing it with the purp weed he bought from Big Ed. "Sure don't. And speaking of Mary, I hope you got some in here 'cause don't nobody want to hear no shoot 'em up bang-bang." "It should be some in that black CD book on the backseat," Slim said, licking the blunt. Ivonne was surprised to see a CD book full of R&B CDs. "Slim, I didn't know you like R&B music this much. You got all the jams up in here. Now we talking," Ivonne said, pulling out a best-hits CD by Mary J. "I'm a lil versatile I guess," Slim said, thanking his momma for her love for R&B. *If Vonne only knew that not a single CD in that book goes into the CD player while I'm in here, she probably wouldn't have said any of that,* Slim thought to himself then hit the power button on the remote, knowing that his momma left some R&B in the radio. And just like he thought, Mary J. and Method Man's "You're All I Need to Get By" song came blasting through the speakers. *I knew it,* Slim said to himself. "I love this song," Ivonne said, singing along with Mary. By the time Ivonne pulled in front of her house, every CD with Mary's name on it got played. Slim didn't mind. He loved watching Ivonne bobbing her head, trying her best to match Mary's vocals. Not really wanting to leave Ivonne's side but knowing he had business to tend to, Slim promised to call her later. Ivonne grabbed Slim's face and said, "You better." She kissed him on the cheek and climbed out the truck and walked inside. "I think I'm in love already," Slim said, watching Ivonne walk into the house before he pulled off.

Chapter 3

Over the next few weeks, Slim and Ivonne kept in touch with each other more than they both intended. Ivonne even invited Slim over for dinner one night to show off her skills in the kitchen. "I guess you believe in the saying 'The way to a man's heart is through his stomach,'" Slim told Ivonne after eating the last bite of his steak, shrimp and potatoes. One day, while riding back from the mall, Slim asked Ivonne to be his girl. "Slim, as bad as I want to be with you, I just, umm, I just know that you're not ready to settle down and commit yourself to one person. And I don't want to play second to anybody," Ivonne told Slim. "How do you figure that I ain't ready? Look, Vonne, I've never felt this way about another female. And I'm not saying that just because either. I'm saying that because I mean it. The more time we spend together the more I feel that you're the one for me. And as far as you playin' second to someone, NEVA! I'll never put another female before you," Slim said with the most sincere look in his eyes. "Well, we'll work on that. Let's just take it slow right now and see what happens, okay?" Ivonne said, believing every word Slim just told her. "Aite, we can do that. But I'm tellin' you now that it ain't no way I'm lettin' you escape me." And Slim meant every word he said too. Meanwhile, on the other side of town, Fresh was having problems with the law. "Sorry, Mr. Morgan, but your licenses are suspended," A female officer was telling Fresh. "I just got my licenses six months ago, so how could they possibly be suspended, Ms. Coolwaters?" Fresh said, reading the officer's name tag. "I have no idea, sir. That's something that you have to take care of at the DMV. I'm not going to write you a citation as long as there isn't anything in this truck that shouldn't be. Is there?" Ms. Coolwaters asked Fresh. "Nawl, ain't nothin' in here," Fresh said, nervous as hell because of the large amount of money that was in his console and the P-89 Ruger that was on his waistline. *Shit, I'm fucked. Maybe I can bribe my way out of this one. Shit!* Fresh said, thinking fast. "I'm going to need you to step out of the vehicle while I search, and if everything's clean, you're good to go Mr. Morgan." Opening the door on the Ram truck, Fresh slid out, hoping that Ms. Coolwaters didn't search him first. *If she search the truck and find the money first, I'll have a better chance at bribing her.* Fresh thought. "How have yo day been so far, Ms. Coolwaters?" Fresh said, trying to play it cool. "It's been fine. Now step back over there while I search please," Ms. Coolwaters said, pointing toward the back of the truck. After about a quick forty-five seconds of searching, Ms. Coolwaters opened the console and pulled the large Ziploc bag full of money out. "What are you doing riding around with this much cash on you, Mr. Morgan? You know that this money can be seized if you don't have legal proof of where it came from, right?" Ms. Coolwaters asked the two questions in one sentence. "Yea, I kno." "What do you do for a living, sell drugs?" Ms. Coolwaters asked. "Nawl, I'm a rapper." Fresh lied. "I've heard that one before. What's your rapper name because you don't look like nobody I've seen on TV?" "I'm Fresh. The CEO over at Bankroll Records. Look, I was on my way to a real important business deal. That's twenty-five thou all hundreds in that bag you holding. I'll give you ten of it to look the other way," Fresh, said hoping she take the bait. Fresh figured that if she didn't take the $10,000 and decided to search him and find the gun that he'll be spending that if not more on lawyer fees anyway and have a gun charge on his record. "Trying to bribe an officer is another charge, Mr. Morgan. You do understand that, right?" Ms. Coolwaters asked. "But what you say fifteen thousand to look the other way?" "Yea, that's what I said," Fresh replied, noticing the extra $5,000 Ms. Coolwaters added onto the ten he offered. "Okay, then here's what I want you to do," Ms. Coolwaters said then gave Fresh specific orders in which to get the money to her. "I want it done this way because I can't just walk back to my car with it. There are too many eyes out here. So nine o'clock sharp. Be there, or you will hate me dearly," Ms. Coolwaters said, walking back to her police car. "Damn, that ass phat in them uniform pants, gurl," Fresh called out, staring a hole through her pants. Ms. Coolwaters heard that and felt wetness between her legs instantly. *Shit, for $15,000, you might get to see this ass naked,* Ms. Coolwaters thought to herself, getting into her car and pulling off. Needing someone to talk to about what just happened, Fresh called Kilo, "What's good, my nigga?" Kilo said, picking up the phone. "Man, you ain't gone believe what just happened to me. How 'bout I'm comin'—" "You ain't in no life or death situation right now, are ya?" Kilo asked, cutting Fresh off midsentence, knowing how reckless Fresh will talk on the phone. "Nawl, I'm straight now. I just got—" "Aite, meet me at the Fish Tank and tell me 'bout it there. I'm like five minutes away. Everybody's 'pose to be meeting up there to talk about a surprise party for Quick," Kilo said before hanging up. Pulling up at the Fish Tank, Fresh killed the engine on his truck, opened the ashtray, and grabbed the half of blunt that he was smoking on before he went inside Mikayla's house. "Glad she didn't find this," Fresh said, firing the blunt back up. Fresh got out, knocked on the door, and was let in by Cutt. "What it's lookin' like, my nigga?" Cutt said, giving Fresh some dap. "Same shit. What's happenin'? Where 'erbody at?" Fresh asked. "They in the back." Sitting around, passing a blunt back and forth Kilo, Slim, and Benjamen turned their attention to Fresh as he walked in. "What's going on, Fresh?" Kilo asked. "Man, I got pulled over and damn near got caught with my burner on me." "Word. What happened?" Slim asked, passing the blunt. Fresh told them everything from why he was on the other side of town down to how Ms. Coolwaters wanted to meet up with him later on to pick the money up. "Damn, cuz that bitch want $15 thou to keep her mouth shut? What you gone do? If it was me, that bitch wouldn't get shit," Benjamen said. "I thought about sayin' fuck her, but then she would just make it her business to harass me. And I ain't tryna have that. Besides, I would have spent close to that on lawyer fees anyway." "Yeah, you right, Fresh. I would give it to her to if that was me. Harassment from the law is the worst type of harassment. Freedom is priceless. Remember that," Kilo told Fresh. "That's real, my nigga. But what's up with this surprise party for Quick? What we doin' for him? Ima tell ya what we need to do, and that's fly down to Atlanta and rent that strip club called Onyx out for that nigga. I heard they be havin' all types of bad bitches up in there shakin' that ass topless," Fresh said, thinking about how many bitches he was going to try to fuck in one night if they went. "I wouldn't mind hittin' the A, but we got something better brewin' in the pot. We goin' to Vegas!" Kilo said. "Vegas? Get the fuck outta here. You mean to tell me we goin' to Nevada?" Fresh, said forgetting about the A that fast. "Yeah, that's where we're headed. We figured since Quick birthday is a week after Heavy's, we'll just fly down there and celebrate his with Heavy's. And whatever he wants to do when we get back, we'll do that too," Kilo said, grabbing the blunt from Benjamen. "It's a must that I go. What about you, Cutt?" Benjamen asked, getting excited about going to Las Vegas, the city that never sleeps. "Hell yea, I'm goin'. This a once-in-a-lifetime thing for a nigga in the streets. Tomorrow ain't promised to a nigga like me," Cutt said, rubbing his hands together, thinking about his first trip ever out of town. "We still got like two and a half weeks until we leaving so keep ya'll mouth shut around Quick about this. Fresh, just grab you some spending money. Everything else is on me since you just took a lost," Kilo said, getting up headed for the door. "Ima holla at ya'll a lil later. I got some moves to make." Later on that night, Fresh pulled into the movie theater's parking lot and parked in the seventh row in the third parking spot. Reading the clock on the dash, Fresh saw that he was eight minutes early, so he decided to roll himself a blunt up. Three minutes til nine, Fresh was firing the blunt up. At nine o'clock sharp, a white Optima with dark-tinted windows pulled up beside him and parked in spot four. Waiting a few seconds to see if Ms. Coolwaters was going to get out and get in his car, Fresh kept smoking. "Damn, I should have told him to bring it to my car," Ms. Coolwaters said aloud, thinking about pulling in spot two so she can grab it through the window. *Fuck it. For fifteen thousand, I'll get into his car,* Ms. Coolwaters thought, getting out of her car. "That's right. Get yo ass out and get in here" were Fresh's thoughts while unlocking the doors. "Damn, that's some loud-ass weed!" Ms. Coolwaters said, getting into the car. "I like everything loud especially my women," Fresh said, chuckling. "Now hold this for me while I run through this check again," Fresh said, grabbing a bag off the backseat. "I see you got a fleet of cars, Mr. Morgan," Ms. Coolwaters said, rubbing the dashboard on Fresh's brand-new Mustang. Fresh didn't respond or look up from counting the money. He was flicking through the money faster than a money machine, and this was making Ms. Coolwaters wet. "That's one hundred and fifty $100 bills. But nawl, I don't have a fleet of cars. This a rental," Fresh lied. "Now pass me that blunt back. I'm tryna get high." To Fresh's surprise, Ms. Coolwaters grabbed his lighter off his lap and fired the blunt back up herself. "It smelt too good. I had to take a puff. Sorry," Ms. Coolwaters said, handing Fresh his blunt. "Sorry? Shit, don't be sorry. I wish I would have known you smoked. I would have brought a box wit me." "Yeah, I puff a little every once in a while." "You wanna finish the rest of this blunt with me before you roll out?" Fresh asked Ms. Coolwaters, hoping she said yes so that he could try to talk his way into her panties. "Sure," Ms. Coolwaters said, thinking that she hadn't smoked anything this strong in a long time. They sat in the movie's parking lot, smoking and talking like they've known each other for years. Fresh, being the womanizer he was, found out damn near everything about Ms. Coolwaters. Her first name, how many kids she got, why she chose to become a police officer, even the high school she graduated from. *She must really be feeling the effect of this weed because she's talking willingly now. I wonder how much of it is true,* Fresh thought to himself. After the blunt was gone, Mrs. Coolwaters sat for a few seconds, getting her thoughts together because the only thing she was thinking about now was fucking the shit out of Fresh. *Why this nigga gotta be cute with money? And he's just like I like them. Thugged the fuck out, dreads hanging, and chain swanging. DAMN, why I smoke that blunt.* "So when you gone let me take you out and show you a good time, shawty. You just gotta nigga outta fifteen large. The least you can do is let me take you out so I won't feel like a trick that got played," Fresh said, causing Ms. Coolwaters to laugh. "I'll even take you to Cincinnati to get away from Youngstown. How is that?" *'Shit, you can get a suite now and fuck this pussy all night long if you want, mister,'* Ms. Coolwaters thought to herself but said, "I guess we could make that happen. But I'm only off on Wednesdays and Saturdays. And Saturdays I spend at home or at the park with my son." "Wednesdays are cool with me, Ms. Coolwaters." Fresh said, looking at Ms. Coolwaters for the first time that night, realizing how pretty she was out that uniform. "Okay, I'll call you one Wednesday I'm off, and please stop calling me by my last name. It's okay to call me Monica, please." "How about I call you by your middle name?" "That's if you remember it, Mr. Morgan." Ms. Coolwaters said, laughing at her own joke. "Aite, if we're going by a first-name basis, then call me Fresh, please. Nicole," Fresh said, imitating Ms. Coolwaters. *And he listens well,* Ms. Coolwaters thought. "Don't call me that, Fresh. I didn't think you were listening when I told you my middle name." "I listen to everything. But answer this question for me, Monica. Where did you get a last name like Coolwaters?" "I have no clue. It came from my mother's side of the family," Ms. Coolwaters said. "Is that thing cool and wet as water?" Fresh asked, feeling himself. "That's a good question. But if I told you the answer, I'll have to put you in handcuffs to keep you away from it," Ms. Coolwaters said, then opened the door and got out. *'Damn, that nigga got my panties wet. Damn that bitch got my dick hard.'* Ms. Coolwaters and Fresh thought simultaneously, pulling out the parking lot. Fresh decided to call Shan to burn her head up while Ms. Coolwaters decided to go home and masturbate on top of her money. "May I speak to Shan?" Fresh spoke into his phone. "I'm on the other line. Who is this? I'll have her to call you back," Rita said, lying in her bed. "Tell her Fresh called." "Fresh? What the hell you doing calling my daughter at ten something at night?" Rita asked, being nosy but already knowing the answer to her question. "Uhh, I was just checking on her. I ain't heard from her lately." "Yea right, boy, save that lie for a fly and see if it listens. I know you calling trying to get between Shan's legs 'cause you're scared of what I got between mine," Rita said, rubbing her pussy through her panties. "Scared? I ain't neva scared. I might be a lil too much for you, tho." "Boy, please, I'll put this pussy on you and have yo young ass gone on in the head," Rita said, sliding her panties to the side and playing with her lips. "Talk is cheap. I'm all action," Fresh said, cutting the small talk. "So what's up?" "I guess Ima have to show yo young ass. Where you at rite now?" Rita questioned. "Wherever I need to be. Tell me where I need to be." "In front of my house in fifteen minutes," Rita said and hung up. Twenty minutes later, Fresh was pulling in front of Rita's house, talking on the phone. Without him having to blow the horn or call the phone, Rita came walking out the house, dressed in a long black trench coat. *Damn, this bitch must smell dick. I hope she ain't got nothing on under that trench,* Fresh thought. "Ima call you after while, baby girl," Fresh told the female on the phone and hung up in her face. Rita opened the car door got in and said, "It took you long enuff." "My bad. I didn't think you was waiting, but wait right here while I holla at Big Ed next door to grab something to smoke on," Fresh said and hopped out. After getting the weed and getting back in the car, Fresh glanced over and saw Rita's coat halfway open. "I know that ain't Fresh's Mustang out front," Shan said looking out her window after hearing a car door shut. "Let me call and make sure." "So where we headed, Rita?" "You driving, not me." Shan dialed Fresh's number only to get the voicemail on about the seventh ring. "I know he saw me calling," Shan said out loud, hitting the redial button. Fresh looked at his phone, smiled, and said, "I know just the place to knock the bottom out that thang." Fresh took Rita to the same hotel he took Shan a few months ago. Hearing the phone ring, Shan thought that maybe it was Fresh returning her call. "Was that you parked outside my house, Fresh?" Shan asked. "This ain't Fresh. My name Charles. Is Rita in?" A deep voice said back into the phone. "Oh, I thought you was somebody else. Hold on. Let me check. Momma!" Shan yelled. "Momma just left out the front door, wearing a long ugly black coat," Her brother Lil Timmy said, walking upstairs to his room." *I thought that was her. I knew that was Fresh too. Two can play that game,* Shan thought before picking the phone back up. "Is she expecting you over or something 'cause she's in the shower," Shan lied. "Yeah, actually she is," Charles said. "Well, come on over, and I'll let you in if she's not out by the time you get here." "I'm two blocks away, so I'll be there in a second." "Okay." Walking inside the hotel room behind Fresh, Rita shut the door and dropped her trench. Standing in front of the door in nothing but a red thong and black heels, Rita said, "Are you sure you're ready for all this woman?" "A dark-skinned devil in a red thong and heels? You damn right I'm ready," Fresh said and stripped down to his boxers and socks. *'Let me find something sexy to put on before he gets here,'* Shan said to herself and walked into her mother's room. Not having much time at all, Shan pulled her undersized T-shirt over her head, exposing her perky brown breast and the pink-and-black boy shorts. Hearing a knock at the door, Shan grabbed the closest piece of clothing, which was Rita's bathrobe. "Perfect." Opening the door for Charles, Shan told him that Rita was still in the shower and she said for him to wait for her in her room. "I see you get your looks from your momma. You're such a pretty girl," Charles told Shan, peeking at her breast that was hardly covered by the robe. "I get a lot from my momma, and the looks ain't half of it," Shan said, letting Charles into her mother's room and going in behind him, shutting the door. Shan dropped the robe and stood there in nothing but her pink-and-black boy shorts. Caught off guard by this, Charles just stood there stunned. "I know you come to get between my momma's legs, but how about we do something a little different and I let you get between my legs?" Shan said, rubbing her titties together then sticking her nipples in her mouth one at a time." "I don't know about that . . . Where's . . . uh . . . uh . . . Rita at?" Charles said, feeling himself become aroused watching Shan. "She's gone. She left with another date. I won't tell if you won't tell. Besides, I know you want some of this young wet tight pussy I got. So be a good boy and strip," Shan said and wiggled out her boy shorts and started playing with her pussy and moaning lightly. "Well, lay back on that bed and let me give you some of this grown woman head I got that I'm sure you've never had," Rita told Fresh who obeyed like a puppy does his master. Rita strutted toward the bed, rubbing her nipples then stopped at the edge and crawled between Fresh's legs doggy style and popped his dick out his boxers using her mouth. "I see you're working with something down here," Rita said, wrapping her lips around the head of Fresh's dick and sucking it like a baby would a pacifier. "Damn, that feels good . . . Shit, gurl, you really know how to do it with no hands, don't ya?" Fresh said, wrapping his hands around Rita's head. Rita then started to put a little bit more of Fresh's dick into her mouth inch by inch until the whole thing was inside her mouth. Then she grabbed his balls and rotated them gently before sucking her jaws together and coming back up slowly, stopping at the head then sucking it like a pacifier again. Rita did this over and over until she felt Fresh's dick start to twitch and his body stiffen. "I'm 'bout to . . . ohh shit, gurl . . . suck that dick . . . here it cum . . . gur . . . ohh shit catch it," Fresh said, pushing Rita's head down. Rita caught and swallowed everything Fresh spit out. "Damn, that head fye. I ain't neva had a bitch suck my dick like that." "You think my head fye wait til you feel how wet this pussy is and how tight these muscles get," Rita said, then turned around and put her ass in the air and said, "Fuck the shit outta this pussy, or don't fuck it at all." Rita then put her face in the pillow and arched her back making her pussy come into full view. "Ahh . . . ahh . . . ahh . . . ahh . . . ohh . . . umm . . . shit . . . fuck me . . . fuck meee . . . fuck this pussy, daddy, umm!" Shan moaned, laying in the middle of Rita's bed with her legs wide open and Charles in the middle of them. "You like this dick, don't ya?" Charles said, ramming his dick in and out of Shan's pussy. "Ummhumm, yes, it . . . feels so .. so . . . uhh, fuck. I'm both to cum." "Cum all on daddy's dick then. Damn, this pussy tight, warm, and wet . . . Cum all over it," Charles said then started long stroking Shan. "Ahh, shit, I want to cum all over your face, daddy . . . I want . . . ummm . . . you to taste how sweet it is." Charles flipped Shan over and let her ride his face and cum all over it. "That was some of the best pussy I've ever had. Even better than your momma's. What made you seduce me?" Charles asked, putting his clothes back on. "It's a long story. Now hurry before my mother gets back," Shan said, glad that Rita's room was the only one downstairs because of all the noise she was making. "Gydelee Rita, I see why you got so many kids. That pussy feels like a massage parlor for dicks. If I didn't know any better, I'll make you mine," Fresh said, walking in the bathroom to wash off. "Boy, you crazy. Now hurry up so I can wash off and get back home. I was having company over tonight," Rita said, getting off the bed still naked. Fresh washed off, put his clothes back on, then rolled a blunt, waiting on Rita.

After Charles left, Shan straightened up Rita's room then went upstairs to take a shower. Fresh dropped Rita off at a quarter till midnight and headed home. Rita got in and tried to call Charles but no answer. "Did somebody come by or call me, Shan?" Rita asked, talking over the shower water. "Yeah, some guy came by. I saw you leaving the house earlier and didn't know where you was going. I didn't want to get you caught up by saying something wrong, so I sent him home sleepy. I mean I sent him home, saying that you were sleeping," Shan said, holding her laughs back behind the shower curtain. "Okay, thank you baby. Is this my bathrobe sitting on the sink?" Rita asked, not remembering leaving her bathrobe in the bathroom. "Oh . . . uh . . . mine's dirty, so I grabbed yours. You can take it if you need it," Shan said, saying the first thing that came to her head. "Oh, no, you're fine baby. Just make sure you return it when you're done," Rita said, turning to leave out the bathroom. *'I wonder what Shan would think of me if she found out I just had sex with one of her lil boyfriends,'* Rita wondered while walking down the stairs. Drying off and rubbing baby oil all over her body, Shan said to herself, '*It must be true that birds of a feather flock together because I'm just like my momma minus the kids.*' The next day Quick called Kilo and told him what he was thinking about doing for his birthday. "What you think about taking a trip? I wanna hit one of these vacation states like Florida or some shit." "Yea, Florida would be nice. I've been to Tallahassee once. You talking 'bout bad bitches it's bad bitches everywhere you go. Even their prostitutes are bad," Kilo said, sitting on the couch next to Kenya, watching *Why Did I Get Married?* "I am sitting here, Keon. A little respect wouldn't hurt," Kenya said, turning her face up. "My bad, boo, I wasn't trying to be disrespectful. You know you'll always come first." "Uh-huh." "You better watch your mouth, nigga. Kenya ain't going for that," Quick said, laughing. "I wear the pants in this relationship. But you thinking about taking a trip, huh? I don't know about that one. I gotta see what my money looking like after Friday," Kilo said. "Aw, man, come on with that one, Kilo. You and I both know how straight yo money is. You the man round here." "Nawl, I don't want that title. I'm just tryna survive." Kilo said rubbing Kenya's leg. "What 'pose to happen Friday anyway?" Quick questioned, getting off the turnpike. "Kenya school tuition is due, and you know that schooling ain't cheap. Especially not when you're trying to become a head doctor," Kilo said then smiled at Kenya. "I'm not going to school to become a head doctor. It's called brain surgeon. I'm already a head doctor let you tell it," Kenya said, unzipping Kilo's pants. "I know it ain't cheap going to school, but if you ever need to hold some bread, I got ya, homie. I'm just planning on doing something different this year. I ain't got nothing but what a week and a half, two weeks left?" Quick said to Kilo who was slouched down on the couch with his eyes closed. "Don't worry but nothing. Something will fall in place for you," Kilo said, grabbing a handful of Kenya's ass. "Yea, I know, but let me call this nigga and tell him I'm out front with his package," Quick said then hung up. Kenya continued being a head doctor using her mouth and hands. After sucking every ounce of semen from Kilo, Kenya asked, "Baby, why did you lie to Quick about paying for my schooling?" "Because we've planned a surprise party for that nigga down in Vegas. And I didn't wanna tell him, so I lied about having to check my money." "Baby, why didn't you tell me about this? Please tell me I'm invited. Please . . ." Kenya said, getting excited about going to Vegas. "Only if you're a good gurl," Kilo said. "I'm always good. Now come on to the bedroom so I can be a bad gurl."

Over the next few days, Kilo began to get things set up for the trip. He booked the flights, made the room reservations, he even made reservations for two show models to entertain Quick the entire night. Kilo spent a little over ten grand on his, Quick's, and Fresh's stay in Las Vegas. *'I'll make it back,'* Kilo thought to himself, giving Kenya the money to pay for the flight and the hotel reservations. At the airport, Kenya was stopped by a guy who she asssumed was a rapper or something because of the jewelry he wore and the two men that was following him around. "How you doing, good-looking? My name Heavy. What's yours?" "Thanks for the compliment. I'm Kenya," Kenya said then started to walk toward the counter. "Can I have a minute of your time, if you don't mind, Kenya?" Heavy said, walking behind Kenya. Kenya looked over her shoulder and said, "Sorry, but I'm kind of running behind. Besides, I'm engaged." "I understand. But if yo man ever give you problems, ask somebody that know somebody what's Heavy number," Heavy said, then turned, and walked away. *'That nigga was fine and seemed to have some manners. He probably would have had a chance if I wasn't with Kilo,'* Kenya thought. "Next person in line please," the lady behind the counter said. Kenya paid for the reservations and left with nothing left to do for the day. So Kenya called Ivonne, "What's up, gurl? What you got going on today?" "Nothing much. I was just doing a little studying. What you doing?" Ivonne asked, getting up, stretching. "Out running errands for Kilo. I'm on my way over. We got some catching up to do," Kenya said. "Catching up on what? We ain't been separated from each other, gurl." "Somebody been keeping secrets tho, I see. I'll be there in no time. Just be ready to fill me in," Kenya said and hung up. *'What in the world is Kenya talkin' 'bout now?'* Ivonne thought, picking her books up off the floor. Half an hour later, Kenya was knocking on Ivonne's door, walked in, and went straight to the kitchen. "What are we 'pose to be catching up on 'cause I'm lost," Ivonne said, standing in the living room. "You tell me. I heard Kilo and Slim talking the other day, and Slim was saying that ya'll been hanging out lately," Kenya said, pouring some pineapple juice into a glass. Hearing Slim's name, Ivonne started to miss him a little.

"Oh, it was nothing like that. We just went out for lunch a few times. Gurl, it wasn't nothing to tell." "Let that be the reason. I heard him tell Kilo that he's inviting you to go to Vegas with us," Kenya said, gulping the pineapple juice down. "Vegas? He ain't told me nothing about going to Vegas. When is this supposed to happen?" "I think I just ruined a surprise. Oops. Next week tho, gurl, for Quick's birthday. It's a surprise to him too. I can't wait to see the bright light city," Kenya said, ready to see Las Vegas for the first time. "I wonder when Slim was gone ask me because he show ain't said nothing about it. Are you sure about this? I'll hate to get worked up for nothing. Now stop playing, Kenya," Ivonne said, thinking that Kenya was making all this up. "Gurl, I'm dead-ass serious. As a matta fact, let's go do a little shopping for new outfits. You could use it to get out this house a little anyways," Kenya said, rinsing out her glass in the sink. Four and a half hours later, Kenya and Ivonne were leaving the mall with one too many shopping bags apiece. "All this shopping has made me hungry. What about you?" Ivonne asked Kenya who was driving around, singing along with Jasmine Sullivan." "I'm always hungry for some reason now. I think my metabolism done went up or something," Kenya said. "Your metabolism my ass. You sure you're not having an offspring developing in your uterus?" Ivonne questioned. "What you tryna say? I'm pregnant?" "If you're eating more than normally, then it's got to be something. Unless you done started smoking and just got the munchies," Ivonne said. "Smoking? Of course not. You know how I'm against that. But let's go to the chicken shack and eat. I got a taste for some chicken," Kenya said, changing the subject back to food. *'I know I'm not pregnant because I haven't missed my period,'* Kenya thought and made a mental note to stop by the drugstore after she dropped Ivonne off. *'I'll buy a test to make sure.'*

After eating, Kenya dropped Ivonne off and drove to the nearest drugstore. Kenya hid the pregnancy test in her shopping bags to keep all suspicion away from Kilo. *'What if I am pregnant? How would Kilo take it? Do he even want kids right now? Would it be a girl or boy?'* All these thoughts raced through Kenya's head while driving home. Seeing that Kilo was home, Kenya grabbed her bags and headed in and dreaded not telling Kilo about the pregnancy test she bought. "Hey, you still here? I thought that you would be out with your boys or something. It feels good out," Kenya said, shutting the door with her ass. "Nawl, boo, I'm cooling rite now. Let me help you with them bags," Kilo said, getting up from the couch. "I got them, baby. It's just a couple, but lock the door back," Kenya said, not wanting Kilo to go through her bags. "A couple? Shid, it look like you bought something out of every store in the mall. Let me see what you got." "I want to look nice for you when we're down in Vegas, baby, you'll see," Kenya said, walking to the bedroom. Kenya put the pregnancy test in the dresser under her panties and bras. Knowing that Kilo never went through her belongings, Kenya stripped down and headed for the bathroom to soak in some steaming hot water. *'A bubble bath is exactly what I need to take my mind off this baby thing,'* Kenya thought then lit the vanilla-scented candles around the tub, turned on the water, then poured some bath beads from Victoria's Secret into the tub. Sinking down into the tub, Kenya let her thoughts drift. "Have you seen the news?" Slim asked Kilo over the phone. "Un-un. What happened?" Kilo questioned, turning the television station to ABC to watch the worldwide news. "The DEA took down a Mexican cartel earlier today. Said they recovered sixteen thousand kilos of cocaine and over $18.3 million in cash," Slim said. "Gyde damn! Fa real?" Kilo said, not believing his ears. "Yea, fa real, my nigga. They said it's the biggest drug bust since the early 2000s." "I hope shit don't start to dry up round here. But do you have everything set for the party? We leaving Thursday," Kilo said. "Yea, I'm ready. Ima ask Vonne if she wants to go today. I hope she say she does because everything paid for already," Slim said. "You ain't asked her yet? What you waiting on the day we're leaving so she can tell you she already made plans to do something else." Kilo said trying to catch the news. "Ima call and ask her soon as we get off the phone. If she done made plans already, I bet she'll change them to go to Vegas," Slim said. "You right. Gone handle yo bizniz tho my nigga, and hit me when you're done," Kilo said, getting up from the couch looking for Kenya. "Aite, one," Slim said and hung up. Slim called Ivonne to see if she had plans for the weekend. "Well, I just made plans today. Thanks for the invitation to Vegas, Slim. I'm glad you chose me," Ivonne said, letting it be known that she already knew about the trip. "Hold on. How do you already know about this, Vonne?

'Cause I show'll can't remember telling you," Slim asked, confused. "I got my sources. Just know that my girl ain't gone leave me in the dark about nothing. That's all I'm saying," Ivonne said. "Kenya! But how do she know I was gone ask you if you wanted to come? I know Kilo ain't tell. She musta been eavesdropping. Well, since you know already, how about a little shopping before we leave? My treat." "You're too late for that. Me and Kenya just got back about an hour ago, and I'm all worn out. I think I'm gone take me a nice bath and relax a little. We're leaving Thursday, and it's Tuesday now," Ivonne said, lying in the middle of her bed, staring up at the ceiling. "You know more than I do about this trip I see. Well you just be ready 'cause I'll be there bright and early picking you up," Slim said, pulling into his mother's driveway. "I don't know why you're coming so early and the flight don't depart until two thirty in the afternoon," Ivonne said, picking with Slim with the information she already knew. "Just to see your face Ms. Know-it-all. How about that?" Slim said, laughing. "You can see my face now if you promise to rub my feet after I get out the tub." Ivonne said taking her cloths off. "I'll rub yo feet if you promise me that they're not ugly," Slim said. "I promise." "I'll be over there as soon as I leave from my momma's house, eating me a plate." "Bring me one and tell my mother-in-law I said hi," Ivonne said a little too late because Slim had already hung up. Slim sat and ate his food quietly with Ivonne on his mind. "You sure are quiet, Isaac. Is everything okay?" Ms. Cook asked, sensing that Slim had something on his mind. "I'm just thinking, Ma, that's all." Slim said, biting into his baked pork chop. "What are you thinking about? Is there anything I can help you with, son?" Ms. Cook asked. Ms. Cook, like any other single mother with a son, tried her best to be there for her son in every way possible. But she knew that only a man could teach a boy how to become a man. "It's this girl that I've been seeing lately, Ma. I can't seem to shake her. I mean she's always on my mind. She seems so perfect for me," Slim said, looking at his mother, waiting on her response. Slim knew that he could talk to his mother about anything, and she'll always tell him the truth about what she knew or felt about the situation. "Now, Isaac, I'm gone tell you something that I want you to always remember. Just because a female has something so good between her legs doesn't mean that she got a good head on her shoulders. You have to make sure a person's intentions are good before you just up and decide that you want to be with them. It's a lot of people in the world today that just want to be with somebody because of who they are or what they got," Ms. Cook told Slim. "Yea, Ma, I know, but me and her haven't had sex yet. I'on even think we had a conversation about it. I feel comfortable when I'm with her and I know it's not a money thing either because I just tried to take her shopping and she declined and asked for a foot massage instead." "Really? Well, what is it that she do for herself as far as work?" Ms. Cook asked. "Because any woman who declines a shopping spree for a foot massage has to be mature and stable." "She's going to school, studying law. She wants to become a lawyer. I'm not sure if she works or not. I've never asked. But, Ma, I know a hood rat and a sack chaser when I see one, and she's neither," Slim said, scraping the last bit of baked apples and macaroni and cheese together then eating it. "And what's her name?" "Ivonne." "Well, I'll like to meet Ms. Ivonne as soon as possible," Ms. Cook said, cleaning the kitchen table. "Aite, Ma, but where's Tia?" Slim asked, wondering where his lil sister was. "She said she was going over to her friend's house for a little while." "I can't never catch her at home. Is Tia dating, Ma?" Slim asked. "Not that I know of. She haven't said nothing about it or brought nobody home. So I'm not sure. Why you ask?" "Just wondering. How about her schooling? Have she decided where she wants to go?" "We're supposed to be going to Nashville next month to do a tour of Tennessee State University. That's where she wants to go," Ms. Cook said. "Let me know if ya'll need help with any expenses and tell Tia I said to call me," Slim said, getting up from the table. Slim hugged and kissed his momma and was out the front door. Thursday morning Kilo was up early, packing a few things he thought he might need. *'Man, something don't feel right. I hope everything go as planned today,'* Kilo thought to himself. "You're up pretty early. What time is it?" Kenya said, pulling the covers up. "It's seven thirty-eight. Get you some rest. I'm just making sure everything set to go." Kilo told Kenya then leaned over and kissed her on the forehead. "Okay, baby, but don't let me oversleep. Wake me up at nine o'clock please," Kenya said, then rolled over, and went back to sleep. Still feeling like something wasn't right, Kilo rolled a blunt to try to ease his mind. *'Maybe I'm just paranoid or something. Whatever it is, I ain't gone let it ruin my nigga trip,'* Kilo thought while smoking his blunt and flipping through the channels. *'I wonder if I should call and let Quick know that we're going to Vegas today as an early birthday present. Nawl, I'ma keep it a surprise.'* An hour later, Kenya was in the kitchen, cooking breakfast. Kilo walked up behind her and kissed her lightly on the neck and said "Good morning, boo." "Good morning, baby. You was on the phone when I walked by, and I didn't want to disturb you. Besides, I woke up with an appetite out of this world. I've been eating a lot lat—" Kenya said, catching herself in midsentence, not wanting to tell Kilo about the crazy cravings she had been having. "Baby, can you hand me some butter out the fridge please?" Kenya said, hoping Kilo didn't catch her last sentence. "Cooking breakfast in your T-shirt and panties will get you in trouble. You know that, right?" Kilo said, handing the butter to Kenya. "Is that so? Well, how about I cook breakfast in nothing at all?" Kenya said then pulled the shirt over her head, throwing it at Kilo. "This was all you had on anyway, huh?" Kilo said, admiring Kenya's body. "Damn, you got one hellava body, boo. You haven't been sneaking to the gym on me, have ya?" "Nope, but maybe I should to get this little gut off," Kenya said rubbing her stomach that got just a tad bit of baby fat on it. *'Or maybe I shouldn't,'* Kenya thought. "Gut? Don't you mean butt? 'Cause that ass stick out way farther than yo gut, boo," Kilo said, grabbing Kenya's ass and making it jiggle. The two ate breakfast then lounged around the house till around one thirty. "I think we better gone head and get ready. I told Fresh and Slim that we'll meet up here at a quarter till two," Kilo said, and as soon as the words left his mouth, Fresh was calling his phone, telling him that he was out front. Slim called a lil while later, announcing his arrival with Ivonne. "Aite, now that we're all here, what do ya'll think is the best way to tell Quick about this?" Kilo asked. "I think we should keep that nigga in the dark about the trip and let him find out when we get there," Slim said. "Yea, don't tell him shit. Let's just pick him up and take him with us. If he ask any questions, we'll just say it's a business trip," Fresh said then noticed that everybody in the room had their woman with them. "I'm feeling kinda left out being that I'm the only one without a female with me. Call one of yo homgurls for me and tell them everything on me, Kenya," Fresh said. "I don't have any. Ivonne the only one I got," Kenya replied. "Ya'll be quiet for a sec while I see where Quick at,"

Kilo said, calling Quick from the home phone. "Hello," Quick answered. "Where you at, fool? I need you to take a trip with me. It's bizniz," Kilo said into the phone. "I'm down the street from the Juice Box. Give me ten minutes flat, and I'll be there," Quick said, turning his car around, and headed towards Kilo. "Aite, just hurry up. I'll be waiting." "Do I need to grab my toaster?" Quick asked, getting the feeling that something was wrong. "Nawl, you won't need it," Kilo said then hung up. "He's on his way. Let's wait out in the parking lot for him." By the time they made it to their cars, Quick was pulling up and Kilo's phone was ringing. "Speak," Kilo spoke into the phone. "Me and Cutt decided not to go this time. We gone save some money up to ball like the Big Dawgs next time," Benjamen said, sitting in the kitchen at the Fish Tank. "Good choice. There's always a next time," Kilo said, clipping his phone back to his waist. Quick hopped out his car, wondering what was going on. "Kilo, what's good, my nigga? Why do you need me when Slim and Fresh is here?" "It's a bizniz trip, and everybody needs to be there," Kilo said. "Trip? Where to?" "Vegas. Now get in. The plane leaves at two thirty, and it's two eleven now." "Shit, I wish I would have known we was going to Vegas. I would have grabbed 'bout ten extra bands to play with. I'm glad you called rite after I made my lil play, tho. I got sixty-five hundred to play with," Quick said, climbing in the backseat of Kilo's Magnum. They made it to the airport just in time to board the plane. On the plane, Quick sat by the window and Fresh sat next to him. Kenya, Kilo, Slim and Ivonne sat behind them. "Who the hell are we 'pose to be meeting down in Vegas?" Quick asked Fresh after the operator said what she said over the intercom. "The connect is all I know," Fresh said, feeling the plane take off. "Why in Vegas, tho? And why did Kilo bring Kenya and Slim bring Ivonne?" Quick questioned. "Ion know. But check out that fine-ass stewardess right there. I gots to have her before we get to Vegas," Fresh said then flagged her

down. "How you doing you video vixen you?" "I'm fine, sir. Can I get you anything?" The stewardess asked, blushing. "Nawl, I'm good right now. I just wanted to let you know that you're very attractive. And was wondering if we could get to know each other a little better. My name is Fresh by the way," Fresh said to the stewardess who liked the way Fresh wasn't cutting corners trying to get to know her. "That's so kind of you. I'm Layla, and I'm engaged, sorry," the stewardess said then asked Quick, "Can I get you anything, sir?" "Yea, let me get a bottled water if you don't mind." "I'll be right back with it, sir." The stewardess said and walked off. "Damn, my nigga, I ain't seen you get turned down since high school," Quick said, laughing at Fresh. "It's cool. I see her anywhere else I bet she'll go. That bitch probably tryna keep her job. But did you peep her accent? She sound like she Latin or some shit," Fresh said. "You can look at her and tell she's from another country," Quick was saying as Layla was walking back up the walkway. "Here you go, sir," Layla said, handing Quick his water. "Thank you, miss. If you don't mind me asking, what's your race?" Quick asked. "The West Indies," Layla said with pride. "So you're Dominican, huh?" Fresh asked. "Yep!" Layla said then walked off. "You dropped something," the guy next to Fresh said, pointing at the ground. Fresh picked up the folded piece of paper, unfolded it and read, "Meet me in the bathroom in one hour." "It's hard for a bitch to pass me up. Read this," Fresh said, giving the note to Quick." "Get the fuck outta here. Ion believe this," Quick said after reading the note. "I'll tell you all about it once I'm finish," Fresh said, getting the last laugh. Feeling somebody poking him in the side, Kilo woke up and said "Are we there yet?" "Yes baby, we just landed. You've missed everything. Especially the good part of flying over the city and seeing all the tall buildings and bright lights." "It ain't even dark. How you see some bright lights, boo?" Kilo said. "Everything still seemed bright. Don't hate because you missed it," Kenya said, standing up to stretch her legs. Exiting the plane, they all climbed into the limousine Kilo had waiting on them. "We pulling up to meet the new supplier in a stretch navigator. This nigga connected to the mob, ain't he?" Quick said to no one in particular. "Just sit back and keep a clear head for me, Quick. Can you do that?" Kilo said. "Yea, I got you. It's just that this shit happened so—" "Quick!" Kilo snapped. "Aite, dawg." After about a twenty-five-minute drive, the limousine pulled in front of the Marriott Hotel then stopped. The driver, a big black Jamaican-looking dude got out and opened the back door. "We're coming right back out, sir. We just checking in and dropping our stuff off," Kilo told him. "Okay, my man. The name's Xson," The driver said, shaking hands and helping people out. After everyone checked into their room, they all met back up in the lobby then climbed back into the limousine. "Take us to the biggest mall around here, Xson." "No probleem," the Jamaican said back in broken English. "A yo, Kilo, I got one question and I'm done with the matter," Quick said. "What's that?" "Who in the hell paid for that suite for me?" Quick wanted to know. "The connect wanted to know how many rooms we was gone need, so I told him four." "That's what's up, and how did you meet this guy?" "You said you had one question, not two. Now just sit back and enjoy yoself," Kilo told him. "I just like to know everything that's going on. Ion like being in the dark about nothing." "You're in good hands. Don't worry." The rest of the way to the mall, they all took shots of Remy Martin from the built-in mini bar that was in the limousine. Fresh was filling Quick in on how the stewardess didn't want to let him fuck on the plane because he didn't have any condoms. "But she sucked the hell outta my dick tho, nigga. She stay in Cali. I got her number and told her I'll keep in touch," Fresh was saying as the limo was coming to a stop. "Dhis the biggest mall down here," Xson the limo driver said through the middle window that separated the front and back. After walking around the mall for two hours straight, they all decided to hit the room and chill out for a while since everyone was tired from the plane ride anyway. Kilo told Kenya she can hang out if she wanted, but he was checking in for the night. Kenya checked in right behind him. And so did Slim and Ivonne. "I guess it's just me and you. You checking in too?" Fresh asked Quick. "Nawl, not just yet. Let's find us some of the best weed Vegas got and ride around and do a little more sight seeing," Quick said, hopping back in the limo. The next morning Kilo called both Fresh and Quick but got no answer. He tried back around 11:30 a.m. and still didn't get an answer. "I know these niggas ain't still sleep," Kilo said, putting his cell phone on the charger. Kilo called Slim and got an answer on the third ring, "Hello." "Who dis? Vonne?" "Yep, and good morning to you, Mr. Carter," Ivonne said, calling Kilo by Kenya's last name. "Good morning to you too. Where's Slim?" Kilo asked. "He's in the shower. You want me to tell him to call you when he get out?" "Yea, have him to hit me." Kilo said then hung up. "Yo, gurl, must be feeling my nigga, boo." "Why you say that?" Kenya said, pulling Kilo's T-shirt over her necked body. "'Cause she's answering his phone and everything. I hope she ain't going through his pockets while he's in the shower," Kilo joked, flopping down on the bed. "Vonne's not like that. She did tell me she's feeling Slim, though." A few minutes later, Slim was calling Kilo back. "What's good, my nigga?" Slim asked, rubbing cocoa butter on his legs. "Have you heard from Fresh or Quick this morning? Them niggas ain't answering the phone." "Nawl, I ain't heard from 'em. I just got up not too long ago," Slim said. "Aite. Ain't no telling what them fools did last night. I'm funa go to their room and check on them. Hit me back after you finish getting yo self together," Kilo said. "Aite, one." Kilo slipped his jeans and shoes on and walked four doors down to Quick's room and knocked on the door but got no answer. So he knocked harder, and there was still no answer. *'Maybe that nigga crashed in Fresh room last night,'* Kilo thought, then walked two more doors down, and knocked on Fresh's door. *Knock, knock, knock.* No answer. Kilo knocked a little harder, then put his ear to the door, and heard the TV playing. "Yea, they gotta be in here." *Boom, boom, boom.* Kilo used the tip of his shoe to knock this time. "Man, who the fuck is that bangin' at the door like that?" Fresh said and rose up. "Who is it?" he hollered. "Kilo, nigga, open the got damn door." Fresh got out the bed in his wife beater and boxers and saw Quick laid out on the other bed with a bitch beside him. Then he looked back and saw another one in his bed. "This nigga funa trip off this," Fresh said, opening the door. "I thought you was the police the way you bangin' on the door." 'If ya'll niggas pick up ya'll phones and state that everything's aite, I wouldn't have to bang on no door," Kilo said, walking into the room. Looking around, Kilo said, "I see ya'll did a lil extracurricular last night." "I can't wait to tell you about this one, nigga. Some serious freaking went on last night," Fresh said. "Tell him about it now. Maybe he'll want to join in so I can pull his dreads while he's fucking me," the girl lying in Fresh's bed said. "It's like that, huh?" Kilo said, sitting down at the table in the corner of the room. Picking up a bag of weed that looked like something out of a magazine, Kilo said, "Where ya'll get this shit from? This shit look good enuff to eat." "Wait till you fill yo lungs with it. Three or four puffs it's all it takes." By this time, Quick was up, getting his thoughts together. "Get yo ass up, nigga. It's going on one, and ya'll laid around like it's cool," Kilo said, laughing. "I had one hellva night fucking with Fresh,"

Fresh and Quick told Kilo about everything that happened last night. They were talking as if the two females weren't still in the room with them. But that didn't do anything but turn the females on. They tried to push up on Kilo once, but Kilo refused, telling them that if it was another place and time, he would've knocked the bottom out of both their pussies. "Man, I'm 'bout to get up outta here. I gotta get myself together. Ya'll niggas need to be doing the same thing 'cause we're leaving to handle bizniz 'round eight," Kilo said, getting up from the table. "I'm about to get up outta here too. I need to wash my ass. I got juices all over me," Quick said. "Let me do the honors and lick them off. It's probably my juices anyway," the girl in Fresh bed said. After another orgy Quick left, and so did the two females whose names still remained unknown. The only thing known of the two females was they were foreign. *'It's cum all around this room. Let me go see if they got another room available on the same floor,'* Fresh said to himself after taking a shower and debating on what to wear for the night. Picking a blue-and-brown Akoo outfit and some all-white midtop Air Force Ones, Fresh grabbed his chain and watch and was out the door, heading for the lobby. "Baby, do you think this look right?" Kenya asked Kilo, holding up a gray and black Coach dress and some gray open-toe heels. "You know you look good in anything you rock, boo. Besides, that ain't nothing but two colors. Why wouldn't it look right?" "I know it matches. I want to know it if it's appropriate or not," Kenya asked. "You got my approval if that's what you're asking. Just make sure that ass is phat to give them niggas something to look at," Kilo said, grabbing a towel and washcloth to take a shower with. "You're crazy, baby. Why you want another man looking at your woman like that? Wouldn't that make you mad?" Kenya asked, following Kilo to the shower. "Ion get mad. I know a nigga gone look, which just let me know that I got something they want but can't have." Kilo said cutting on the hot water. "Must be a man's thang," Kenya said, sliding in the shower right behind Kilo.

"You gone kill 'em tonight in that all black Prada skirt set Vonne. I'on think they ready for that yet," Slim said, telling Ivonne how cute she looked in something so simple. "Thank you, baby. You're not a bad look on the eyes either," Ivonne told Slim. Slim decided to keep it simple himself and rock a Black Label outfit and the solid-black

Air Max 95s he bought from the mall. "The simpler the better. I like to feel comfortable when I'm out," Slim said, putting his chain around his neck. Around seven fifteen that night, Kilo called Xson and told him that they will be ready around eight. "I'm out front, my man," Xson called Kilo's cell phone at eight sharp and said. The limo pulled in front of the MGM Grand Casino and stopped. "What kind of bizniz meetings are held at casinos?" Quick wanted to know. "This ain't no bizniz meeting, nigga. This a early birthday present. HAPPY BIRTHDAY, FOOL!" Fresh said, not able to hold back the surprise any longer. "Aw, shit, so this what this is all about. Man, ya'll let me come down here with $6,500 to spend for my birthday. Really $4,500 'cause I spent $2,000 at the mall," Quick said, cheesing from ear to ear. "Nigga, don't worry 'bout nothing if you run out of money. It's mo where that came from. Now let's go have some fun," Kilo said. "Yea dawg, don't worry 'bout nothing. Enjoy yoself tonight," Slim told Quick, stepping out the limo. "HAPPY BIRTHDAY, QUICK!" Kenya and Ivonne said one after the other. "Thanks." Inside the casino, Kilo gave Kenya $5,000 and told her to enjoy herself tonight win or lose. Not knowing if Ivonne had some spending money, Slim counted out twenty $100 bills, folded them in half, then asked Ivonne for a hug, and slid them in her purse without her knowing. "Let's grab us something to drink then go find Heavy and his entourage to wish that nigga a happy birthday," Kilo said, making his way toward the bar. "Look at all these beautiful bitches in here. I don't see how niggas can just settle for one. It's too many," Fresh said, observing the crowd walking through the casino meeting and greeting people, some they knew and some they didn't. They found Heavy and his crew piled up in the VIP section surrounded by bottles of champagne, weed smoke, and a bunch of women. Slapping fives with Heavy and Jimmy, Kilo told Heavy happy birthday. Heavy then got everyone's attention that was in the VIP and introduced Kilo and his boys. "A . . . A . . . A . . . LEMME GET EVERYBODY'S ATTENTION!" Heavy said, causing everybody to look at him, then started introducing Kilo to everybody in the room. "And this rite here is my nigga Fonzi and that nigga there is JD," Heavy said, pointing to Fonzi and JD. *'Damn, what a coincidence, I've bumped into two niggas who name I've always heard but could never put a face to it,'* Kilo thought to himself. "Kilo gone be the next big thang to blow the city a new asshole," Heavy said. "Ion know about that we just trying to eat like everybody else," Kilo said, putting emphasis on *we*, letting them know that his niggas played a part in everything he did. "Enuff with the small talk. Let's get this party started!" Lil Jimmy hollered, holding a bottle of Ace of Spades in the air. "We came to celebrate, not converse," One of Heavy's homeboys yelled out, putting his arm around one of the half-dressed girls in the room. "Well, let's do it like real niggas do and let the dice roll. Anybody feeling lucky?" Heavy said, leading the way to the crap table. Making their way to one of the tables, Heavy told the young lady that was stationed there that she could take a few hours off. "I'm not allowed to leave this area, sir, sorry." "I'm the renter of this casino for the night babygurl, so your boss won't mind. I promise." The young lady left, and the gambling began. "We shooting regular dice to fuck that casino shit. Fifty dollars I shoot, $50 I hit," Heavy said, pulling out a knock of $100 dollar bills. "Shoot, nigga! I got the hit and the fade," Fonzi said, peeling a $100 dollar bill from his bankroll and throwing it on the table. "Just like old times, huh?" Heavy said picking, up the dice and shaking them. Heavy rolled the dice and they came two deuces. "Four. I bet a hunnet I ten or four to anybody," Heavy said, dropping his bet. "I got a hunnet you don't," Quick said, dropping two fifties. "Six fo' fa tha po' one," Heavy said, then threw the dice, and crapped straight out. "I knew you had a seven in ya. Next man with oil," Quick said while he and Fonzi picked up their winnings. They sat around shooting dice, talking shit, drinking, and smoking six hours straight. Kilo hit eight points in a roll before he crapped out. Feeling some hands wrap around his waist, Kilo looked back and saw Kenya standing behind him. "What's up, ma? You run outta money?" "Nope! I've actually been winning. Me and Vonne been tearing them slot machines up. I was just checking on you making sure you're okay, baby," Kenya said then kissed Kilo on the lips. "I'm good. Do me a favor boo, and go get me another bottle of Ace of Spades from the bar." "Okay, is that all you want, baby?" Kenya asked, looking up to see who was doing all this hollering and for what. Kenya made eye contact with Heavy for the first time that night and told herself, *'How could I be that dumb not to put two and two together to know that this would be his party? I know this nigga didn't just wink his eye at me.'* "Kenya, did you hear what I just said?" "Sorry, baby, I was trying to see what the commotion was all about. What did you say?" Kenya said, drawing her attention back to Kilo. "I said bring me a few bottled waters too." After the dice game, everyone sat around the VIP area kicking the shit. Before leaving the casino that night, Kilo told Heavy and Lil Jimmy that he'll be to see them within forty-eight hours of their plane landing. "That lil nigga got some real potential of playing in the major league with the right guidance behind him," Heavy said after Kilo left. "The only one that might cause problems or draw unwanted attention is Fresh. That nigga is way past flamboyant. I like his style, tho," Lil Jimmy added. *'I think I'm gone take that young nigga under my wing and give him the game,'* Fonzi thought to himself.

Chapter 4

It was back to the basics as soon as the plane landed in Youngstown for Kilo. After making sure everything was the way he left it at home, Kilo called Benjamen at the Fish Tank to check on his loot. "Everything's everything, my nigga," Benjamen said. "Aite, I'll be there in a second to grab that." Jumping on his motorcycle, Kilo zoomed to the Fish Tank to pick his money up. "I'ma have Slim hit ya'll with some mo as soon as I re-up," Kilo told Benjamen and Cutt before he left. Kilo called Slim before he hopped back on his motorcycle to tell him that he just picked the money up from the Fish Tank. "I need you to swing by the Juice Box and check on things there then meet me at my spot." "I'm funa handle that now. Then I'm coming straight to ya," Slim said. "One." "One." Kilo flung the knapsack on his back, hopped on his bike and sped off. Back at the house Kenya was on her hands and knees with her face in the toilet, throwing up. *'I'm gone have to take that test to find out the truth because this is real unusual for me,'* Kenya thought, getting up to brush her teeth. *'I'm gone take me a long hot shower. Then I'll find out my fate,'* Kenya thought then got her things together to take a shower, wondering, *'What if I am pregnant? Would I be a good mother? How is Kilo gone take it?'* Standing under the showerhead, Kenya rubber her belly over and over trying to imagine her life with a child, picturing herself and the baby having good times together at the park. Kenya was brought back to reality by a knock at the door. Sticking his head in the door, Kilo asked, "How much longa you gone be in there, boo?" "I just got in about five minutes ago. Why? Do you need me to do something, baby?" Kenya asked a little startled. "Nawl, I was just gone let you know that me and Slim will be in the living room." "Oh, okay, thanks for letting me know because I was show'll coming out in my birthday suit," Kenya said. Kilo knew that Kenya loved to walk around in her panties and bra and sometimes nothing at all, so he made sure to tell her when someone was coming over. Kilo and Slim sat at the kitchen table stuffing money into the money machines that Kilo promised he was going to get. "You ain't got nothing to smoke?" Kilo asked Slim. "I got a half a quarter of purp in the car. I didn't bring it with me 'cause every time we counting money, we counting money ain't no time for smoking," Slim said, putting a rubber band around $10,000 in fifties. "We got time now thanks to these money machines. Go grab that so we can blow one. While you doing that, I'ma call Heavy to tell that fool we ready." Slim got up from the table to go get the smoke sack, and Kilo called Heavy. "Yo what up, fam?" Heavy spoke. "Same shit, different time. It's a beautiful day to go fishing at the bank. You going?" "Nawl, the lakes all dried out. You ain't seen the news?" "Yea, I saw that last week, but I know we can catch at least five of them thangs at the lake," Kilo said, remembering the Mexican Cartel that got busted last week. "It ain't even one at the lake. My fishing pole been sitting since yesterday and I still haven't got a bite. But soon as I do, I'll hit yo phone and let you know something," Heavy said. "Aite, one," Kilo said then hung up. *'What the fuck am I gone do now?'* Kilo asked himself. Ever since Kilo began doing business with Heavy and Lil Jimmy they were always able to fill his order, so he never considered having a second supplier. *'Smoking on purple to ease my mind.'*

Slim walked back into the house, singing. "Man, you ain't gone believe what Heavy just told me," Kilo said, still sitting at the kitchen table. "What? That the prices went up so he can get some of the money back he spent throwing his party?" Slim said, sitting back down with the purp and cigar in hand. "Shit, that would've been better than him saying he ain't got none at all. I'm guessing that his supplier was connected to that Mexican Cartel that just got busted because he said something about it. I couldn't really get to much detail over the phone," Kilo told Slim. "That nigga got something. He just sitting on it till he's able to see what's gone happen. But fuck that nigga. He ain't the only nigga with dope. Let's shop elsewhere." Slim said, sitting down at the table rolling the blunt up. "That's the thing. We've been dealing with the same nigga since we got started, so who else is there to shop with? I don't feel comfortable spending my money with anybody, not knowing what the product is," Kilo said.

"Damn, I didn't think about that. So what we gone do?" Slim asked, firing the blunt up. "Ion know just yet. We might have to wait on them depending on how long they take. Or we could go through Quick's connect to get something to hold us over til Heavy get straight," Kilo said, grabbing the blunt from Slim. "Yea 'cause I spent damn near twenty grand in Vegas and I'm tryna get all that back then some." Kilo called Quick and asked him to call his people and see if they were straight. And if they were to grab five extra bricks when he re-up and he would give him the money back. Quick told Kilo that he was just about to call him to buy a few bricks. "I was just funa call you. My people said it would be a couple of days before they get back straight," Quick said. "My people saying the same thing. Keep an ear open and let me know if you hear anything," Kilo said, passing the blunt back to Slim. "Aite bet," Quick said then hung up. "It look like more than one connect was affected by that bust," Kilo said. *'Please don't let Kilo walk in here while I'm taking this pregnancy test,'* Kenya thought after removing the test from the box. Taking the urine cup, Kenya squatted over the toilet and peed in it. Not knowing what to think, Kenya just wanted to get it over with and know the truth. Dipping the stick into the pee, Kenya waited on the results. *'I would pray, but I'm not sure if I want a baby or not,'* Kenya thought. Reading the instructions on the back of the box, Kenya waited three minutes then pulled the test stick out, and saw a dark pink line across it. *'This thing can't be right. I should have bought two of them, but wait. Why ain't I happy, and why am I second-guessing this preg'*—Kilo knocked on the door. Throwing everything under the sink then pouring the pee that was left in the cup in the toilet, Kenya said, "Hold on, baby, I'm almost done in here." "You ain't gotta rush, boo. I was just letting you know that I'm about to head out for a little while. I'll be back later," Kilo said through the door. "Okay baby, just don't make it back to late. I hate being here by myself at night," Kenya said back. "I won't." After Kilo left, Kenya made sure she cleaned every piece of evidence up and promised herself to take another pregnancy test. If that one came back positive, then she was going to get a checkup. Hopping in Kilo's Magnum, Kilo and Slim ended up posted on the block after riding around the city trying to get their hands on some coke. "Somebody 'round here got some dope. I don't believe everybody was connected to the same socket," Kilo said, leaning against the front of his car. "Shit, the way things looking, that one Cartel supplied the whole state. We done contacted erbody that's somebody 'round here and still can't find nothing," Slim said, standing on the sidewalk, looking up the street. "Some bullshit like this would happen after a nigga done jacked off close to forty thou down in Vegas," Kilo said, looking up the street trying to figure out what the hell Slim was staring at. "Who the fuck is this creeping up the street in this dark green 750 LI?" Slim said, putting his hands behind his back to get closer to the Glock 40 that he had tucked there. "I got mine on me too," Kilo said, noticing Slim. The dark-green Benz came to a stop right beside Kilo's Magnum, and the passenger window rolled down. "What's a nigga like you doing hanging on the block?" A voice said out the window. Ducking his head to see who was driving, Kilo grinned. "Aw shit, we didn't know who you was nigga. I'm out here tryna get my hands on something. I know you know where it's at," Kilo said, leaning in the car to give some dap. "If I knew where it was, I would tell ya, but you know I don't mess around nomo. What my man and 'em talking 'bout?" "It's ugly on their end to," Kilo said. "That drug bust the DEA just did fucked a lot of shit up I heard. Ain't no telling when shit will get back straight on that end. But on another note, come ride with me and let me holler at you." "I'll be right back. I'm funa ride with this nigga for a sec. Here go the keys to the whip case you need to pull off," Kilo told Slim, then tossed him the keys and hopped in the dark-green Benz with Fonzi. Fonzi drove Kilo all over the city, throwing questions at him, trying to see where his head really was. And after about an hour of talking, Fonzi got the vibe that Kilo had the mind state of a leader and told him the same words Martin Luther King Jr. spoke. "I can't lie, Kilo. I see in you what my mentor saw in me before he died," Fonzi said, pulling up to a gated house way on the west side of town. "And what's that?" Kilo wanted to know, wondering who house they were pulling up to. "Leadership. But always remember that a genuine leader is not a searcher for consensus but a molder of consensus. Once you get the full understanding of that, the better off you'll be as a leader," Fonzi said, remembering the day his mentor told him those exact same words. "That's some real shit, and it's the truth. Yo roots run deeper than I thought," Kilo said. "Everything I tell you will be the truth. I only lie to the judge and the police." "So why you come looking for me?" Kilo wanted to know. "Or was you just passing through and happened to see me out there? And who crib is this?" Kilo asked all three questions at once. "I was passing through to holla at Norman and just happened to see you out there. I liked the way you carried yourself at Heavy's party and told myself that I was gone give you the game like it was gave to me," Fonzi said, putting the car in park. "But it's on you to put some sponges in yo pockets and soak this game up 'cause I can only tell it to you. And this is just one of my cribs by the way. Now come on, let's go inside," Fonzi said then climbed out. Inside the house, Kilo was kind of shocked at how spacious and clean everything was. *'This nigga can't live alone. It's too clean in here. Marble and zebra stripes everywhere,'* Kilo thought. "Make yourself at home. You want something to drink?" Fonzi asked, pouring himself a shot of Remy. "Nawl, I'm good. It's too early for me. You got some bottled waters in there?" Fonzi came out the kitchen with a half of glass of Remy Martin VSOP and a bottled water for Kilo. "Too early? It ain't never too early for some of this here," Fonzi said then tossed Kilo his water. "You looking at the game of life like you know something about it." "Nawl, Ion know nothing about it really. I've never learned how to play," Kilo said, picking up the black king and sat it back down. *'This shit feels like déjà vu,'* Fonzi thought then said, "It's not that you've never learned how to play. No one has never taught you how to play. See, the game of life is just like the dope game. You must be taught in order to reach great heights. I'ma teach you how to play the same way I was taught, with street terminology," Fonzi said, sitting down on his $4,500 dollar sofa that had real zebra fur around it. "I'm always willing to learn something new," Kilo said. "Well, Ima teach to you the names of the pieces and how they move first," Fonzi said then took a sip of liquor from his glass. "Aite, now pay attention. These pieces right here are called Pawns, but we call them foot soldiers in the game. We call them that because if its king guides them in the right direction. They can grow up to be whatever they want to be when they make it to the top," Fonzi said, pointing to the top of Kilo's side of the board. "Pawns are real valuable in the game just like foot soldiers. Aite, now these pieces right here are call Rooks, but we call them pack runners in the game. We call them that because they can stretch across the board as far as you need them to and come back. It also can move from side to side like this," Fonzi said, demonstrating what the Rooks can do. "So how do the Pawns move?" Kilo asked. "The Pawns move forward only. Either two steps on the first move and one after that or one step all the way out. The only time a pawn can kill another piece is when the other piece is in front of it like this," Fonzi said, showing Kilo the only way a Pawn can take another piece. Kilo nodded in understanding, and Fonzi went on. "Okay, now these pieces right here are called Knights, but we call them robbers in the game because every time you look up one of these pieces is bending the corner taking something. The Knights move in an L shape and is the only piece on the board that can jump over another piece. Like this," Fonzi said then jumped the Knight over a Pawn. "Those pieces can become very dangerous once you learn how to use them. Aite, now these pieces right here are called Bishops. They are the sharpshooters in the game. They move in a diagonal direction and can shoot across the board to kill another piece as long as it stays on its color. One on black and one on white. Then you got the Queen, which we call a bad bitch in the game because she can do whatever the hell she wants to do on this board. The only thing she can't do is jump over other pieces. The Queen is the most powerful piece on the board. Kinda like in real life to 'cause ion care what they say it's power between the legs of a woman," Fonzi told Kilo then took another sip from his glass. "Don't let that shit called pussy fuck your vision up, Kilo. Women are real sneaky, devious, and conniving. Don't let a pretty face and an innocent personality fool ya. You feel me?" "Yea, I feel ya. But do you have a Queen in your life? If you don't mind me asking," Kilo said, thinking about Kenya. "Yea, I got one. She's in France right now, studying to become a dermatologist. She should be back by the end of the year," Fonzi said. "All okay. I was just wondering, that's all. Okay, so the Queen can move however she want to, just can't jump over other pieces," Kilo said, sensing that Fonzi missed his girl from the tone of his voice and his facial expression when he spoke of her. "Yea, she can do whatever she want to. And this piece right here is the King, or to the niggas in the game, he's considered 'The Man.' All he do is sit back and orchestrate things. He move one step at a time anywhere he want to. This is you. You gotta use everybody around you to win, not just one piece. You have to make sure that every time you move somebody, you have protection for them. You have to make sure that all your moves are calculated. And keep your eyes on your opponent's moves at all times. The object is to keep yourself out of harm's way but attack and checkmate your opponent at the same time. Just like in real life. You gotta strategize your way to success. Now run it back by me the names of each piece and how it moves," Fonzi told Kilo then swallowed the rest of the liquor that was in his glass. Kilo named off each piece and the moves it made as if Fonzi told it to him more than once. "I see that you listen pretty well too. Now let's play a quick game to see where your thinking skills at," Fonzi said. "Let's do it and don't take it light on me. Play me fa real," Kilo said back and straightened his pieces. "White moves first, so take off." Kilo's first move: he pushed the Pawn that was in front of his King up one spot. Fonzi did the same. Kilo then pulled his Bishop out two spots. And Fonzi did the same. "You wanna do everything I do, huh? I got something for that. Watch this," Kilo said. Fonzi beat Kilo five games straight before his phone rang. "Hello . . . yes, I'm still interested . . . okay, I'll give you a call Monday morning . . . okay and thanks again," Fonzi said, sounding like a totally different person. "You gotta cool game on you for a beginner," Fonzi told Kilo after he hung up. "I see you rising to the top a whole lot quicker than the average person in the game," Fonzi said. "I've always been a thinker. But on some real shit Fonzi, I need to get my hands on some coke. I ain't got nothin'," Kilo said, still thinking that Fonzi knew somebody that had some. "Honestly, Kilo, I cut all ties to the drug game two years ago, back when Norman first told me that you were trying to get in the game," Fonzi said. "Yeah, whatever happened to you getting back at me anyway? I was waiting like hell to hear from you." Kilo said sitting back on the couch. "My bad on that. I should've bumped down on you and told you the business. But around the time Norman told me I was on my last run and didn't want to meet no new people to supply. I was tying up all loose ends and paying all dues to make a clean exit from the game," Fonzi told Kilo. "What made you wanna leave the game?" Kilo wanted to know. "The game is meant to be played, not lived. Remember that. I had a good ten-year run in the game and made enough money to live off for the rest of my life. I felt I didn't need the game anymore, so instead of getting greedy, I gave it up and switched my grind up. Everything I do now is legit. Once you're ready for the game on the corporate level, Ima give to you on that level. Until then, Ima teach you everything I know about the dope game." Kilo and Fonzi sat around, talking a little while longer then Fonzi told Kilo that he had to pick his son up from his mother's house. Pulling back up on the block, Kilo gave Fonzi some dap, then hopped out and told him that he would call him later on. "Have you heard anything from anyone?" Kilo asked, walking up on Slim who was on the phone, leaning against an abandoned house fence. "Man, I haven't heard shit. Ion know who's holdin' on to the dope, but I'm startin' to get mad," Slim said after he got off the phone. "We might have to stuff a couple duffels and hit the interstate if we don't get our hands on something soon. And the way it's looking 'round here, we might need to be hitting the interstate headed south anyway. I'm tired of payin' twenty-two a brick when we can be gettin' those thangs for eighteen or something," Kilo said. "I'm ready to move whenever you are. Just tell me when." Slim said. "Shit, we might be moving in a couple days if Heavy don't come through." Just as Kilo finished his sentence, his phone rang. "Here go Quick callin' back now. Hopefully, he got some good news. Hello," Kilo answered the phone and listened to what Quick was saying. "Aite. I'm on my way over there now," Kilo said then clipped his phone back on his hip. "What that nigga talkin' 'bout?" Slim asked as soon as Kilo hung up. "He said meet him at the Fish Tank. I think he found something," Kilo said. "Let's go see what he done got his hands on then," Slim said then tossed Kilo his keys. On their way over to the Fish Tank, Kilo stopped at the Chicken Shack to grab a bite to eat and was trying to figure out where Quick could have found some dope at. "I wonder where this nigga done found some dope at and I've been lookin' high and low for it and still haven't found any," Kilo said, putting the car in park. "You gotta remember that's how he got the name Quick. The nigga stay with something goin' on," Slim said, hopping out the car. Inside the Fish Tank, Quick was at the kitchen table breaking some dope down, when Kilo and Slim walked in. "What's up, fool?" Kilo said, walking into the kitchen where Quick was. "Tryna break this bitch down so I can whip some up to see what it do," Quick said, smashing a bag of powder with the bottom of an anchor jar. "Droppin' it in the water is always the scary part. Who you get this from anyway?" Kilo asked, picking up a chunk of the cocaine to examine it. "Ion know if you know Leroy or not, but I ran into him at the gas station and asked him where the dope was, and he hooked me up with his cuzzin'. He said his name was Moon," Quick said. "You talking 'bout Leroy that use to be on the Hill?" Kilo asked. "Yea, that's him." "Yeah, I remember that nigga. What was the ticket? It couldn't have been too much 'cause this here is some oil base. It ain't nothing like that fish-scale dope we usually get that jumps out the pot fa no reason at all," Kilo said, putting the cocaine down. "I just gave him twenty-eight for one. It was all I could find around here," Quick said, cutting the stove on. "Tell me about it. I've been on a goose hunt myself and still haven't got my hands on any. I ain't paying twenty-eight, tho. Me and Slim taking a trip down south tomorrow to try to find some at a cheaper price," Kilo said. "What's up with Heavy and 'em?" Quick asked. "The well's dry over there. I'm about to get outta here tho. It's getting late. I just wanted to see what you was working with. What's up Slim, you rollin' or chillin'?" Kilo asked Slim who was sending somebody a text message. "I'm rolling. I gotta get my whip from yo crib," Slim said. Before Slim hopped in his car and pulled, off Kilo told him that tomorrow they were going to Georgia to see if they could find better plug. "So wrap up $25,000 in hundreds, and I'ma take $25,000. That's just to test the quality. If it's good, we'll go back for more." "I hope you ain't planning on driving to Georgia. We might as well fly and drive back. Which part of Georgia, Atlanta or Savannah?" Slim said, grabbing half a blunt from his ashtray. "I was thinking Savannah since it's a little farther down south," Kilo said. "Aite bet. What time we leaving, and how long we staying?" Slim asked then fired his blunt up. Kilo told Slim that they would leave around one to catch some daylight in Georgia. "I ain't tryna ride around with fifty grand at night trying to come up on a plug. We might be down there for a couple days, so if you wanna pack a luggage, cool." "Aite, I'll meet you at the airport 'round noon then," Slim said, starting his car up. The next day Kilo was sitting at the edge of his bed, counting money, when Kenya walked in. "Hey, baby!" Kenya said then kissed Kilo on the cheek. Kenya was on her way to the clinic to get a checkup, and seeing Kilo kind of surprised her. "What's up, boo? What you got going on today?" Kilo said, looking up from the pile of money in his lap. "Oh, nothing. Me and Vonne about to go to the nail salon and get us a manicure," Kenya lied. "You sure is glowing, boo. You need some money?" Kilo asked. "No, baby, I got it this time. I forgot my cell phone on the dresser," Kenya said, looking at the digital clock on the nightstand noticing she had fifteen minutes to get to the clinic. "Do me a favor before you leave baby, and run to the store and get me some rubber bands. I ran out of them again." "I'm gone be late for my appointment baby, and I hate rescheduling. Plus Vonne is waiting for me in the car," Kenya whined. "Gone head then, boo. I'll run to the store in just a second," Kilo said then continued to count his money. After counting everything, Kilo hopped in his Magnum and shot to the corner store and got a box of cigars and ten bags of rubber bands. Kilo was five blocks from his house when he saw them blue light behind him. *'Woop! Woop!'* "What the fuck. Damn, you can't even go to the store without the laws on a nigga ass," Kilo said, checking himself, making sure he was clean. *'Shit I ain't got nothing on me plus I'm DL'd up,'* Kilo thought as the female officer approached his car. "Good afternoon, sir. Licenses and registration please," The female officer said to Kilo as he dropped his window. "I got everything right here in my glove box. Can you tell me the reason I'm being pulled over mam?" Kilo asked, handing his licenses and registration over. "You failed to yield at that yield sign back there. Now just hold tight while I run your information. If everything checks out and you're clean, I'll let you go citation free," The officer said, then turned and went back to her cop car. After what seemed like thirty minutes to Kilo, the officer walked back to the car and told Kilo that his licenses had been revoked but if his vehicle was clean she would let him go. "I'on see how my licenses are revoked and I haven't never been pulled over but gone head and search. Everything's clean. Ain't nothing in here," Kilo said, then got out, and let the female officer search. Searching Kilo first, the officer then searched his car and found a loaded Glock 40 under the driver's seat. "I'm gone need you to put your hands behind your back, sir. You're under arrest. Anything you say or do can and will be used against you in the court of law unless you can come up with $15,000," The female officer said. Kilo was so caught up in a trance that he didn't even hear the last words the police officer said. The only thing he heard was "Put your hands behind your back." "That gun ain't mine! I'on know where that came from," Kilo said. Then it hit him. *'Slim! That's Slim's gun.'* Kilo thought. Assuming that Kilo didn't have the $15,000 to save his ass, the female officer cuffed and took him to jail. Once Kilo found out his bond, he made a collect call to Kenya. "Hello," Kenya answered her cell phone not recognizing the number. "You have a collect call from Keon. To accept, dial zero and hold to decline dial." Kenya hit zero before the recording stopped. "Hello, baby, what's going on? Why are you calling me from jail? Are you okay?" Kenya asked, already in tears. "I need you to come post my bail. It's $25,000. I'll tell you about it later. But fa now, I need you to come get me out," Kilo said, knowing not to say too much on the jail phones. "I'm on my way, baby," Kenya said through her tears. Kenya paid Kilo's bond within the next hour and was sitting beside the jailhouse, waiting on him to come out. *'I guess the good news I received from the doctor will outweigh the bad news he's about to tell me,'* Kenya thought as Kilo was getting in the car. "What happened, baby? Why did you go to jail?" Kenya asked. "I got pulled over, and the police found a gun under my seat. I gotta go to court in two weeks," Kilo said, noticing the time. "I'm supposed to be meeting Slim at the airport in forty-five minutes. You think you can make it?" "Sure, it's only fifteen minutes away." "Good. Stop at the house first." Sensing that Kilo didn't want to talk about his situation anymore, Kenya decided to tell him what went on at the clinic. "Guess what happened to me today baby," Kenya said, trying to cheer Kilo up a little. Seeing the look in Kilo's eyes and the expression he made, lifting his eyebrows up as if to say "What," Kenya thought against telling him and said, "Never mind baby. I can see that you have a lot on your mind right now. If there's anything I can do to help, just let me know and I'll do it." "Everything's fine, boo. I'ma hire me a lawyer soon as I get back. It's good to know that you are here for me tho boo," Kilo said then thought to himself. *'How in the fuck could Slim be so careless and leave his gun in my car? My car! Shit!'* 'I'ma need one more favor from you while I'm gone, baby." Kilo told Kenya. "Anything you need baby, I'll do," Kenya said. "I need for you to pick my car up from the pound. I'm not going to have time to before I leave," Kilo said. Kenya pulled into the apartment complex and waited for Kilo while he ran in the house to handle his business. On the way to the airport, Kenya asked Kilo how long he was going be gone. He told her no longer than three days. At the airport, Kilo kissed Kenya and then got out and called Slim,

"Where you at? I'm out front." "I'm on the inside, waiting on you. Where you been at? It's twelve fifty," Slim said. "I'm walking in now," Kilo said then hung up. Not wanting to ruin the trip, Kilo decided to wait till after they got back to tell Slim about what happened. "I didn't know what was going on with you, nigga. I've been blowing yo phone up. It's been going straight to voicemail tho," Slim told Kilo as they were getting on the plane. "My phone went dead on me. I forgot to charge it last night." Slim noticed how concise Kilo was being with his words and figured something was wrong. "Is everything aite? You seem a lil uptight about something. Look fool, if it's Kenya you worried about missing, don't feel alone 'cause I'ma be missing Vonne too. I finally got her to give me a chance," Slim said humorously. "So she finally broke, huh? I betcha that trip to Vegas did it. I'm good tho, just thinking about how this trip gone play out. You know how it is stepping into the unknown," Kilo said, sitting down in his seat. "Yeah, I feel ya on that. We is kinda putting our heads out there." The rest of the plane ride was mostly quiet besides the small talk Slim made about him and Ivonne. Two hours later, the plane was landing. "Let's flag one of these cabs down and go get us a rental car," Kilo said, standing on the sidewalk outside the airport. "Whatever we get, we make sure the car gotta GPS system because we'll be lost if we don't," Slim said back then flagged down a taxi. Inside Hertz, Kilo gave Slim half on the car then told him that he was going to the restroom. Kilo did this to avoid putting the car in his name because he thought that his licenses were revoked. "I chose a platinum-gray Yukon for us to cruise the city in. It comes with a built-in navigation system," Slim told Kilo as he was walking up on the counter. Leaving Hertz in the Yukon, Slim decided to ride around Atlanta for a little while then hit Savannah. As they stopped at Chantrell's to grab a bite to eat, their search ended just as fast as it started. They met a nigga named Zo that was able to fill their order. "We just paid thirty-six for two whole ones, and we ain't been down here a full four hours yet. I say we have us a little fun and tear the mall down," Slim said, ready to see what the down south atmosphere really felt like. Under any other condition, Kilo would have balled with his nigga but after what happened earlier, he just wasn't feeling it. "I'on know, Slim. I say we save the partying for later and handle our bizniz now. The quicker we get back, the quicker we can get rid of these two bricks we just bought. Then the quicker we can get back down here to get some more. Ya feel me?" Kilo said. "You wanna roll out now?" Slim questioned. "Ain't no point of waiting around. Let's go fill this tank up and get on down," Kilo said. "Let's make this thug move then, my nigga," Slim said, finding the nearest gas station. They put the gas tank on Fat Joe, then typed their destination into the navigation system, and were on their way. Kilo thought about telling Slim about what had happened earlier but didn't want Slim thinking about how careless he was and lose focus on getting them home without any traffic stops. "Would you call getting our hands on some coke that fast a coincidence, or would you say it was meant to meet a nigga like that?" Slim asked Kilo who was a million miles away in his head. "Everything happens for a reason. So I think it was meant for us to come down here and meet Zo the way we did," Kilo said. "That nigga seemed cool as hell. Do you plan to keep shopping with him and make him the new connect, or are we just shopping for the time being?" Slim asked. "It all depends on the type of deal he work with us on shipping them. Because I ain't gone keep taking the risk of riding up and down the interstate with a trunk full of bricks," Kilo said. "Me either. This right here is Cutt and Benjamen's job." Slim said switching lanes. "We'll see if he got a driver. Then we'll go from there. Even if he don't we can pay somebody to make this trip," Kilo said then let down his window to spit. Slim drove through Tennessee and halfway through Kentucky before getting tired of driving. "You might wanna take over from here, Kilo. I'm starting to see doubles." Not really wanting to get behind the wheel because of his license situation, Kilo kind of hesitated but got behind the wheel anyway. Making it home without any problems from the law, Kilo pulled into his apartment complex and got out and stretched. "We made it in one piece. Now let's get some rest," Kilo said to Slim who barely had his eyes open. Kilo grabbed the dope from out the trunk and went inside. To his surprise, the lights were on, and there were two wine glasses sitting on the living room table. "I know she ain't disrespecting me like this." Kilo told Slim who just shook his head. Kilo walked to the bedroom and put his ear to the door. The only sound heard was the TV playing. Then he heard a giggle and flung the bedroom door open. Jumping up at the sound of the door opening, Kenya screamed, "What are you doing sneaking up on me like that, nigga? I thought you was gone be gone for a few days, so I invited Ivonne to spend the night with me." "My bad boo, I didn't mean to scare you. What's up, Vonne?" Kilo said. "Hey, Kilo. Kenya told me about your day. I hope everything works itself out for you," Ivonne said, lying across the bed next to Kenya. "I 'preciate that. I gotta surprise for you in the living room, Vonne." The next morning Kilo was up before everybody else and needed some milk to eat him a big bowl of Pops. *'I'll go to the store while they still sleep instead of waking them,'* Kilo thought, double-checking himself to make sure he had nothing on him. Kilo hopped in the Yukon and went to the store. "This shit gotta be a fucking dream," Kilo said, seeing the police lights flashing behind him again. "Ain't no fucking way in the world that this is happening." Kilo pulled over and went through the same procedures as yesterday. Only difference was the car and the officer. Kilo gave the police officer his licenses and asked the reason he was pulled over. The police officer told him that the Georgia tags on the car looked suspicious. The police ran Kilo's licenses, came back to the car, and told Kilo that his licenses are valid and that he was good to go. "What are you doing with Georgia tags and an Ohio licenses, sir, if you don't mind me asking?" The police officer said. "Me and my wife had our honeymoon down there and rented this car and drove back," Kilo said." You got to test drive it before you buy it. Remember that, son," The old white officer said then walked off. *'So if my licenses are legit, why did that other officer lie? This is where my lawyer come in at,'* Kilo told himself on his way home. Later on that evening, Kilo hired the best lawyer the city of Youngstown had. Sitting in the law firm, Kilo's lawyer Jack Holland told Kilo for $10,000 he could get the case dismissed. "As long as what you told me is true, you have nothing to worry about," Jack told Kilo. "Well, I guess I ain't got nothing to worry about then, do I? I'ma give you $5,000 now and the other $5,000 at court. Is that cool?" Kilo asked. 'That's fine with me," Jack said, taking the money from Kilo. "I'll see you at court." After Kilo left from his lawyer's office, he called Slim and asked him where he was. Slim told Kilo that he was on the block, chilling. Kilo told him not to move and that he was about to pull up. Kilo pulled up twenty minutes later and told Slim that the 40 Glock he left under his seat a few days ago was now a charge on his record. A little confused by what Kilo was saying, Slim said, "What you mean by that?" "You left yo gun in my car, didn't ya?" Kilo asked, trying not to lose his cool because this was his nigga he was talking to. "Aw, shit, cuz I thought that I told you to get it from under there. Damn, when did this happen?" Slim asked, feeling fucked up because Kilo caught a gun charge from his mistake. "It happened the same day we went to Georgia. I didn't say nothing because I +didn't want to mess nothing up. But don't worry 'bout nothing. I got Holland on the case. He said he was gone beat it," Kilo said. "That shit is all my fault. The least I can do is pay the lawyer fees. How much is it?" "He want ten. I gave him five already and told him I'll give him the other $5,000 at court." "Well, I'ma reimburse you on the $5,000 you already gave him and pay the other $5,000. I don't know how I could've been so damn careless and thoughtless," Slim said, beating himself up over the matter. "It's all good, baby boy. We all make mistakes. You just gotta be a lil more cautious next time. I got court in two weeks. I'm planning on taking one more trip before then," Kilo said. "Let me know when. I'm ready to move when you move," Slim said. "Aite, we'll take that trip the day after tomorrow. But I'm funa get up outta here. I gotta move to make." "Aite, get at me later then and a . . . I apologize for that mistake too," Slim told Kilo before he pulled off." "Where in the fuck is this nigga at?" Slim said, talking about Fresh who said he was ten minutes away forty-five minutes ago. Two days later, Kilo and Slim were traveling back down the interstate with one hundred and forty thousand in the trunk of a Chrysler 300 they rented. After meeting with Zo and discussing how much extra it will cost to get the dope delivered to them instead of them picking it up, Kilo and Slim dropped the rental car off then hailed a taxi down. "Where to?" The taxi driver asked. "The airport," Kilo said back. The plane touched down around ten forty-five in Youngstown, and Kilo called Kenya to come pick them up. With the shipment of dope coming tomorrow morning, Slim decided to call Ivonne and chill with her for the night while Kilo called Fonzi to chop it up with him about the situation he was in. "It's always gone be something or somebody pulling you back. The shit can get rough at times, it will either break you or make you. No matter what you do, you gotta keep striving because failure is not an option when you headed to the top," Fonzi told Kilo over the phone. "You right. I just don't understand why the police officer lied like that about my licenses being revoked," Kilo said, sitting in his living room, flicking through the channels. "I can only see two reasons why. One, somebody set you up, or two the officer is crooked and was hoping you had some money on you. Why else would she lie?" Fonzi said. Fonzi and Kilo talked a lil while longer before hanging up. The next day Kilo and Slim were waiting at the McDonald's on the east side of Youngstown for the drop-off. Seeing the black minivan pull into the McDonald's and park on the other side of the restaurant, Kilo backed out and pulled beside them. The driver of the minivan got out and went inside the restaurant, and Slim got out and followed him. The side door slid open on the van, and a heavyset man hopped out and climbed in the backseat of Kilo's car. With no words being exchanged, the heavyset man dropped a duffel bag in the passenger seat then got out, and climbed back into the minivan. Kilo unzipped the duffel and counted the bricks that were wrapped in the black-and-gray duct tape. Slim came out of McDonald's with some food in his hand, talking to the driver of the minivan then gave the driver some dap and got back in the car with Kilo. "Ya'll talking like ya'll know each other. You know that, nigga?" Kilo asked Slim after he got in. "Nawl, I was just making small talk. You get the work?" Slim asked Kilo. "Yea, it's in that duffel on the backseat." Kilo said, pulling out the restaurant. Slim and Kilo sat at Kilo's spot, breaking the dope down and cutting it. They stretched the eight bricks to nine then took five of them to the Fish Tank for Benjamen and Cutt to distribute. They then took two of the bricks to the Juice Box and kept one a piece for their personal sales. "Ion know how long this work gone hold us, but I got court comin' up, and I ain't makin' nomo moves until I get that situation settled," Kilo told Slim. "We just will have to make what we have do what it do then. You got court next week, don't ya?" "Yea, on the eighteenth," Kilo said. The eighteenth came around way sooner than Kilo had expected too because before he knew it he was sitting next to his lawyer in the courtroom, listening to him eat his case up, telling the judge that the officer didn't have a probable cause to search his client's car because his licenses weren't revoked like the officer said they were. "Your Honor, I ask that this case get thrown out due to the fictitious story the officer gave to search the vehicle," Jack Holland said at the end of his argument. "You know, Mr. Holland, I totally disagree with how the officer went about searching Mr. Campbell's vehicle with the fictitious story as you said. But I am also against crime and violence, and there was a loaded handgun found in the process of this fictitious story. So throwing this case out is out the question," The judge said then gave a slight wink at the DA. Or at least that's what Kilo thought he saw the judge do. Hearing the judge's last words made Kenya nervous. Slim, Fresh, Quick, and Ivonne were all there to show their support for Kilo. Fonzi even came out to support his man. "I'll give Mr. Campbell a choice to either serve one year in prison and the charge disappears, or he can serve three years on probation. Whichever he choose is fine with me. I'll take a fifteen-minute recess for the two of you to discuss the matter," The judge said before stepping down. Kilo already had his mind made up on what he wanted to do before the lawyer asked. "In actuality, this case is supposed to be retired. But evidently, the judge is doing what he pleases today," Jack said to Kilo who was lost in his thoughts. "Yea, I know, but there's a reason for it I guess," Kilo said, then looked back at his supporters, and grinned. "So do you know what you want to do? If not, we can try to get it continued until another day," Kilo's lawyer said. Kilo told his lawyer what he wanted to do, then sat back, and waited on the judge. "Mr. Holland." The judge said. "Yes, Your Honor." "Has your client decided his fate?" "Yes, he has, Your Honor," Kilo's lawyer said then looked at Kilo to make sure this is what he wanted to do. Kilo nodded, and Jack Holland went on, "My client Keon Campbell has decided to serve one year in prison instead of the three years on probation." The courtroom broke out into a small chaos and soon after Kilo was handcuffed and led to the back with his head held high.

Chapter 5

Walking out the courtroom, Fonzi caught up with Kenya and them then introduced himself. "I'm Fonzi, a friend of Kilo. Ya'll probably remember my face from Heavy's party," Fonzi said. "Yea, I know who you are. Kilo spoke good words about you," Slim said, holding a weeping Kenya around the shoulder to console her. "I just wanted to say if there's anything I can do to help make his time easier, let me know, and I'll see that it gets done. I know you're hurt right now baby girl, but everything's gone be aite. You gota stay strong for that nigga. He gone need his woman strong while he's gone. And like I said, if there's anything you need, give me a call," Fonzi said then handed Kenya his business card and walked off. Kenya took the card and stuffed it inside her purse without even looking at it. Not really wanting to be bothered with anybody, Kenya put $400 dollars on Kilo's books for commissary and $200 dollars on his phone account then dropped Ivonne off and went home. Slim, Fresh, and Quick met up at the Fish Tank to discuss business as far as who should take over Kilo's operations until he gets out. "How about we all operate the Fish Tank and the Juice Box?" Fresh said, being rational. "We could, but it ain't enuff money for all of us to get a fair share. Besides that, the dope seems to be drying up around here, and that's gone make it even harder for the three of us to make a decent profit from either one of those spots. So I say that Slim take over since he's been the one help run things over there anyway," Quick said. "However ya'll want to play it, it's cool with me. I'm just mad that he took the time instead of probation," Slim said thinking about Kilo. "Me too. If it was me, I would've took the paper and been done with it. I know I can stay out of trouble for three years. That ain't nothing," Fresh said. "He did what was best if you ask me. Why deal with them white folks for three years when you can deal with them for one? If he would've took the probation, then he would've had a felony on his jacket. That's where things got tricky, so he came out on top really," Quick said. Then said "But what's up with that connect ya'll found down in Atlanta? Shit done got real ugly 'round here." "As far as I know, everything should be good on that end. Me and Kilo just came from down there 'bout a week and a half ago," Slim said. "Call that nigga and find out if he's good or not. What was the ticket on them things down there?" Quick asked. "Seventeen five," Slim said then unclipped his cell phone. "Damn! Ya'll was paying seventeen five? I'm spending everything I got on this re-up," Quick said. "Shit, me too. I got like fifty thou to spend," Fresh said, taking advantage of the situation. Quick put up $80,000 and Slim put up the money from the Fish Tank and the Juice Box. All together they had $270,000 to spend with Zo. "Call and see if he'll sell us sixteen of them things for what we got." Quick said. Slim made the call to Zo and asked the price on sixteen bricks. "Pickup or delivery?" Zo asked. "Delivery," Slim said back. "The best I can do right now on a sixteen piece is two eighty-five. That's the lowest I can go on the delivery, but the pickup I can do for two seventy-five," Zo said. Slim placed the order to have the dope delivered to them at the same spot. "It'll be there around noon tomorrow," Zo said then hung up. Sprawled all out in the center of the bed, Kenya felt like her whole world was on pause. *'How could he be so selfish and only think about himself? What about me? What am I supposed to do now?'* Kenya was thinking. Without Kilo being home, Kenya was still able to provide for herself financially, but knowing that she was pregnant, she wanted Kilo home to support her mentally. *'I guess I'm gone have to stand up and go through this pregnancy alone. I can make it. As long as my baby's good, I'm good.'* Kenya thought, rubbing her stomach and thinking about Kilo. Hearing the phone ring, Kenya snatched it off the hook, hoping it was Kilo calling. "Hello." "What's up, girl? How are you feeling?" It was Ivonne calling to check on her. "Oh, what's up, Vonne? I thought you was Kilo calling. I don't know why he ain't called yet," Kenya said. "He'll call. He's probably still getting processed. You know how slow the system is," Ivonne said. "Yea I know, I just wish he would have came home instead of taking that time," Kenya said. Ivonne told Kenya that from a lawyer's point of view, Kilo took the better option. "If he didn't take the time, that would have left him with a felony on his record and you and I both know how bad a felony can be especially for a young black man." Ivonne said closing her books. "But now I got to go through this preg—" Kenya started to say then caught herself because she forgot that she hadn't told anyone about her pregnancy. "You're not gone have to go through your pregnancy alone. I'm always here for you," Ivonne told Kenya, picking up on her sentence. "Girl, I'm not pregnant. What you talking about?" Kenya tired to lie. "I've known you all my life Kenya, and the way you're putting on weight, eating everything in sight, says it all. Now like I said, you're not alone." After talking on the phone with Ivonne, Kenya felt better about the situation she was facing. *'I'm strong enough to take care of business while Kilo's gone. But it's going on nine o'clock. Why haven't he called yet?'* Kenya thought to herself, getting ready to take a shower. The next day Slim and Quick were waiting at the McDonalds for the delivery. "Man, what the fucks taking these muthafuckas so long? We've been sitting here damn near forty-five minutes, and they still haven't pulled in. Call that nigga and see what's up," Quick said, becoming impatient. "If they don't pull up in another ten minutes, Ima call," Slim said, scanning the parking lot with his eyes. "I hope these niggas ain't on no funny shit 'cause I didn't bring my burner with me." Quick said wishing he grabbed his gun from out his car. "Ion think they're on nothing stupid. They probably caught a flat or something. But if they do try something, I got mine on me. It stay with me like my nuts," Slim said, lifting his shirt showing Quick his nickel-plated .45. "Is that them right there?" Quick asked, pointing toward the other side of the restaurant. "Yea, that's them. You remember what to do, don't ya?" Slim said, then backed out and pulled beside the minivan like he and Kilo did the first time. Quick got out and went inside the restaurant and the driver of the minivan got out and did the same. The only difference was it was a white girl that got out the driver's seat this time. The side door slid open on the minivan, and the same heavyset man got out and into the backseat of Slim's car. The heavyset man dropped the duffel bag in the front seat then grabbed the two duffels on the backseat, unzipped them, looked inside, zipped them back and opened the door. "Zo said that this might be the last run until he's able to work out some technicality with his plug," The heavyset man said before getting out. Back at the Fish Tank, Fresh and Quick got what they paid for and left. Slim sat at the kitchen table thinking,

'Damn, now that Kilo's gone, I'm gone need another spot to cook and cut this dope. I can't have Benjamen and Cutt all in my business. Maybe I can get Vonne to let me use her spot.' Slim then called and asked Ivonne where she was. Ivonne told him that she was at Kenya's house keeping her company and that if he wanted to see her that it was cool to come over there. Slim told Ivonne what he was trying to do and even though Ivonne disagreed with what Slim was doing, she agreed to let him use her house. "You better be lucky I have an unconditional love for you already, or the answer would have been no," Ivonne told Slim. "Is that your way of saying you love me? If so, I love you too." Slim picked up Ivonne's house keys and went straight to work. Instead of turning the eight bricks into nine like he and Kilo did the last time, Slim turned them into nine and a half. *'I might as well stretch it 'cause ain't no telling when I'ma be able to get my hands on some more,'* Slim told himself, remembering that Zo said something about a last run. After Slim finished, he cleaned up his mess he made then took a brick and a half to both the Juice Box and the Fish Tank and left the rest of the dope at Ivonne's house. Slim told Benjamen not to sale no weight only ounces 'cause things weren't looking too good. "But what if they want more than one?" Benjamen asked. "Then sell it to them. They can buy as many singles as they want but ain't no weight being sold right now. We need every dollar. I think we might be coming up on a drought 'round here." Slim left the Fish Tank and headed over to Kenya's house to see if she talked to Kilo yet. Plus he wanted to spend a little time with Ivonne. On the way, Slim stopped and got him something to eat then swung by Big Ed's weed house to get himself something to smoke. *'It's gone be a long year without my nigga,'* Slim thought pulling into the apartments where Kilo lived. Getting out his car with a cloud of smoke trailing him, Slim walked up the flight of stairs to Kenya's door. *'Knock, knock, knock! Knock, knock, knock! I know that they're here. I just left,'* Slim thought before he heard a male voice ask, "Who is it?" Slim checked the door number to make sure he was at the right apartment then answered, "Slim." After about a minute or two of waiting, he heard the locks being unlocked, and the door opened. Standing in the door was a nigga dressed in a white shirt, some blue Levi's and some solid white midtop Air Force Ones. "What's up, my nigga? Who are you?" Slim asked, not recognizing the face in front of him. "I'm

Murda, Kenya's brother. She told me about what happen to Kilo, so I dropped by to check on her," Murda told Slim, stepping to the side so that Slim could get in. "That's what's up. I'm Slim, Kilo's homeboy. I was swinging by to do the same. Where's Kenya at?" Slim asked, walking into the living room. "She's in the back. I'm about to get up outta here. Tell Kenya I'll call her later on." "Aite, my nigga, be careful out there," Slim told Murda before he left. Slim locked the door behind Murda then walked to the back to find Kenya. *Something ain't right about that cat,* Slim thought, sticking his head in the bedroom door. "Slim!" Ivonne yelled excitedly then jumped off the bed and into Slim's arms. "Hey, baby. You seem happy to see me. What's up?" Slim said, scooping Ivonne off her feet. "I'm always happy to see you," Ivonne said then kissed Slim on the forehead. Ivonne was like a white girl trapped inside a black girl's skin. Her speech, personality, and sense of humor all matched that of a white girl, which made Slim like her even more. "I like her because she's green to a lot of things but still has beauty and brains," Slim once told Kilo. "What's up, Ms. Kenya?" Slim said, putting Ivonne back on her feet. "Nothing much. Still waiting on Kilo to call," Kenya said, sitting up on the bed. "Where did my brother go?" "Oh, he told me to tell you that he was out and that he would call you later. But I didn't know you had a twin. That nigga look just like you," Slim said. "Yea, I've heard that a lot. But he's actually four years older than me. He stay in Toledo and barely comes around. Kilo met him a few times," Kenya told Slim then checked her phone to make sure there was no missed calls. "I don't know why Kilo haven't called yet. I know that he have had the chance to use the phone by now," Slim said. "Me either. I put some money on his commissary and his phone account, so that can't be the reason he hasn't called. I just hope everything is okay with him in there," Kenya said, sounding a little worried. Kenya made sure she kept her phone with her everywhere she went so that she wouldn't miss Kilo's call. She even forwarded the house phone to her cell phone just in case he called while she was out one day. "Whenever he do decides to call, tell him I need to speak bizniz with him. Other than that, how have you been holding up?" Slim asked. "I'm fine. Thanks for asking, Slim. But my only concern is making sure Kilo's fine, and until I hear it from him, I'ma be worried," Kenya said, getting emotional. "One thing that I'm certain about Kilo is he's straight in any situation he's in. He knows how to handle himself, so don't worry yourself to death about his well-being. He's good. Take my word for it." Slim sat and chopped it up with Kenya and Ivonne a little while longer before rolling out. A few days later, while at the gas station filling up his car, Slim somehow bumped into Murda again. "What's up, Slim?" Murda said, walking into the store. Slim was at the cash register, paying for his gas, when he heard the unknown voice. Looking up to see who was speaking to him, Slim gave Murda some dap. "What's good, my nigga, you aite?" Slim asked. "I'm better than some and worse than others you know how that go. But I need to holla at you about some bizniz fool," Murda said. "Yea, well holla at me when you're done getting what you need. I'ma be pumping my gas," Slim said and walked out the store. Slim already knew what type of bizniz Murda wanted to talk about. He just wondered which angle Murda was going to come from. *'Is he trying buy or have some fronted to him?'* Slim thought, putting the gas nozzle back then leaned against the back end of his car and waited on Murda to come out the store. Murda came swagging out the store with a box of Newport and a box of cigarillos in his hand. "What type of bizniz are we talking?" Slim asked Murda as he walked up. "I only know one type of bizniz and that's bizniz that's lucrative," Murda replied. "I hear ya, so what we talking?" Slim asked, getting straight to the point. "I was doing bizniz with Kilo before he got knocked, getting lil nine pieces and shit. But now that he's gone, it seem to have dried up around here for me." Murda said. "So what you trying to do, nine of them thangs?" Slim asked, talking about nine ounces of cocaine. Slim figured that Murda was okay since Kilo used to serve him. "Nawl, I'm trying to get half a brick this time. I got a few people trying to get their hands on a few zips so I might as well grab enuff to serve them to. Ya feel me?" Murda said, opening the pack of Newports. "Cool, but everything's getting singled out right now because of this lil drought so the prices have jumped up to fifteen hundred a zip." Slim said. "Damn! Fifteen hundred? Kilo would give them to me for twelve all day. Drought or not," Murda said, trying to get Slim to drop the price. "Kilo ain't here, and bizniz is bizniz. This ain't nothing personal. Take it or leave it," Slim said, walking toward the driver's side of the car. "Aite, cool, let me get nine of them thangs from you then," Murda told Slim. Slim got Murda's cell phone number and told him to expect a call within an hour. Slim pulled off and headed to Ivonne's crib to get Murda's package ready. Sitting in Ivonne's living room, weighing and bagging up nine ounces of dope for Murda, Slim glanced up and noticed a picture frame sitting on the end table with a dude and a little girl in it. Picking the picture frame up, Slim wondered who was the little girl that looked so much like Ivonne and who was the dude with his arm around her. '*Maybe she has a little sister that I don't know about, and that's her uncle or brother or something. Wait, that's Vonne and her brother that she said was locked up for something he didn't do,*' Slim thought, then sat the frame back down then took and placed the dope he bagged for Murda into the freezer. Then he took the rest of the dope and hid it before his phone rang. "Hello . . . yea, I'm good . . . They like fifteen a piece . . . Nawl, you want four . . . Okay, give me thirty minutes, and I'll be there . . . One." Slim hung up, then took half a brick out his hiding spot, took four ounces of cocaine out, then put the rest in the freezer. '*Let me call Murda to see where he's at so I can go get my peoples straight to,*' Slim said, talking to himself. Slim dialed the number Murda gave him and Murda answered on the first ring. "What up? Dis Slim. You ready for me?" "Yea, I'm ready. Where do I need to meet you at? I'm out by the Chicken Shack right now," Murda said. "Damn, you're right around the corner," Slim said then thought to himself '*Should I tell this nigga where I am or meet him somewhere? Hmmm . . . I'll let him come to me since he's Kilo's people.*' "Where you at?" Slim told Murda the address to where he was instead of going out to meet him. '*I want that nigga to know Vonne's mine anyway just in case he don't know already,*' Slim thought, wondering how much Murda knew about Ivonne. Ten minutes later, Murda was knocking on the door. Slim let him in and led him straight to the kitchen where the nine ounces were sitting on the counter. "Who crib is this?" Murda asked. "This my crib. You got that bread on you?" Murda pulled out a grocery bag from out his pants and sat it on the counter. "It's all there. You can count it if you want to," Murda said, then grabbed the cocaine and sniffed it. "I'll count it later, if it's short, I'll call and let you know. I gotta make a move right quick," Slim said, then took the four zips of cocaine out the freezer and stuffed them down his pants. "Aite, but I might be calling you back before you call me because half of this already sold,"

Murda told Slim as they were walking out the door. Slim locked the door behind him, gave Murda some dap, hopped in his car, and pulled off. After delivering the four ounces, Slim called Quick to see what he was doing. But Quick didn't answer, and neither did Fresh. "Ain't no telling what them niggas got going on," Slim said before placing his phone on his car charger and cutting the music up. With nothing to do, Slim started to go back over Ivonne's house but decided not to because she wasn't there and he didn't want to be laid up by himself. That probably would have been his best option instead of hopping out on the block and losing a $1,000 dollars shooting dice. Feeling like he needed some company, Slim swung by the Fish Tank to smoke and kick the shit with Cutt and Benjamen. Two and a half hours later, Slim was starting to feel his stomach rumble from the purple weed Benjamen smoked with him. "Ya'll niggas be easy. I'm funa get up outta here. I'm starving like Marvin." "Aite, nigga we 'bout out of work to so keep yo phone on," Benjamen told Slim as he was leaving. "Just hit me whenever ya'll ready," Slim said then left. Having the taste for some soul food, Slim called his momma to see what she cooked. "I cooked some baked pork chops smothered in gravy, macaroni and cheese, green beans, and some cornbread. Are you coming over for dinner?" Ms. Cook asked. "Yea, you're right on time. I gotta taste for everything you just named." "Okay, good because Tia was supposed to be inviting one of her friends over but it don't look like she's coming. You can bring Kilo or Fast with you because it's more than enough," Ms. Cook said. Laughing, Slim said, "His name is Quick Mama, not Fast." "Quick, Fast, Swift, or whatever his name is. You know who I'm talking about." Ms. Cook said chuckling because she could never get Quick's name right. "It's Quick Ma, but you know Kilo got locked up a few weeks ago. I'll bring somebody with me tho. Somebody special," Slim said. "I don't even want to know what he's locked up for as long as he's not dead. I'm gone have to call Ms. Campbell to make sure she's okay. But you just come on before the food gets cold." "Okay, I'll be there, Ma." Slim said, then hung up and called Ivonne to see if she was hungry. Ivonne declined because she didn't want to leave Kenya by herself but Kenya insisted that she go saying that she'll be okay. Ivonne told Slim that she'll go grab a bite to eat as long as he didn't take her anywhere expensive because she wasn't dressed to go out. Slim told her not to worry about anything because her beauty makes up for her dress attire any day. Slim pulled into Kenya's apartment twenty minutes later and honked the horn. A few minutes later, Ivonne came down the stairs in a light-blue dress, some light-blue and white Coach slippers, and her hair pulled back in a ponytail. "Damn, she look good," Slim said as Ivonne was walking toward his car. Ivonne got in and looked at Slim sideways. "What's up with the mean mugging, boo?" Slim asked. "What's up with you blowing the horn instead of coming to get me? You blow the horn at your jump-offs." Ivonne told Slim who was mad at himself for not thinking that. "I apologize, boo. It won't happen again. But you're looking good," Slim said, trying to steer the conversation in another direction. "Thanks, so where are we going?" "There's a new restaurant in the middle of downtown that just opened called Ms. Cook's. I figured we would try it out." "Well, I hope it's nothing upscale and I hope they got some soul food 'cause I sure gota taste for some," Ivonne said. "I guess two hungry stomachs think alike 'cause I got the taste for the same thing." Slim and Ivonne made small talk the rest of the way to Ms. Cook's house. Slim pulled into the driveway, parked and said, "We're here! Ms. Cook's finest." "Whose house is this?" Ivonne wanted to know. "I thought we were— oh, so you tricked me into meeting your mother. I get the whole 'Ms. Cook's' thing now. But I wish you would have told me so I could've put on something more appropriate and at least done something to my hair. The first impressions are the best impressions, you know," Ivonne said, looking in the mirror. "The best impression is any impression from you. Now come on, let's go do some meeting and greeting and fill our stomachs," Slim said, then got out and walked around the car and opened Ivonne's door. *'Bet she wasn't expecting that,'* Slim thought. Slim knocked on the front door and was greeted with a big hug and a big kiss from his baby sister Tia. "Hey big brother, who is this you have with you? She's pretty." "Thank you. My name is Ivonne, and you must be Tia. The little sister Issac talks so much about," Ivonne said calling Slim by his real name. "Yep, that's me." "Ya'll two can sit right here and have girl talk as long as ya'll want to but I'm about to starve. Is Mama done cooking?" Slim said, making his way into the living room. Tia ran down the hall yelling, "Momma, Slim gotta girlfriend, and she's pretty too! Momma!" "What are you yelling about now, child?" Ms. Cook asked

Tia as she came into the kitchen. "She's just yelling to be yelling. You know how she do," Slim said, walking into the kitchen with Ivonne behind him. Slim hugged and kissed Ms. Cook on the cheek then introduced Ivonne. "Momma, this is Ivonne. Ivonne, this is my momma." "Hi," Ivonne said the one word as if she was shy. "How are you doing, darling? You have to excuse my son's manners. I don't know where he picked his up from, but they sure didn't come from me," Ms. Cook said, wiping her hands on the apron she had on. "Tell me about them. I thought I was the only person that noticed he didn't have any manners," Ivonne said, then looked at Slim and smiled. "We ain't here to talk about my flaws and mannerism. Let's talk about something that's more convenient, like food," Slim said, rubbing his belly. "Boy, you better hush up while I'm talking to this fine young lady. Maybe she'll let me in on her secret to beauty." Ms. Cook said taking a liking to Ivonne already. "Yea, me too 'cause I sure could use the advice with me starting college in August," Tia said. Tia wasn't a bad look on the eyes herself with her shoulder-length black hair with gold highlights and a baby face that resembled Rudy from *The Cosby Show.* "I think the two of you are already pretty. There's not too much more a secret could do. But thanks for the compliments," Ivonne said then sat down at the table in the chair Slim slid out for her. Ms. Cook prepared everybody's plate then sat down and said grace before they ate. Ms. Cook and Ivonne carried on a conversation like they've known each other for years. They jumped from subject to subject with Tia asking question after question. After dinner, Ivonne helped Ms. Cook clean the table and wash the dishes. Before leaving, Ivonne gave Tia her number and told her that she could call her anytime she wanted to and that they could go out sometimes when she wasn't studying. Tia smiled and gave Ivonne a hug. "Ya'll be careful. And, Issac—nawl, matter of fact, Ivonne—if he does anything wrong, I want you to call me as soon as you're through letting him have it so I can let him have it," Ms. Cook said, standing in the doorway. "Once I get finish letting him have it, he won't have nothing else to have," Ivonne said, smiling at Slim. "So that's how we doing it Ma, you taking her side over mine?" Slim asked. "Yep! I sure am. Because you're going to appreciate this one. She has manners and respect, so I'm telling you now I'm on her side," Ms. Cook said then smiled at Ivonne. "I don't know what kind of spells you've done casted on my peoples to have them taking your side over mine, but it showl worked," Slim told Ivonne once they were in the car. "I don't know how to cast no spells. I'm just a likeable person that has a charming personality. Besides, good women know good women when they see them," Ivonne said then blushed the most seductive blush Slim had ever seen. Slim couldn't help but smile and say, "Ivonne, if I told you my true feelings right now, you would probably think that I'm either deranged or crazy or you may even think I'm lying. But trust and believe me when I tell you that my heart's into you 100 percent." "All I'll ever ask of you when dealing with me is to be a man in every situation and not a boy. If you can prove that to me, then I won't have any trouble believing and trusting in you," Ivonne said, then leaned over and kissed Slim on the lips. That was Slim's first time ever feeling Ivonne's lips against his and now he was wondering what her other lips felt like. "You have my word on that. All I want is to make you happy. Now lean over here and let me feel them soft-ass lips of yours again," Slim said. Ivonne leaned over and gave Slim another kiss then whispered "I got something that's even softer and wetter than these lips." That got Slim's attention real fast— so fast that it left him speechless. *'I can't wait to feel them,'* Slim thought. Ivonne picked up her cell phone to call Kenya and tell her about the dinner she just ate at Ms. Cook's but Kenya didn't answer. *'Maybe she's sleep or on the other line with Kilo,* Ivonne thought before putting her cell phone back into her purse. "Have you ever thought about opening up a restaurant for your mother because her food is good enough to sell. You know that, right?" Ivonne asked. Slim told Ivonne that he has plans of opening a restaurant for his mother just as soon as his money gets right then asked Ivonne if she was going back over Kenya's or if she would spend the rest of the day at home with him as her company. "I guess it wouldn't hurt anything to chill out for the rest of the day." Slim covered the distance from his momma's house to Ivonne's in no time, eager to spend as much time with Ivonne as possible. Slim pulled in front of Ivonne's house and instantly felt that something wasn't right. Making sure that he was strapped, Slim got out and walked Ivonne to the door. "Don't be standing there looking like you don't have the key to the door," Ivonne said, sensing that something was on Slim's mind. "Oh, my bad, boo. I almost forgot." Slim unlocked the door and was shocked at what he saw. Ivonne walked in behind Slim and stopped midstep. "What in the heck have you been doing here? It looks like you've had a party and forgot to clean up." Ivonne said wondering what Slim done to her house. "I didn't leave this place looking like this. When I left, everything was exactly the way you had it. Stay right here and let me make sure our intruders are gone," Slim said, pulling out his gun to check the house. Once he cleared the rooms, Slim came back up front and went to the freezer and like he expected, his dope was gone. "Shit." Slim checked his hiding spot and was relieved a little to see that whoever this intruder was didn't find his main stash. Slim told Ivonne that whoever broke into the house broke in through the bathroom window and that everything in the back seemed not to be messed up too badly. "I might not know who broke into my house, but I know why. Now all I'm asking is that you be a man about this situation and fix it," Ivonne told Slim. Thinking that Ivonne would be mad or even terrified about someone breaking into her house, Slim asked, "Aren't you mad?" "No, I'm not mad. I knew that something like this was capable of happening once I gave you permission to come here and do whatever you needed to do. I just didn't think that it would happen so soon," Ivonne told Slim on the verge of tears. Hearing this, Slim knew that Ivonne had his back and made a vow to himself at that very moment that he would give his life to save hers. "Don't worry about none of this, baby. I'm gone take care of everything." Slim helped Ivonne pack a few of her belongings and told her that they would come back tomorrow to get the rest. Slim grabbed the rest of his work and took it to his momma's house before paying for them a suite at the Marriott downtown. On the way up to their room, Slim and Ivonne bumped into Fresh coming down the stairs with a D. Woods lookalike on his arm. "I should've known to call every hotel in town, and I'll find you. Let me holla at you for a second. It's important," Slim told Fresh. "Sit right here for a second. I'll be right back," Fresh told D. Woods lookalike. Slim and Fresh walked out of earshot from Ivonne and the lookalike. Fresh was about to open his mouth to tell Slim how good of a dick the lookalike can suck until he saw the facial expression Slim made. "What's up, fool? Everything all right?" Fresh thought that Slim was bringing Ivonne to the room to have fun instead of laying low. "I got robbed today. I think I know who's behind it too. I'm just waiting to make sure." Slim didn't want to tell Fresh that the only person that knew he had some dope stashed at Ivonne's house was Murda because he knew how Fresh liked to talk. "Don't tell nobody about this," Slim said, putting emphasis on *nobody*. "Aite bet. But what they get from you?" Fresh wanted to know how much Slim got robbed for. But Slim didn't really want to say. "It wasn't much," Slim said. "Just let me know what the bizniz is. I'm riding no questions asked," Fresh told Slim. "I already know you is but just do me a favor and keep your ears open and mouth closed," Slim said, then gave Fresh some dap and told Ivonne to come on. Slim didn't get much sleep that night, thinking about how Murda doubled back and robbed him. "I knew that nigga wasn't straight." Slim decided to wait to talk to Kilo and see what he had to say about the situation before he did anything. "Let's go take a shower and come back and lay down so I can relax your mind a little, baby," Ivonne told Slim, knowing that he could use a little affection as well as herself. Ivonne gave herself to Slim for the first time that night, and Slim enjoyed every minute of it. They made love to each other, had sex, and fucked each other to sleep.

Chapter 6

"You have a collect call from Keon, an inmate at . . ." Was all the recording said before Kenya hit zero on her keypad. "Hello," Kilo said in a raspy voice. "Hey, baby! Why are you just now calling me? I've been worried sick waiting to hear from you. Are you okay in there? Did you—" An excited Kenya was about to go on and on until Kilo cut her off. "Yea, boo, I'm fine. I wasn't able to use the phone because of a facility lockdown they was on before I got here. But what's up with you? How you holding up out there?" Kilo asked Kenya who was now sitting straight up in the bed with her back against the headboard. "I'm okay, baby. I was a little frustrated and discouraged at first, but now I'm starting to cope a little better. Ivonne was staying here with me until her and Slim moved in together." "Slim and Ivonne live together now? Wow, that happened fast. I haven't been gone a full two months yet, and they've decided to move in together. I can't wait to clown Slim about this one. So what else been happening, boo?" Kenya filled Kilo in on everything that Ivonne told her and the things she heard about while getting her hair and nails done at Susan's. The information Kilo was hoping to hear wasn't anything Kenya told him. He knew that in order to hear about what's been going on in the streets, he'll have to talk to one of his niggas. So right before the phone hung up, Kilo told Kenya to tell Slim to come and visit him. Kenya told Kilo that she'll be up there to see him as soon as possible. "Aite boo, love ya," Kilo said. "I love you" Was all Kenya got out before the phone hung up. After talking to Kilo, Kenya's stored-up energy came rushing out at once and now she was ready to get out the house. So she called the only friend she had and asked if she wanted to hang out for a little while. "Girl, you had to have just gotten off the phone with Kilo because you seem a little spunkier from the conversation we had yesterday," Ivonne said, noticing that Kenya was in a cheerful mood. "Is it that easy to notice that the man of my life has finally called?" Kenya said, still gleaming from talking to Kilo. "Apparently so if I called it out. I'm glad that he called, though. Now you will hopefully be yourself again. Now let's get out and do some walking because you and I both know that you could use it," Ivonne said, snickering. "Like you couldn't use a little walking. Now come on and pick me up because I don't feel like driving," Kenya said then said, "Hold that thought. Maybe I should drive over there to see your new house. Yeah, that's what I'm going to do. Now what's that address?" Ivonne gave Kenya the address to the house that she and Slim moved into last week. "Girl, don't go anywhere. I'm on my way now." Kenya took a quick shower, then threw on some sweatpants and a T-shirt, pulled her hair back into a ponytail, and headed out the door. Opening the door, Kenya jumped at the sight in front of her. "I didn't mean to scare you, my bad. You was coming out as I was about to knock." "OMG, you scared the daylight out of me. Don't you be sneaking up on me like that," Kenya said playfully. "My bad, I was coming to check on you to make sure everything was aite." "Yea, I'm fine. I just got off the phone with Kilo. If you would've come by an hour earlier, you would've caught him. I'll tell him you stopped by the next time he calls." "Okay, do that. Did he say he needed anything?" "Nawl, he just wanted to know what's been going on. He didn't really ask for nothing," Kenya responded. Quick pulled out a bankroll, peeled off five $100 dollar bills, and handed it to Kenya. "That's just in case he needs something. Tell him I said call me," Quick said, walking down the hallway with Kenya. Outside, they jumped in their cars and sped off in different directions. *'Let me call Slim and ask him have he heard from Kilo,'* Quick thought, then pulled out is cell phone and dialed Slim's number. Slim didn't answer but called right back. "What's up, fool? I was in the other room doing a lil organizing when you called and didn't get to the phone in time." "You and Ivonne putting that thang together I see," Quick said. "You know how women are. They want everything the way it's supposed to be in twenty-four hours. Have Fresh told you what happen?" Slim asked Quick. "Told me what? I haven't talked to Fresh in a few days. I was calling you to see if you've heard from Kilo," Quick said, switching lanes. "I haven't heard from Kilo yet but meet me at the Fish Tank. I got some important shit I need to holla at you 'bout, fool." Slim said, lowering his voice so that Ivonne wouldn't hear him. "Okay . . . ummm . . . I'll be there less than thirty." "I should be right behind you. I'm leaving out now." Slim hung up the phone with Quick and told Ivonne that he'll be back. He grabbed his car keys and pistol then headed out. Feeling like he was about to go on a rampage, Slim took out B.G.'s *Heart of tha Streetz* CD and popped in Lil Boosie's *The Return of Bad Azz* CD and turned it to the last song on the album. "Welcome to the Mind of a Maniac" came blasting through the speakers, and Slim rapped the song word for word on his way to the Fish Tank. Slim pulled up to the Fish Tank lost in his thoughts. Looking around, he noticed that Quick hadn't made it there yet, so he sat in the driveway and rolled a blunt. Just as he was about to put some fire to the blunt, Quick pulled up and hopped out. Honking the horn once to let Quick know that he was sitting in the car, Slim fired the blunt up. Quick hopped in the car, gave Slim some dap and said, "Man, don't tell me that this drought got you acting stingy with yo weed. Why you ain't in the trap blowing?" "Nawl, it ain't nothing like that. Matta fact, I'm still living how I been living. This shit ain't affected my pockets. It's just that what I'm about to tell you ain't for everybody to hear. Feel me?" Slim said then pulled on the blunt before passing it. "Yea, I feel ya, my nigga. So what the bizniz is?" Quick asked, grabbing the blunt. Slim told Quick detail for detail what happened the other day. He told him how he first met Murda as he went to check on Kenya right down to Murda being the only nigga that he served out Ivonne's house. "So it had to be him. I mean didn't nobody know I had my shit over there but Ivonne and I know that she ain't gone cross me out like that." Slim said, feeling his anger rise. "From everything I've just heard, this cat Murda is our main suspect. What you wanna do about it? You know that if nothing is done about it, then he'll try you again," Quick said. "I'm 'pose to go see Kilo Saturday, Ima see what he thinks. But no matter what he say, something's gone get done. Believe that! Ain't no bitch in me." Slim and Quick sat in the car talking for another hour and smoked another blunt before Quick told Slim that he had a move to make. "Aite my nigga, be careful," Slim told Quick "Fa show. But get back at me after you holla at Kilo and let me know what's up," Quick said, then got out, hopped in his whip and pulled off. Slim called and checked on Ivonne then went inside the Fish Tank to check and make sure business was good. Satisfied with how things were looking, Slim left the Fish Tank and headed over to the Juice Box.

After having to put two bitches out that was there for pleasure instead of business, Slim told Lucky, the nigga Kilo had running the Juice Box, that the Juice Box was a business, not some place to be playing around. "This shit ain't personal, but if you don't tighten up, I gotta replacement," Slim told Lucky. "I got you, Slim. You ain't gotta worry 'bout that nomo. It just got slow 'round here so I called some hoes over. I think a new nigga done opened up a spot 'round here somewhere 'cause one of my snaps said I was in competition," Lucky told Slim before he left. Slim told Lucky not to worry about anything and to keep doing what he was doing. Leaving the Juice Box, Slim rode around the area to see if he could find some unusual traffic going on. And just like Lucky said, two streets over, he saw junkies going in and out of this one house. *'Damn, I see how the police seem to always know where the dope coming from,'* Slim thought to himself, looking on from a distance. *'I wonder whose spot this is and how long have they been pumping right here.'* Slim caught the next junkie headed in that direction and stopped her. "What's up, ma? Where you headed?" "With you if the price is right. How much you tryna spend is the question," The junkie asked Slim, walking up on his car. "I got fifty for you if you can tell me who's running that trap house right there," Slim said, waving a crispy $50 dollar bill in the air. The junkie saw that $50 dollar bill and immediately got to talking at the chance of getting paid without turning no tricks. "I think his name Killa or something like that." "You don't get paid for thinking. Either you know it or you don't," Slim said, acting like he was putting the money back into his pocket. "It's Killa, Homicide, Murda, or something. That's it. It's Murda. That's his name—guaranteed!" The junkie said with confidence sticking her hand out. Hearing Murda's name caught Slim by surprise and caused his blood to boil. Slim was ready to bust in there with his gun out but thought against it. "I guess you tryna act like you didn't hear me tell you his name, so you ain't gotta pay me, huh? Youa real nigga, ain't ya? Well, keep ya word like one," The junkie said, feeling like she got played. "Nawl, I heard you. I was thinking about something. Here you go." Slim handed the money over and the junkie damn near broke her wrist grabbing it out his hand. Slim shook his head, then drove off and headed home with murder on his mind. *'I can't leave this nigga breathing after I do something to him because I know he'll try to retaliate. So that leaves me one option.'* Slim was so lost in his thoughts that he didn't even realize that he had his strap in his lap with his finger on the trigger the whole way home. Getting out the car, Slim tucked his strap and made his way inside the house. Unable to get his mind right, Slim pulled out an ounce of kush and a box of cigars and sat down in the living room and rolled one up. *'Ivonne must still be out with Kenya,'* Slim thought, remembering her say that she and Kenya were about to go out. Halfway through his blunt and halfway through the movie *Shottas*, Slim's phone rang. Seeing that it was Fresh, Slim picked up. "What up, fool?" "You know, another day another dollar and a different model," Fresh said. "I hear ya nigga, but don't let these stack-chasing-ass bitches be the death of you," Slim told Fresh who actually just dropped a broad off. "I tell myself the same thing, fool. But I ain't call you to be talking 'bout how much pussy I be getting. I'm tryna get my hands on something else. I'm out," Fresh said, trying to get some more coke from Slim, but Slim really didn't have enough dope to serve Fresh, so Slim told him that he would call him right back. "Let me call around and check my sources to see what's up." "Aite, hit me back and let me know something," Fresh said, then hung up, and called Quick. Quick's phone was going straight to voicemail, so Fresh hung up and waited on Slim to call him back. Fifteen minutes later, Slim was calling Fresh back. "Man, it's dry everywhere. Even down in Atlanta. They saying that the well is dry right now to. But I told them niggas to hit me back as soon as things get right," Slim told Fresh. "Aite bet, hit me when you hear something," Fresh said then hung up. Slim fired his blunt back up, sat back, and got to thinking about where his next shipment of coke was coming from since nobody seemed to have any. Saturday morning Slim was up bright and early on his way to see Kilo. He was dressed in a blue-and-white LRG outfit and some fresh white shell toes. "You can't go this time baby, but I'm coming back to get you," Slim said, talking to his brand-new Glock 40 before putting it in the dresser. Not wanting to wake Ivonne up, Slim slid his chain on then bent over, and kissed her on the forehead and was out the door. All the way there, Slim wrestled with the thought of firing a blunt up but didn't want the guards tripping on the smell, so he didn't. After getting through the procedures it took to visit an inmate, Slim was led to the visitation room by a female guard who seemed a little too friendly for her job. "You sure smell good. Is that Cool Water you're wearing?" The guard flirted, saying the only men's cologne she probably knew. "Cool Water?" Slim said, chuckling. "Nawl, boo, this that UR. Usher Raymond. I didn't know niggas still wore Coolwater." Feeling a little embarrassed, the guard said "Oh, my daddy still wears Coolwater, and it kind of smells like that. That's why I asked, but who are you here to see your brother or something?" *'Damn, you sure is nosy to be somebody that 'pose to be showing me to the visitation room,'* Slim thought. "Nawl, just a friend of mine," Slim said. "The visitation area is right through those double doors," The guard said. "I hope you have a good visit. My name is Ms. Jackson if you need anything." "My name is Slim. Thanks for showing me how to get here," Slim said, walking into the visitation room. "My pleasure." Slim stood at the front and scanned the room looking for Kilo. Unable to locate him, Slim went and found Ms. Jackson and asked her to call for a Keon Campbell. Ms. Jackson told Slim that Kilo was on his way out and that he could pick any table to sit at. This time, when Slim returned to the VG, he saw Kilo being led in by another female officer that looked a little too fine to be working at a prison. Walking toward the same table,Kilo was seated at, Slim cracked a smile once he got up on Kilo. "What's up, fool? How you living back there?" Slim asked Kilo who stood up to embraced Slim. "I'm cool. Ain't shit changed with me but the fact that I'm missing my freedom, money, and fam. What's good with you, tho? I see you looking good, smelling good. Kenya told me that you and Ivonne got ya'll a lil spot together now. What's up with that?" Kilo asked, still tripping off the fact. "Yea man, it's true. We've been living together for almost a month now." Slim and Kilo kicked the shit a lil while longer with Slim clowning Kilo for not shaving his beard, which made him look similar to Rick Ross and Kilo clowning Slim for spraying cologne on to come see him like he was coming to see his bitch or something. "See this that grown-man shit that you don't know nothing about. I bet I can fuck the guard that work up front off this smell alone. She already let that be known," Slim said. "Who Ms. Jackson? Get the fuck outta here. She's too stuck-up. But I'm glad you brought that up. You got some bread on you?" Kilo asked. "Yea, I got some. Why what's up, you need some?" "I need like $500. You remember that guard that brought me in here? Ms. Blackwell?" Kilo said. "You talking about the pretty one that looks like she should be working at a dentist office instead of here?" Slim asked. "Yea, her. Check this out. I've been in the bitch ear, trying to get some pussy since I've been here, and the other day she tell me she'll let me bust one for five hunnet." "I got you, fool. Don't worry. But this Ms. Jackson bitch I'ma rock her ass to sleep for free then send you some ass shots of her," Slim said sliding Kilo five $100 dollar bills under the table. "Good-looking, but what's been going on in the streets? From what I've been hearing in here, it's a drought out there." Knowing that he had to break the news at some point, Slim told Kilo everything that's been happening and the real reason he and Ivonne moved in together." "You know Murda, Kenya's brother?" "Yea, I know that nigga. Don't fuck with him. He's a jackboy from Toledo. He use to fuck with Heavy and 'em until he crossed them and they cut him off. Why you ask?" "Cause the nigga told me that you use to serve him and that ya'll been doing bizniz. So I took the initiative to conduct bizniz with the nigga on the strength of you and the nigga double back and hit the spot where I served him which happened to be Ivonne's crib. That explains why we're now living together." Slim told Kilo. "Hold up a sec. You mean to tell me that Murda robbed you, fool?" Kilo said it like he was shocked. "He got me for twenty-three ounces you might as well say 'cause he paid for a nine piece and got that money back along with another fourteen zips I had in the freezer. He didn't find the other stash I had, tho," Slim said, noticing Kilo's facial expression change from being content to angry. "Damn, I hate it for Kenya but something gone have to be done about this. You know that, right? If not, that nigga will try you again." Kilo let Slim know. "I already know it. I was just waiting to let you know the scoop before I did anything. He got something coming, tho. And the nigga got enuff balls to open a spot two streets over from the Juice Box like I wasn't gone find out about it. I'm putting a plan together now for this clown," Slim stated. Seeing the look of seriousness on Slim's face, Kilo told him to be careful with whatever he chose to do and to keep his mouth closed about doing it. "Mr. Campbell, visitation times over," Ms. Blackwell, the guard that escorted Kilo out, said. "No doubt. Stay up back there, and I'll be back up here to let you know the bizniz," Slim said, standing up to embrace Kilo before leaving. "Take care of yourself out there and remember what I told you," Kilo said. "Fa show. Do you need anything else?" "Nawl, I'm still cool right now, but do me a favor and test Kenya loyalty for me," Kilo said, rushing his words. "What you mean by that?" Slim asked, confused. "Send a nigga she don't know her way to see if she'll fuck him. If her brother got some conniving ways, I'm wondering if she has some too." "Mr. Campbell! Visitation time is over. Now tell him you'll call him later and bring your ass on," Ms. Blackwell, said smiling. "Aite, here I come, boo. Chill. But take care of yourself and handle yo bizniz and don't forget to do that with Kenya for me," Kilo said, walking off. "I got ya, fool." On the way out, Ms. Jackson, the guard that worked up front stopped Slim and asked him how his visit was. "Not long enuff and hurtful" Was Slim's only words. "Not long enough I can understand but hurtful?" Ms. Jackson wanted to know. "Long story. Just know that I miss my nigga." "Oh, I see. Well, how about we hook up sometime and maybe I can help ease the pain a little by taking your mind off it for a while?" Ms. Jackson said. Slim got her number and promised to call. Sitting in his car outside the prison parking lot, Slim broke down a cigar and filled it with weed. *'I didn't realize how much I missed my nigga until I seen his face. This gone be the longest year of my life,'* Slim said, then fired his blunt up and made his way to the interstate with Kilo heavy on his mind. Slim rode around the city in complete silence, trying to get his thoughts together, smoking blunt after blunt, and winding up at the Chicken Shack with a five-piece chicken snack dinner sitting in front of him, half eaten. Slim was thinking about what he was going to do to Murda when the waiter came up and said something that sealed the deal to his plan. "Would you like a refill, Slim?" Hearing the waiter call him by his name, Slim questioned, "How you know my name?" "You do eat here two or three times a day and most of the time you're with . . . umm . . . Kilo. I think that's his name, but I haven't been seeing him lately," The waiter said. "You musta been doing some research or something 'cause you're showl on point." Slim told the waiter. "You don't seem to be yourself today is one of the reasons I asked to refill our cup. I really wanted to tell you that I can be the key player to solving your problems," The waiter said. Slim heard that and smiled. "I wish you could solve these problems, baby girl. But I think that these problems right here are a little too immense for you to solve." "Not when I can get to the person you're after quicker than you can." Slim looked on, stunned. "I know what's going on. I overheard him talking about what happen the other day while he was in here eating. He gave me his number and told me to call him whenever I was ready to fuck with a real nigga," The waiter said it like she was committed to Slim. Needing to know if she knew what she was talking about, Slim asked her. "Who is he? Do he got a name?" The waiter looked at Slim sideways as if to say, "What you think I'm lying?" Then mouthed Murda's name as if she didn't want anybody to hear her. "Check this out. What time do you get off?" Slim asked. "Eight. Why?" "I'll be here to pick you up at eight sharp. We need to talk in private." Slim had to see what it was that the waiter actually knew. "Okay, but don't be late," The waiter told Slim. "I'm not, but ain't it only fair that you tell me your name since you know mine?" "My name is Jazmine, but I told him it was Isabelle." "Aite, Jaz, I'll be here at eight to get you," Slim said, then pulled out a bankroll, and left a fifty on the table and told Jazmine to keep the change. Ten minutes till eight, Slim was sitting in the parking lot, waiting on Jazmine to walk out the door. Jazmine came out the Chicken Shack a few minutes after eight, untying her waiter's apron looking around like she was lost, Slim flashed the lights on his car. "How was your day?" Slim asked Jazmine after she got in. "It was okay I guess. I can't complain. It gets the bills paid," Jazmine said. "I gotta question to ask you before we pull off. What made you tell me the things you did?" "Because I don't want to see nothing happen to you," Jazmine said. "But you don't even know me, so how could you possibly care? How do I know that you ain't tryna bait me in for him? For all I know, ya'll could be working together." Jazmine convinced Slim that she and Murda had nothing going on by calling him on speakerphone and letting Slim hear the conversation. "Yeah," Murda said answering his phone. "Yeah? That's such a rude way to answer your phone, don't you think?" Jazmine said. "It all depends on who's calling. I don't recognize this number, but the voice sounds familiar. Who dis?" Murda said. "This is Isabelle. You gave me your number the other day. I work at the Chicken Shack," Jazmine said then looked at Slim. "That's why I don't recognize the number then. You're just now calling. What's good with you tho, lil momma?" "Nothing much. I was just making sure you didn't give me the wrong number," Jazmine said, not knowing what to say. "As fine as you was in yo work clothes, I would've been a fool to mislead you like that because I now the beauty goes much deeper than that." Slim glanced at Jazmine's face features and thought, *'You is a pretty lil something.'* "That's nice of you, but I'm not into game being ran. I may look a little green, but I was raised in the hood too." Jazmine said. "Ain't no game, ma. It's the truth. But what you doing tonight? You wonna hook up?" Murda asked. "Umm . . . umm . . ." Jazmine said looking at Slim. Slim shook his head no. "Uh, I don't think tonight's a good night. I told my momma that she didn't have to watch my kids because I'm off tomorrow. Maybe we can hook up next week if that's okay." "Yea, that's cool. Just give me a call and let me know when." "Okay, I will call to let you know." "Aite, baby gurl," Murda said then hung up. "Now do you believe that nothing suspicious is going on with me and him?" Jazmine asked Slim who was staring at her. "I guess so since he didn't say nothing out of the ordinary. I'm just tryna figure out what are you getting out of telling me this. That's what I'm trying to figure out," Slim asked trying to put it all together. Jazmine told Slim what her intentions were and why she was telling him so much. She told him it was nothing personal and that she saw an opportunity to make some money. She told Slim she'll do everything it takes to leave Murda dead as long as the money was right. "I'on know about that. How much money are we talking?" Slim questioned, wondering if Jazmine had what it takes to kill a man and live with it. *'If she does, her heart is as cold as ice.'* Jazmine was raised in Winter Hill Housing Projects with her mother being the only parent after her daddy abandoned them after she was. Jazmine was seventeen years old when she saw her mother who provided and protected her by any means get shot to death by a heroin addict who was trying to get his next fix. Unable to deal with the fact that the heroin addict wasn't arrested for killing her mother, Jazmine killed him with a butcher knife, stabbing him thirty times in the face and chest. "Fifteen thousand. Half up front and the other half after I've killed him," Jazmine said, talking like killing somebody is her specialty. Slim wanted to know if this was something that Jazmine "did" or something she was trying to "do" to make herself some money. "Have you ever killed anybody before?" Slim had to ask. The way Jazmine answered Slim's question told it all. "Real killers don't speak on the past. Don't let the cute face and slim waist fool ya." Slim and Jazmine talked an hour straight with Slim trying to figure Jazmine out. From the conversation Jazmine was giving, Slim was sure that Jazmine was capable of getting the job done. His only worry was if she would hold her tongue if she got caught. "So do you want your problem solved or what?" Jazmine asked, getting to the bottom of things. "How long will it take you to handle your bizniz?" Slim asked. *'I mightas well send a hit,'* Slim thought. "If you can get me half the money tonight, I can have your problem solved this time next week. I could have it solved earlier, but I don't want him to get any strange thoughts. If you know what I mean." Slim was sure that he didn't have half of the money on him now, and he didn't want to swing by his house with Jazmine in the car. "Shit . . . umm . . . didn't you say you had to pick your kids up from your mother's house?" Slim asked. "I don't have any kids. I told him that because that's the first lie that came to mind. I don't have a mother either. She was killed when I was seventeen. Why you ask?" Jazmine said. "I'm sorry to hear about your mother. I asked because I don't have all the money on me right now, but I was gone pick it up and drop it off to you. If that's cool." "Well, I guess it is since you don't want me knowing where you stay." Jasmine said peeping game. Slim dropped Jazmine off then swung by his house, got the money, and called Jazmine right back. "I'm on my way." Slim pulled up at Jazmine's house and blew the horn. Jazmine peeked out the window then called Slim's cell phone. "Uh, if you don't mind, will you bring it in? I just got out the shower." Jazmine met Slim at the door dressed in a bathrobe. "Come in. I got some nosy neighbors." Jasmine told Slim who was trying to hand her the money and leave. Slim stepped in and was surprised at how clean and organized Jazmine's house was. "You have to excuse my house. I'm not use to having company over, so I clean it to my satisfaction." "Your satisfaction must have some high standards 'cause it looks like you just finished cleaning up. But here's that bread," Slim said, reaching in his pocket. Jazmine got the money and turned around, then placed it on top of her entertainment system which caused her robe to rise a little, showing the bottom of her ass cheeks. Slim caught a glimpse and had to keep himself in check by telling himself, *'I can't mix business with pleasure. But goodness, that ass looks like its soft as a pillow.'* Jazmine turned back and said, "I trust that it's all there and don't be sneaking no peeks at these cheeks. You know that B&P don't mix. Even if it did, I wouldn't want to have you pussy whipped over this wetness and not make it home to your girlfriend." Jasmine said bluntly. Slim couldn't do anything but laugh at Jazmine's bluntness. "I see you got jokes. But if P did mix with B then we would find out who'll be whipped. Phat as that ass is, I'll bend that rule a little but only after the bizniz is taken care of," Slim said. "This time next week, the business will be taken care of and that's my word," Jazmine said. Slim left Jazmine's house and headed home. The next morning Slim was awoken by the sound of his phone ringing. *'Who in the hell is this calling me back to back like they ain't got no fucking life?'* Slim said, grabbing his phone off the nightstand. Seeing that it was Quick blowing his phone up Slim sat up, stretched and yawned then noticed that Ivonne had already gotten up. Slim called Quick back to see what the problem was. "What's up, my nigga. You aite?" "Hell nawl, I ain't aite. I need to holla at you but not over the wire. I need to holla at you face-to-face. How long will it take you to meet me at the Fish Tank?" Quick asked. Slim heard it in Quick's voice that something was seriously wrong, so he told Quick to give him forty-five minutes to get himself together. "Is that cool?" "Yea, that's straight. Just meet me there when you're finish getting yourself together. It's kinda early," Quick said, looking at the clock on his dashboard that read 7:45 a.m. Slim got out the bed and hopped in the shower. *'I wonder what done happened with Quick,'* Slim thought, drying off. After getting dressed and putting his strap on his waistline, Slim made his way into the kitchen where Ivonne was sitting eating her breakfast and studying. "Good morning, baby. You're up early studying and eating. You was gone let me sleep the day away, wasn't ya?" Slim said, kissing Ivonne on the cheek then picking up her fork and eating a forkful of her eggs. "Good morning to you too sleepy face, and put my fork down and get your own. I made enough," Ivonne said, reaching for her fork back. Slim ate almost everything Ivonne had on her plate and was out the door. "Baby, I'll be back. I gotta go holla at Quick. He seem to be facing some type of dilemma this morning," Slim said, giving Ivonne another kiss. "I seen him calling you this morning, but I didn't answer. I didn't know why he was calling so early and consistently. If I'm not here when you get back I'll be with Kenya. I told Tia that I'll come and get her today too," Ivonne told Slim. "Be careful and call me if you need anything," Slim said before he left. Pulling up at the Fish Tank, Slim hopped out and walked to the porch where Quick was talking on the phone in a heated conversation. Getting within earshot, Slim heard the name Murda and knew this couldn't be good. "I don't give a fuck who this nigga is or what he's about! He done put his self in a fucked up situation now. But good looking on that info. I'ma hit you back," Quick said then hung up. "What's going on, fool?" Slim asked, giving Quick some dap. "I bumped into this nigga while I was leaving from getting my face lined up yesterday, right?" Quick said, pulling out a pack of Newport and fired one up. "Yea, I hear ya." Slim said, already knowing where this story was headed. "The nigga fade me like he use to do bizniz with Kilo before he got locked up and since Kilo been gone, he hasn't been able to find no dope. So I give him my number and tell him to hit me whenever he's ready. The nigga called me at seven o'clock this morning trying to buy a brick, so I hopped straight up didn't brush teeth, wash face or nothing, and shot straight to him," Quick was saying. "What he do get you with some counterfeit money or something?" Slim asked, trying to get to the bottom of the story. "The nigga got in the car with me and acted like he was about to pull some money out and pulled a gun out and put it to my head. I couldn't do nothing about it. I was slipping and didn't even think to grab my strap before I left," Slim told Quick that a cake has been baked for Murda because he robbed him too. "So don't even worry 'bout the nigga 'cause his days are numbered. I got somebody on top of that as we speak. But you know that the game is about to get shady now that this lil drought hit. So watch who you do bizniz with." Slim told Quick. Slim and Quick talked a lil while longer before Slim said that he was about to bounce. "I gotta go check the trap to make sure my money still flowing. I'ma get at you later on," Slim said, shaking Quick's hand. "Aite bet, but before you re-up let me know so I can re-up with ya. That was my last brick that fool robbed me for," Quick said. "Cuz I'on even know who got it right now to re-up with. All my sources talking like they still waiting so they got me waiting. So you might wanna try and see where it's at too cause its ugly on my end. I'm down to my last lil bit." Slim said. "I'ma keep my ears open and let you know if I find something," Quick said, still pissed off. "Aite, do that," Slim said then went inside the Fish Tank to make sure everything was running properly. Satisfied, Slim pulled off and headed toward the Juice Box to check on things there. Lucky told Slim that business has been remarkably slow for the last couple of days and that somebody opened a crackhouse a few streets over. Slim in return told Lucky not to worry about the business being slow and to just keep doing what he's doing and that things will pick back up. In need of some more coke, Slim left the Juice Box and called Heavy to see what was up. Heavy told Slim that he was about to shop with some new niggas from Akron, Ohio. "You can send some money up the road with mine if you want to. This my first time doing business with these niggas so I'ma send something light to see what it do. If shit blow over right, then I'll send some mo," Heavy told Slim. "When is you making the move?" Slim asked. "Here in a minute. You want to make a test run?" Heavy asked. "Yeah, but give me a lil time to see what I'ma send. What's the ticket anyway?" "They want thirty-two apiece. I'm tryna give them thirty," Heavy said, lying trying to make an extra $2,000 off each brick Slim buy." "Damn, they taxing but give me a few minutes and I'ma call you back and let you know what's up," Slim said, then hung up and called Quick to see if he wanted to send some money blindly up the highway. "I'on know about that one. What's the ticket?" Quick asked, feeling kind of hesitant about the situation. "Thirty-two apiece. Which they probably want twenty-nine or thirty. That's just the price Heavy gave," Slim said, already knowing how the game go. "I might have to take a chance. The city is dry and it ain't no telling fa how long. I want two of them to test the water," Quick said, not really feeling the idea of sending $64,000 thousand up the road. "Aite, get yo bread together and call me when you're ready," Slim said then called Fresh to see if he wanted to get in on the action. Fresh wasn't really digging the plan either but since he needed some coke, he sent for one. Slim hung up with Fresh, then called Heavy back and placed an order for six of them thangs. "Aite well, meet me at my crib with the money and we can watch it leave together," Heavy told Slim. Slim showed up at Heavy's house with $192,000 thousand stuffed in two duffel bags. Heavy met Slim at the gate and let him in personally. "I showl hope this go right cause $192,000 would be a hellava lost especially at a time like this," Slim said, getting out his car and shaking hands with Heavy. "I got a quarter mill invested on this trip, so you know how I feel about it. Taking chances is part of the game tho, no matter the risk," Heavy said then told Big Blu to grab the duffel bags off Slim's backseat and load them into the trunk of the Chevy truck he rented just for this occasion. Heavy then told Big Blu to do the speed limit and call him if anything happens. "I got you, boss." Was all Big Blu said before getting into the driver's seat and pulling out the gate. "All we can do is wait on the outcome now. It shouldn't take him no longer than an hour and a half to get there. Once he gets there and everything goes right, I got another rental and another driver that he'll give the dope to that's already up there, waiting on him. I did that just in case these niggas on some jack shit," Heavy told Slim, which made Slim feel just a tad bit better. "Good thinking, but ain't no sense in sitting out here thinking and talking about our money. That's when things tend to go wrong. I know you got some of the best dro round here. Smoke something," Slim said, not trying to think about all the things that could go wrong with his money. "I keep that fire. My bitch just came back from Cali with some shit called Moon Rocks. The shit looks goldish green. You ever heard of it?" Heavy asked Slim as they were walking back toward the house. "Moon Rocks? Hell nawl, I ain't neva heard of it. I'm tryna get my lungs dirty from smoking it, tho," Slim said. "One fat blunt of that Moon is all a nigga need. That shit have a nigga high all day." It took Slim and Heavy damn near an hour to smoke the whole blunt of Moon Rocks. They were so high afterward that neither one of them was worried about the money they sent on the road. They were too busy discussing how much of a profit they were about to make back off each brick. In the middle of their discussion, Heavy's girlfriend Holly came into the den holding two large meat-lover pizzas from Papa John's. "Here you go, baby. The delivery guy just left," Holly said, looking a lot like one of the Kardashians. "I almost forgot about that pizza. I was starting to feel my stomach rumble, tho. What about you, Slim?" Heavy said, getting up to get the pizza from Holly. "I ain't forgot about shit. It seem like they forgot about us as long as they took. I thought I was about to die, hungry as I am," Slim said, causing Holly to laugh. Slim then asked Heavy where the bathroom was so he could relieve his bladder. "Straight up the hall on the left. It's the first door," Heavy said, stuffing his face with a slice of pizza. Heavy was too occupied with the pizza to notice Holly licking her lips then winking her eye at Slim. *'I know she didn't just do what I think she did. Man, that weed got me tripping,'* Slim thought on his way to the bathroom. Heavy was on the phone when Slim came back into the den so Slim went straight

THE LONGEST DROUGHT EVER

for the pizza sitting on the table. Heavy hung the phone up and said, "The first part of the deal went through. Blu said he made the transaction with the other driver and they're both getting on the highway headed back this way." "That's what I'm talking about," Slim said, taking a bite of pizza feeling a lot better about the deal." Slim called Quick and told him that everything went through with the deal. Now they were just waiting on it to make it back. Almost two hours later, Blu pulled up to the gate with the same exact truck behind him. Heavy and Slim watched everything on the surveillance screen Heavy had mounted on the wall in the den. Heavy hit a button on a remote that was sitting on the table and the gate opened. Blu and the driver of the other vehicle, which looked like a woman to Slim got out and entered the house. Blu and the woman carrying a duffle bag apiece walked into the den where Heavy and Slim were. "Everything's all here. I checked each brick myself," Blu said, handing the bag to Heavy. "How was the drive, Luni?" Heavy asked the woman who looked like the twin of Holly's. "A piece of cake to a professional like myself. Now where's my niece so I can get my kisses and hugs before I leave?" Luni asked and then said "And who is he?" Talking about Slim. "This my nigga Slim." "What's up with ya?" Slim said with a mouthful of pizza. "I'm Luni, Holly's sister. Nice to meet you," Luni said. "You too." Was Slim's reply. Heavy told Luni that Holly got her money for making the drive for him upstairs with her. And just as soon as Luni entered the room, she exited it. "Now let's see what we working with," Heavy said, then took one of the bricks out the duffel and busted it open. "Looks like they hit us with some oil base. But the coke doesn't look like its cut up or anything." Slim checked the work out and was content with the dope being oil base instead of fish scales because he knew that cocaine in the city was scarce right now. "It's all good. It's gone sell like fish scale 'cause ain't no dope in town so niggas gone buy it or starve," Slim said. Before Slim left he told Heavy to let him know when he was talking a trip to Cali again. "Aite my nigga, I'll do that but don't blame me if you go broke smoking that shit," Heavy said, grinning. "I ain't going broke on that shit. I just need me a few pounds for personal use only," Slim said, talking about the Moon Rock weed Heavy smoked with him earlier that still had him high as a kite.

Chapter 7

"Baby, did you hear anything I just said?" Ivonne asked Slim who was zoned out, thinking about the time that he and Kilo would sit in the same restaurant, buzzing off some killer weed they would smoke before coming to eat. "My bad baby, I kinda got side tracked thinking about something, but what was you saying?" Slim asked Ivonne who now seemed upset because Slim wasn't paying her any attention when she was trying to explain to him how she felt about him. "Nothing. I wasn't saying nothing at all, Isaac. Nothing too important to have caught your attention anyway." Ivonne pushed her plate of shrimp and lobster pasta to the center of the table. "Don't act like that, baby. You know you mean the world to me. It's just that I've been having a lot on my mind lately." Slim kept Ivonne away from all his illegal activities and told her little to nothing at all about what's going on in the streets, so if the police ever bumped down on her, she honestly wouldn't know anything. "I understand, baby. I just want the time that we're together to have some meaning and value because as of lately you've been hanging out in the streets a lot more than you used to. So the time that we are together would make me feel a lot better if I got some attention," Ivonne told Slim. *'Every woman loves attention I know, but am I really starting to show her less attention because of the streets?'* Slim thought to himself. "I apologize for not giving you the attention you deserve, boo. I promise to do better. That's my word." Slim and Ivonne enjoyed the rest of their meal together and made plans to go see a movie later on that night. On the way home, Ivonne asked Slim to take her over Kenya's house so she could spend some time with her bestie. Dropping Ivonne off was right up Slim's alley because he had some business that he needed to take care of. "How has Kenya been doing anyway? I haven't heard from her in a while," Slim asked. "She's been doing okay. She's doing better than I probably could if you were to leave me for a year,"

Ivonne told Slim, then leaned over and kissed him on the cheek. "I ain't tryna leave your side for a day if I don't have to," Slim said, then dropped Ivonne off and told her to tell Kenya he asked about her. Just as soon as Ivonne was out the car and headed up the stairs to Kenya's apartment, Slim was calling Jazmine to make sure the plan was still going down tonight. The phone just rang then went to voicemail. "Hi, you've reach Jazmine. Sorry that I'm unable take your call right now, but if you leave me your name and number, I will gladly return your call. *Beep.*" Slim hung up and thought, *'Damn, she sure sound like an innocent, sweet young lady on her voicemail. I hope she ain't tryna trick me out some money, acting like she can get the job done.'* A few seconds later, Jazmine was calling Slim back. "Hey, sorry, I missed your call. I'm at work and was filling an order. But what's up?" Jazmine asked, sounding the same as usual, like she wasn't about to commit a crime that could put her away for the rest of her life. "My bad, I should've known that you were working. Call me when you get off," Slim said. "No, you're fine. I just took my break." Jazmine said sitting down at a table. "I was just calling to make sure that party was still gone be thrown tonight and to ask if you would need any party supplies," Slim asked, talking in codes. "Nope. I got it all under control, but thanks for asking. I'll tell you all about it if you don't make it," Jazmine said, letting Slim know that the hit he put out on Murda was still going down tonight and that she had everything set up just the way she needed it to be. Slim told Jazmine that he couldn't wait to hear about the party and that he hoped she have fun. As soon as Slim hung up the phone with Jazmine, Fresh called. "What's good with ya Mack Daddy Fresh?" Slim said. "Man, shit ain't looking too good right now. I need to holla at you 'bout something," Fresh said, sounding real sedated. "What's up? Can you speak over the phone, or do we need to meet up?" "We need to meet up. I don't wanna talk over this phone. Meet me at the Chicken Shack in twenty minutes." Not wanting to meet up at Jazmine's job discussing business, Slim told Fresh to meet him at his momma's house instead. Slim pulled up to his momma's house, and Fresh was already there waiting on him. Fresh hopped out and hopped in the car with Slim. "What's up, fool? What you need to holla at me about that you couldn't over the phone?" Slim asked Fresh. "I just got robbed for a half a brick and $10 bands. Some nigga name Murda did it. I swear once I catch this nigga I'ma kill 'em! No ifs, ands, or buts about it. I'ma—" "Slow down a second and tell me how do you know who robbed you," Slim said, putting two and two together in his head. *'This nigga musta known something about us hanging with Kilo because he done robbed all three of us. Ain't no telling how long he been watching us,'* Slim thought. "'Cause when I served him, I had this lil bitch I be fucking in the truck with me and she said that him and her use to mess around when she lived in Toledo. But when she moved here, they lost contact," Fresh said. "Look, check this out." Slim said then told Fresh that he believed Murda robbed him because the same nigga got him and Quick. "But don't worry 'bout nothing tho. I gotta plan already in motion for his ass. He'll be meeting his Creator by nightfall." "I want my muthafucken money and my dope back. I ain't taking no lost like that," Fresh said, mad at the world, ready to kill. Slim didn't think about getting his money back. He just wanted Murda dead especially after Quick got robbed and now Fresh. A thought popped in Slim's mind, and he told Fresh that he knew a way to get their money back but it would probably take some more killing. "Man, I don't give a fuck who dies. I want my bread!" Fresh snapped. "Aite look me, you and Quick gone hit the spot that Murda been operating out of while he's getting his world rocked. So tonight 'round eight, we gone meet up and handle our bizniz like real niggas do," Slim said. "Have you talked to Quick about this yet?" Fresh asked. "Not yet, but I'ma run everything by him as soon as I leave from here." "Aite well, where are we meeting up at?" Fresh asked. Slim thought about it for a second then said, "We gone meet at the Juice Box. That way we can stick and move without being noticed that much. His spot is just a few streets over from there, so it's not going be nothing to hit his spot with a surprise attack. My only concern is who's gone be in the spot," Slim said. "We'll find out once we hit it, we just have to be fully prepared," Fresh said then gave Slim some dap before he got out. "Eight o'clock sharp. Be there," Slim said, then got out and went inside his mother's house to check on things there since he hadn't seen her since he and Ivonne moved in together. After visiting his mother, Slim called Quick and met up with him. Slim told Quick everything he and Fresh talked about, and Quick was down with it all. After leaving Quick, Slim decided to go home, and collect his thoughts and prepare himself for the action that was taking place later on that night. While Slim was sitting in his living room smoking a blunt and letting the TV watch him, Ivonne called and said that she and Kenya were going to hang out tonight. "I thought that we was supposed to be seeing a movie tonight," Slim said. "Oh, baby I forgot all about tonight. I'm sorry. I'll tell Kenya that I want be able to hang out," Ivonne said, wondering how she could have forgotten about her and Slim's plan for tonight. "Nawl boo, you don't have to. You just spend a little time with Kenya because I'm sure she needs it. We can always go tomorrow night," Slim said, freeing himself so he could handle his business tonight. "Are you sure baby, because—" "I'm positive, boo. Now go enjoy yourself," Slim said, cutting Ivonne off midsentence. "That's why I love you so much because you're always rational about things and you're very understanding," Ivonne said. "I love you too, and I'll see you when you get here," Slim said then hung up. Around 7:30 p.m., Slim was leaving out his front door dressed in black from head to toe, carrying a Tek .45 and a Glock 40 he bought a few weeks back. Slim pulled up at the Juice Box at 7:48 p.m. and killed his headlights. Not even five minutes later, Fresh turned the corner in his truck with Quick right behind him. They both hopped out, sporting all black as well and got in the car with Slim. Slim went over the plan they were going to use to make sure each one of them remembered how it was going to go down. "So let's get this straight. We gone send a smoker in there to buy some work then kick the door behind them?" Quick asked. "Yeah, and once we get in, we tie everybody up and then get what we came fo," Slim said. "To make things a lil easier on our end and to have the ups on them, I'm gone play the part of the smoker and go in like I want to buy some dope. By the time you and Fresh kick the door, I'll have my pistol out," Quick said, changing the plan up just a little. Fresh had some clothes in the backseat of his truck that Quick took and ran through the dirt to try to disguise his identity. Before they left, Slim called Jazmine to make sure her plan was in motion. The way Jazmine answered the phone threw Slim off for a second. "Hey Momma, what's up?" Slim took the phone from his ear and looked at the screen to make sure he had dialed the right number. "How are we looking?" Was all Slim said back. "Okay Momma, but I might be in a little late because I'm on my way to the movies right now. I'll call you as soon as I leave and let you know that I'm on my way." Slim caught on to what Jazmine was telling him and hung the phone up. "Aite, ya'll niggas ready to do this?" Slim asked, thinking about how he was about to kill two birds with one stone. "Let's do it," Quick said, looking like a in-the-closet smoker with dirt all over him and his dreads all over his head. Slim led the way around the house of the Juice Box and into the backyard where they had to jump over a fence and sneak through the neighbor's backyard and around their house. They blended in with the night with the only light coming from the streetlights as they crossed the street and snuck around another house crouching down behind it. Slim pointed to a small white house two houses down from where they were and said, "That's the house right there. And from the looks of it, somebody's home. All the lights are on, so ain't no telling how many people are inside. We gone have to hit them quick. Ya'll ready?" Slim asked. To answer his question, both Fresh and Quick cocked their guns back, putting a bullet in the chamber. Walking down the small alley, they cut into the back of Murda's dope house that didn't have any type of entrance protection around it. *'So unorganized,'* Slim thought. Creeping along the side of the house, they heard the front door open and ducked down immediately. Someone had let the same sell out the house that told Slim whose dope house it was. "Aite now look, we coming in two minutes after they shut the door behind you," Slim told Quick who was making his way to the porch. Quick nodded, then set his stopwatch for two minutes, then knocked on the door. "Who is it?" A voice asked from the other side of the door a few seconds later. "Jonny," Quick said the first name that came to his mind. The chains could be heard sliding off the door like they knew who Jonny was. The door opened and a guy who resembled a smoker himself asked, "Who the hell are you?" "Gena told me that I could find some good dope here." "Who the hell is Gena?" The guy said, looking Quick up and down. "The prostitute that just left from outta here. Me and her use to get high together," Quick lied and gained entrance into the house that easy. There was a long table sitting across the living room floor so that whoever came to buy dope from them couldn't go past that area. There was two niggas sitting behind the table, passing a blunt back and forth. "What you tryna cop?" One of the niggas asked. "How much is the grams?" Quick asked, stalling, trying to see if anybody else was in the house. "They seventy apiece. You want one?"

The other nigga said, cutting the scales on and pulling out a Ziploc bag full of crack. "Gena told me ya'll got $50 dollar grams," Quick said, thinking how much of some amateurs they were. "Well, Gena lied. Now do you want it or not, bum-ass nigga?" "Nawl, man, I'm cool. I'ma go holla at dude a few blocks over. He got grams for $50," Quick said, ready to pull his burner out and stick it in Mr. Smart Mouth's mouth. "I'll let you get one for sixty-five. That's the lowest I'm going. I got that straight drop," The first nigga said. "Nawl, I'm straight. I'on got nothing but fifty really forty-six 'cause I had to get me some cigarettes," Quick said then turned to leave just as the front door came crashing in. "What tha fu—" Was all the door man got out before Slim and Fresh were in the house with their guns out. Quick spun around at the sound of the door being kicked in and had his pistol out and in the nigga's face at the table. "Move and feel how hot these .45 slugs get," Quick said, throwing his head back to get his hair out his face. "Come pat these pussies down to make sure they ain't got no heat on them, Fresh," Quick said, realizing that he just told the niggas Fresh's name. "Ya'll must not know who the fuck ya'll fucking with," The second nigga said, raising up but was pushed back down from the force of the .9 mm bullets Fresh hit him with. *'Boom, boom, boom.'* "Sit yo bitch ass down, nigga!" *Boom!* Fresh shot him one last time in the head, killing him instantly causing blood to squirt all over his partner. Slim turned his gun on the door man and made him lie face down on the ground and found an old .357 in the small of his back. "What was you gone do with this?" Slim asked then pointed it at the other nigga who was scared to death. "Nigga tell us where the dope at or leave out this bitch the same way yo homeboy left," Slim said, staring in the eyes of the other nigga that was sitting behind the table. "Everything's in the kitchen man I swear. The dope is in the cabinet next to the refrigerator and the money is stuffed in the couch cushion right there," He said pointing at the couch. "Check the kitchen for the dope, Fresh. Quick, check the cushion while I make sure these fools don't try nothing," Slim said. Fresh ran into the kitchen and found the dope right where Scary said it would be. "Jackpot," Fresh said grabbing a garbage bag off the counter to put the dope in. "It was seven of them thangs stacked in the cabinet," Fresh said, walking back into the living room. "Toss me that bag 'cause the money is here too," Quick said. "Is that all that's in this house, or is there something we're missing?" Slim asked Scary. "Man, that's everything I swear. Please just—" "Shut the fuck up, nigga. You starting to sound like a real bitch right now," Fresh said, sticking his pistol in Scary's face. "Chill out, Fresh. This lil nigga aite. Now are you sure we got everything?" Slim asked. "Yeah, man, that's everything." *'Boom, boom, boom, boom!'* Slim's Tek .45 put holes in Scary's head the size of nickels. "I know this nigga didn't expect to live after seeing our faces and hearing out names," Slim sad. Quick walked over the top of the door man and put two single slugs through the back of his skull with no words said. That night they each caught their first body, and neither one of them seemed to be worried about it. Meanwhile, Jazmine and Murda were leaving a Sports Bar & Grill in Cincinnati where Murda chose to hang out at because after robbing so many people in Toledo and in Youngstown he couldn't really be seen around certain parts of town without being shot at. "You ready for the after party, Isa?" Murda said, full of that yac. Murda and Jazmine sat at the bar, having a casual conversation, until about Murda's fifth shot of Hennessy. Jazmine thought Murda was a totally different person after he got that liquor in his system. He went from trying to get to know her to telling her that he was the man round town and that if she wanted to get on the winning team she better fuck with him because pretty soon the whole Youngstown will belong to him. Jazmine just sat there, sipping her ice tea, stroking his ego, telling him everything he wanted to hear. "I don't know. It depends on who's all attending the after party," Jazmine said, making sure it was just him and her afterward. "Just me and you boo, in a well-secluded area," Murda said, rubbing his hand up Jazmine's skirt. Jazmine opened her legs a little so Murda could feel how phat her cat was. Then she leaned over and whispered in his ear. "Do you think you can handle all that?" Murda told Jazmine that he was going to fuck her so good that she'll catch four nuts at once then beg him to make her do it again. Before they left the bar, Murda ordered two more shots of Hennessy and downed them one after the other. Staggering outside toward his car, Murda continued to talk shit about his position in the dope game, "I'm the muthafucken man 'round here. If it wasn't for me, half of these niggas would starve to death." *'I think you got it twisted, mister, because if it wasn't for the niggas you'll starve to death,'* Jazmine thought to herself, knowing that Murda was surviving off robbing people. "I'm glad that I'm with you then Murda, 'cause I love to be on the winning team and not the losing," Jazmine said. "Is that right? We're going to the hotel right next to the Bengals Stadium where the big cats play and the big dogs watch," Murda said, hitting the unlock button on his keys to unlock the car doors. Murda drove like a bat out of hell to the hotel almost causing a few wrecks on the way. Pulling up to the front door, Murda pulled out a wad of money and gave Jazmine a few hundred-dollar bills to pay for them a room. *'This is going to be easier than I thought'.* Jazmine paid for the room, came back out, and gave Murda his change. "Here's the change. The room wasn't expensive because there aren't any football games this week." "Put it in your purse then baby gurl, and accept it as a gift. What's the room number?" Murda drove around the back of the hotel and parked. "I got to piss like a racing horse. Grab that weed and them blunts out the console for me." Murda and Jazmine got out and headed to room 228, which was on the top floor. "The last room on the walk. Perfect," Jazmine said, opening the door. Murda rushed straight in and went directly to the bathroom. Jazmine sat her purse on the table along with the weed and cigars Murda told her to grab. Looking around the room as if she was going to find a hiding camera, Jazmine slid a seven-inch hunting knife under the crease of the blanket just as Murda flushed the toilet. Murda walked straight out the bathroom without washing his hands and saw Jazmine flatten out one of the pillows. Thinking that Jazmine was trying to set him up, Murda said, "What are you hiding under that pillow?" Jazmine looked up like the words Murda just spoke offended her and said, "What do you mean hiding? I'm not hiding nothing. What are you trying to say that I'm hiding something under this pillow to harm you with? 'Cause if that's what you're thinking, then you can take me home. I came to enjoy myself, not be accused of hiding something." "I'm not accusing you of anything. I've seen a lot of movies that play out like that. You know where the nigga has been set up and killed by a broad. I can't go out like that. I got too much to live fo. This has nothing to do with you," Murda said then lifted the pillows off the bed to make sure Jazmine wasn't trying to do him in. "I think that you've had a little too much to drink. How about we both strip naked and take a shower together?" Jazmine said, guiding Murda away from the bed. "I think I'm too full of it to take a shower. How about

KEITH L. BELL

we soak in the Jacuzzi while I smoke a blunt?" Murda said, sitting down at the table to roll him a blunt. After Murda finished rolling his blunt, Jazmine stood up and unbuttoned her skirt, letting it fall to the floor then pulled her shirt over her head and stood there. "Damn, that body banging, boo! I don't see a single stretchmark and you say you got how many kids?" Murda asked, staring at Jazmine like she was a piece of raw meat and he was a hyena that hadn't eaten in days. "I got two. But once you get inside this love tunnel of mine and see how tight, warm, and wet it is I guarantee you'll be trying to make number three," Jazmine said rubbing her vagina through her panties. "Let's hurry and take a bath so I can find out if you're 'bout what you talking 'bout then," Murda said, getting an erection looking at Jazmine play with herself. Leading the way into the bathroom to turn the Jacuzzi on, Jazmine got completely naked and climbed in. "Are you going to get in with me, or are you going to just stand there staring, looking like a lost puppy?" "You got me caught in a trance with that body of yours, boo. I can't lie. I can't wait to get all up in them guts," Murda said, almost tripping over his pants leg trying to take them off as quick as possible. After soaking in the Jacuzzi and fondling with each other for damn near an hour, Murda was ready to release some pressure. "Let's take this to the bed so I can finish what I started," Murda said, climbing out the Jacuzzi. "I hope you're as good with this as you are with your hands," Jazmine said, reaching around Murda to grab his dick. "I'm even better." Jazmine layed Murda down on his back, then sat Indian style between his legs and started to softly stroke his shaft with the palm of her hands. As Murda began to get hard, Jazmine leaned over and popped the head of his dick in her mouth and sucked lightly. "Damn, that shit feel good, gurl. Don't stop." Jazmine continued to stroke Murda while the head was still in her mouth. Murda closed his eyes and said, "Do that shit then, gurl." Jazmine stroked a little faster and made her mouth wetter, causing Murda to tense up a little. Seeing that this had Murda on the verge of cumming, Jazmine stopped and slid up Murda's body and layed on top of him. "How did that feel?" Jazmine said in Murda's ear. "It felt good, but now I'm trying to see how good that pussy feel wrapped around me," Murda said, squeezing Jazmine's ass cheeks with both hands. "I'm gone show you how wet it gets before you even put it in. Watch this." Jazmine said, then arched her back so that her ass was

108

in the air, then reached down and placed Murda's dick between her pussy lips and ass, and started to grind up and down real slow. Feeling herself becoming wetter and wetter, Jazmine sped up and tightened her thighs so that Murda's dick wouldn't slid inside her. Murda was so high and drunk that he didn't even realize that it was only Jazmine's pussy lips and juices that she was using to fuck him. "Gyde damn, Isabelle, this pussy fye! Oh shit, gurl . . . ride that dick." "You like that, daddy . . . huh? Do you like the way I put this pussy on you . . . huh . . . daddy?" Jazmine asked, busting a nut all over Murda's public hairs. "I love it . . . Don't stop, boo . . . make daddy cum. I want to cum all inside of this pussy, baby . . . oh shit . . . make daddy cum." "Tell momma when you're about to cum, daddy . . . umm . . . umm . . ." Jazmine said, bouncing her ass in Murda's lap. Jazmine positioned her hands flat on the bed beside Murda's head and felt for her knife. Getting a grip on the handle, Jazmine said, "Fuck this pussy, baby . . . fuck me harder, daddy. I'm about to cummm . . ." Murda grabbed Jazmine by the waist and thrashed himself harder. "Here it come, baby . . . ummm . . . I'm about to cum . . ." Were Murda's last words before Jazmine took the hunting knife and slit his throat wide open with one swift slice. "Not tonight you're not. Maybe next time." Murda tried to hold his neck to stop the bleeding, but it was to no avail. It was too late. The damage was done. The knife cut through his esophagus and his windpipe, leaving Murda grasping for air. Jazmine gathered all her belongings including Murda's car keys then thought about how she was going to get rid of his body. *'Good thing I didn't check in under my real name.'* Before Jazmine left the hotel room, she wrapped Murda's body in a sheet then drenched the sheet in some fingernail polish remover she had in her purse. Taking the lighter Murda left on the table, Jazmine lit the end of the sheet and watched it go up in flames then left. That night Jazmine showed her loyalty and worth to Slim and in return Slim made her a part of their entourage as their official hit woman. The next day the media had it all over the news, saying that there were four people murdered last night. Three of which they believed was drug related and the other one they had yet to find a motive for. "I feel sorry for whoever that was in that hotel room. They said the body was burnt so bad that the only way to identify the body was the teeth," Kenya said into the phone. "Umhum . . . things are starting to

KEITH L. BELL

get out of control around here. You're not safe nowhere. Not even in your own home," Ivonne said, lying next to Slim, watching the news. "That's why when Kilo come home, I want to get away from here and move somewhere like Florida where the sun always shininng." "Girl, it's drama everywhere you go. No matter where you go, it's going to always be a hood. But I wouldn't mind getting away from here either," Ivonne said, laying her head on Slim's chest. Kenya hung up the phone with Ivonne then got herself together so she would be on time seeing her man. After trying on almost everything in her closet, Kenya settled for a yellow sundress and her yellow-and-white Prada slippers. *'I can't fit nothing in my closet anymore. I must be getting fat. I wonder will Kilo notice,'* Kenya thought to herself stripping down to take a shower. It took Kenya ninety minutes flat to bathe, put on all her accessories, do her hair, and check herself in the mirror twice before leaving the house. Making sure she had everything she needed, Kenya locked the door behind her and headed out. Jiggling the key in the car door to open it, Kenya felt as if she was being watched so she looked over her shoulder and into the eyes of a stranger a car over from hers. "How you doing today, sexy?" The stranger asked Kenya who didn't notice that she was no longer trying to get into her car. "Fine." Was the only thing that Kenya mustered up before hearing her door unlock. "You look like you're on your way somewhere very important, so I'm not going to take up much of your time. I just wanted to let you know that I think you're beautiful." "Thanks," Kenya said, opening her car door. "My name is Justice by the way. I apologize for not stating that first." "I'm Kenya. Nice to meet you, Justice," Kenya said, wondering why she just gave a stranger her real name. *'At least he was a cute stranger,'* Kenya thought closing her car door. Kenya was a little early by the time she pulled into the prison gates for visitation, so she checked herself over in the mirror before getting out and going into the building to see her man. "I'm here to see Keon Campbell," Kenya told the female guard at the front desk. "Just sign in right here and clear that metal detector then stand over there so I can research you," The guard told Kenya who looked at her like she was crazy. "You want me to do what now?" Kenya asked, not understanding why she had to go through so much to visit her man. Kenya was new to the jail system, so going through all this was like trying to understand a foreign language. "Sign here,

110

clear that, and stand there. Three simple instructions," The guard said being smart. Kenya held her composure and went through the procedures it took to see her man. Sitting down in the visitation room waiting on Kilo to come out, Kenya became impatient after twenty minutes of waiting. Especially after seeing people come in that came after her. Kenya got up and asked the guard if Keon Campbell had been informed about his visit. The male guard working visitation called on his walkie-talkie and informed another officer about Kilo's visit. "Ten Four. He's in route," The dispatcher said back. "He's on his way now Ms." The guard told Kenya sizing her up with his eyes. Kenya sat back at the table and waited another ten minutes before Kilo came out. "Hey, baby!" Kenya said, standing up to hug Kilo. "What's up boo, how you been?" Kilo said, kissing Kenya. "I've been fine, baby. Just missing you like crazy and going to school every day is all that's on my agenda. Haven't much changed since you left," Kenya said. "I'm glad to know that you're still going strong out there without me. You're still looking good, so I know you're talking care of yourself," Kilo said, staring Kenya in the eyes, astonished at the way she was glowing at the table. "Baby, please don't tell me you're studying Muslim now." Kenya asked serious as a heart attack. "It's Islam, not Muslim baby. You can't study Muslim. But why you say that?" Kilo said. "Because you are starting to look like Rick Ross by the face and I know that's how a lot of Muslims look," Kenya said. Kilo busted out laughing because he knew that Kenya was serious and the worried voice she had showed it. "What's funny?" Kenya asked, smiling. "You crazy boo. Nawl, I'm not studying Islam. I just chose not to cut my face with those clippers they use to cut every inmates hair with. That's unsanitary especially when half the people back there are nasty," Kilo said. "Oh, okay. Do you want something out the vending machines? I brought some money with me," Kenya asked, hoping that he did because she did. Ever since Kenya found out she was pregnant, she couldn't smell or see somebody eating without getting a craving for something. "Get me a soft drink and a couple cakes, some chips and some hot wings," Kilo said. Kenya got up to get the items Kilo wanted and could feel the eyes of the guards watching her. Kilo scanned the visitation room when Kenya left to see if there was a bitch he fucked in the free world there visiting some other nigga. If there was, he was going to clown the nigga as soon as visitation was over. Not seeing any familiar faces, Kilo focused his attention back on Kenya who was slightly bent over, getting the chips out the vending machine. *'Damn, that ass done got a little fatter. Come to think about it, she looks like she done picked up a lil weight. It might just be that dress that got her looking like that tho,'* Kilo thought to himself. Kenya came back to the table and asked Kilo if this was all he wanted. "Yes, baby, 'preciate it." "No problem." Kenya and Kilo talked about how much they loved and missed each other for majority of the time until the guard yelled, "Fifteen more minutes and visitation is over." "I can't stand that cocksucker," Kilo said under his breath. "When you coming back to see me, boo?" Kilo asked. "Whenever you want me to baby. I just don't like the procedures and the attitudes these female guards have. But that's not going to stop me from coming back. I think she was just jealous because I look better than her. It's not my fault I woke up like this," Kenya said, singing Beyonce's "Flawless" song. "That's probably the case. I can't stand none of them either. But to kill the hassle a lil bit you could just come every other week. That way you want have to deal with them as much," Kilo said. "Forget them! They're not stopping me from seeing my baby. I'll just have to deal with it and they will to because I'll be here every week until you're back home with me," Kenya said. "Five minutes!" The guard yelled. "That's what's up, boo. What Slim and them been doing? Have you talked to them lately?" Kilo asked. "I talked to Slim a few days ago. And Quick and Fresh came by the house also. Oh . . . I don't know if ya'll watch the news back there, but they found four people dead last night," Kenya told Kilo just as the guard yelled, "Visitation's over! Say your good-byes, give your kisses, and let's go ladies." "Yeah, I seen that. But you take care of yourself out there boo. I love you!" Kilo said, standing up to kiss and hug Kenya. "I love you too, baby," Kenya said then bursted out in tears. "Don't cry baby. Everything's gone be okay. I need you to stay strong for me while I'm in here," Kilo said, holding Kenya wiping her tears away. "I'm sorry, baby. I just miss you and want you home with me that's all," Kenya said, wrapped in Kilo's arms. "I'll be home soon baby. Don't worry." "Let's go! Visitation time is over, Mr. Campbell," The guard yelled at Kilo who was the last inmate standing in the visitation room. Seeing Kenya break down and cry in visit made Kilo realize just how much he missed her. Lying back on his bunk, thinking about all the good times he and Kenya shared together made Kilo smile. "What's up, fool? What you up there smilin' for? You musta played with that cat in visit," A nigga named CP said. CP was about the only nigga Kilo fucked with in there besides a few people he knew from the hood. "Nigga, don't be sneaking up on me like that interrupting my train of thoughts. That's how the graveyard got started fool," Kilo said, joking with CP. "Nigga, you ain't gone kill nothing or let nothing die. How was that visit tho, playboy? Tell yo ol' lady to hook a nigga up with something. I know she gotta pretty lil friend for a nigga. Birds of a feather flock together," CP said, sitting down on the stool in Kilo's cell. "The visit was cool. Shawty just broke down crying at the end. What's up tho, my nigga? Ain't you 'pose to be in education somewhere?" "I pasted my GED test, fool. I ain't gotta go to class nomo. I been meaning to tell you that." "Word. That's good my nigga, but the question is, is you gone get out and put it to use?" Kilo asked CP. CP been locked up two and a half years and had another year to do before he went up for parole. "Yeah, I'ma do something with it believe that. You know how I spend my time in here studying, nigga. Small business, real estate, franchises— they ain't gone able to miss me out there," CP said. CP had a real business mind and was smart bookwise and streetwise just like Kilo. Which was another reason the two clicked so well. CP also held his own weight in the streets, which let Kilo know what type of nigga he was. "I'ma hold you to that my nigga, but where that chessboard at? Let me smash ya before count time," Kilo said. "Nigga, you can't fuck with me on that board. I'll beat you without my bitch on the board," CP said back. If Kilo wasn't working out or reading, he was playing chess with either CP or a Muslim brother named Salim who would literally read his Quran and beat the shit out of whoever sat down in front of him. "Don't ever insult my game like that. You know the outcome of CP versus Kilo. Quit playing," Kilo said, setting up the chess pieces. The two played four good games before the same guard that worked visitation yelled out, "Lockdown!" Standing in Kilo's doorway, the guard told CP to get to his cell before he caught a write up. "You show'll got a nice-looking woman out there. I wonder who's keeping the cobwebs out that thang while you're in here?" The guard said to Kilo, trying to make him mad. "I don't know who that could be, but I do know that it ain't you for two reasons. One, your money ain't long enuff and two she's just like me, don't fuck with the police," Kilo said then smirked. "Real funny. Truth is, it's probably one of your so-called homeboys that's sticking dick down her throat while you're in here, fucking your hand." "If you only knew," Kilo said, grabbing a honey bun off his shelf, thinking about all the times he and Ms. Blackwell had sex in the mop closet.

Chapter 8

Slim, Fresh and Quick all sat at the FishTank table contemplating where their next supply of dope was coming from. The dope they took back from Murda didn't last two full weeks and Heavy told them that his people in Akron weren't picking up the phone right now, so that left them back at square one, trying to find some more dope to keep their money flowing. "What's up with lil buddy down in the A?" Quick asked Slim. "I tried to call him a few days ago and the operator picked up, saying that the number was disconnected so I don't know what the bizniz is with him." "Damn, it's ugly out here. Somebody got something, tho. I don't believe that ain't nobody got shit!" Quick said, going through his phone. "This lil bitch I be fucking on told me her cuzzin be doing some hustling out of Detroit. She didn't really say too much about him tho, just that most of her family is from up there and she grew up around it," Fresh said. "Call that bitch an see if she can hook us up with her cuzzin then. Shit, drastic times causes drastic measures and right now shit seems as drastic its gone get," Slim said. "Her cuzzin probably slanging dog food 'cause that's what most of them niggas in Detroit sell," Quick said. Fresh called the chick and asked her if she could holler at her people in Detroit for him. "I'll have to call my brother and get his number because I don't have my cuzzin number programmed in my phone," The chick said. "Aite, do that for me. Tell him that your ol man tryna get his hands on something," Fresh said, then hung up and waited on her to call back. "Roll a blunt up. This shit is starting to give me a headache. Whoever thought that tryin' to buy some fucking dope would be this hard?" Slim said to no one in particular. It took the female Fresh was on the phone with almost forty-five minutes to call back, but when she did, she said something that was music to his ears. "He told me to tell you that everything was gravy and to give him a call. Whatever gravy mean," The female told Fresh then gave him her cuzzin number.

"Aite. And to show you my appreciation, I got something special in mind for you to do. So soon as I handle my bizniz, I'ma come scoop you up and treat you like the queen you are," Fresh told the female lying through his teeth. If she was to ask Fresh her name right then and there, he probably couldn't tell her because her contact name in his phone said Green Eyes. Fresh remembered each female he talked to by one of her features, and that feature was what he saved her name as in his phone. Fresh hung up with Green Eyes and called her cousin. "Yo," A voice answered. "What up, money? This Fresh. Yo cuzzin gave me your number and told me to holla at you," Fresh said. "What's good, Fresh? I'm Shoob. What you tryna do something big or small? Danyel told me about cha." "I'ma big nigga, so that's how I like to eat as long as the food is good," Fresh said. "The food is good no need to worry about that. I cooked it myself. I got plates for twenty-nine. But if you want to feed your dogs, I got some food for them too. The plates are a lil higher doe," Green Eyes's cousin said, talking in codes. Fresh caught on to what Shoob was saying then said, "Nawl, I ain't tryna feed my dogs. We gone eat off the same plate. I'ma call you right back and tell you the type of meal we want," Fresh said then hung up. "What in the hell was ya'll talking about?" Slim asked. "He kinda had me confused for a second too, but I caught on. He told me he got plates for twenty-nine, meaning it's $29,000 a brick. Then when I said something about food, he thought I was trying to cop some heroin and said if I was tryna feed my dogs he got food for them too," Fresh said. "He want twenty-nine a brick? That's cheaper than what Heavy's people got it for. The question is how we gone make the transaction? 'Cause I ain't taking no risk driving back from Detroit dirty," Slim said. Once they discussed how much dope they wanted and how they were going to get the dope back, Fresh called Shoob and placed the order. He told Shoob to give him two days to get shit situated with his driver and all. "Aite, just call when you get here," Shoob told Fresh. After talking to Shoob, Fresh called Shan and asked her if she wanted to make some money. "What kind of question is that? That's like asking you if you want some pussy," Shan said. "Funny. But look, I got two grand for you if you drive to Detroit and back for me." "That's all I have to do is drive?" Shan asked. "I know you ain't asking freaky-ass Shan to make this trip. I told you I got a driver for the job," Slim told Fresh then called Jazmine. Fresh hung up with Shan and said, "My fault. I forgot." Jazmine told Slim that she would be more than happy to make the trip to Detroit for him, just let her know when. "We're leaving in the morning 'round nine. Do you have to work?" Slim asked. "Nope! I'm off tomorrow, so I'll be ready." Jazmine said, lying about not having to work. The next morning Slim, Fresh and Quick were piled up in a black Hummer H2, trailing behind Jazmine who was driving a white G6 that Slim rented along with the H2. After stopping one time to get some gas and take a restroom break, they arrived at their destination. Pulling into a Burger King, they all got out and stretched. "I didn't think we would ever make it. Thanks to the man who invented GPS because I didn't have a clue as to where I was going," Jazmine said, seeing Quick and Fresh faces for the first time. "Okay, who's Fresh and who's Quick?" Jazmine asked. "I'm Quick and he's Fresh," Quick said firing up a cigarette. "Call this nigga and see where we are meeting him at. I'm tryna get it and go," Slim told Fresh who took out his cell phone and called Shoob. "He ain't answering," Fresh said. "Call his ass back. We didn't make this trip for nothing," Slim said. Fresh tried calling Shoob two more times only to get his voicemail. "Man, I don't know what his fool got going on. He still ain't answering." "Let's go get a room and chill for a minute then. Shit, that might be a sign or something. Ain't no sense in rushing," Quick said. "Yeah, you right. That drive drained me anyway," Slim said. Finding a suite that was suitable for everyone, they sat around smoking some of the best weed Detroit had. Jazmine even took a few hits from one of the blunts and fell straight to sleep. "She gotta be new to this the way she just passed out. Either that or that drive kicked her ass," Fresh said, sizing Jazmine's shape up. *'I'll bust that pussy wide open,'* He thought. "I really don't like the type of vibe I'm getting from this Shoob cat. He ain't conducting bizniz like a boss do," Slim said. "I was thinking the same thing. He could have at least called back and let us know something," Quick said on the verge of falling asleep himself. "What we gone do then? We could hit the streets and try to find a connect—" Slim said. "We can leave the money here and go looking' cause this nigga don't seem like he gone come through," Fresh said, cutting Slim off. Slim thought about what Fresh was saying and didn't see anything wrong with it. "I guess we could do that. What's up, Quick, you rollin'?" Slim asked Quick who was dead to the world sleeping like a baby. "Look like it's just me and you, fool. Grab the room key off the table and let's go see what we can come up on," Slim said. Just as they were heading out the door, Fresh's phone rang. "Look who decides to call back now. It's Shoob." Shoob told Fresh that he saw him calling but was unable to answer the phone because of a business meeting he was in. "I figured you would be here a little later on, my bad. But everything's still gravy if you wanna come on by." Fresh took the phone away from his mouth and told Slim what Shoob was saying. "Ask him where do he want to meet at?" Slim said. "Yeah, I'm tryna come through now. Where do I need to come to?" Shoob gave Fresh an address to some apartments and told him that there would be two females there to make the exchange. "Everything's gravy with the gals, my nigga. I told them to be expecting you, so they should still be waiting." Fresh hung up with Shoob and told Slim the address to the apartment and that they weren't meeting Shoob personally. "He said some broads would be there to make the exchange." "Some broads? Who this nigga think he is, Don Juan of the dope game? Man, I swear I don't like the way this nigga been conducting bizniz. Make me think we're walking into a trap," Slim said, not really feeling this Shoob cat at all. "But then again, it could be the way these niggas hustle in Detroit." Slim said. "I'on know how these niggas get down up here. That's why I brought my strap," Fresh said. "This could be an opportunity and I would hate to miss out on it by not taking the risk, so I'ma chance it. But if I sense anything funny, I'm coming off the hit with it," Slim said, patting his pistol. "You wanna wake Quick up?" Fresh asked. "Nawl, let that nigga rest. We can handle this." Slim grabbed the money that was stuffed in a knapsack off the bed and the keys to the G6 Jazmine drove off the table and they were out. It took them seventeen minutes flat to get to the apartment Shoob gave them from the hotel room. Before they got out the car, Slim told Fresh to make sure his shit was off safety and ready to shoot. "Hold up before you knock," Slim whispered then put his ear to the door to see if a conversation could be heard. Slim knocked on the door three times then stood back after not hearing anything in the apartment. A short dark-skinned chick dressed like a dude opened the door and said, "Wuz up?" Sounding real thuggish. "Shoob sent us. Said you knew we was coming," Fresh said. "You must be Fresh then," The thugged-out chick said. "Yea, that's me and this my nigga Slim," Fresh introduced Slim then stepped inside the apartment. Slim followed him inside and took in the whole layout of the apartment in less than five seconds. *'Bathroom door closed, bedroom door open, closet cracked, binds shut, TV volume low—hold on. Where's the other chick that's 'pose to be here?'* Slim thought. "Shoob gave specific orders to count the money first before I put anything in yawl's hands," The thug said. "The money part is all good, but I hope you don't plan to count out $150,000 by yourself. We ain't got all day. We tryna hit and move. Ya feel me?" Slim said. "I'm just telling you what I was told to do. That's all, my nigga. And I got help counting the money she's using the bathroom," Ms. Thugged Out said, getting a lil gangsta with it. The toilet flushed in the bathroom and out stepped a high-yellow redbone in a tennis skirt and tank top. "I thought I heard you talking to somebody out here, girl. They must be who Shooby had us waiting on." It took everything in Fresh not to say something sexual to the redbone who was cute and shaped up just like he liked them. "Yeah, that's them. I was trying to let 'em know that bruh said count the money before we give them anything." "Well, let's run it through the machine he brought by and make this quick as possible 'cus I got somewhere to be in twenty minutes," The redbone said then walked into the bedroom to get the money machine. "Can one of yawl come grab this for me? It's too heavy and I don't want to break a nail." Since Slim had the money and Fresh's hands were free, he walked in behind the redbone to grab the machine and caught her bending over, exposing her white lace panties. "Let me grab that as I can see you need some help with it," Fresh said, indicating the word *as* as her ass literally. Fresh picked up the money machine and brought it back into the living room and sat it on the table. "Once the money is counted, you can check the product to see if you want it or not," The thug told Slim who still wasn't feeling the way they do shit in Detroit but knew he had to do it their way in order to get what he wanted. "Cool," Slim said, then opened the knapsack and pulled out a stack of money. He popped the rubber band on it and ran it through the machine to make sure the money counter was accurate. "That's just $10,000. Where's the rest?" "I got fourteen more $10,000 dollar stacks right here," Slim said and ran the rest of the money through the machine. After everything was accounted for, the redbone went back into the bedroom and came back out with a suitcase. "Now you're free to check the product out," The stud said, opening the suitcase. Slim touched each individually wrapped brick and split it open to make sure the product was cocaine and not baby mix. "It's straight we want it," Slim said, then took the bricks out the suitcase, and put them in the knapsack. *'I guess these niggas up here are straight,'* Slim thought, making his way towards the door. "Tell Shoob we'll be getting at him in a few days. This was just a test run," Slim said, then opened the door, and was forced back into the apartment by three assassins wearing blue bandanas, holding assault rifles. "Nigga, get the fuck back into the room or feel how hot these muthafucken chopper bullets get!" The first assassin said, pointing the AR-15 he held directly in Slim's face while the other two assassins trained their weapons on Fresh. "Nigga, I wish you would even act like you funa reach for something so I can hit you with this cannon and knock a limb off yo ass," The second assassin said, talking to Fresh who was inching toward his waist. Feeling like they were in a lose-lose situation because of the heavy ammunition that was pointed at them, Slim gave in knowing that if he was able to get out of there alive he'll be able to retaliate. But if he was to try to stand a shootout being caught off guard like he was then, he would surely die. "Ya'll got that, my nigga." Slim said. "Shut the fuck up and put yo muthafucken hands in the air, nigga. Didn't nobody ask you to speak. You too, nigga! Get yo muthafucken hands up!" The first assassin snapped. "Nina, pat these clowns down. I know they packin' some heat." The thugged-out chick walked over and patted both Fresh and Slim down and took their pistols. "Yawl want be using these. Take and get rid of them. I'll call you and Sara when we're done," The leader of the assassins said. The redbone chick followed the thugged-out chick out the door and the assassins weren't too far behind them. Once they took the knapsack with the dope in it and the money that was in the suitcase, they were out too. "I ain't gone kill yawl this time, but if I catch yawl 'round here tryna find out who I am, it's a wrap. Lights out!" Before the assassins left the apartment, they tied Fresh and Slim together so that they would have enough time to make their getaway. "Man, I can't believe this shit. We walked straight into a mufucken trap. I knew something wasn't right with this cat. I could feel it. But they fucked up and let us live. Payback's a bitch!" Slim said, wiggling his arms to get the rope over his head. "And we got some names. Whoever Sara and Nina is they're just as dead as the punk-ass niggas that robbed us," Fresh said, freeing himself of the rope. "Come on, let's get up outta here before these fools realize they made a mistake and let us live," Slim said getting up off the floor headed for the door. Back at the hotel, Quick didn't believe what Slim and Fresh were telling him. "Please tell me it ain't so. I know we didn't take this long-ass trip to be set the fuck up and robbed. Did ya'll see some faces, hear some names or anything?" Quick asked. Slim then broke down the story for Quick for the fourth time. "So let me get this right. The niggas was wearing flags over their faces and the two bitches' names were Nina and Sara, which are probably some made-up-ass names that they came up with to throw us off. It's looking to me like we're fucked." Quick said ready to kill. "If ya'll don't mind me asking, who turned ya'll on to these people?" Jazmine asked after listening to them rave violently about killing whoever had something to do with them getting robbed. "You got straight to the bottom of this with that question, Jaz. Fresh, I think that bitch you called knew all about this. I wouldn't be surprised if setting niggas up was her job," Slim said, looking at Fresh. "You right, so she don't get away either." Fresh said. After coming to an agreement on leaving well enough alone for now, they all decided to stay at the hotel for the night and hit the highway first thing in the morning. Meanwhile, Kenya was receiving some devastating news about her brother from the mortuary. The mortician told Kenya that Murda was identified by his dental records and that she was the only immediate family member they were able to contact. Kenya felt a sense of grief overcome her body and tears started to form in her eyes, so she told the mortician that she will be down as soon as possible to identify and claim the body. Knowing the type of person her brother was and the things he did to survive, Kenya told herself, '*God has a reason for doing everything he does, and maybe God took my brother away to give my baby life.*' Taking the palm of her hand, Kenya wiped the tears from her eyes then called her mother to see if she knew what had happened to Murda. Kenya's mother broke down crying before Kenya finished telling her everything the mortician said. After asking the Lord why he had to take her baby from her over and over, Kenya's mother said through her sobs and tears in a voice that sounded like life had no purpose at all, "I [sniff] had a [sniff, sniff] feeling something was wrong with him. He usually calls and comes by at least twice a week [sniff], and I haven't been hearing from him," Kenya's mother said. Kenya knew how close her mother was to Murda and could only imagine the pain her mother was feeling. "I told the people that I will be down there to claim the body as soon as possible. Do you want to go with me?" Kenya asked her mother. "No. I don't want to see my son or whatever's left of him in the condition he's in. Just be sure to have him cremated." Not really knowing what else to say to her mother because the relationship they had wasn't as pure as the one she shared with Murda, Kenya told her mother that she'll always be her daughter no matter what. "And I will always love and respect you." In return, her mother told her that even though the two of them hadn't been talking much, she would really like to start. "There's something I want to tell you Mama," Kenya said, letting the tears that formed in her eyes fall freely. "I'm listening, baby," Kenya's mother said, still crying. Kenya started crying because she felt that her mother should have been the first person she told the news to. But because of their past relationship, Kenya wasn't concerned with telling her mother anything. "I know that Murda's death has brought pain that's unbearable to your heart because it's done the same to mine. But behind every curse, there's a gift. You'll be a grandmother soon." Kenya's words took a second to dawn on her mother, and when they did, it brought joy to her heart instantly. Kenya's mother was so excited that she changed her mind about not wanting to go with Kenya to claim her son's body. "You know what Kenya, before you go down to claim Murda's body come and get me. I want to go with you." After making arrangements at the funeral home, Kenya and her mother stopped and got themselves something to eat an did a little catching up on each other. "So how has Kilo been doing?" Kenya's mother asked after hearing Kenya tell how happy her life has been up until this point. "Dang Ma, we haven't been talking for real because Kilo is locked up," Kenya said, wishing and knowing that if Kilo was out he could somehow make all her worries and pain disappear. "Ohh . . . I guess we haven't been keeping up. How long have he been locked up?" Kenya's mother asked, a bit embarrassed. "Almost five months now. He have to be in there a year before he's able to come back home." Kenya said missing Kilo like crazy. "Do he know about his unborn child? I know he's so happy and can't wait to spoil him!" Kenya's mother said excitedly. "I haven't told him yet, Mama. And how do you know that it's not a girl?" Kenya said. Kenya's mother then went into the physics of how a mother always know what her child is having even before it's possible to tell. Kenya was twenty weeks pregnant, but by looking at her, you wouldn't be able to tell mainly because of the flannel dresses she wore. "To be five months, you still look your natural self. Your nose hasn't swollen, fingers aren't fat or nothing. Well, I guess you have put on a few extra pounds. Have Kilo noticed?" "He haven't said anything about it if he have. I haven't been to see him in almost two months, but we talk every day on the phone," Kenya said then made a mental note to go visit Kilo. After spending a little more quality time with her mother, Kenya became tired and dropped her mother off with promises to keep in touch. Before Kenya could get in the house good enough to get off her feet, Ivonne was blowing her phone up. Kenya answered and told her about her brother's death and how her mother and she reunited. "I'm about to take me a nap. I'll call you when I get up, girl. I'm tired as hell. My fat ass been up all day." "Okay. Don't forget either 'cause I got something I need to tell you," Ivonne said, then hung up and walked in the bedroom where Slim was on his knees, leaning on the bed counting his money. Not wanting to interrupt him, Ivonne stripped down and walked into the bathroom. Hearing the shower come on, Slim continued to count his money, thinking about the loss he took in Detroit. $90,000 of the $150,000 they got robbed for belonged to him and to make matters worse, he was still unable to re-up. Twenty minutes later, Ivonne stepped out the shower and heard Slim through the closed door going off on whoever was on the phone. "I just lost ninety muthafucken grand and the bitch that set this shit up ain't nowhere to be found, done changed numbers, probably skipped state and you telling me to be cool everything's gone be alright? You gotta be fucking kidding me, right? Ain't shit cool about getting fucked out yo bread, fool!" Slim snapped then hung up. Hearing Slim talk in such a delirious way made Ivonne want to be there for her man even more to let him know she got his back no matter what. Wrapping a towel around herself, Ivonne came out the bathroom and sat down on the bed next to Slim. "Baby, I know that you are frustrated right now but know that I'll always be here for you. I'll never turn my back on you. Whenever you need me, no matter the reason, baby, I'm here." Slim tried to speak only to feel Ivonne's finger cover his lips, hushing him. "No words needed, baby. Now lay back and let me ease your mind," Ivonne said, forcing Slim to lie back then undressed him. The next week Kenya was sitting across the table from Kilo with tears in her eyes, telling him about her brother. "It's okay to cry, baby. You don't have to hold it in. I know how you feel. I just wish I was out there with you to console you in your time of need," Kilo said, reaching out to hold Kenya's hands. "I really need you home with me, baby [sniff, sniff]. I've been holding on, going strong for the both of us. There isn't a day that passes that I don't think of you. [Sniff] I love you and will do everything in my power to keep you in my life," Kenya said, debating if she should tell Kilo about her being pregnant. Not wanting to put any more stress on Kilo that he may already have, Kenya kept something that she should have told him to herself. Instead, Kenya told Kilo about Murda's funeral that was being held tomorrow morning. Kilo encouraged Kenya to stay strong then tried to lighten the mood by telling her that she's starting to look like Ms. Piggy. "I can tell eating is all somebody been doing. That let me know you've found something to do with your time since I've been gone," Kilo said, thinking that would make Kenya laugh a little. But hearing that embarrassed Kenya because she knew that she have gained some extra weight, but that was only because of Kilo's seed she was carrying. "Don't make fun of me, baby. I'm going to lose it by the time you come home, I promise," Kenya said. "Well, you got six months to be losing it, so don't rush. I kind of like the lil weight 'cause now that ass suuppaa fat!" Kilo said, stretching the word super. "I see you are still obsessed with my booty, huh? Well, I got something else that I know you miss that's even tighter and wetter," Kenya said. Kilo looked back to make sure the guard wasn't looking then reached his hand under the table and under Kenya's dress. "Boy, you is crazy!" Kenya said after Kilo removed his hand. "Yeah, crazy about you. You know I'ma put a punishing on that pussy when I come home, right?" "I sure hope so. It's been so long that you might get inside and cum immediately as tight as this thing is," Kenya said, feeling herself become wet just thinking about how Kilo used to put it on her. "Visitation time's over!" The guard yelled. "Damn." Kilo and Kenya kissed each other, said their I love yous, and just like that, they were separated again. After the visit, Kenya stopped by

Ivonne's house to see if she was in the mood to help her find something to wear to Murda's funeral tomorrow. As Kenya was pulling up, Slim was leaving out. "Hey, Slim! Is Ivonne home?" Kenya asked. "What's up, Ken? Yeah, she's in there. Have you talked to Kilo?" Slim questioned, noticing that Kenya had put on some weight. "I just came from seeing him this morning. He's doing okay." Slim told Kenya to let him know if she needed anything, then hopped in his car, and pulled off. After Murda's burial the next day, Kenya just wanted to be alone but didn't want to be in the house, so she left the burial and ended up at the park, sitting on a bench watching the ducks. As she thought about how she and Murda used to always fight as kids and how their mother would always take his side, a smile came to Kenya's face. Wondering if there really was a heaven for people like Murda, Kenya lifted her head toward the skies above and said a prayer for her brother, "Dear, Heavenly Father, I know my brother, Melaki Lamar Carter, wasn't the godliest man on earth, but I'm calling you, asking that you please have mercy on his soul. I'm also asking that you give me and my mother strength to carry on. In Jesus's name I pray. Amen." Kenya wiped the tears from her eyes, still smiling then muttered the words, "I love you, brother." "Those must be some tears of joy." Startled by the voice behind her, Kenya jumped a little and turned around to stare into some eyes that looked very familiar. "I didn't mean to distract you, Kenya. I believe that's what you told me your name was. But I left your brother's funeral around the same time you did, hoping to catch you so I could give my condolence and tell you that I'm sorry about your loss. But you kinda got ahead of me, so I followed you, thinking that you would stop to get gas or something and I could tell you there. But you came straight here." Kenya was trying to figure out where she knew this face and set of eyes from but couldn't remember. "Thanks. But have we met?" Kenya wanted to know. "We have but not as precisely as I would have liked to. I was in some . . . I guess your apartment and happened to see you getting in your car and spoke. My name is Justice." Kenya thought about it for a second then remembered exactly what he was talking about. She was on her way to see Kilo that day. "Aww, okay, I remember now. How did you know my brother?" Kenya asked. "Me and Mel use to go to school together," Justice said then asked Kenya if she would mind if he sat down. Not knowing his intentions but feeling like he didn't mean any harm, Kenya told Justice that she didn't mind. Kenya and Justice sat and talked for well over an hour, talking like they'd known each other for years. Feeling herself becoming hungry, Kenya told Justice that she appreciated him for caring enough to talk to her and making sure that she was okay but she had to get home. "I think I should be headed on out myself. I just want you to know that if you ever need somebody to talk to, I'll always be here," Justice said then gave Kenya a tight and secure hug. Kenya felt Justice's strong arms wrap around her and his chest pressed against hers and instantly became wet between the legs. *'What am I doing getting wet at the touch of another man? And why am I resting my head on his shoulders?'* Kenya thought to herself. Kenya didn't know if it was her pregnancy that had her hormones acting up the way they were or what, but since Kilo has been gone and she found out about being pregnant, she's been masturbating at least three times a day now. Justice wrote his number down on a napkin from out his glove compartment and handed it to Kenya before they got into their cars. Kenya accepted the number with no intentions to use it then got into her car and pulled off. Realizing that she left her phone in the car on the charger while sitting at the park, Kenya checked it to make sure she didn't miss a call from Kilo. Seeing that Ivonne and her mother were the only missed calls she had, Kenya told herself that she would call them later. Making it home a little after five, Kenya grabbed her a bite to eat then ran her some water for a long hot bubble bath. Soaking in the bubbles, rubbing her belly, Kenya thought about the times she and Kilo shared together. *'I can't wait for my baby to come home and reclaim what's his,'* Kenya said out loud, moving her hands from her belly to down in between her legs. Rubbing around her second set of lips, Kenya let out a soft moan, "Umm . . ." Then she thought about how she used to lay Kilo on his back and climb on top of him slowly. "Oohh . . ." Kenya moaned after sticking her middle finger inside of herself and pressing her thumb on her clit while her finger was still inside. Kenya started to rotate her thumb slowly. Kenya then closed her eyes and tilted her head back, imagining that it was Kilo playing with her pussy instead of her. Spreading her legs open wider and moving her middle finger in and out while still rotating her thumb over her clit, Kenya was on the verge of cumming. Moving her fingers faster and moaning louder in pure ecstasy like she was getting the real deal, Kenya came back to back all over herself. *'Shit, Justice,'* Kenya sai catching herself, realizing that the image she just masturbated to wasn't Kilo's image but Justice's. Kenya became bashful and felt very ashamed. *'How could I masturbate to another man's image? That's just like cheating. I don't even know him well enough to be envisioning his face while I'm playing with myself,'* Kenya thought and then let the bathwater out and took a shower. After showering, drying off, then applying lotion, Kenya returned her mother's and Ivonne's calls. "Hi, you've reached Kerry Carter. Sorry that I missed your call but if you—" Kenya hung up before her mother's voice message was over and called Ivonne. "Now you decide to call," Was Ivonne's way of answering the phone. "I had a lot on my mind earlier, so I decided to go to the park to try to find a peace of mind," Kenya said back then thought about telling Ivonne about Justice but didn't. "So that's where you headed to after the funeral. I tried to catch you, but you left so fast that by the time me and your mother finished talking you was gone. How are you doing? Are you okay?" Ivonne asked. "Yeah, I'm fine. Just tired that's all." Kenya said back. "Do you need me to come over there? Because you know I'll drop everything and come quick like Creg daddy was told to do in one of them Friday movies," Ivonne said, causing Kenya to crack up laughing. "Girl, you is crazy. I'm fine though, I promise. I'll probably be sleep before you get here anyway girl," Kenya said then asked, "Where's Slim at anyway? You know he be having you on house arrest." "Girl, no he do not! You know I runs this here over here. Don't do me!" Ivonne said in her Remy Ma's voice, trying to sound hood, hard and ghetto. Ivonne knew that Kenya was going through it right now because of the loss of her brother and her man being locked up, so she did her best to comfort her. "Now you know you ain't got a lick of hood in you, girl. The only time you get some hood in you is when Slim is in you," Kenya said laughing, making Ivonne laugh even harder once she caught on to the joke. Ivonne knew that she had a white-girl side to her but didn't care because she knew that's what made her versatile. "That was a good one. I didn't get it at first. But Slim haven't been his self lately. From the small things he tell me and the conversations I've overheard, he's been taking some losses, some big ones too. I think Slim misses Kilo being out here with him," Ivonne said.

Chapter 9

"Who dis?" Slim asked, answering his cell phone. Slim had just got up, washed his face, brushed his teeth, and was sitting down at the kitchen table eating breakfast with Ivonne and their daughter. "Dis Kilo. I need you to come get me from the jailhouse. They just let me go." "What? Quit playing, nigga. You don't get out until next month," Slim said, not believing Kilo. "Nawl, I'm fa real, fool. They let me out a month early on good behavior. You coming, or do I gota call Quick to come get me?" "I'm leaving out now, fool. Give me ten minutes and I'll be there, cuz." Slim said, getting up from the table. "Don't tell nobody you coming either. I wanna surprise them, so come alone," Kilo said before he hung up. Slim slipped on his shoes and shirt, grabbed his keys then told Ivonne he'll be back and was out the door. Doing seventy-five miles per hour the whole way to the jailhouse, Slim got there in seventeen minutes flat when it normally took him thirty-five. Slim pulled up, hopped out, and gave Kilo the biggest hug he could give. "Damn my nigga, loosen yo grip a lil bit. I know you don't miss a nigga that much," Kilo said humorously. "My nigga, you don't know the half. Shit ain't been the same since you left." "Well I'm back now nigga, and better than ever. Society—nawl, these white folks owe me for that year I just did. I got some thug moves to make. But before I do anything, swing me by the crib so I can see my bitch," Slim and Kilo pulled off and headed to Kilo and Kenya's apartment. Once they got there, Kilo let himself in with the same keys he got locked up with. '*At least the locks ain't changed,*' Kilo thought then walked in with Slim right behind him. Slim was so happy that his nigga was home that he still had a smile on his face. Entering the living room, what Kilo saw turned his heart cold instantly. "Is this what the fuck you call going strong and hard for the both of us? Huh? What the fuck is this, Kenya? You gotta nigga in my shit!" Hearing Kilo's voice unexpectedly caused Kenya to jump.

"Kilo? Baby, what are you doing home?" Kenya asked, getting up. "What am I doing home? Bitch, what the fuck is you doing 'in' my home is the question," Kilo snapped. "This is not what it looks like, baby, I promise. He's just—" Kenya tried to explain after Kilo had seen her sitting next to some nigga breastfeeding a baby." "I don't give a fuck who he is! Why the fuck is he here?" "Look man, this shit was—" Now the dude tried to speak. "Nigga, shut the fuck up! I didn't ask yo bitch ass to speak. You must not know who the fuck I am. Matter fact I'm trippin', you can have this bitch. I'm out my element for even getting mad," Kilo said then walked toward the back. Slim didn't know what to say or do, so he followed Kilo and told him that the dude in the living room was his brother. "You in on this shit too, nigga? You've known about your brotha fucking my bitch and ain't told me? What type of shit is that? But you my nigga, right? Get the fuck outta here with that bullshit! You just as guilty as them," Kilo told Slim while chipping at the wall in the closet. Kilo then removed a board of dry wall, which was concealing his safe. "Nigga, you should know me better than that. I'll never cross you! Remember you told me to test her loyalty for you? That's what I did. That's what that's all about in there. I just never got back at you because he didn't get back at me," Slim said, letting Kilo know that this was his doing. Kilo stopped removing the money from the safe and apologized to Slim for coming at him sideways. Kenya was busting through the door by this time begging Kilo to let her explain, but Kilo was not hearing none of it. "So did you fuck him?" Was all Kilo asked. "Baby, I . . . I . . . I . . ." Kenya stuttered. "Did you or didn't you? Save all the other shit." Kilo said then said, "What? The cat got yo tongue?" When Kenya didn't respond. "Well, let's ask him." Kilo tore past Kenya and went back into the living room. "Kilo, please let me explain. It's not what it seems. Me and Justice just . . . We just . . ." Kenya said, not finishing her sentence. "Ya'll just what? Gone head and say it, Kenya. Ya'll fucked, didn't ya?" Kilo said, turning back to face Kenya in the hallway. "Kilo, please don't do this to me. I've been going through a lot and—" "I don't give a fuck what you've been going through. When the truth comes out and you've had sex with this nigga, I'm out! Point-blank, period!" Kilo said, then turned and proceeded toward the living room. Walking up on Justice, Kilo said, "Check this out, my nigga. Slim already gave me the bizniz on you. Now have the mission been accomplished?" Justice was holding Kenya's baby when Kilo walked in. "What do you mean have the mission been accomplished? And what mission did Slim give you?" Kenya asked, dumbfounded, looking at Justice. "This was all set up to see if you and your backstabbing-ass brotha got the same traits," Kilo said, giving Kenya a cold stare. "Kilo, how could you after all we've been through?" "All for one simple reason. Now did she open her legs to you?" Kilo asked, now giving Justice the same cold stare he gave Kenya. Justice handed Kenya her baby then grinned a grin that confused Kilo. Kenya said something to Justice that wasn't understandable because of the sobbing she was doing. "I'ma keep it real with ya," Justice said, looking Kilo in the eyes. "Please just—" Kenya tried to say something, but Kilo cut her off, telling her to shut up. "Like I said, I'ma keep it real with you, man. Me and Kenya—" "Slim! Slim! Wake up, baby. It's almost ten o'clock. Wake up, sleepy face!" Ivonne said, playing with Slim's eyelids. Slim opened his eyes, stretched and yawned, then realized that it was all a dream that Kilo got out early. "Good morning, baby. I cooked breakfast, but I'm sure it's cold now. Do you want me to warm it up for you?" Ivonne asked, sitting down on the bed. Slim noticed that Ivonne was in a real good mood this morning. "What's up with you, boo? You seem overly excited about something," Slim said, stretching again. Ivonne told Slim that she'll forever be excited for as long as he was in her life. "I just had a crazy dream, boo. I dreamed that Kilo called and told me to come pick him up from the jailhouse while me, you and a little girl that I assume was ours because she looked identical to the both of us was sitting at the kitchen table, eating breakfast," Slim said, not really being able to remember much else from the dream. "Well, you know dreams come true." Ivonne said then went and warmed Slim's breakfast. After showering and getting dressed, Slim sat at the table eating the breakfast that Ivonne had warmed up. "You must have been thinking about having a child last night if you're dreaming about one," Ivonne said the statement in more of a question. Slim thought about what Ivonne said before he replied, "I haven't been thinking about having any children, but that doesn't mean that I don't want one. Or two. Or three," Slim said, laughing at his own joke. "You must been thinking 'bout havin' some," Slim asked Ivonne. "Well, of course I've thought about it. But I think it would be best if I finished school before I have kids," Ivonne said then paused for a second. "Unless you want some now, I'll sacrifice schooling, for you baby." Slim peeped the last statement Ivonne made and knew right then and there that Ivonne's love for him was real and that she'll do whatever it took to please him. "Nawl boo, I can wait as long as you can. I ain't in no rush. Gone head and do what you gotta do to finish school and fulfill your dreams of becoming a doctor," Slim said. "Not a doctor, a lawyer, baby." "I know. I was just kidding." After Ivonne and Slim were done eating, they lounged around the house for a little over an hour before Kenya called and asked Ivonne if she wanted to hang out for a little while. Ivonne told Kenya to give her some time to wash up and put some clothes on then she would be right over. Ivonne hung up with Kenya then asked Slim if he would mind if she went over to Kenya's for a while. "Of course not, boo. I got some runs I need to make myself. You just be careful and call me if you need anything," Slim said. "I'm always careful, baby. You just make sure you're careful out there in those streets because it's a dirty, dirty world that we live in," Ivonne told Slim. Slim heard that and cracked up laughing. "What you know about that?" Slim asked. "I heard it in one of those songs you always listen to, baby. It's the truth because this is a dirty world. Even the people that are supposed to bring justice to the people are dirty. That's why I'm becoming a lawyer to help those that get treated unfairly." Ivonne said. "You can't save and help everybody tho, boo." "I know I can't. But if I can help and save just one person and they change and do the same, then I'll feel as if I accomplished everything I've been working so hard for," Ivonne said. *'I got me a real soldier,'* Slim thought. Slim grabbed his keys, tucked his gun on his waistline, gave Ivonne a kiss, and was out. Slim hopped in his truck and headed straight to the gas station. Pulling up to the pump, Slim got out and walked inside the store to pay for his gas. "Let me get forty on pump . . . uhhh . . . seven," Slim said looking out the window to see which pump he was at. "And a box of cigarillos please," Slim said to the lady cashier who was eyeing him. "It's $42.50, sir." Slim peeled off a fifty and handed it to her. "Keep the change, baby girl." Leaving the gas station, Slim called Big Ed and got him something to smoke on then pulled up on the block where he saw Fresh sitting on the trunk of his car, talking on the phone. Slim got out and crossed the street to where Fresh was. "Man, you ain't gone believe who I just got off the phone with!" Fresh said as Slim got up on him. "Shit, if it wasn't somebody from a Mexican Cartel talking 'bout some work, then you wasn't talking to nobody important," Slim said, opening the box of cigarillos he bought at the gas station. "That was Danyel, fool!" Fresh said. "Who the fuck is Danyel nigga? You said her name like she's somebody to know. I'on know no Danyel, fool," Slim said, dumping the tobacco from the cigars on the ground. "That's the chick that turned us on to them niggas in Detroit . . . Said that she didn't have nothing to do with us being robbed, and the only reason her phone been off was because her bill was due and she couldn't pay it until today when she got paid. I just went along with her, telling her that everything was all good," Fresh said. "I'm glad you did because she's gone be the one that get us our money back," Slim said, rolling up his blunt. "I'm 'pose to pick her up in about an hour or so. We can hold her hostage and interrogate her ass 'cause I still feel like she know something," Fresh said. Slim fired up the blunt and took a big pull from it, letting the weed smoke coat his lungs. Exhaling the smoke, Slim told Fresh to set everything up and let him know where he was taking her. "But what you doing out here. You got some work or something?" Slim asked Fresh, handing him the blunt. "I bought a nine piece from Quick just to make some type of profit. I've been out here all morning, piecing this muthafucker just like old times," Fresh said, grabbing the blunt and taking a pull. "Where Quick at anyway? I ain't heard from that nigga in two days." "He said he was funa shoot to Cincinnati when I hollered at him earlier. He didn't say fa what, tho. He just dropped the work off and said that he'll pick his money up once he got back." Fresh said scrolling down his contact list. "Let me call this nigga to see what he got going on in Cincinnati," Slim said, taking out his cell phone to call Quick. "What up, nigga?" Quick answered. "That's what I'm tryin' to figure out. What you got going on, fool?" Slim asked. "Not shit really, just down here in Cincinnati networking a lil bit, tryna come up. What up, tho?" "Same shit. I'm out here with Fresh, he told me where you were headed, so I called to tell you if you find something let me know," Slim told Quick grabbing the blunt back from Fresh. "Aite bet," Quick said and hung up. "Dude, stay on the move putting something together," Slim said. "I know. That nigga can't sit still fa shit. But who is gal coming out the cut, fool?" Fresh asked, pointing to the cut ready to test his macking. "Man, that's Red dooty ass. She use to fuck with Mannie a few years back. I'on know where she been at, tho." "I got her watch this," Fresh said, then crossed the street to where Red was and said a few words that made her laugh. Slim stood back and watched Fresh go to work. *'He'll never learn about fucking everything he see,'* Slim thought, still smoking the blunt he rolled. Not even five minutes later, Fresh was coming back across the street saving Red's number in his phone. "I'ma try to first night her. She was too easy!" Fresh said, smiling. "Why you want it if it's easy then, nigga?" Fresh told Slim that all bitches are easy to a nigga like him. "I'm too advanced for them. See, the bitches I be fucking you probably couldn't fuck unless you come off that bankroll you got. I just use my mouthpiece," Fresh said. "Don't let pussy be the death of you nigga," Slim told Fresh. "Shid, we all gotta die from something." Fresh and Slim sat on the block, kicking the shit with all the other niggas that were out there getting their grind on. "A Fresh, I'm 'bout to bust a move. Gone head and set shit up with ol' gal and call me when you ready," Slim told Fresh then made his way toward his truck. "Aite. Keep yo phone on. I'm funa set shit up now, so I'll be calling you shortly. I done made a cool lil profit. I'm about to bounce too," Fresh said. Slim sat in his trunk outside the Fish Tank for a few minutes thinking about how he could get his hands on some more dope. Coming up with nothing, Slim got out and went inside where Cutt and Benjamen sat in the living room, serving. "What up, Slim? What it's looking like? I hope you got something else for us because we're damn near through with what you dropped off the other day," Cutt said, giving Slim some dap. "Shit not looking good right now, but I still got a lil something. Just let me know when ya'll ready. How much work ya'll got left anyway?" Slim asked. "It's like seven or eight zips in the freezer plus the two that's right here," Benjamen said. "But the way the sells been coming, I'll say we will be out by the end of the night," Cutt said, grabbing a Newport off the table and firing it up. Slim was down to his last half of brick and knew that he had to be real precise on how he got rid of it. "Aite, check this out. Don't serve anything over a half ounce at once. And for every half sold, cut it with two grams of baking soda," Slim said, not really wanting to cut the dope but knew he had to stretch it. Slim left the Fish Tank and was headed to the Juice Box when Fresh called. "I'm about to pick her up now and take her to the hotel across the street from the Chicken Shack. Room 121. I should be there in less than twenty," Fresh said into the phone before hanging up. Slim swung by the Juice Box to check on things there then headed straight to the hotel where Fresh said he would be. *'Where the fuck is this nigga at?'* Slim thought after sitting three doors down from room 121, waiting on Fresh. After about eight minutes of waiting, Fresh pulled up with Danyel on the passenger side of his car and hopped out. *'I wonder did that fool see my car parked right here,'* Slim thought to himself, watching Fresh opening the door to the room. Inside the hotel room, Danyel was telling Fresh how much she missed him while Fresh acted in tune sitting at the table, rolling a blunt. "Why don't you show me how much you miss me instead of talking 'bout it?" Fresh said. In one swift motion, Danyel pulled her shirt over her head, unstrapped her bra and pulled her pants off. Standing there in nothing but her panties, Danyel started toward Fresh and dropped to her knees right in front of him. Fresh licked the end of his blunt then fired it up. Danyel, still on her knees, reached up and unbuckled Fresh's belt buckle and pants then pulled them down around his ankles. "Ohh, I'm gone show you all right," Danyel said, playing with Fresh's manhood with her hands. Opening the hole in his boxers and pulling his dick out, Danyel looked up at Fresh who was taking a pull from his blunt and said "I bet you miss this, don't you?" Danyel said, then dropped her head in Fresh's lap, and started giving him some of the sloppiest head ever. Sucking, licking, and spitting on Fresh's dick then cleaning it all back off with her mouth, Danyel was doing her thing—or so she thought. *'This bitch never could suck a dick, but her pussy feels like heaven,'* Fresh thought, blowing weed smoke all in Danyel's face. Grabbing a handful of Danyel's hair, Fresh guided her head up and down at the pace he wanted. "Just like that, gurl! Now suck them jaws in and make a nigga cum." Fresh came all in Danyel's mouth, knowing she hated it when he did that but to his surprise, she swallowed everything he shot out. "That's how much I've missed you! Now let's take a shower so you can show me just how much you've missed me," Danyel said, getting up off her knees and taking her panties off. *'I just showed you how much I've missed you. I let you swallow my kids,'* Fresh thought smiling at his inside joke. Fresh didn't want to get in the shower with

Danyel because he knew he had to let Slim in, so he told Danyel that he bathed before he picked her up. "But you get in and let me do the honors of washing you up." "As long as you promise not to miss a spot," Danyel said, rubbing her pussy lips. Danyel got in the shower, and Fresh was just about to lather her body with some body wash that she brought with her when Slim knocked on the door. "Someone's knocking at the door. Did you order room service, baby?" Danyel asked. "That must be my surprise I had delivered just for you. I'll be right back," Fresh said, then handed Danyel the rag he was holding, and walked to the door to let Slim in. "She's in the shower, washing off. I told her that I had a surprise for her. So you're the surprise. When she get out, just play along with me, aite?" "Yeah, aite," Slim said, walking into the room and sitting at the table where Fresh was smoking and getting his dick sucked at. Slim picked the half-finished blunt up out the ashtray and fired it up. "Who was it, baby?" Danyel asked, rinsing the suds off her body. "That was your surprise, boo. Now come on out of there and see if you like it." Fresh handed Danyel a towel and helped her out the tub. "I'm sure I'll like any surprise that comes from you," Danyel said, wrapping the towel around her body. "I hope so," Fresh mumbled. Slim had his feet propped up on the table when Danyel and Fresh came out the bathroom. Danyel saw Slim and stopped. "Who is he, Fresh?" "That is your surprise. Dis my nigga, Slim. I brought him in to make things a lil more interested. I want you to show him how good that head is, boo," Fresh told Danyel. Danyel wasn't feeling that Fresh's surprise was an extra party which whom he wanted her to flex her skills on. "I . . . I don't know him like that, baby. I wouldn't feel comfortable going down on him," Danyel said. Fresh tried to convince Danyel into giving Slim some head by saying that she must not love him like she claimed because if she did then she would do it. Danyel was just about to give in to Fresh's commands until Slim spoke up, "It's all good, baby girl. You ain't gotta break a nigga off none of that top piece. Just tell me where yo bitch-ass cuzzin at with my money!" It took Danyel a few seconds to comprehend what Slim said. "I promise I don't have anything to do with what happen. I promise!" Danyel said, backing into Fresh. "Fresh, tell him I didn't have anything to do with that, baby. Tell him." Danyel said sounding like she was about to cry. "I'on know if you did or didn't have something to do with what yo cuzzin did. All

I know is you turned me on to him, and he robbed us," Fresh said, pushing Danyel off him. "Now, we can make this easy, or we can make it hard. Simple and plain. All you gotta do is get yo cuzzin on the phone and let me holla at him, or you can keep yo mouth closed and take a bullet for him. Either one is cool with me," Slim said, pulling his gun out. Danyel saw Slim's gun and his facial expression and knew he wasn't playing. "I'll have to call my brother to see if he know how to get in touch with him because I tried to when Fresh told me what happened but his number had been changed," Danyel said, scared for her life. "Don't try nothing stupid on that phone. That's my only warning," Slim said and cocked his gun back. Danyel sat down on the bed with the towel still wrapped around her and went through her purse, looking for her phone. "Put him on speakerphone. I want to hear everything," Slim told Danyel as she was dialing some numbers. "I ain't heard from that nigga, lil sis. Why you looking for him fo? You aite?" Danyel's brother asked. "I'm fine. I just . . . just wanted to visit Grandma next week that's all." "Why don't you call her then? I'm sure she wouldn't mind." "She . . . she haven't been answering the phone. That's why I was trying to catch Shooby to tell him that I'll be headed that way next week," Danyel said nervously, pulling the towel up around her breast. Danyel's brother told her that he would call their other cousin and try to get a number for Shooby for her. "Okay, thank you, brother. I love you," Danyel said then hung up. "No one can get in touch with him. I don't even think my grandma knows his whereabouts, and he lives with her," Danyel said, giving up too much information. Slim heard that and a plan popped into his head immediately. "I tell you what, since can't nobody seem to get in touch with him, what's the address to yo grandma's house? He'll drop by there eventually if that's where he lives," Slim said. Danyel didn't want to get her grandma involved in what her cousin had going on, so she tried to plead with him, "Please don't do nothing to my grandma. She don't have anything to do with this. She's clueless to what's going on." Slim didn't plan on harming the old lady. He was just going to hold her hostage inside her own house until Shooby showed his face again. "You ain't gotta worry about yo grandma. I don't prey on the weak. She will be perfectly fine, but I can't say the same thing for yo cuzzin if he don't have my money." Danyel wasn't worried about Shooby's fate because he controlled that. Her only concern was for her grandma. Slim pointed the gun at Danyel and told her that he wasn't going to ask for the address to her granny's house again. "Speak now, or forever hold your peace." Feeling like she had no other choice, Danyel gave Slim the address. "Fresh, please don't let nothing happen to my granny. Please!" A now crying Danyel begged Fresh who didn't have much to say. "She gone be aite" Was Fresh only words. "Aite look Fresh, this how we gone do this," Slim started to say until Danyel's phone went off. "It's my brother calling back. Do you want me to answer it?" Danyel asked. Slim thought about it for a second. "Yeah, answer it. He might gotta number for yo cuzzin." Danyel picked up the phone, and just like Slim assumed, her brother had a number for her. "Okay, thank you again, brother." Danyel hung up with her brother and looked at Slim. "Call him," Slim said. Danyel dialed the number her brother gave her then handed the phone to Slim. Slim grabbed the phone and waited on Shooby to answer. "Yo," A male voice said after the phone stopped ringing. "Short time no see, my nigga," Slim said into the phone. "Who da fuck is this calling my phone talkin' 'bout short time no see?" "Cut the tough talk. You got something of mine, and I got something of yours." Slim said into the phone. "And what the hell is that? Who the fuck are you anyway?" Shooby wanted to know. "You gotta hunnet and fifty thou of mine and I want every dime of it back, or your cute little cuzzin I got right here at gunpoint dies," Slim told Shooby. It took Shooby a few seconds to respond to what Slim said. "You must be that green-ass nigga from Ohio who fell for the oldest trick in the book," Shooby said, chuckling into the phone. "Green? Nigga, the only thing green about me is my money! Now, either you cough up 150 thou you stole, or you'll be using it for yo cuzzin's casket," Slim said with a little aggression in his voice. "Shooby! Please give these people their money back. I don't want to die like this," Danyel yelled into the phone, crying. "Now do what's right for the sake of Danyel, my nigga!" Slim said. Shooby's next words were a total shock and told his true character. "Shit, Danyel gotta brother thata deal with yo ass if you kill her, so I ain't worried about that. Do what you gotta do 'cause I ain't coming off shit!" Shooby said then hung up. Slim looked at the phone then at Fresh. "Dude is one coldhearted muthafucker," Fresh said. "What do you think we should do?" Slim looked at Danyel, wondering if he should kill her or not. "I say we pay this nigga a visit.

He thinks he's safe the way he just left her to die like that," Slim said, unintentionally pointing his gun at Danyel. Danyel screamed and jumped back on the bed. "Please don't kill me! I didn't do it . . . I didn't have nothing to do with it either," Danyel said, holding her hands out in front of her like her hands could stop a bullet. Fresh told Slim that he believed Danyel really didn't have anything to do with it so she didn't deserve to die. Slim didn't plan on killing Danyel right then and there but knew that if they killed her cousin she would have to die too. "I'on think she deserves to die either." Hearing this, Danyel jumped off the bed with the towel falling off and gave Slim a half-naked hug. "Thank you so much for not killing me," Danyel said happier than she's ever been. Danyel then dropped down to her knees in front of Slim completely naked now and tried to give him some head, but Slim turned her down. "I'm good, baby gurl. You don't have to degrade yoself like that. You wasn't comfortable doing it at first. I know you 'preciate me, but I'ma let you and Fresh continue on," Slim said. "Come on cuz, at least hit that pussy. That thang get stupid wet," Fresh said, trying to get Slim to toss Danyel with him. "Nawl fool, I'm straight. Just hit my phone when you're done. I gotta holla at you about something," Slim said, then helped Danyel off her knees, and smacked her ass cheeks when she turned to get on the bed. Danyel just looked at Slim and smiled. "Don't touch it if you ain't gone fuck it," Fresh said. "Youa fool, Fresh. Gone handle yo bizniz and hit me when you're through," Slim said before leaving. "I don't know too many niggas who'll pass a chance to climb behind this big o' ass you got, gurl," Fresh told Danyel while peeling off every stitch of clothing he wore besides his socks. Danyel instantly grew a mutual respect for Slim for not making her degrade herself like most men would have. Back at the house, Slim was putting together a plan to deal with Shooby when his phone rang. Seeing that it was Quick, he picked up, hoping that he had found some work. "Tell me something good." "I met a nigga down here talking 'bout he can get his hands on a few of them thangs, but he wants thirty-six apiece," Quick said. "Thirty-six apiece? Gyde damn! He got some raw shit straight off the leaf don't he? Shit . . . is that the lowest he going?" Slim asked. Quick told Slim that the nigga was saying thirty-eight at first. "I tried to get him to go down to thirty-two, but he said that he wouldn't be making nothing at that price, so the best he could do was thirty-six." Quick said. "He must be the middleman then. But are you sure you can trust this nigga 'cause you know this lil drought got these niggas starving and trying to eat?" Slim asked Quick. "Yeah, I trust him. I don't got no funny feelings or anything. I'ma get me two of them thangs for now. What you gone do?" Slim told Quick that he wanted two bricks also. "Aite well, call Fresh and see what he want to do and then meet me halfway and we'll come back together," Quick said. "Bet. Remind me to tell you what's going on once we meet up," Slim said, then hung up and called Fresh. "I knew you would change yo mind on hitting that pussy. Come on back. We still here," Fresh said with his dick still inside Danyel. "Nigga, you gotta think with yo big head sometimes." Slim said tripping off Fresh. Fresh had a sense of humor that kept his niggas laughing. "Nigga, that is my big head," Fresh said, pulling out of Danyel. Slim told Fresh what Quick told him and asked him if he wanted to test the water again. Fresh told Slim to get him one and he'll pay him for it when they got back. "Aite bet. But check this out. Hit or miss, I want my bread nigga." "Aite, I got you, fool." After counting out the money for three bricks, Slim called Quick and met up with him. Slim hopped in the Charger with Quick and headed to Cincinnati where they met some DMX lookalike at a gas station. Quick made the transaction with the DMX lookalike who was driving a goldish-colored Explorer in less than five minutes, then hopped back in his Charger and pulled off. "Everything's there. I checked it," Quick said, giving the backpack with the five bricks in it to Slim. Slim unzipped the backpack and checked each brick himself. "It's coke, but the prices are too damn high. I guess that's because whoever we just got this from is from up north and is getting taxed for it," Slim said, zipping the backpack back up. "That's the exact reason why. But what's this you had to tell me about? What's going on?" Quick asked. "Aw, yeah, check this out," Slim said then told Quick everything that went on at the hotel including the phone conversation he had with Shooby. "Who do this nigga think he is? Like he can't be touched or something. When do you plan on checking this address out to see if it's the right one? I can't wait to see how gangsta he is with a gun in his mouth," Quick said, speeding a little thinking about what Slim was telling him. "Slow down a lil bit, fool. You know we're riding dirtier than UGK." Slim said. "My bad, fool. Just thinking about how this nigga was gone sale his own blood out got me heated." Quick slowed down just in time to let two cars turn out in front of him. One of them being a police car. Quick switched lanes and got on the interstate. "Right before you called, I was thinking about sending Jazmine back up there to deal with his ass. Since she's a girl, he probably wouldn't be expecting much," Slim told Quick after making sure they weren't being followed. "Shit, tryna give him a dose of his own medicine might not work because that's how he got us with some bitches. So he might not fall for it," Quick said, getting behind an eighteen-wheeler. "That's exactly why he will fall for it. He'll be expecting some niggas just for the simple fact that it was a hundred and fifty thousand that he got us fo. So he's expecting war," Slim said. "You might be right about that. But do you think Jaz can handle him and get our money back?" Quick questioned. The way Jazmine took care of Murda, Slim was confident that she could. "I think she can. I'ma call her and see what she thinks," Slim said then called Jazmine and got her voicemail. "She must be at work 'cause she didn't answer." A few minutes later, Jazmine texted Slim and said, "@ wrk call on brk." Slim and Quick made it back safely with no run-ins with the law, and Quick dropped Slim off at his car and told him to call him and let him know what the business was with Shooby. "Aite, be careful, nigga." Slim hopped in his car and pulled up at the Fish Tank to bust each brick down. *'Let me call this nigga right quick,'* Slim told himself, walking into the Fish Tank. "Where you at, fool?" Slim questioned. "I'm at the Chicken Shack, getting something to eat. I'm hungry as hell. That bitch was so grateful that you spared her life that she sucked and fucked the life outta me," Fresh said, pulling into the drive-thru. "I got that for you at the Fish Tank whenever you're ready for it," Slim said, giving Cutt and Benjamen a nod, walking into the kitchen. "I'ma swing by the house to grab that bread then swang straight to ya," Fresh said, looking at the menu as if he didn't know it by heart already. "Aite bet," Slim said then hung up. Slim sat at the kitchen table, breaking the bricks down. "A, Cutt, let me use those scales right quick," Slim hollered into the living rom. Cutt brought the scales in the kitchen and sat them on the table. "Ya'll ain't got no bags in here?" "It should be some in one of these cabinets," Cutt said, looking through the cabinets above the stove. "Here they go right here." Cutt sat the bags down next to the scales and sat down. "What we looking like?" Cutt asked referring to the cocaine Slim had in front of him. "The quality is good, but the price was fucked up, so you know what that mean. I'ma stretch this shit like Laffey Taffey's like Jeezy said." By the time Slim was finished cutting and mixing the dope, Fresh was pulling up. "What up, Fresh?" Cutt said, giving Fresh some dap as he came in the kitchen. "What's happening, fool?" Fresh said. Slim told Fresh that his work was in the freezer on the side rack. Fresh grabbed the dope out the freezer and sat it on the table, then pulled a Ziploc bag from the front of his pants, and handed it to Slim. Slim took and put the money in the bag the dope was in then put his dope back into the bag. "You straight, ain't you? I'm funa get up outta here?" Slim asked Fresh. "Yea, I'm good. I ain't gone be long. I'm waiting on Quick to swing by to get his bread then I'm out." "Aite then, hit me if you need me," Slim said. Cutt told Slim before he left that they'll probably need some more work later on. "Call and let me know when," Slim said. On his way home, Slim called Jazmine back to see if she could handle the job he had for her. Jazmine answered the phone apologetically, saying that she hadn't been able to take a break yet because she was the only cashier working. "Okay, well call me when you get off or whenever you get the chance. I need to holla at you about something real important," Slim said. "I get off at seven. Do you want to pick me up so we can talk then?" Jazmine asked Slim. Slim glanced at his watch and saw that it was a little after three and told Jazmine to call him around six thirty to see what he was doing. "I don't want to tell you I'll be there at seven and can't make it. So if you can, just call ahead of time." "I'll tell you what, how about I call you when I get home and you just come by there?" Jazmine said. "That's even better. Call me when you get there," Slim said then hung up. After dropping his work off and calling Ivonne to check on her, Slim stopped by his momma's house to check on things there and winded up falling asleep on the couch after eating some of Ms. Cook's famous cooking. Hearing and feeling his phone constantly going off, Slim woke up in a daze. *'How in the hell can I have the same exact same dream twice?'* Slim thought, checking his phone to see who was calling. Seeing that it was Jazmine calling, Slim checked the time and saw that it was a quarter till eight. *'Damn, how long have I been sleep?'* Slim asked himself, calling Jazmine back. "What up, Jaz? You made it home yet?" Slim asked Jazmine when she answered the phone. "I've been here for almost an hour now. Where have you been?" "I fell asleep on my momma's couch. I musta been tired, but I'm on my way now," Slim said then hung up. Ms. Cook walked in at the end of his conversation and said, "I hope that was Vonne you saying you're on your way to." Slim stood up, stretched and changed the subject. "Mama, what does it mean when you have the same exact dream twice in one day?" "I don't know, but I do know that dreams come true. What were you dreaming, that you and Vonne got married and had me some grandbabies?" Ms. Cook asked. "Ma, you sure do like Ivonne, don't you?" Slim asked already knowing the answer. "Yeap, she's a good girl with both Bs—beauty and brains—so you treat that girl right," Ms. Cook told Slim. "I am. But I'ma 'bout to head on out, Ma. Love you," Slim said, giving his momma a hug and a kiss on the cheek before leaving. Not even twenty minutes later, Slim was sitting on Jazmine's couch, smoking a blunt, talking business. "Okay, taking care of him and getting the money back if he has it is no problem. The only place the problem come in at is I have no earthly idea what he looks like," Jazmine said, sitting across from Slim in her silk pajama shorts and a tank top. "I'm on top of all that. I got pictures being sent to me as we speak." Slim said. "Okay, so when do you want this done?" Jazmine asked grabbing her water off the table. "I want to handle this as soon as possible just in case this nigga gotta spending habit," Slim said, blowing a cloud of weed smoke out his mouth. "I'll take off work tomorrow and hit the highway first thing in the morning then. How about that?" Jazmine said. Slim wondered why Jazmine was still working for minimal wage when she was getting paid good money taking on jobs for him. "I'll have you a rental car and a G to take care of any expenses you might need while you're handling yo bizniz. If you need any assistance once you get there, call and let me know and I'll get you some," Slim told Jazmine, dumping the ashes from his blunt in the plastic cup he was drinking out of. Jazmine told Slim that she wouldn't need any help handling her business because she knew how most niggas think with their dick and not their brain. Slim thought about Fresh when she said that. "Besides, I'm eye candy to the eye but a fatal attraction to the soul," Jazmine said, reminding Slim that killing was nothing new to her. Jazmine stood up and grabbed an ashtray off the top of her TV stand. "You don't have to keep using that cup as an ashtray. You could've asked for one, you know?" Jazmine said, then sat the ashtray down on the table and picked Slim's cup up and threw it away. "My fault, baby gurl. I forgot you be tryin' to smoke," Slim said, watching Jazmine's ass move freely in the silk shorts she had on. *'She can't have no panties on the way that ass bouncing,'* Slim thought. "I don't be trying to smoke either." Jazmine said, stressing the word *trying*. "I just don't smoke as much as you." Jazmine grabbed the blunt from Slim and took a long pull from it and gave it back. "Like I said, 'trying' to smoke." Slim finished his blunt with Jazmine, taking a few more pulls from it before it was gone then decided that it was best that he leave before he tried something with Jazmine. "Look, I'm funa get up outta here. Everything will be ready for you in the morning. Just call me when you get up." When Slim got home, Ivonne was sitting on the couch, watching *Girlfriends*, talking on the phone. "Hey, baby!" Ivonne said, looking up at Slim. "What's up, boo? How long you been here?" "About an hour. I cooked dinner. It's in the oven if you're hungry." "Okay, I'm funa take a shower right quick, and then I'll eat." Slim said, leaning over the couch to kiss Ivonne on the cheek. "Tell Slim Kilo said come visit him when he get a chance," Kenya told Ivonne. Ivonne relayed the message, and Slim told Ivonne to tell Kenya to tell Kilo that he'll be there next week. "How much longer Kilo got anyway, girl?" Ivonne asked. "He got five months left, and I can't wait! This has been the longest year of my life," Kenya said. "I know it have been, but you've been doing good for yourself while he's been gone. Aren't you expecting to drop in a few months?" Ivonne asked. Kenya was seven months pregnant but didn't look no more than four. "Yeap! I had my checkup last week. The doctor said that the baby might be premature but healthy. Kilo gets out in five months, and the doctor said that I should be dropping in two," Kenya said, excited about the arrival of her unborn seed. Ivonne thought about what Kenya was saying about her baby being premature and prayed for her baby. "Girl, you are small to be seven months. I don't see how though, and you eat everything you see." Ivonne and Kenya talked for a couple more minutes. Then Ivonne told Kenya that she had to get ready for school tomorrow. "All right, girl, call me on your break," Kenya told Ivonne before hanging up. Ivonne warmed Slim's food then made her way to their bedroom. Slim was sitting on the bed, rubbing lotion on his legs when Ivonne walked in. "Let me do that for you, baby," Ivonne said and took the bottle of lotion out of

Slim's hand then pushed him back on the bed. "Be my guest," Slim said then told Ivonne what his momma was saying about them getting married and having her some grandbabies. "Do you think she really meant that?" Ivonne asked, rubbing lotion on Slim's chest. "That lady loves you. She swears you're an angel or something. What you do to my mama to have her feeling this way about you?" Slim said, enjoying the touch of Ivonne's fingers on his chest. "I didn't do nothing, baby. It's just that a good woman knows a good woman after being in the presence of a good woman, I told you." "Yeah, aite, let me find out you know voodoo," Slim said. Ivonne pinched Slim's nipples for saying that and told him that she wasn't into witchcraft. After eating and watching the movie *South Paw*, Slim winded up falling asleep with Ivonne on his chest. The next morning Slim was up around seven, getting ready to go get the rental car for Jazmine, when she called. "I'm leaving out now," Slim said. "Okay, well I'll be waiting on you to get here," Jazmine said back. It took Slim a little over an hour to get the car and take it to Jazmine. Jazmine dropped Slim off at home and got straight on the interstate, heading to Detroit. Once she got there, she checked into a hotel room under an alias and left right back out. Typing the address Slim gave her into the GPS the rental car had built in, Jazmine pulled up to a brown brick house with a short bush-like fence around it. *'So this is where Mr. Wrong stay,'* Jazmine said to herself, thinking about how she was going to get inside the house. Just as she was about to pull off, the door opened, and out walked Mr. Wrong. Jazmine opened her purse and looked at the picture Slim gave her and said, *'This is going to be easier than I thought.'* As Mr. Wrong was coming through the bush-like fence, Jazmine got out the car and told him that she wasn't from around there and seemed to have gotten lost. "Where was you tryin' to get to?" Mr. Wrong asked, looking Jazmine up and down. *'Damn, I wish I would've put on something that showed off a little more body,'* Jazmine thought following Mr. Wrong's eyes with her eyes. "The mall. A friend of mine said that Detroit has some of the best malls to visit." "They aite I guess for the ones that ain't from here. But once you've been there more times than the workers, it gets boring. So where you from, ma?" Mr. Wrong asked, catching Jazmine off guard with the question. Jazmine didn't want to tell him Ohio because then he might get suspicious. "I'm originally from Tallahassee, but I've been living in North Carolina since I was four," Jazmine said, smiling a sinless smile. "Do you have a bathroom I can use? If you don't mind? I've been holding it all day." *'I might as well go for it all while the time presents itself,'* Jazmine thought. "I do, but I don't even know your name, so that makes you a stranger and I don't let strangers in my house, ma," Mr. Wrong said. "Isabelle." Jazmine said. 'Follow me then, Isabelle," Mr. Wrong said, turning and walking back toward his granny's house. "My name is Shoob by the way." Jazmine told Shooby to let her get her purse out the car first so it wouldn't get stolen. Inside Shooby's grandmomma's house, Jazmine let her eyes roam from room to room, trying to figure out if there was some money in the house and where it would be. "The bathroom is right here," Shoob said, opening the door for Jazmine. "Thank you," Jazmine said, smiling. In the bathroom, Jazmine was trying to come up with a plan to take care of Shooby and search the house for the money. *'I know how to play him.'* Jazmine then pulled her pants down and sat on the toilet like she was using it. Then she took and hid the tissue that was in there. Cracking the door a little, Jazmine called Shooby's name. Shooby, acting like he wasn't standing by the door, answered. "What's up?" "There's not any tissue in here." "Check the closet," Shooby said, wondering if he could talk Jazmine out her panties. Jazmine located the closet then told Shoob that she couldn't reach it without getting up. "Can you come grab it for me?" Jazmine said back. Shooby heard that and grinned. "You sure you want me in there while you're using the bathroom?" Shoob said halfway in the bathroom. "I don't mind. I'm sure you've seen a woman's goods before. Besides, you're in here now." Shooby got the tissue out the closet and turned to face Jazmine standing there in nothing but her bra with her hands behind her back like she was about to unbuckle her bra. Shoob just stood there. "If you like what you see, you'll unbuckle your pants and let them fall," Jazmine told Shoob who complied. "Now if you want to see me totally nude, you'll close your eyes while I unfasten my bra." *'That had to be my worst line ever!'* Jazmine thought. But to her surprise, Shoob complied with this also. *'He must be thinking with his little brain,'* Jazmine said to herself. Jazmine walked up on Shoob with one hand still behind her back and with her free hand, Jazmine played with his balls. Shoob tilted his head back and Jazmine struck like a snake, slicing his throat wide open.

Chapter 10

Twenty-four hours later, Slim and Jazmine were sitting in the Waffle House, eating and talking. Jazmine was explaining to Slim how things went down in Detroit. "You telling me you wasn't in town for a full hour and handled yo bizniz?" Slim asked. "Yeap! He couldn't resist the thought of getting some. You know how ya'll think," Jazmine said sipping her tea. "You can't categorize me with the rest of these niggas. But you said you got the money back too, huh? How much was it?" "I don't know. I didn't count it. But it's at my house." After they finished eating, Slim followed Jazmine to her house and counted out the money she found in Shoob's granny house. Slim counted out $75,000, which was half the money back that Shooby robbed them for. Slim gave Jazmine five extra grand for her service, then put $40,000 up for himself since he took the biggest loss in Detroit, and split the other $30,000 between Quick and Fresh. "Jaz don't play no games when it comes to getting the job done. Niggas better be careful," Quick said. Slim handed Quick his money then said, "That's why I'm glad she's on our team. Kilo want me to come see him this weekend. You wanna go? I know you ain't seen that nigga in forever." "Hell yea, I wanna go. It seem like forever since I seen that nigga fa real," Quick said. "Aite, we going Saturday. Be ready." Saturday morning Slim and Quick were sitting in the visitation room, waiting on Kilo to come out. "Check out ol' gal sitting two tables down from us in that white, that ass supa fat," Quick told Slim. "Yeah, I peeped her when we first came in. Look at the brown-skinned chick sitting behind us in the black. That bitch been eyeing a nigga since we came in," Slim said. Quick tried to play it off and look behind him and caught eyes with a fly lil Pueto Rican chick that was dressed in a pink-and-white Cache outfit. "Yeah, she cool. But check out that Spanish broad sitting at the table across from her. I think I know her from somewhere," Quick said, trying to remember where he knew the Spanish chick from. "Yeah, I seen her to. Whoever dude is she's visiting haven't cracked a smile yet. He looks like some type of Mexican boss or something. Like he's tied into the mob or a cartel," Slim said, glancing in their direction. "I swear I know her from somewhere. I just can't remember where," Quick was saying as Kilo came out into the visitation room. Kilo spotted Slim and Quick sitting toward the front of the visitation room and made his way toward them dressed in his blue prison uniform with the numbers 00413123 stamped across his shirt. "Aww, shit! My nigga got the Freeway and the Bob Marley going on. What's up, fool?" Quick said as Kilo got closer to the table. "Yea, yea, yea, you know, I had to switch the swag up in here. I can't us these nasty-ass clippers, and I ain't got enuff time to let one of these niggas twist my shit down even tho it's some niggas back there that will have a nigga looking like he just came from Susan's. What up tho, Slim? Tell me something good," Kilo said, giving Quick and Slim some dap and a hug before sitting down. "I can't call it, fool. I'm waiting on shit to get greater. What's up with you, tho, nigga. You aite?" Slim asked Kilo. "I'm straight. I'm just waiting on my time. This was nothing but a minor setback for a major comeback. Ya dig?" Kilo said rubbing his hands together. "It's ugly out there now. Niggas tryna charge thirty-five, thirty-six apiece. The streets is dry," Quick said. "I heard about the prices out there. That shit's ridiculous. I got something up my sleeve for that, tho. And if everything goes as planned, shit's gone get real plentiful," Kilo said, leaning on the table, trying not to be heard. "Don't look, but it's a Puerto Rican cat sitting behind us. His name Jose Sanchez. He's the *real* man behind a cartel called the El Dorado. I can't go into detail, but I got something going on with him," Kilo whispered. Quick heard the last name of Jose and remembered exactly where he knew the Spanish broad sitting at the table with him from. "That's Maria Sanchez sitting at the table with him then. I knew I knew her face," Quick said. "Who the hell is Maria Sanchez 'pose to be?" Slim asked. "That's the same chick that was in my fourth-period math class back in middle school. She used to like a nigga." "I'm not sure if that's his wife or sister. This my second time seeing her up here. There's usually a short petite Puerto Rican chick visiting him every time I come up here," Kilo said. "I'ma find out their relation after visit, don't worry. But what's been going on with you, fool?" Quick said. "It's the same shit every day in here. Don't nothing change: push-ups, read, and write like Yo Gotti said. If I ain't doing one of those three, I'm playing chess or lying in that sack, thinking about some money," Kilo told Quick. Slim asked Kilo if he wanted something out of one of the vending machines before they ran out of the good stuff. 'Yeah, grab me a water and two of those chicken wings things, fool." "You straight, Quick?" "Yea, I'm good," Quick said. While Slim was at the vending machine, Quick was giving Kilo a rundown on the things that's been going on since he's been gone. "Then we take a trip to Detroit and take a loss there." "In Detroit? What kind of loss?" Kilo wanted to know. "Some chick Fresh was fucking with set that shit up. Long story short, we get there and get robbed, but Slim send Jaz back, and she took care of the biz." "Who is Jaz?" Kilo asked as Slim was coming back to the table. "You ain't told him about Jaz yet, fool?" Quick said to Slim as he was sitting down. "Nawl, not yet. I had to make sure she was official first plus I aint been up here in a sec," Slim said. Slim then told Kilo the whole story of Jazmine from how he first met her at the Chicken Shack up until now. "Ms. Jazmine don't play no games I see. I got to meet her. She gotta be attractive to the eye if she's catching niggas in her web. So which one of ya'll done tapped her? Let me guess, Fresh?" Kilo said. "I don't think nobody out the click fucked her. But I ain't gone lie I was real close one night," Slim said. The rest of the time in visit, the trio sat and kicked the shit with one another, reminiscing on old times. "So what's up with the Juice Box and the Fish Tank, Slim?" Kilo asked. "The Juice Box really ain't doing too much, but the Fish Tank still going strong. I was thinking about shutting the Juice Box down and just operating out the Fish Tank since the Juice Box ain't really turning over a hellava profit," Slim told Kilo. "Do whatever you think is best, my nigga," Kilo said right before the guard yelled that visits were over. "Visitation time is up! Say you're good-byes and let's go," The guard said, walking around to each table." Damn, fa real? How long is visits?" Quick asked. "'Pose to be a hour but a lot of these pussies be cutting visit short sometimes," Kilo said, standing up to give both Slim and Quick a hug and some dap. "I'ma swing by the house and drop some bread off to Kenya for you when we leave from here fool," Slim told Kilo before they left. Out in the parking lot, Quick was waiting on the Spanish broad to come out so he could find out if she was Maria Sanchez from his math class in middle school. "There she go right there fool," Slim said nodding toward the front door of the prison. "I be right back," Quick said, then got out the car, and walked toward the Spanish chick. Slim sat in the car and rolled a blunt, watching Quick the entire time. *'That must be Maria,'* Slim thought after he saw Quick lock her number in his phone then give her a hug. "That had to be her the way you getting in this bitch grinning," Slim said, pulling off. "Yeah, that was her. She talking like she miss a nigga," Quick said, shutting his door. "Who was that she was visiting?" Slim asked. "Aw, she said that was her brother. He gotta life sentence was all she said about him," Quick said. "Play yo cards right with her, and she might be able to get our ass in," Slim said, firing up the blunt he rolled. After Slim dropped Quick off at home, he drove by Kenya's to drop some money off for Kilo. *"Where the hell is Kenya at?'* Slim thought to himself after knocking on her door and not getting an answer. Thinking that she was with Ivonne, Slim called Ivonne's call phone and asked her if she was with Kenya. Ivonne told Slim that she hadn't heard from Kenya all day. "Why are you looking for Kenya? Is something wrong, baby?" Ivonne wanted to know. "Nawl boo, ain't nothing wrong. I was just trying to give her some money for Kilo that's all," Slim told Ivonne. Slim left from Kenya's house and stopped by the Barbeque Pitt and got himself a to-go plate then headed to the Fish Tank. Sitting on the couch eating and watching *Blue Hill Avenue,* Slim was debating on shutting the Juice Box down since the spot wasn't really bringing in any money. "A Ben, call Lucky at the Juice Box for me and tell that nigga I said to lock everything up and swing by here for a minute," Slim told Benjamen. Benjamen dialed Lucky's number and waited on him to answer. "Slim said lock everything up and swing by the spot so he can holla at you for a second . . . I'on know . . . Aite, one." Benjamen said then hung up. "What he say?" "He said he was on his way." "Aite. What ya'll smoking on? I know ya'll got something rolled up," Slim said, closing the Styrofoam tray. "I ain't smoked shit all day. Cutt was 'pose to go holla at Big Ed 'bout an hour ago and still ain't left," Benjamen said. "I'm waiting on that nigga to call me back. He said he wasn't there when I called," Cutt said. Almost fifteen minutes later, Lucky pulled up to the Fish Tank with a worried look on his face. "What up, Slim? What's this about?" Was Lucky's first words because he knew something wasn't right because usually Slim would come by the spot when he wanted something. Slim told Lucky that he was shutting the Juice Box down because of the drought that they were facing. "So what am I 'pose to do now?" Lucky asked like he heard the most devastating news a man could ever hear. "I'on know. That's all on you. Hopefully, you've been stacking instead of jacking yo money so you can do your own thing," Slim said then told Lucky to give him the keys to the spot. "How much mo work left?" Slim asked Lucky who really didn't have much money saved up. "It's probably two and a quarter in the freezer and the bread is in the same spot it's always at. I wish you would've gave a nigga a heads-up or something," Lucky said, giving Slim the keys to the Juice Box. "If I could've told you in advance, I would've. But since this was a decision that was just made, I wasn't able to." While Slim was getting shit together on the outside, Kilo was getting shit together on the inside. After the last chow was served, Kilo headed back to his cell to do some reading. Since his homeboy CP was in the hole for six pounds of tobacco, he didn't come out his cell much. Sitting at the small desk that was attached to the wall, Kilo felt somebody staring through his cell door window and looked up to see Jose standing there with two more Mexicans standing behind him. *He finally got my message, huh?'* Kilo thought as he opened the door. "You want to speak with me?" Jose said in plain English. "I do. It's bizniz," Kilo told Jose, looking him in the eyes. Kilo knew that he would have only one chance to lay a foundation with Jose, so he made his first impression his best. Jose turned and gave the two Mexicans a nod and on cue, they both put their back to either side of the door frame. "Let's talk inside," Jose said then walked into Kilo's cell. "What kind of bizniz are you talking about?" Kilo told Jose straightforward what he was trying to do when he got out of jail. "I've been watching the way you move and carry yourself in here, Kilo, and I think you have what it takes to be a leader. But once you do buznuz with my family, you do buznuz for life!" Jose said, letting that sink in for a second before saying, "You'll never be able to get out once you're in. Think about that before you make a decision." Jose left out the cell leaving Kilo to think about what he just said. After Jose left, Kilo sat down on his bunk and focused his thoughts on what Jose told him about not being able to leave the drug game once he did business him. *'I knew this*

Jose cat had big feet, but I didn't know they were this big,' Kilo thought to himself. That night Kilo tossed and turned all night long with Jose's words repeating over and over in his head, "Once you do buznuz with my family, you do buznuz for life!" Kilo weighed his options that night and the next day decided to let Jose know what was up. "What's up, Kilo?" A dude named Lou said. "What's up, Lou? Where the brown at?" Kilo asked, referring brown to tobacco. A code name the convicts used. "I think OG got some 'round there. You want me to go see?" Lou asked. Lou was one of those niggas that's always trying to fit in with the crowd so he'll run errands, watch out for the police, or do anything that he thought made him look cool. "Yeah, see if he got some left. And if he do tell him, I said sell me a pack for $50," Kilo told Lou, then reached in his pocket and pulled out a crispy $50 bill. "I'll be in the dayroom," Kilo said, walking toward the stairs. Before Kilo could get up the stairs, he bumped into Ms. Blackwell at the top of the stairs, threatening to write an inmate up for disrespect. "Cut all that out, Ms. Blackwell. You know we don't do no write-ups," Kilo said once he was close enough to see what was going on. "Yeah, well we are about to start if this clown don't watch his mouth," Ms. Blackwell said. Kilo told the nigga that Ms. Blackwell was talking to that he would take care of things and that he had nothing to worry about. "I ain't worried 'bout no write-up, Kilo. She just need to learn how to mind her fuckin' business!" The nigga said then walked off. "What was that about?" Kilo asked. "He mad 'cause I caught him coming out the cell with Coco," Ms. Blackwell said then laughed because everybody knew that Coco was the biggest punk in the jail. "And I thought that nigga was a aite dude. That's fucked up. But what's up with you and all that ass you got poking out back here?" Kilo said then grabbed a handful of Ms. Blackwell's ass. Kilo used to fuck Ms. Blackwell every night she worked until she started catching feelings. "You know what's up with this ass, nigga. What's up with him down there is the question," Ms. Blackwell said, pointing with her eyes at Kilo's crotch. It's been almost three months since Kilo had sex with Ms. Blackwell, and hearing her talk like she wanted some made Kilo want it. "Come get me to clean up tonight and it's going down," Kilo said then walked into the dayroom where half the "niggas" were watching Telemundo just to see the Mexican chicks dance around the stage in their swimsuits, talking a language that neither one of them understood. Kilo walked past them to a table where AB and Silver were playing chess. Kilo met AB through CP and Silver through AB and felt they were some real cats his first time talking to them and have been messing with them ever since. "What's up, Kilo?" AB said after taking Silver's Bishop with his Knight and saying, "Check." "Shit, I can't call it. What's good, Silver? I see AB getting the best of you on that chessboard," Kilo said. "Every dog has his day. He ain't doing nothing I haven't done already. But where that brown at? I know you know," Silver said, moving his King out of check. "I sent Lou to holla at OG for me. He should be on his way up here. What's up you tryna blow one?" Kilo asked Silver. "Yeah, I need one the way AB been kicking my ass on this board," Silver said. "I still can't seem to understand why ya'll niggas still filling ya'll lungs up with that bullshit, knowing that it's a slow death," AB said. AB didn't smoke. All he did with his time was work out, read, and play chess. AB was locked up on some drug charges because somebody in his circle ratted on him after they got caught up on some drug trafficking charges. Silver, on the other hand, was the complete opposite of AB because he never worked out, and all he did was smoke. Silver was locked up for killing his daddy for beating his mother half to death when she didn't come home one night. While AB was built like a trainer, Sliver was tall and skinny but was good with his hands, so both of them were well respected around the compound. "I'll quit smokin' one day but until that day comes—" "Here go that pack of brown, Kilo," Lou said, handing Kilo his cigarette. "Ima keep smokin'," Kilo said, finishing Silver's sentence for him and cuffing the pack of cigarettes Lou was handing him. "OG said come holla at him when you get a chance," Lou told Kilo. "Aite, I will. Come on, Silver, let's go put one in the air." Kilo said, walking out the dayroom. After smoking a cigarette with Silver and Lou in Lou's cell, Kilo decided to go do some studying, so he told Silver that he would holler at him later. "I'll catch ya'll niggas later on. I'm funa go soak up some of this knowledge out this book I had my bitch send me." "Ain't nothing wrong with that. Knowledge is power. But only when you take the knowledge you learn and apply it to your life will it become real power. Remember that," Sliver told Kilo before giving him some dap and leaving out the cell. Kilo told Lou that he would get up with him later on then headed to his own cell where he had a letter and a money order for $200 dollars from Kenya lying on his floor. Kilo read Kenya's letter and smiled. *'What in the world is she talking about twice the love twice the life and twice the fun?'* Kilo thought, folding the letter back and putting it in the envelope. Kilo thought about Kenya and the life they shared and wondered if she would be the one that he spent the rest of his life with because he loved Kenya wholeheartedly and knew that she loved him just the same, but he told himself that if she ever cheated or showed any sign of infidelity, then everything they've worked for to build history together would be over at the blink of an eye. "There are two types of people to always watch out for son, and that's a disloyal or a lying man and an unfaithful woman," Kilo's mother would always tell him. Kilo thought about one of his niggas being disloyal but couldn't see either one of them crossing him, so he grabbed the book *Think and Grow Rich* by Napoleon Hill that he had Kenya send in and began reading and winded up falling asleep with the book on his chest. Dreaming that he was out and doing his thing with Jose supplying him with whatever he asked for, Kilo started to really take over. Then the whole dream changed to him sitting in front of two Puerto Ricans with Slim, Fresh, and Quick on the side of him. Kilo could tell from the vibe that the Pueto Ricans were giving that something wasn't right, so he tried to ask what was going on but couldn't speak. *'Why do they have tape over my mouth?'* Kilo asked himself in his dream. *'And why is my hands and feet tied together?'* The door in front of him opened, and a silhouette that Kilo thought was Jose appeared. Kilo was squinting his eyes, trying to figure out who was standing in the door that opened, when he heard somebody knocking on his cell door, waking him up. "Get up, nigga! It's almost four o'clock and you in here sleep. What's wrong, you stressing nigga?" It was Silver coming back to see if Kilo was going outside on the rec yard. "What's up? You hitting the yard or what?" Silver asked Kilo through the door. "Nawl, I ain't fuckin' with it. It's too hot out there," Kilo said sitting up on his bunk. *'What kind of message was behind that dream?'* Kilo wondered, opening the door for Sliver. "It's too hot? Nigga, you ain't gone melt. Bring yo ass on." "I'll be out there in a minute. Let me use the phone first," Kilo said, still thinking about that dream he just had. Kilo called Kenya to thank her for the money order and to ask her what she meant by twice the love life and fun, a saying that she's been writing in all her letters now but Kenya didn't answer, so Kilo called Slim. "What up, nigga?" Kilo said after Slim pressed zero to accept the call. "You already know what it is. I shut down the Box and moved everything to the Tank. The Box wasn't nothing but a headache," Slim told Kilo. "It's all good. I told you to do whatever you thought was best. I ain't tripping, but what it's looking like out there?" Kilo asked. "It's still fucked up, cuz. You know shit ain't getting no better if Quick can't get his hands on nothing and he stay on the move." "I ain't got much longa, fool. I be home soon to put the sun back in the sky," Kilo told Slim. Kilo talked to Slim a few more minutes before hanging up and going outside. "What's up, Kilo? Let me hold sumthin'?" Some nigga that Kilo didn't know from Adam said. "I should be asking you that big homie," Kilo said to the niggas that looked like he just wanted to be down. "Kilo!" Sliver yelled from across the yard. Kilo looked to his left and saw Sliver waving his arm in the air, signaling for him to come over there with him and AB. "I got next," Kilo said, sitting down on the bench where AB and Sliver were playing chess. "So what you gone do when you get back out there, Kilo?" AB asked Kilo. Kilo didn't have to think about his answer because he planned on picking right back up where he left off. "I'm doin' the same thing I was doing before I took my time. Ain't nothing changed. Why? What's up?" Kilo said. "I was just asking because I know you're on your way home that's all. So you say you're right back to the basics, huh? Look, I know you haven't made enuff money to consider leaving the game yet, but once you have made it to that point, do you think you will?" AB asked, looking up at Kilo. "I don't know. I haven't thought about that. What you getting at, tho, fool?" "I asked that to say and tell you that the game is meant to be played, not lived. Once you try to live the game, you wind up in one or two places—either dead or in jail—and that's something you already know. I'm just reminding you because I see you elevating in the game a lot faster than most." Kilo heard that and remembered Fonzi telling him those same words. '*Man, I hear those same words everywhere I go. They gotta be true,*' Kilo thought. "And I don't want to see you make the same mistakes that me and a whole lotta other niggas done made by still selling drugs when we've made more than enuff money to leave the game alone and do something legitimate," AB told Kilo. Kilo thought about what Jose said about not being able to give the game up once he started doing business with him and then thought about what AB was saying. "That's some real shit, my nigga. A lot of niggas don't even think that far ahead. All they see is the money, power, and everything else the game has to offer. See, once a nigga get so much money, he automatically start to accumulate power, which a lot of times we use for the wrong reasons," Sliver said. Kilo sat and listened to AB and Sliver give him the game from their perspective until the rec yard closed. "You are the master of your faith and the captain of your soul, Kilo. Remember that," AB told Kilo as they were walking back into the building. After working out the next day, Kilo was on his way to the showers when one of the Mexicans that was with Jose the other day stopped him. "Ose tell me tell you he wants to see you," The Mexican said. "Tell him I'll be to see him as soon as I finish showering," Kilo said, wondering what Jose wanted. After showering, Kilo put his things down then went to see what Jose wanted. Turning the corner to where Jose's cell was, Kilo saw the same two Mexicans standing around outside his cell. As Kilo got closer, one of the Mexicans said something in Spanish in the door then shook his head no. "Is Jose in there?" Kilo asked. The same Mexican that stuck his head in the door and said something in Spanish then made a gesture for Kilo to enter the room. "You wanted to see me?" Kilo asked. Jose was sitting at the desk when Kilo walked in. "Yes, my friend. There's something I forgot to tell you about joining the El Dorado family." Jose then stood up so that he and Kilo would be eye to eye. Kilo just stood there, waiting on Jose to say whatever it was that he forgot to tell him. Jose told Kilo before he could plug him into the family he had to prove his loyalty. "What do you mean by that?" Kilo asked. Jose then told Kilo that he would have to kill the leader of the El Dorado's rival before he could even attempt to do business with him. "It's the only way for you to get accepted by the rest of the family. Loyalty is everything." Kilo thought about what Jose was saying then thought to himself, '*So he want me to prove my loyalty by killing his rival, and once I'm plugged in with his family, I'll never be able to get out. Man, this shit serious.*' "If you don't think you can get the job done, don't try. I understand," Jose said, seeing that Kilo seemed to be in another place. "It's not taking care of the rival that I'm thinking about. It's this lifelong distribution that got me cogitating" Was what Kilo wanted to say but didn't want Jose to get the impression that he wasn't fit for the cartel, so "I can handle whatever comes my way. That's not a problem" Was what Kilo said. Kilo and Jose talked until the guard came down the walk, telling everyone to lock down. "It's count time! Lockdown!" "Damn, it's count time already? I'll holla at you later on so we can finish talking," Kilo said and left out Jose's cell. During count, Kilo was in deep contemplation about tying not only himself but his niggas into the El Dorado's cartel for life. All type of stuff was going through Kilo's head, but the main thing that kept repeating itself was if his niggas would commit themselves to the cartel forever. *'Fuck it. If the number is good enuff on each key, then I'm in,'* Kilo thought, making a decision that would change his life for good. *'It's for the better or worst. Which one? I don't know yet, but this is a chance of a lifetime. An opportunity that I'm willing to take a chance on.'* While Kilo was coming up with a plan to put himself on top of the game, Slim and Quick were sitting in Big Ed's weed spot, talking to him about buying one thousand pounds of weed. "One thousand pounds? Where in the hell am I 'pose to get that much weed from?" Big ED asked. "From yo connect or whoever you be getting yo weed from," Quick said. Quick came to Slim with the idea of buying a bulk of weed big enough to make a profit off earlier that day and thought that Big Ed could supply them with the quantity of weed they needed. "Shit, I ain't getting nothing but one hundred of them thangs. I'm not sure if the niggas I'm fucking with can getta nigga a thousand pounds. I can check on it for ya tho," Big Ed said, knowing that the dope game was all messed up and that Slim and Quick were trying to make a profit. "Most niggas wouldn't have done that for a nigga 'cause they don't want to see a nigga with nothin'," Quick said. "Ain't no hate in my blood, fool. I wanna see every nigga eat," Big Ed said, grabbing his cell phone off the table. Big Ed dialed some numbers on his phone and put it to his ear. "Hati, what up? This Ed," Big Ed spoke into the phone after a few seconds. "My peoples tryna get a thousand of them thangs and want to know if you can fill the order . . . yea, they good I put my word on them . . . Okay . . . okay. What's the ticket? Six?" Big Ed told Slim and Quick that he wanted six hundred a pound, and they told him they wanted it. "Aite, they said they want it . . . Same spot? Aite, give us thirty minutes." Big Ed hung up and told them to go get their money and meet him at the shopping plaza downtown.

Slim and Quick left Big Ed's spot and were both sitting in Quick's Charger in front of the shopping plaza twenty minutes later with the money for the weed on the backseat. "They gotta nigga sellin' weed again fool, you know it's fucked up out here," Slim said, trying to figure out the last time he sold a nigga some weed. "I was thinking the same thing fool, but fuck it, as long as the numbers adding instead of subtracting, I'm with it," Quick said. Big Ed pulled up next to Quick's Charger and a black Pontiac GT with black tints pulled alongside of Big Ed. Big Ed called Quick's cell phone and told him to hop in the car next to him with the money. Quick grabbed the money off the backseat, got out and walked around Big Ed's car and got into the black Pontiac. "Hey, mon, I'm Hati," A black-ass Jamaican-looking dude with big thick nappy dreads said. "I'm Quick," Quick said, damn near choking from the thick cloud of weed smoke that was in the air. "Is the weed I'm smelling the same weed I'm buyin'?" Quick asked. "Yes, mon, som of Hati bess," Hati said, then reached under his seat, and pulled out an ounce of the weed and said, "This what it looks like, mon." Quick looked at the weed, then stuck his nose in the sack and told Hati he wanted it. "You have to follow me to get it, mon. I not ride with thousand pounds of weed." Quick weighed his options then asked Hati where he would have him follow to. Hati told Quick that he had a spot uptown where he kept his weed. "It's thirteen minutes away," Hati told Quick. Quick told Hati that he'd follow him to the stash house as long as his partna was cool with it. Quick called Slim and told him that Hati didn't have the weed on him and that he wanted them to follow him to get it. "We'll tell that nigga to pull off and I'll hop in the driver's seat and follow ya'll," Slim said, climbing over the seat. Quick hung up with Slim and told Hati that Slim was going to follow behind them in his car and he was going to ride with him. Before Hati pulled off, he gave Quick the ounce of weed he had under his seat and told him to roll up. Hati pulled up to a dark-brown small wooden house with a tent in the front yard, and Slim pulled in behind him. "Come on, mon," Hati said and got out the car. Quick got out and grabbed the money, then looked back and gave Slim the "come on" nod. Slim tucked his strap, got out and followed Quick and Hati to the door. "I'm Hati," Hati said, looking back at Slim while sticking the key in the door, opening it. "I'm Slim," Slim said, walking into the house. "Wait hea. Me be rite back, mon." Slim and Quick both stood by the door, taking in the setup of Hati's living room. Two couches, a coffee table with a China bowl full of weed on it, a lawn chair, and a big flat screen TV hanging on the wall were everything that was in the living room. Hati came back into the living room, holding two large trash bags in his hands. Following Hati, holding another two trash bags, was a dark-skinned Jamaican lady wearing a black T-shirt and some black tight stretch pants that looked as if they were painted onto her tiger-like body frame. The Jamaican lady sat the trash bags she was holding down and turned and walked off. "It's two fifty in each bag," Hati said, pointing at the trash bags that were brought in. Quick opened all four bags to make sure everything checked out. Satisfied with what he saw, Quick asked Hati if he had another thousand pounds to sell. Slim looked at Quick as if to say, "A thousand mo'?" "You want one thousand mo' pounds rite now, mon?" Hati asked. "If you got it, I do. But if not, I'll wait," Quick told Hati then told Slim, "We might as well get it while the gettin' good." Hati told Quick that he had more than another thousand pounds if he wanted it as long as the money right. "The money is good. Just give me thirty-five to forty minutes to go grab the bread for the other and I'll be right back to pick them up," Quick said, handing the money to Hati. "Suni!" Hati yelled in a deep raspy Jamaican accent, and the Jamaican lady reappeared a few seconds later and said, "Yos, papi?" Hati handed her the money that Quick handed him. "Damn, I love her accent," Quick said aloud, not really meaning to. Suni looked Quick in the eyes and smiled, then turned and walked off, ass bouncing. "You con't handle ha in bed, mon. She like tiger," Hati said then grinned. "Where she from? Jamaica?" "No, mon, ha from Haiti. Same place me from." "Is all the women over there shaped like her?" Quick asked. "Yea, mon. Big boodee big titties errwhere!" Hati said. "I'm going to Haiti real soon if all the women are as thick as she is. You with that, Slim?" Quick asked Slim who was still watching Suni ass bounce down the hall. "Hell yea I'm with it, but you know them Haitian niggas crazy," Slim said. "Mee well-known in Haiti. Nobodee touch you. When yous ready to take trip, I go with you and show you good time." After talking to Hati, Quick and Slim took and put the trash bags full of weed in the trunk of Quick's Charger. "You funa buy another thousand pounds, fool?" Slim asked Quick as they were getting into the car.

"Six hunnet a pound, fool. We need to be tryin' to buy two thousand mo'. Just think niggas paying eleven or twelve hunnet a pound, so that's five or six hunnet off each pound easy," Quick said, backing out of Hati's yard. "I've did the math on that already. I'm just tryna figure out where we gone put all this weed at," Slim wondered. "I got a spot for that already," Quick said. Doing the speed limit back across town. Quick pulled into his sister's backyard and pulled beside a rusty '73 Cutlass sitting on bricks. "Man, I've been wondering what you did with this cut dawg," Slim said, getting out the car. "It's been sitting back here for damn near two years now. I've thought about fixin' it up. I just ain't had the time. This bitch came in handy, tho. Two thousand pounds can be stashed perfectly in the trunk of this thang," Quick said, trying to find the key to his Cutlass on his key ring. Quick popped the trunk and he and Slim loaded the trash bags of weed in there and shut it. "Don't nobody know about this but me, you and my sista so we straight. Now let's go grab that other thousand from this Hati cat," Quick said. After getting the rest of the weed from Hati and putting it in the trunk, Quick and Slim took twenty pounds apiece to hit the streets with. Quick dropped Slim off at his car and told him to call him in a hour and he would have a key made to the Cutlass for him. Slim hopped in his truck and drove straight to the Fish Tank. "So ya'll think ya'll can move the weed?" Slim asked Benjamen and Cutt. "For a rack apiece, man, we might run through the weed faster than the dope. Last time I heard a pound of some mid was twelve hunnet," Benjamen said, telling himself that he was going to charge niggas eleven fifty a pound just to get it off quick. "Aite, well, check this out. I got 10 p's of some killa in the truck and got plenty mo' elsewhere. So once them ten gone, hit my phone and I'll bring ten mo'," Slim said. Riding through the hood, Slim spotted Tila, a young nigga that was known for selling weed standing out and pulled over. "A Ti, let me holla at you for a sec," Slim said, letting the window down on his truck. Tila looked up at Slim, hoping that he heard him right. "Yeah, you. Let me holla at you right quick," Slim said after seeing Tila point to himself as if to say "Who me?" Tila crossed the street and walked up on Slim's truck with his heart beating from not knowing what Slim wanted but knew if a nigga like Slim rolled up and asked to holler at you then nine times out of ten, it was about some money. "You ain't got nothing on you do you, lil nigga?" Slim asked Tila as he got up on the truck. "Nawl, I don't keep nothin' on me, but I got some killa in the cut. What's up you tryna get you something to smoke?" Tila asked, eager to sell Slim some weed just to say he had done it. "Nawl, I ain't tryna cop none. But hop in and bend a couple blocks with me." Tila jumped in the truck with Slim without thinking twice about it. Slim pulled off and immediately started talking about hustling to see where Tila head was at. "How long you been out hea grindin', lil nigga?" Slim asked Tila after finding out that he had a real motive behind being out in the streets doing what he had to do to make a dollar. "Me, my mama, and my lil sister moved here from Memphis when I was eleven. By the time I turned thirteen, my mama was out there on drugs bad, leaving me and my sister to fend for ourselves. I been out here damn near four years doing what I gotta do to feed my lil sister. Nah mean?" Tila said, looking Slim in the eyes. Slim saw the pain in Tila's eyes and felt where he was coming from and decided to take the lil nigga under his wing and fuck with him. "I feel yo struggle lil nigga, so I'ma keep it real with you as long as you keep it real with me." Tila didn't say a word, just listened. "How much weed you buyin'?" Slim asked Tila who had his poker face on. "I might buy me a pound and a half every other day. Just depend on the price. These niggas been taxing lately." "Don't worry 'bout them niggas taxin' you nomo. What they been charging you eleven and twelve hunnet a pound?" Slim asked. Tila nodded and said, "Something like that. Sometimes $1250 and thirteen hunnet." "Them niggas ain't tryna let you eat. I'm gone give it to you $800 a pound on fronts. Keep yo money and pay me when you done," Slim said, pulling into the Burger King. "Eight hundred a pound! I can really get this money now. I 'preciate you fuckin' with me, Slim. Ain't nobody never showed love to me like that. I owe you one." Tila said. "Now I can get me and my lil sister new clothes and shoes for school. I can't wait to tell her. She gone be happier than she's ever been." Slim noticed how Tila mentioned doing for his sister every time he mentioned doing something for himself and knew that it must be hard doing for both of them when he was only buying a pound of weed. "How old is your sister, Ti?" Slim asked. "Leah is fourteen. Three years younga than me. Why you ask?" Tila asked Slim, a little defensive. Tila was very protective of his little sister and Slim could tell. "I just wanted to know. When school start back?" Slim asked Tila. "In two weeks," Tila said back, thinking about how fast those two weeks were going to come. "Okay well, don't worry 'bout buyin' ya'll nothing new. Next week I'ma take both of ya'll shoppin' for back-to-school clothes. Matter fact, I'ma bring my ol lady with me so her and Leah can go their own way in the mall and we can go ours. I hate shoppin' with women. They take too long," Slim said. Tila couldn't believe what he was hearing. "I can't believe this. It started off with me lookin' forward to just sellin' you some weed, to you supplin' me with it. Now you tellin' me you gone take me and my lil sister shoppin'. What's this all about?" Tila wanted to know. "It's about me helpin' you and giving back. Count it as a blessing," Slim told Tila before dropping him back off.

Chapter 11

"Everything seems to check out just fine, Ms. Carter. Have you been having any problems?" Kenya's doctor asked. Kenya was lying on the medical bed with her legs in the air, getting a pap smear. "No, not really. Everything's fine I guess," Kenya said. Kenya's doctor helped her sit up on the bed then asked her if she was sure she didn't want to know what she was having. "I'm positive. I want to wait till the day that he or she is delivered to find out." "That's unusual. What do you want, a boy or girl then?" The doctor asked. "I haven't really thought about it much. I just wish she hurry up!" Kenya said, signing the clipboard her doctor held out in front of her. "It's a girl that you want if you're wishing 'she' hurry up!" Kenya's doctor said, hearing Kenya tell on herself. "That slipped! You weren't supposed to hear that." Leaving the doctor's office, Kenya decided to stop by Susan's to see if her girl Tasha had enough time to squeeze her in for a pedicure and a manicure. *'Two seventeen on a Tuesday, she better have time,'* Kenya thought, jumping on the interstate and getting off ten minutes later and was at Susan's in another six. Kenya walked into Susan's and immediately felt like she was the center of attention the way the tone of conversations lowered. "Hey, gurl! Where have you been?" Tasha asked Kenya, sitting the curling irons down. "I've been around, girl." "I show'll haven't seen yo face in a while. Let me find out you done found you a new beautician and watch how fast I burn the back of that neck with these curlers," Tasha said, grabbing the curling irons out the iron oven and dangling them in the air. The girl in Tasha's chair looked back and said, "Gurl, watch them irons. You know they hot!" "I ain't gone burn you, boo. I got this." "Tash girl, you ain't missed me with all the business you be having. Now cut it out. I come by to see if you could fit me in somewhere. I just want a pedi and a mani." Tasha told Kenya that she had one person waiting, but all she wanted was a relaxer and had one other person scheduled to come in at three forty-five to get a touch-up. "I can get you in after the relaxer if you want to wait." Kenya told Tasha that she would wait since she didn't have anything else to do. *'That's what I get for walking in and not calling,'* Kenya thought, sitting down in the waiting section of the shop where three other girls were waiting. Kenya grabbed a *Jet* magazine off the table and could feel the eyes of one of the girls on her. "Hi," Kenya said to the girl then leaned back in her chair. The other two girls were carrying on with their conversation like they didn't have a care in the world, talking about some dude that they both had sex with. Kenya listened to them talk and wondered who they were talking about and how could they talk so openly about having sex with the same person. The doorbell chimed, *'ding dong!'* Kenya looked up to see Fresh walk into the shop, looking like a rap star. "Look who just walked in, gurl." One of the girls said that was sitting by Kenya. "Speaking of good dick, it walked straight in. Ain't that sumthin'?" The other girl said. *'I know they weren't just talking about Fresh,'* Kenya thought. You could tell that Fresh was a regular at the shop the way every beautician and some of the clients spoke to him. "What's up Susan, I'm next ain't I?" Fresh asked, stopping at Susan's booth. "You were supposed to be here an hour ago. Where you been?" Susan said in her Nigerian accent. "My bad, Susan, I got tied up." Fresh said. "You always tied up, boi. Go sit in the chair under the sink and I'll be over as soon as I finish putting this wrap on." Fresh walked past the waiting area and saw Kenya sitting with three other girls, two of them looking real familiar. "What's up, Ken? What you doing in the waiting section?" Fresh asked, giving Kenya a hug. "Hey, Fresh! I did a walk-in today instead of calling, and you know how that go. But Tash got me in there." "A, Tasha, you know we don't do this waiting shit! My peoples better be next in that chair or we gone have some problems!" Fresh yelled across the room to Tasha. "Boy, don't worry 'bout that one. She's next, so you just sit down under that sink and get ready to get those funky dreads washed!" Tasha yelled back, smiling. "Boy, you crazy. I don't mind waiting. I didn't have anything else to do," Kenya said, sitting back in her chair. "I know. I like fucking with Tasha ghetto ass. Have you talked to my nigga?" Fresh asked. "I talked to him earlier. He didn't say he needed anything. So he should be okay," Kenya said, getting envious stares from the two girls that were talking about Fresh before he walked in. "Tell that nigga I said to call me if he need something," Fresh said and walked off without saying anything to either one of the females that were speaking highly of his sex game. Kenya just shook her head. "I know he seen me sitting here. Why he tryin' not to speak?" One of the girls was saying before Tasha called Kenya. *'Saved by Tasha! Whew! Because I did not want to hear any more of their gossip about Fresh,'* Kenya thought, sitting the *Jet* magazine down and grabbing her purse. Kenya was gone by the time Susan was finished twisting Fresh's dreads. *'Damn, I forgot to ask her something,'* Fresh thought. Fresh paid Susan $150 dollars and gave her a $50 dollar tip before he left. After sitting in the shop, getting his hair done and listening to all the gossip that went on inside a beauty shop, Fresh felt like smoking. "What you smoking on?" Fresh asked Quick over the phone. "I got some cool lil mid you ain't heard? Me and Slim. Meet me at the Fish Tank so I can put you on game," Quick told Fresh then hung up. Quick was leaving out the projects, dropping off ten pounds of weed to a chick named Candy who was known around the projects for selling weed, when Fresh called. Quick pulled up at the Fish Tank in a white 2015 Impala that he rented just to ride around and get it out of. Fresh pulled up a few minutes later and hopped in the car with Quick. "You bought you a new whip, didn't ya?" Fresh asked Quick hopping in the car with him. "Nawl, this a rental. I just felt like getting out that charger for a sec. Have you talked to Slim?" Quick asked, grabbing the Newport box out the console. "I talked to cuz two days ago seeing did he have a half of slab he wanted to get rid of. Why you ask that?" Fresh questioned. "I figured that he would've told you 'bout the lil weed connect we ran across. It's been so ugly tryin' to find a nigga that can keep a constant supply of dope that I said fuck it and bought some weed to flip for the time being," Quick said, cracking his window to let the cigarette smoke out. "He didn't say nothing 'bout that. I think he was in front of somebody 'cause he kinda rushed off the phone. But ya'll niggas sellin' weed now?" Fresh asked surprised. "You know me. I'ma sell whatever's sellin'. I don't care what it is. As long as I can make a dollar off it, Ima sell it. I'll sell a nigga a bundle of socks as long as I got a quantity of them to make a profit," Quick said then told Fresh about the weed connect. "If you wanna shake it with the weed, we got enuff to give to you for the same price we're getting it at," Quick said. Fresh told Quick to sell him forty pounds so he could test those and see what they did. Quick sold Fresh forty pounds out his stash and noticed that Slim's sack looked a little small. *'I hope sis boyfriend ain't been back here snooping around,'* Quick thought, shutting the trunk on the Cutlass. "Let me make sure," Quick said then called Slim. "What up, fool?" Slim answered. "Not shit. Just makin' sure you been the one in yo sack and not sis boyfriend," Quick said, hopping back in the Impala with Fresh. "I've been runnin' back and forth so much it should be a trail. I got them bitches sellin' like bean pies. I'ma need another hunnet in a minute," Slim said. Earlier that day Tila called Slim and told him that he got a nigga wanting five pounds, then turned around, and called him back a few hours later with a nigga wanting to buy four more pounds. That's not including the extra ten pounds he dropped off at the Fish Tank. "That makes two of us then. I'm ready to re-up whenever you are," Quick said, pulling out his sister's yard. "That's a bet. But what you doing Friday night?" Slim asked. "Nothin' too much. Why. What's up?" Quick asked. "Ivonne's sister 'pose to be coming in town for her birthday and Ivonne wants to throw her a party at the club," Slim said. "Shit, just let me know when and where, and I'm there. You know Fresh will be there too. No questions asked." Slim got off the phone with Quick and continued to count out the money he made off the weed so far. *'This weed money might be slow money and nothing like dope money, but it's still fa show money,'* Slim thought, putting rubber bands around the money then stashing it. "Slim said he want us to hit the club with him Friday for Ivonne's sisters birthday. You going?" Quick asked Fresh before he got out the car. "Ivonne's sister birthday? Hell yeah, I'm goin'. I didn't even know she had a sister. If she look anything like Ivonne, I'ma try to give her ass some birthday sex," Fresh said, getting out the car, hopping in his truck. Fresh pulled off and called Mikayla, the same chick he's been fucking with since grade school. "Hello," Mikayla answered on the first ring. "What's up, boo? Where you at?" Fresh asked. "I'm at the house waiting on the cable man to come fix my cable. My channels aren't showing." "Okay, well, don't leave. I'm on my way over there," Fresh said then hung up. Mikayla was one of the few girls from the hood that decided to do something with herself instead of letting where she came from hold her back and Fresh respected that and kept it real with her. Even though Fresh would never admit to loving Mikayla, he had feelings for her that went beyond one of his sayings: "All hoes are good for two things, and that's dick in their mouth and dope in their house." "Open the door, boo. I'm outside," Fresh told Mikayla over the phone, then grabbed the forty pounds of weed off the back seat and went inside. "Hey, baby!" Mikayla said, hugging Fresh as he came into the house. "What you got in that bag, a skunk?" Mikayla asked, pinching her nose. "Nawl crazy," Fresh said, chuckling. "It's some weed that I need you to put up for me." Mikayla really didn't want the drugs in her house, so she told Fresh he could keep the weed in the shed behind her house as long as he promised not to bring anybody to her house. "You know I know better than that, baby. I'll never bring a nigga to where my Beautiful Black Queen lives," Fresh said staring at Mikayla, wondering how she still looked the same as she did in school. The only difference being that she's mature and has developed the body of a grown woman. "You looking at me like you're admiring what you see." Mikayla knew that Fresh liked her but also knew his reputation with women, so she kept her feelings in check because she liked Fresh too. "I got caught up in your beauty for a second, but let me get the key to the shed," Fresh said just as the cable man knocked on the door. "That must be the cable man at the door. Put that skunk bag in the bathroom until he leaves," Mikayla said, walking toward the front door and opening it. "Hi, my name is Will. I work with Comcast. You called in about your channels not working." The cable guy said staring into Mikayla's eye's. "I did. When I cut on the TV, the screen is blue, saying something about my service provider," Mikayla said. "Do you mind if I come in and take a look?" Fresh was coming out the bathroom the same time Mikayla was letting the cable man in. The first thing the cable man said was "Man, it smell like some loud in here. Who's smoking that?" Fresh told him that he burned one about an hour ago then asked him if he smoked. "Do I? Shit, that's all I do when I get off. Me and my homeboys," The cable man said, turning on the TV in the living room. "Is all of your TVs doing this?" Will asked Mikayla. "Yes, all of them are showing the same thing." Mikayla replied. "Okay, I'ma have to reset your service so it may take twenty to thirty minutes after that for the stations to pop back in," The cable man said, then called in and had the company reset Mikayla's service. "Everything's good to go. Give it a few minutes before you cut the TV on," Will told Mikayla while gathering his tools. Before the cable man left, Fresh told him that he had that weed he smelt for sale. "Fa real? I got a partna that be selling it. I'll let him know about you. What you charging a pound?" "A stack. Tell that nigga he better get it while the getting's good, tho," Fresh said. "A $1,000 a pound. Shit, he gone love you. What's yo number? I'ma call and let him know as soon as I get off." Fresh exchanged numbers with the cable man and soon as the door shut, Mikayla said, "Don't be setting up no business deals in my house, punk! I do all the business making in here," Mikayla told Fresh playfully. "You need to be making it yo bizniz to make a nigga something to eat then. I'ma 'bout to starve," Fresh said, rubbing his stomach. "I got something for you to eat," Mikayla said. "Is that right? Well, bring yo sexy ass over here and let me taste you," Fresh said, tackling Mikayla on the couch and wrestling her pajama pants off. "Move, Fresh, stop punk! I was just playing," Mikayla said, laughing kicking and screaming at Fresh who was ticking her biting on her neck trying to strip her at the same time. "Nope! You wanna play, let's play!" Fresh said, getting Mikayla out her pants. Mikayla flipped Fresh on his back and winded up in his lap with just her panties and shirt on. "Don't start nothing you can't finish," Mikayla said, then pulled her shirt over her head and hit Fresh in the face with it, then stood up to show Fresh what he could come home to every day. Mikayla stood about five feet six inches and weighed 130 pounds all ass, thighs, and titties. "Man, I swear you gotta body of a goddess and a face of a model, boo. Why you gotta be so fuckin' fine?" Fresh said, admiring Mikayla's skin color, flat stomach and fat ass. "I don't know, but come on, let's go get in the bed," Mikayla said. Out of all the times that Fresh and Mikayla had unprotected sex, she never got pregnant but today will mark the day of change for them, and they will find out about it nine months later. Friday morning Slim, Ivonne, Tila, and his younger sister who he introduced as Leah were all piled up in Slim's truck on their way to the mall. "Aite, check this out, Vonne. I already know how much you love to shop and how long you can spend in one store but me and my man's," Slim said, pointing at Tila. "We ain't tryna be in here five hours and ya'll ain't bought nothing but two outfits." "Well, me and my girl Lele, Ms. Lele that is, gone take our time when we shop because when we step out everything got to be on point," Ivonne said. Leah could be heard snickering in the backseat so Slim turned around and said, "I guess your giggling confirms that you agree with Ivonne, Ms. Le...Le?" Leah shook her head at Slim and kept smiling. "Yep." Inside the mall, Slim and Tila went one way and Ivonne and Leah went the other. "Let's go get us some kicks first. Then we'll tear the clothing stores down for some outfits," Slim told Tila, walking inside Footwear. "Where do you want to start, in the cloths department or the shoes?" Ivonne asked Leah who was still smiling from ear to ear. Leah was fourteen years old and never stepped foot inside anything close to a mall. All her clothes either were hand-me-downs or came from the Goodwill. "Ummm . . . ummm . . . let's get some clothes first." "Good choice. That way, we will know which colored shoes to get. So what's your favorite color, Lele?" Ivonne asked, giving Leah the nickname Lele that will stick with her for the rest of her life. "I like a lot of colors. I like pink, purple, orange, red, green, blue, white. But my favorite color is yellow," Leah said, naming off the colors on her fingers. "You like a lot of colors like you said, don't you?" Ivonne said, taking a liking to Leah's personality already. "Yep," Leah said. "Why is yellow your favorite color?" Ivonne was curious to know. "Because it's the color of the sun and the sun is bright. It brightens up the whole day just like me!" To not have had much of a life growing up, Ivonne noticed that that didn't hurt Leah's pride or steal her joy. After asking a numerous of other questions, Ivonne found out that Leah was a straight A student in school and wanted to become a famous tennis player to make a lot of money so she could take care of her brother. "You see anything else you want in here?" Slim asked Tila. "Nawl, man, I think I've got enuff stuff." They had been at the mall for a little over an hour, and Slim and Tila were already done shopping, but Ivonne and Leah were just now starting to shop for shoes. "Let's go to the food court and get something to snack on then because I know they are still shopping," Slim said. Carrying seven or eight bags apiece with only two bags belonging to Slim, they stopped at the ice cream shop then sat down. "Man, I can't wait till school start back! I'ma be the freshes' nigga in there," Tila said. "If you don't do something with that hair of yours, you ain't," Slim told Tila, causing both of them to laugh. Tila had his hair braided in eight big braids to the back that looked like they'd been up two weeks to long. "I think I'ma get me some dreads once I find out where this shop called Susan's at," Slim told Tila that he knew exactly where Susan's was located at and that he would take him there to get his hair done before school started. "Let me call Ivonne and remind her that her sister was supposed to be flying in today," Slim said then called Ivonne's cell phone. "We're almost done, baby. Give us a few more minutes," Ivonne said as soon as she picked up. "Yeah, I bet ya'll are. But I was calling to tell you not to forget about your sister flying in." "Shoot, I've been having so much fun shopping with Lele that I've forgot all about Irish coming in today and the party at the club tonight. We'll be through in a minute baby, I promise," Ivonne said then hung up." "We might as well take our bags to the trunk then come back and help them because I know they probably got twice as many bags as us." Slim and Tila took their bags out to the truck and smoked the half of blunt Slim had sitting in the ashtray. On their way back in, Slim bumped into Fonzi as Fonzi was leaving out the mall and stopped to talk to him mainly about Kilo. "Tell Kilo I said to get at me when he gets home," Fonzi told Slim before he left. After helping Ivonne and Leah put their bags in the truck, Slim dropped Tila and Leah off and made his way home to get ready for tonight. The whole way home, Ivonne was telling Slim how much she liked Leah and how she planned to keep in contact with her to make sure she's okay and still in school. And to make sure she kept in contact, Ivonne bought Leah a cell phone and told her that she would pay her bill every month for her. Slim pulled up to their house and grabbed the shopping bags off the backseat before he got out. "It's almost six and Irish still haven't called. I hope she's okay," Ivonne said, checking the caller ID on the house phone. "Why don't you try callin' her, boo?" Slim said, sitting the bags down on the couch then walked into the kitchen to get himself something to drink. Ivonne called Irish on her cell phone and found out that her plane was delayed, but she was at their airport waiting on her to come pick her up. "I just got off the plane and cut my phone on not even a full fifteen seconds ago. I was just about to call you," Irish said. "I started to get worried, but give me a minute and I'll be there," Ivonne hung up and asked Slim if he wanted to ride with her to the airport to get her sister. "I'ma swing by the barbershop before they close. I'll just meet ya'll back here at the house when I'm done." Slim said looking into the mirror hanging on the living room noticing that he needed to get his face shaved. Ivonne picked Irish up from the airport and was stunned at her sister's new look. "Girl, look at you with the Halle Berry look going on!" Ivonne said, hugging her sister in the middle of the airport. Irish and Ivonne hadn't seen each other since Irish moved to Florida to pursue her nursing career two years ago. "I got tired of dealing with it. Plus it's nothing but sunshine down there and all that hair made me hot. How do I look?" Irish asked, turning her head from side to side. "I like it even though I don't think I could get away with short hair," Ivonne said, grabbing one of the pieces of luggage Irish had. "If I can get away with it, trust me you can too. I mean we look just alike." Irish and Ivonne did favor each other face wise but bodywise, Irish was a little thicker. She was also a whole lot lighter. Back at the house, Slim was sliding his chain around his neck, talking on the phone with Quick, letting him know which club the party was going to be at. "Call Fresh and let him know which club we gone be at and tell that fool I said don't start no shit tonight," Slim was telling Quick as Ivonne and Irish were coming through the door+. "Slim!" Ivonne yelled. "I need to freshen up before we leave, Vonne. Where's the bathroom?" Irish asked, sitting her luggage down beside the door. Slim came from out the back dressed in an all-black True Religion outfit and some fresh black Air Max 95s with his chain hanging. *'She's cuter than I thought she would be,'* Slim said in his mind. *'I see sis got a little taste. I'm glad she doesn't have some bum living with her,'* Irish thought about Slim. Ivonne introduced Slim and Irish before her and Irish got ready for the club. "Slim, this is my sister Irish, and sister, this is the man of my life, Slim." Slim gave Irish a brotherly hug, wished her a happy birthday then told Ivonne that he and Quick were riding together tonight so he would meet them there. "Is Kenya going?" Slim asked Ivonne on his way out the door. "She said she was. Why you ask, baby?" Ivonne asked looking around the room for her phone so that she could call Kenya to see if she was still going. "So I can let whoever's working the front door know to let the three of ya'll straight in instead of standing in line," Slim said before leaving the house. Slim and Quick met up at the Fish Tank to smoke something before they hit the club. "I gotta zip of purp from Big Ed 'bout an hour ago just to smoke in the club," Quick told Slim. After smoking a blunt of the purple weed, Quick and Slim hopped in Quick's Charger and headed to the club. "Let me call Fresh to see where this fool at," Slim said. "I'll be there in less than fifteen. I'm in motion now," Fresh said, locking his truck up and getting in his '73 Impala. "Aite well, we should get there 'round the same time. We getting on the interstate now." Slim told Fresh. Quick and Slim pulled up at the club and didn't have anywhere to park. "The whole city came out didn't they? I wonder who they got performing tonight," Slim said, looking at the crowd of people trying to get in at the door. "Ion know, but whoever it is they got this muthafucker packed. There ain't even no parking spots on this side of the street," Quick said, leaving out the club parking lot to park across the street. Quick and Slim got out and leaned against the front of Quick's car and watched the crowd waiting on Fresh. While they were waiting, Slim called Ivonne and told her that they might have to park across the street from the club because the club parking lot was full. "There go Fresh right there," Quick said pointing down the street. "He had to pull his whip out. Is that him beatin' up the block like that?" Slim asked, hearing somebody's stereo system sound like it was about to bust the trunk open. "Yea that's that fool soundin' like that. Knowin' him he probably done put some bigger speakers and a bigger amplifier in there," Quick said, watching Fresh hold up traffic. Fresh pulled into the parking lot where Slim and Quick were parked and hopped out, leaving his door open and radio blasting Webbie's *Savage Life 2* CD. Dressed in royal blue and gray, the same colors as his car, Fresh had on his watch, bracelet, and all six of his chains ready to get his shine on. "What we waiting on? Let's go pop a couple bottles!" Fresh said after parking his car. They crossed the street to the club, all thinking the same thing. *'Damn, this line long as hell.'* "I ain't waiting in no line. We goin' straight to the door," Slim said. "That looks like Heavy's boy Blu workin' the door. I know he can get us in," Quick said, walking to the front of the line. "Blu, what's up bossman?" Quick said. Blu saw Slim, Quick and Fresh standing in front of the line and waved them over. "What's up with yawl?" Blu said after searching and letting a half-dressed female through. "Man, we tryna get in this bitch. But ain't tryna wait in line. What its gone cost?" Slim asked Blu. "Give me $150 apiece for these VIP passes." "One hundred fifty? Damn, who in this bitch, Obama?" Fresh said, pulling out a wad of money. "Rick Ross, Meek Mill, and Wale 'pose to hit the stage tonight. Yawl ain't heard?" Blu said counting out the passes. "Look, I got $500 for me and three other females that haven't got here yet," Slim told

Blu, pulling out his bankroll. Blu let them all through with VIP passes and told Slim he would let the females in when they got there. Slim texted Ivonne and told her that there were three VIP passes at the front door waiting for them. Inside the club, it was already crowded from wall to wall and still had over two hundred people still trying to get in. "It's already dunked in here, and it ain't even ten yet. Let's hit the bar to get something to drink," Slim said over the loud music. After being stopped a hundred times from niggas and bitches they knew from the hood they made it to the bar, and all ordered a bottle of Rose. "Let me get two bottles, baby gurl," Fresh told the bartender. The DJ played Meek Mill's "House Party" song, and the club went crazy. "Let's hit the VIP section before one of these niggas jump and bounce the wrong way," Quick said. Walking through the crowd and up the stairs to the VIP section, Slim, Fresh and Quick sat in the back of the room where there weren't too many people. "Can I get ya'll something else to drink or eat?" One of the female waiters asked them a few minutes after they sat down. "Bring us ten mo bottles of this," Slim said, holding his half-empty bottle of Rose in the air. "I'll be right back with your order, sir," The waiter said, turning to leave wondering how much of a tip she was going to get from Slim and his crew. "Make sure they on ice, baby gurl!" Quick yelled over Rihanna's "Rude Boy" song. "Roll some of that weed up, Quick. What you waiting on?" Slim said, catching eyes with one of the broads that were sitting a few seats over from them. Quick rolled two blunts of the purple weed he bought from Big Ed. Passing the blunt back and forth and sipping the champagne had all three of them bussing. "I'll be back. I'm funa go to the bathroom I gotta piss bad as hell," Fresh said, standing up. "Don't get lost fool," Slim told him, then stood and looked over the rail that overlooked the club. The DJ was spinning hit after hit and had the club in full swing. "If you ready ta see Rick Ross hit the stage, let me hear you holla . . ." The club went crazy again. "What about Meek Mill and Wale?" The DJ said making the crowd go even crazier. '*I wonder have Vonne and them made it in yet,*' Slim thought, trying to see if he could spot her in the crowd. Quick was rolling another blunt when Slim sat back down. "The way these niggas acting and Ross 'em ain't performed yet somebody might get shot tonight. It never fails. Black people just don't know how to act." "I already know. I got my strap in, so we cool," Quick said, pulling his lighter out and firing the blunt up. "I got mine in too. I wouldn't feel safe without it." The waiter came back to where Slim and Quick were holding a bucket of ice with five bottles of Rose in it. "I'll be right back with your other five bottles of champagne," The waiter said, sitting the bucket down on the table. Quick and Slim were conversing about buying themselves some more weed from Hati when a big bodyguard-looking dude interrupted them, saying that his man sent him over to ask them if they had some more of what they were smoking. "Tell yo man's all we got is some personal use," Quick said, passing Slim the blunt. "Let me rephrase that. Rick Ross sent me over here to ask if yawl got some mo of that yawl smokin'," The big bodyguard-looking dude said, pointing to the far-right corner of the room. Slim and Quick looked over and saw Ross holding a bottle of champagne in the air with a million sparkles jumping off his wrist and neck, and both threw a fist in the air silently saying, "What's up?" Rick Ross then hand signaled for them to come over there to where he and his entourage were sitting. "What's up with yawl, niggas?" Ross said in his deep Southern voice, shaking hands with Quick and Slim. "I smelled that shit yawl smokin' way over here. Where it at? Lemme burn my chest with it before I hit the stage." Quick pulled out the rest of the purple weed he had and said, "Roll the rest of that up." Ross pulled out a rubber-banded knot of money and tried to pay Quick for the weed, but Quick declined. "Just give us a shoutout while you on stage and one other small favor," Slim told Ross. "What's that?" Ross asked. "My ol lady sister's birthday is today. Call her on stage and wish her a happy birthday." Slim said. "I gotcha, my nigga," Rick Ross said back. Then he and his entourage headed to the back of the club after a waiter told him that the owner wanted to talk with him. Fresh came back up the stairs and into the VIP section followed by Ivonne, Irish and Kenya. Ivonne gave Slim a hug and a kiss and told him that they just passed Rick Ross on their way up the stairs. "Yea, me and Quick just hollered at him. You lookin' good, smellin' good, tho, boo," Slim told Ivonne. "What's up, Kenya?" "What's up, Slim? What's up, Quick?" Kenya said, hugging both of them at once. "You must be the birthday girl," Quick said to Irish. "Yup, my name is Irish, and you are?" "Quick." "I see ya'll have started the party without us," Ivonne said, picking up a bottle of Rose from the bucket of ice. Irish grabbed herself a bottle out of the bucket and said, "Well, let's hit the dance floor then."

"Man, did ya'll see the ass on Ivonne's sister? That ass too fat!" Fresh said after Ivonne, Kenya, and Irish left the VIP room. "She fine as hell too. Who's the oldest?" Quick asked Slim. "I'on know. I think Irish is." "Yeah, she is. She turned twenty-five today. You know, I'm on top of all that," Fresh said, rubbing his hands together. "She might be out yo league, Fresh. She looks and seems a lil sophisticated fool," Quick said. "Out my league? I ain't met a bitch yet that was out my league. I'm Fresh." "I got a rack you can't fuck her tonight then, nigga," Quick told Fresh. "Nigga, my game so cold I can get her and let you get some once I'm done." Fresh was boasting. "Shit, I got five hunnet mo you can't fuck her tonight since you claim you that cold," Slim said, popping another bottle. Fresh took both bets with Quick and Slim, saying that he couldn't fuck Irish tonight. The DJ announced that Rick Ross and his MMG squad were about to take the stage and the club went into a complete frenzy, screaming and yelling. Fresh, Quick and Slim stood by the rail overlooking the club while Rick Ross, Wale and Meek Mill did their thing onstage. "Cut the music, DJ. I gotta shoutout to give," Ross said after about the third song they performed. "Dis right here is for them niggas standing up there in the VIP section poppin' bottles and smokin' strong like real ballers do," Rick Ross said then fired up the blunt of purple weed he got from Quick up while everybody in the club turned to see who Rick Ross was talking about. Slim, Fresh and Quick held their bottles in the air, toasting to what Ross said. "Now I would like to give a special invitation to a young lady by the name of Irish to come join us on the stage." Ivonne, Kenya, and Irish were sitting at the bar, listening to Rick Ross. When he said that, Irish looked around the club, trying to figure out how many other Irishes were in there. "I know he ain't talkin 'bout me," Irish said, hoping like hell that he was. "If your name Irish and yo birthday today and your sister talk to one of those niggas standing up there, now is yo last chance to come up here," Rick Ross said after nobody moved the first time he said it. Irish jumped out her seat, screaming and running to the stage. "Lil momma bad lookin' like a bag of money," Wale said into the microphone as Irish was helped onto the stage by the security guards. Irish rushed right over to Meek Mill, Wale and Rick Ross and hugged them. "I can't believe this . . . oh my god . . . oh my god . . . oh my god . . ." Irish said over and over. "How old you turn today, sexy?" Rick Ross asked

Irish. "I'm twenty-five." "And who is your favorite MMG rap star?" When Ross asked Irish that question everybody in the crowd started shouting out names. "Meek Mill!" "Wale!" "Rozay!" "Umm . . . ummm . . . Wale?" Irish said, hunching her shoulders up. "Okay well, Wale gotta present for you then. But before you get it, tell me yo favorite MMG song." "Umm . . . 'I'm a Boss' by Meek Mill." The DJ played Meek Mill's "I'm a Boss" song, and Meek Mill and Ross turned the club into a club again. After the club closed and the champagne was gone, everybody felt a little rumble in their stomach especially Kenya, so they all decided to go to the Waffle House to eat. In the parking lot, Fresh was straggling toward his car rapping, "I'm a Boss." "Don't think you funa get behind that wheel, Fresh," Slim said as they were crossing the streets. Fresh knew that he was too drunk to drive, so he didn't protest. "You come and drive then, fool. I'on mind ridin shotgun." Slim was too drunk to drive too, and he knew it, so he called Ivonne's cell phone and asked her who drove them to the club. "We all got in the car with Kenya. Why, baby, is there something wrong?" Ivonne asked. Slim told Ivonne to tell Kenya to pull into the parking lot across the street from the club before they left to go to the Waffle House. "We need one of ya'll to drive Fresh's car to the Waffle House. He's too drunk and I am tooo to drive," Slim said, leaning into the passenger-side window. "Ohh, I'll drive. I got my licenses," Irish said once she saw Fresh's car. The entire way to the Waffle House, Fresh was in Irish's ear, spitting game. "So you came up here to have a good time for yo birthday, huh? Well, did you enjoy it?" Fresh asked, slouched in the seat. "This was the best birthday ever!" Irish said, following behind Quick with Kenya trailing them. "An after party of two would make it even mo betta," Fresh said, cutting the TV on in his car. "An after party of two? You must be tryin' to get between my legs, mister? I don't think so. I don't know you like that," Irish told Fresh. Fresh told Irish that it wasn't anything like that and that he was just trying to get to know her a little better. Irish figured that it couldn't hurt anything if she and Fresh got to know each other. Besides, she didn't want to sleep on her sister's couch or in a hotel room by herself, so she told Fresh that she would think about it. Sitting in the Waffle House, all eating at the same table, they had it looking like the buffet had been served. "So Irish, how much money did Wale give you for your birthday?" Ivonne asked, wiping her mouth with a napkin. "I didn't even count it. I just folded it and stuffed it," Irish said, reaching in her purse to get the money out. "He gave me a thousand dollars, girl!" Irish said, folding her money back and putting it up. Irish thanked her sister and everybody else at the table for showing her a good time. Fresh just winked at her. After everyone was done eating, they sat in the parking lot for a while, laughing and joking. "Well, I'm getting sleepy, ya'll. I really enjoyed myself tonight. Thanks for inviting me," Kenya said, getting into her car. "Kenya's starting to look a lil chunky," Slim said, not really thinking too much about it. "You need to put some gas in here. We're almost on E," Irish told Fresh after they left the Waffle House. Fresh leaned over and saw that he had only a quarter of gas and told Irish to pull over at the next gas station she saw. After filling the car up and stopping at Slim's house so Irish could get a change of clothes, Fresh took Irish to the most expensive hotel Youngstown had. "Lemme get one of those presidential suites that's fully loaded on the top floor," Fresh told the elderly white lady that was working behind the desk. "Smoking? Oh, never mind. It's presidential. How many nights would you be staying, sir?" Fresh looked at Irish. "Just one, ma'am," Irish said, looking back at Fresh. "Your total is $673.42, sir." Fresh gave the lady $700 dollars and told her to keep the change. Fresh wasn't tripping on how much the room cost because he knew that he would get that back and some off the bets he made with Quick and Slim. "You sure do like to tell people to keep the change, don't you?" Irish asked Fresh as they were getting on the elevator. "Bad habits." Months later, Kenya was sitting up in the hospital bed, holding her newborn child with her mother and Ivonne at her bedside. "Aww . . . he's so cute. Look at him, looking like he's trying to figure out what's going on, with his little bitty self," Ivonne said, playing with the baby's fingers. "My first grandbaby. Let me hold him," Kenya's mother said, reaching for the baby. "Your first and only grandbaby," Kenya said before she handed the baby to her mother. "Have you thought of a name for him yet?" Ivonne asked Kenya. "Keon Melaki Campbell," Kenya said. "I was going to give him my brother's whole name but I knew Kilo probably wouldn't like that, so I just made his middle name Melaki." After being home from the hospital for a few weeks, Kenya started going to the gym to get her body back right and to lose the baby fat that she thought she had but didn't.

Chapter 12

"You a collect call from, "Keon," an inmate at the Ohio state penitentiary" Was all the operator said before Slim pressed zero to accept the call. "What's up, Slim? How you livin' out there?" Kilo said after the call was accepted. "Slow motion. I'm waiting on you to come home. You on your way, ain't ya?" Slim asked. "You better know it. This shits over for me. I need you to do me a favor, fool." Kilo told Slim. "What you need?" "I need you to go by my momma's house and get her spare key to my crib then swing by my house and get twenty thou out my safe and take it to Jack Holland, my lawyer, for me. I've been tryin' to call Kenya, but she ain't pickin up the phone," Kilo said then told Slim where his safe was and why he needed to get the money to his lawyer. "All you gotta do is turn the knob on the safe back to 7, and it should open right up. If not, 34-16-11-7 is the code," Kilo told Slim. Slim told Kilo that he was about to go handle that for him now. "I'll call you later on then, fool," Kilo said, then hung up and told Silver he was straight. *'That nigga must really fuck with whoever he's giving his lawyer $20,000 for,'* Slim thought, leaving out his house to go get the spare key from Kilo's mother. The DA was trying to give Silver eighty years for killing his daddy mainly because he had a public defender instead of a lawyer fighting his case so Kilo gave his lawyer $20,000 to take his case. After getting the key from Kilo's mother, Slim pulled up at Kenya's apartment and got out. Figuring that Kenya wasn't home, Slim let himself in and shut the door behind him. *'Something ain't right in here,'* Slim's intuition told him as he moved through the house. *'What is all this baby stuff doing here?'* Slim thought, walking past the living room to the hall closet where Kilo said his safe was hidden behind a fake wall. While Slim was bending down, counting out the $20,000 thousand for Kilo's lawyer, he thought he heard some noises coming from the back. Putting the fake wall back and shutting the closet door, Slim was sure he'd heard some noises this time and not just any noises. Slim heard some moaning sounds. *'Who the fuck is that moaning?'* Slim thought, feeling like he had the right to find out since his nigga was locked up. Slim cracked the bedroom door and peeked in and saw Justice who he paid to test Kenya's loyalty for Kilo climbing all off inside of Kenya. *'Damn, bitch, you couldn't wait two mo months?'* Slim wanted to say but just pulled the door back up and cleaned the rest of the money out Kilo's safe for him before he left. *'I wonder how my nigga gone feel about this,'* Slim said, getting into his car and pulling off. Seeing Kenya in the act of getting her back blown out by another nigga, Slim thought about testing Ivonne's loyalty to him but knew that it probably wouldn't work because he was out there with her and not locked up. After leaving Kilo's lawyer's office, Slim called Tila back to see what he wanted. Tila told Slim that he was out of weed and that he needed some more. Slim had started giving Tila five pounds instead of one after about the first month of fronting the weed to him. "That lil nigga move more weed than them niggas at the Fish Tank," Slim told Quick one day. After dropping Tila some weed off on the block, Slim took Benjamen and Cutt some more work to the Fish Tank then headed home to wait on Kilo to call him back. Sitting on the couch next to Ivonne, Slim debated on telling her what he caught Kenya doing but didn't want her asking or telling Kenya about it, so he kept it to himself. "What are you thinking about, baby?" Ivonne asked, seeing that Slim was spaced out. "Nothing really," Slim said. "Ivonne, if you ever felt that you have the need to cheat and be with another man, would you let me know or would you do it and try to keep it a secret?" Slim asked the question and caught Ivonne by surprise. Ivonne looked at Slim like he was crazy. "Why would you ask me that, baby? Do you not trust me?" Ivonne asked, a little offended by Slim's question. "I just want to know. It ain't got nothin' to do with trust, boo," Slim said. Ivonne told Slim that he didn't have to ever worry about her cheating on him for as long as she live, and for some reason, Slim felt that her words were sincere and believed her. Kilo didn't call Slim until the next day and when he did, Slim and Tila were riding around in Slim's truck, smoking a blunt. "What's up, nigga?" Slim said after accepting the call. "You sometimes me. What's good tho, fool? You handle that bizniz for me?" Kilo said, asking Slim if he had taken that money to his lawyer. "Yeah, I did that yesterday. I thought you was goin' to call back. He told me to tell you that he would be to see you one day next week," Slim said, passing the blunt to Tila so that he could make a turn. "That's what's up these white folks tryin' to railroad my nigga I've been fuckin with in here, and I ain't tryna see that happen. But what Fresh and Quick been doin'? I ain't heard from them niggas," Kilo said, winking his eye at one of the female guards. "Ain't shit changed with them niggas. I don't know how I should tell you this 'bout Kenya cuz," Slim said, not really knowing how to break the news to his nigga but knew he had to. "What you mean by that, fool?" Kilo wanted to know. Slim told Kilo about all the baby stuff that was lying around the living room and how he heard some noises and crept up on the door and saw Kenya fucking the nigga he paid to see if he could fuck her. "That explain why she wasn't picking the phone up then. With her indisposed, detached, disloyal, traitorous, ungrateful ass!" Kilo said then let out a light chuckle. "I know you're fucked up behind that, but I had to tell you," Slim said, pulling into the automatic car wash. "I ain't mad. It's her loss. I got seventy days left, so just hold on to that lil bread for me until I get out," Kilo said, like he didn't just hear that his ol lady was caught cheating. Later on that night, while Kilo was lying in his bunk, he thought about what Slim said. *'It was a bunch of baby shit lying around, cuz.' 'Baby shit? That snake-ass bitch been fuckin' since I been in here. That's why she ain't been up here in the last three months. I kinda thought she was getting a lil bigger the last time I seen her. I love her, but fuck her! I'll never give a nigga the chance to say he fucked my bitch while I was in here,'* Kilo thought before falling asleep. Two weeks before Kilo was released, Jose told him everything he needed to know about the El Dorado's rivalry and warned him that it wouldn't be easy trying to kill him. "Ricardo Gomez. He runs one of the most dangerous Mexican Cartels that exist. He operates out of El Paso, Texas. You get rid of him, and every kilo of cocaine I give you will be no higher than $11,000." Before Jose left out Kilo's cell, he wrote down his brother's phone number and told Kilo to call him when he got out. "This is my brother Pedro. He's waiting on you to call." The next morning while Kilo was sitting in his cell reading, the guard came and told him he had a visit. "Who is it up there?" Kilo asked the guard. "Uhh . . ." The guard said, looking at the visitation sheet he had. "Kenya Carter,"

The guard told Kilo. Kilo told the guard that he wanted to refuse his visit and kept on reading. Ever since Slim told Kilo about Kenya, Kilo hadn't talked to her. No phone calls, letters through the mail, delayed messages, or anything. That made Kenya worry because she knew that it wasn't like Kilo to go this long without calling or writing. "Sorry, ma'am, but Mr. Campbell refused his visit," The visitation guard told Kenya. Kenya decided to bring Kilo's son to see him after worrying herself to death. Now the guard was telling her he refused his visit. "There's got to be some type of mistake. Does he know who his visitor is?" Kenya asked. "Yes, ma'am, he does. He asked and I told him, so he's fully aware of who his visitor is." Not wanting to embarrass herself any more than she already was, Kenya picked her baby bag and baby up and left. "I know I haven't been to see him in almost three months, but that still doesn't give him the right to refuse his visit. He hasn't called or wrote me to check on me or nothing," Kenya was telling Ivonne over the phone. Ivonne didn't really know what to tell Kenya, so all she said was "It's going to be okay, girl. He'll be home in what, two weeks?" Kenya talked to Ivonne her whole way home then told her she would call her back once she put the baby to sleep. "How have my nephew been doing with his little bitty ol self, looking just like his daddy?" Ivonne asked Kenya before they hung up. "He's doing him I guess. Just eating up everything. Only time he cry is when he's hungry," Kenya told Ivonne before hanging up the phone. After Kenya washed and fed her baby, she put him to sleep then wrote Kilo a letter, asking why he refused seeing her. "What we doing for Kilo when he get out?" Quick asked Slim. Slim and Quick had just finishing hollering at Hati, getting themselves some more weed, and were putting it up in the trunk of the Cutlass. They were now buying five hundred pounds of weed from Hati every other week. "I'on know. The last time I talked to him, he was telling me not to spread the word of him getting out so throwing a party at the club or anything like that is out the question. We might just have to wait and see what he wants to do," Slim said. "Nawl, I ain't got time to do no playing right now. It's time to go to work," Kilo told Slim sitting on the passenger side of Slim's truck with Fresh and Quick in the back. "It's yo first day out, nigga. I know you want some pussy," Fresh joked from the back. "I was fucking the whole time I was in there, fool. I'm ready to get back to the money 'cause that's about the only thing I wasn't doing while I was in there. All I need to know is if ya'll niggas ready or not," Kilo said. "Is we? Nigga, I been ready since you left and still is ready!" Slim said, happy that his nigga was finally home. "What about you, Quick? You ready?" Kilo asked Quick. "You know I'm ready, cuz. It's so fucked up out here tho, it's gone be hard to find somebody that's gone be able to supply us consistently," Quick said. "I got that under control. I just need to make sure ya'll niggas ready. What up with you, Fresh? You ready?" Kilo asked Fresh. "You know I was born ready, fool." "Okay, now that everybody claims that they're ready," Kilo said, "How many of ya'll are ready to commit to this shit for life?" Kilo asked, causing the truck to get quiet for a minute. Then Slim asked, "What you mean by that?" Kilo then explained everything that Jose explained to him. "So once we're in, we are in. Ain't no getting out. That's the whole catch," Kilo said to everybody in the truck. Everybody was thinking about what Kilo had just told them, so the truck was in complete silence until Quick spoke out and said, "This nigga said that he would give it to us for eleven a brick as long as we take care of some mob boss that his Cartel is into it with, right? Well, where is this mob boss at? 'Cause I plan on sellin' dope for the rest of my life anyway, and to be plugged into a Cartel makes it that much better." Quick said. Fresh agreed with Quick and told Kilo that he didn't plan on changing his lifestyle up so count him in. Slim was in deep thought about it because he wasn't sure if he wanted to sell dope for the rest of his life. "What's up, Slim? I see you over there cogitating on what you wanna do. You having doubts or second thoughts?" Kilo said, looking over at Slim. "Yeah, fool, that right there make a nigga think. I mean $11,000 a brick is a price that's unbelievable and will make a nigga get down, but this for-life shit is what's getting me," Slim said. Kilo told Slim to think about it and let him know something by Friday. "'Cause Saturday we will be on the first flight to Texas. But until then, swing me by my momma's house so I can holla at her for a second. Then I'm tryna hit the mall and ball. Ya'll niggas ain't got no loud rolled up? I'm tryna get high!" Kilo said, lightening the mood. After Kilo left from his mother's house and the mall, he told Slim to take him by Kenya's. "You had a change of heart, didn't you, nigga?" Slim joked at Kilo. "Nawl, I just need to get my whip. I ain't got nothing to drive, fool." Kilo sent Slim in to get the keys to his Magnum once they pulled up to the apartment. "I don't want her to know I'm out even tho I am sure she knows already," Kilo said as Slim got out the truck to get the keys. Slim got back in the truck after getting the keys from Kenya and said, "She know you out, nigga. All she asked me to do was tell you to call her. She was actin' like she ain't done no wrong." Slim said, handing Kilo his keys. "She probably don't know that I know that she done fucked up. Follow me to the car wash, tho. I ain't got time for her nasty ass right now," Kilo said, then hopped out and got in his car. After washing his car, Kilo told Slim that he would get up with them later on. "I'm funa go see if Susan can get me in her chair after I take a shower and change clothes," Kilo said. "Aite, call me when you're done. Here go some bread to put in yo pocket until you come and get your money," Slim said then gave Kilo $4,000 out his pocket. Kilo grabbed the shopping bags out Slim's truck then swung by his mother's house to take a shower and change clothes. It was almost six o'clock when Kilo walked into Susan's, and the shop wasn't packed like it usually was. *'I'm glad it ain't a lot of sack chasers in here today,'* Kilo thought, walking toward Susan's booth. There were four other people in the shop getting their hair done besides Kilo. "Sorry, sir, but we close at six thirty on Mondays unless you have an appointment," One of the beauticians told Kilo. "I'm trying to holla at Susan right quick. Is she in?" Kilo said, knowing that he looked crazy by the head and face. "Susan! You have somebody out here needing to see you," The beautician yelled, looking at Kilo up and down. *'He can't be some bum-ass nigga because he's well dressed. Matta of fact, he kinda looked familiar.'* The beautician thought. Susan came from the back, drying her hands on a towel. "May I . . . help you?" Susan said, squinting her eyes at Kilo, finding recognition immediately. "I'm tryin to get retwisted. What's the earliest you can get me in there?" Kilo asked. "Boi, where have you been? I haven't seen you in here forever. I figured you moved to another state. Come give me a hug," Susan told Kilo then sat him down under the sink to wash his hair. "Lordee have mercy. When the last time you washed your hair, chile?" Susan asked Kilo. "I washed my hair probably four times the whole time I was locked up. It was something about that water that didn't sit well with me," Kilo said, closing his eyes as Susan massaged his scalp as she was washing his hair. After shampooing and rinsing Kilo's hair three times, Susan sat him down at her booth and went to work clipping and retwisting his dreads. "Okay, now come over here and sit under the dryer," Susan said, putting a clip on the last dread. "And please don't let your hair get that nappy again, chile! It felt like I was getting finga cuts twisting those thangs," Susan joked and caused the girl sitting next to the dryer to laugh. "That's funny, huh? Gone head and laugh at a brother that just got out of jail then. The jokes on me today, but I bet not eva-eva-eva catch you with yo do not done or the jokes on you," Kilo flirted with the girl that was sitting next to him that he found rather pretty. "I guess you get a pass since you just got out," The girl said then introduced herself as Lisa White, a professional massage therapist. "Here take this. I know you could use a good body massage after lying on that hard bunk in there." Kilo looked at the card and grinned. "What are the bizniz hours, Ms. Lisa?" Kilo asked. "The shop closes at 6:00 p.m. Monday to Friday, and I don't see any personal client after 9:00 p.m.," Lisa White, the professional massage therapist said. Kilo then asked Lisa if she had anybody on her schedule for tonight, and finding out that she didn't, he asked her if she was available. "I am available. But it's going on seven thirty now, and you're just now sitting under the dryer so that will be another forty-five minutes. By the time you get done, it'll be at least eight thirty, so we won't have much time to work with," Lisa told Kilo. "I know you can make some type of exception for a brother that just got out and is in need of a desperate body massage from someone as cute as you." That made Lisa smile. "If today is your first day home, why don't you let your wife massage your body? If you don't mind me asking?" Lisa asked. "What makes you think I got a wife?" Kilo asked. "I mean we're living in a world where everybody has somebody," Lisa said. "Well, I guess I'm a nobody then 'cause I ain't got nobody. I'm single," Kilo said. Lisa told Kilo that she'll bend her rules for him since today was his first day home. Lisa left the shop before Kilo and told him to call her when he was done. "I see you've met you a new acquaint sitting under this dryer," Susan told Kilo, lifting the dryer off his head to check his hair. "What's up with her, Susan? Is she good peoples, or do I need to leave her where I found her?" Kilo asked Susan. "Lisa has good intentions. She is trying to make an honest living unlike a lot of these females that come through those doors." Kilo thought about Kenya when Susan said that then thought about swinging by Kenya's house after he left the shop but didn't want to hear her try to justify what she was caught doing, so he bought himself a suite at the Hyatt hotel downtown to overlook the city. "Man, bring me an ounce of some of that purple shit we smoked early, fool. I'm at the Hyatt on the top floor room 1114," Kilo told Slim. "Aite, give me about twenty minutes. I just left the Fish Tank," Slim said. Kilo then called Lisa and told her where he was, and she told him that she would be there in a matter of minutes. Slim came and left just before Lisa got there. "I'm sorry for the delay. I had to go back and get something," Lisa said once Kilo let her in. "I hope it wasn't a gun," Kilo said shutting the door back. "It wouldn't be very wise to rob a man that just got out of jail who's staying in a hotel even though these rooms are very much expensive," Lisa said, walking into the room. "You'll be surprised at what a nigga that just got out of jail had before he went to jail," Kilo told Lisa, which made her think twice about judging a book by its cover. While Lisa was getting her things ready to give Kilo a massage, Kilo rolled himself a fat-ass blunt, knowing that he wouldn't be able to smoke it all. "You don't mind me smoking this while you do your thang, do ya?" Kilo asked. "As long as you don't fall asleep while I am relaxing your muscles, I don't. I like the smell of it anyways. But do you want to know my prices before I start because you never asked?" Lisa said. "If I gotta ask a price, that means I can't afford it or is on a budget. And I'm not worried about neither," Kilo said, letting off a sense of confidence and cockiness that Lisa liked. "Well, excuse me, Mr. Kilo, I wasn't trying to offend," Lisa then told Kilo to get in a position that was most comfortable for him while she started with the front of his body. Kilo opted to lie flat on the bed with his shirt off. "I am allowed to take my pants off to since this is a full body massage right?" Kilo asked Lisa. "Yes, you are. Whatever's best for you." Kilo stripped down to his boxer briefs, then lay on his back, and fired his blunt up. "Don't burn or drop ashes on me with that thing," Lisa said then asked Kilo if he would mind her sitting on him while she massaged the top part of his body since they weren't at the shop where the massage table was. "Whichever's best for you," Kilo said, mocking Lisa. Lisa smiled, then climbed on top of Kilo, and poured some type of warm oil all over Kilo's chest. Lisa was dressed in her work uniform, which was a pink and blue scrub outfit that her body filled out perfectly. "Damn, that feels good." Kilo said. "How long have you been

THE LONGEST DROUGHT EVER

practicing this?" Kilo asked. Kilo and Lisa conversed the entire time Lisa was giving Kilo his body massage, Lisa telling Kilo about herself and Kilo telling Lisa about himself. By the time Lisa finished massaging the front part of Kilo's body, the two knew more about each other than was intended. Lisa asked Kilo how he could be so full of life and single, and Kilo told her straight like it was. "While I was locked up, the woman I thought I trusted and loved was giving the cookie to some other nigga, so I left. I hear she gotta baby too." Lisa tried to explain to Kilo that just because she had sex with another man doesn't mean that's who she wants to be with. "Women have needs too, you know. I'm not saying that it was right what she did, but you have to look at it like you wasn't there to give it to her. So you should give her another chance," Lisa said, admiring Kilo's body glistening with the oil she applied. "She had her chance and blew it. You only get one chance with a nigga like me. Either you get it right or get left. Besides, if she couldn't keep her legs closed for a year, she's not worthy of another chance," Kilo said. Lisa could tell Kilo wasn't some regular Joe Blow from the streets and that he was a "somebody" just from being in his presence. After Lisa was finished giving Kilo his massage, Kilo convinced her to stay the night with him. "I promise not to pressure you into doing something you don't want to. I just want to be in the company of a female after being around nothing but niggas for a year straight," Kilo told Lisa after he asked her to stay the night with him. Lisa agreed to stay with Kilo and agreed to something else later on that night. The next morning Kilo woke up to his phone ringing. "Yea," Kilo said, grabbing his pants off the chair. "Why didn't you come home last night?" It was Kenya on the other end of Kilo's phone waking him up. Kilo sat up and rubbed the sleep out his eyes. "I didn't know I had a home. How did you get my number anyway?" Kilo asked, wondering where in the hell was Lisa at. "What are you talking about, Keon? Why are you acting like you don't want to see me? First you refuse my visit. Then you get out and don't come home. What is the reason behind this?" Kenya said, sounding like she had been crying all night and morning. "You want the truth or a lie?" Kilo said, getting out the bed to take a piss. "I want the truth," Kenya said, holding their baby in her arms. Kilo told Kenya everything he knew about her cheating while he was locked up, and Kenya confirmed everything Kilo said with her silence. "You're not disagreeing, so I assume that what I'm saying is true," Kilo said, picking up a note that Lisa left on the table. Kenya still said nothing. "Hello . . ." Kilo said into the phone, thinking that Kenya hung up. "I . . . I'm still here . . ." Kenya said in a voice that was barely audible. "Look, Kenya, I'm not tryin' to belittle you when I say this, but what you did was that of a freak and not a lady. You know how much loyalty means to me, and you wasn't loyal in that department. So I feel as if I can't trust you anymore," Kilo thought that Kenya would try to justify what she did by accusing him for not being there or saying something about the loss of her brother, but what Kenya said made Kilo respect her more. "Baby, I know I've messed up, and I take full responsibility for doing so. I want you to know that there was no passion behind what I did, and even though what I did may cause me to lose you, I want you to know that I will forever love and have your back for as long as I live." Kilo was surprised by what Kenya said and didn't know how to respond because he still loved Kenya more than anything in the world but felt that if she cheated once she'll cheat again. Kilo told Kenya that he would always have love for her and help her out whenever she needed help but thought that it was best that they be friends so he dont become vindictive and hurt her back. "You cheating on me will always be on my conscious, so I'll rather be friends than to do something to hurt your feelings." Hearing Kilo say that let Kenya know that he still cared for her enough not to see her hurting. Before the phone hung up, Kenya told Kilo about his son. "Well, before we hang up, I want you to know that we will always share something else besides the love for each other, and that's the love for our son," Kenya said the words with tears in her eyes. After talking to Kenya and finding out that he had a son, Kilo promised Kenya that the baby would be taken well care of. *'That explains the baby stuff Slim saw when he was there,'* Kilo thought. Kilo left the hotel room after taking a shower, changing clothes and smoking a blunt, then headed to the shop where Lisa worked. Kilo handed Lisa seven folded crispy $100 bills and told her that he would be in touch. After Kilo left the shop, he called Slim to see where he was, but Slim didn't answer, so Kilo pulled up to his old apartment to see if the baby Kenya said was his looked like him. Kilo hadn't seen Kenya face-to-face in almost four months, and when she opened the door to let him in, Kilo saw her face and knew that it was going to be hard not to mess with her on that level again. One look at the baby was all Kilo needed to see that the baby was his. "What's his name?" Kilo asked, staring at the life he created. "Keon Melaki Campbell. He has everything but your middle name," Kenya said, standing back by the door. "You're not going to deny him?" Kenya asked Kilo. "How could I when it looks like I spit him out? How long has he been sleep?" Kilo asked, turning to face Kenya. Kenya walked over and told Kilo that he could wake him up if he wanted to because all he did was sleep. "The only time he cry is when he's hungry just like you use to do," Kenya said. "Let the lil nigga rest 'cause he ain't gone get none once he gets old enuff to hang with me and don't be worried about when we cry, just feed us when we do punk!" Kilo said playfully, punching Kenya. "I ain't no punk! Your son's the punk just like his daddy," Kenya said then punched Kilo in the arm. Kilo sat and talked to Kenya for little under an hour before he left. "I'll be back to see my lil nigga. Don't have some nigga over here around him when I get here either or I'ma show you how much of a punk I am," Kilo said, hugging Kenya in the doorway. After Kilo left, Kenya sat in the living room and cried her eyes out, thinking about how much of a perfect family she could've had. While Kilo was sitting down at the Chicken Shack eating, he called his mother and told her the news about her being a grandmother and told her that he would tell Kenya to bring the baby to see her as soon as she got the chance to. *'I guess lil momma didn't have to work today,'* Kilo thought, looking around, trying to find the chick he used to mess with that worked there. Kilo called Quick once he fnished eating, and the two met up at Quick's house. Quick was on his way to drop some money off. "So what you think about doing bizniz with Jose, fool?" Kilo asked Quick, sitting on his couch smoking a cigarette. "I told you how I feel, cuz. Drug dealing will always be my occupation. Check this out tho, fool. You know I been talking to Maria, José sister, off and on right?" Quick said, counting and stacking his money on the table. "What she talkin' 'bout, fool?" Kilo asked, dumping the cigarette ashes in the ashtray. Quick told Kilo that Maria gave him a little inside information on her brother's archenemy Ricardo Gomez. "She said that he once tried to kidnap and kill her just because she was a Sanchez. But the thing that caught my attention was she said that every Thursday night he's inside of the Cat House. One of the biggest strip clubs El Paso has," "I bet you anything in the world he's a big fat, freaky, nasty-ass mob boss who has low self-esteem and always thinkin' with his dick. If not, why in the fuck is he always in the strip club?" Kilo said. "I'on know, but now we got a starting point to track his ass down." Kilo and Quick formulated a plan to get Ricardo Gomez right where they needed him to be. "If that don't work, then what?" Quick asked, trying to come up with a plan B. "We ain't gone worry about no what ifs. We're going at this knowing it will work," Kilo said with certainty that their plan would work. "Have Slim made his mind up yet?" Quick asked. "Yeah, that nigga told me he's all in. We gone head out Saturday morning." Their plane landed in El Paso, Texas saturday evening, and a limousine was there waiting to pick them up. Kilo told the driver of the limo to take them to the rental car shop where they rented two black SUV trucks. "Slim, Quick, and Fresh get in that truck and follow me and Jazmine to the room," Kilo said so he could lay the foundation of his plan on Jazmine since he hasn't had a chance to fully go over it with her. "Aite, but before we get to the hotel, stop at one of these restaurants. I'm hungrier than a muthafucker!" Slim said. Kilo ran the plan by Jazmine and Thursday night, Kilo, Fresh, Quick, and Slim were sitting in the Cat House, pretending to be watching the strippers, trying to be inconspicuous as possible. "That has to be Ricardo sitting over there surrounded by niggas and bitches and more bottles of champagne than the damn club has," Quick said, cutting his eyes in Ricardo's direction. "Yeah, that's him, and like I guessed, he's big as hell!" Kilo said, sizing Ricardo up to be at least 385 pounds. "We shouldn't have any problems tonight then," Slim said, throwing a couple dollars onstage at one of the strippers. "That bitch at the bar better be lucky we down here on bizniz 'cause I'll have her ass back at my room with her legs in the air after she leave work," Fresh said, making eye contact with the bartender. "All right, I won't yawl to give it up for Isabelle! Dis her first time shaking what her mama gave her in the Cat House, so yawl show her some love!" The DJ announced then played Twista's "Wetter" song, and Jazmine came out in a white doctor's lab jacket with nothing on under it but a fishnet-stocking bodysuit and some red heels. Jazmine took the jacket off and strutted to the front of the stage in the fishnet stocking, turned around, bent over, and made her ass bounce giving the crowd what they came to see. "Damn, look! Look at Jazmine make that ass bounce fool," Fresh said, getting out his seat. "Who is she?" Ricardo asked, watching Jazmine climb the pole and slide down it slow. "The DJ said her name Izebel or something like that. She's new boss," One of Ricardo's henchmen said. Jazmine was on stage, pulling the fishnet stocking off, leaving her in nothing but a black lace thong and the Red Bottom heels she had on which made damn near every nigga in the Cat House get as close to the stage as they could and throw money including Fresh. Jazmine strutted to the front of the stage again, angling herself to face the direction of Ricardo, and slid down into a split, then lifted herself up with her hands and turned around backward while still in the splits stance. "Where she learn all this from?" Kilo said over the loud music. "Man, I'on know, but she got me ready to fuck!" Slim said back. Jazmine then got on all fours and arched her back and started popping her ass, which made her pussy come in and out of view. This really had niggas throwing money all over the stage, trying to let Jazmine know that money wasn't a thing. After Jazmine finished onstage, Ricardo told his henchman that he wanted Izebel over there with them. "Whatever her price is, pay it!" Jazmine came out the dressing room dressed in a different fishnet and was approached by Ricardo's henchman and asked if she would like to join his boss in the private part of the club. "Sure, but only if he's paying," Jazmine said. Ricardo's henchman told Jazmine that his boss specifically asked for her. "So I know he's paying." Jazmine and the henchman passed the table Kilo was sitting at, and Jazmine winked her eye at them. In the private part of the club where Ricardo and his goons were, it was like a club inside the club. "Here she is, boss," The henchman told Ricardo. Ricardo was a short heavyset Mexican with short black hair. "I seen you onstage and think you dance good. You do private dances?" Jazmine looked around and saw at least four other strippers giving lap dances and said, "My lap dances cost $100 dollars a song. Can you afford it, big shot?" Ricardo told Jazmine that he got enough money on him now to have her dancing till the club closed. Jazmine pulled Ricardo off to the side and started teasing him. By the time the first song went off, Ricardo was trying to pay Jazmine a thousand dollars to fuck him right there in the club. "I don't fuck in clubs. I'm a lady." Jazmine leaned back to whisper in Ricardo's ear. Ricardo was so drunk and horny that he offered Jazmine $2,000 instead of the $1,000. "It's dark and crowded, so nobody will see,"

Ricardo said with both Jazmine's titties in his hands. Jazmine told Ricardo that it wasn't about the money. It was her standards that wouldn't let her have sex in the club. Kilo, Slim, Fresh and Quick left the club a few minutes after Jazmine was in the private section with Ricardo and his entourage. After another song of slow grinding her ass all over Ricardo, Jazmine had him under her spell. "I got to pee, poppi. I'll be right back." Jazmine went into the changing room and called Kilo. "What we looking like?" Kilo asked. "I got him ready. I just don't know where he's going to take me, so keep your phone on," Jazmine said and hung up. Back in the private section, Jazmine was in Ricardo's ear, telling him how wet she was and how she wanted him to fuck the shit out of her tight little pussy. "I got a place where we can go," Ricardo said then said something in Spanish to his henchman. The henchman shook his head no and said something back in Spanish that made Ricardo mad and say something that made the henchman change his mind. "He's going to drive us there," Ricardo said, then said something else in Spanish, and all ten of his goons stood up. Ricardo downed the rest of his liquor and grabbed a bottle of champagne then asked Jazmine if she was ready to go. *'I know he don't think I'm leaving like this,'* Jazmine said to herself. "I have to change clothes and pay the owner. I'll be right back." Jazmine came back fully dressed then asked Ricardo if all his soldiers had to be there. "They're just making sure I get out this club safe. You and I are going somewhere special." Outside the club doors, there were three black SUV trucks just like the ones Kilo rented and a black Rolls-Royce lined up. Ricardo grabbed Jazmine's hand with his fat, chubby hand and led her to the Rolls-Royce, which was in front. Jazmine was thinking of a way to get Kilo on the phone to let him know they were leaving the club, not knowing that Kilo and them had eyes on her already. Pretending to get some lip gloss out her purse, Jazmine pressed talk twice on her cell phone to call the last person she talked to back, which was Kilo. "Wow! The inside of your Chrysler 300 is so big," Jazmine said, getting into the back of Ricardo's car. "This is a Rolls-Royce, not a Chrysler. I paid a couple hundred thousand for this car," Ricardo boasted. "So where are you taking me?" Jazmine asked, sitting her purse next to Ricardo so that Kilo could hear his every word. Kilo was on the other end of the phone, listening to Jazmine and Ricardo's conversation. *Jaz slick as hell,* Kilo thought listening to Jazmine pry Ricardo for information. Kilo pulled out the parking lot a little after Ricardo's motorcade left and turned a few cars behind them. "He don't want to tell her where they're goin'," Kilo said out loud. "Keep following their ass then. They gone have to pull up somewhere," Quick said just as the three SUV trucks turned off on a side street. "Where them trucks going?" Slim said, pointing. "I'on know, but I'm glad they turned off. Now it's just us and them," Kilo said, now two cars behind the Rolls-Royce Ricardo and Jazmine got into at the club. "We need to make a move then before it's too late and them trucks pop back up," Quick said "You right. Look, I'm gone get behind them and bump the back of their car and make them pull over. If they pull over, we got them. But if they don't, they might think it's a hit and speed off," Kilo said, switching lanes to get behind the Rolls-Royce. Ricardo was in the back of the car with his hands all over Jazmine when they rammed the back of his car. "What the fuck was that?" Ricardo said in Spanish, turning to look out the window, and saw a black SUV truck and thought that it was one of his men driving it. Ricardo yelled something else in Spanish at his henchman, and he pulled over and got out and threw his hands in the air as if to say "What the fuck!" When nobody got out the truck, Ricardo's henchman walked toward it. "When he gets close enuff, Slim, I want you to gun him down from the passenger side. That way, I'll be able to hit freaky dude if he tries to get out and get into the driver's seat," Kilo said, watching the henchman come closer. Slim flung the passenger door open and came over the top of the door blasting. *'Boom, boom, boom, boom, boom, boom!'* Bullets jumping out the chamber of Slim's .40 cal were the only sounds being made. Slim hit Ricardo's henchman five times in the chest and once in the neck, which caused him to drop. Kilo then hopped out the truck as Ricardo was trying to get into the driver's seat just as Kilo thought he would. *'Boom!'* Kilo let off a shot, hitting Ricardo in the back, causing him to stumble. *'Boom, boom!'* Kilo let off two more shots, hitting Ricardo, making him fall. Kilo walked up on Ricardo without giving him a chance to plead for his life and told him "Lights out!" Then emptied the rest of the clip into the body of Ricardo Gomez, killing him. *Click, click, click.* "Come on, fool, that nigga dead!" Slim said out the driver's side of their SUV. Jazmine was in the back with Quick and Fresh already. Kilo got in, and they smashed off.

Chapter 13

Two weeks after killing Ricardo and his henchman, Kilo, Slim, Quick and Fresh were flown to Washington DC to meet with Jose brother Pedro. Sitting in a penthouse suite across the table from Pedro, Kilo was listening intensively to Pedro talk. Pedro had already informed them that he knew everything he needed to know about them and their families so if anything ever happened, their families would be the ones held accountable. "Now that we have that understood, let's get to business," Pedro said. Pedro then asked Kilo if he could handle a hundred kilos of 100 percent pure uncut cocaine. "How long do we have with them?" Kilo asked. "Two months. I'll be expecting to hear from you in two months," Pedro said then explained that if they needed more time to let him know. "Two months should be enuff time do to what we got to do. The only thing we worried about is getting them from here to there," Kilo told Pedro. "Don't worry about the transport. I'll have them wherever you want them every time. The first shipment will take me a week, but every one after that will get to you the next day," Pedro said. "Oh yeah, my friend José said to tell you good job, and since you took care of the problem so quickly, he wants me to send ten kilos of cocaine on him. I'll have the ten kilos there today," Pedro said before they left. Back home, Kenya, Ivonne and Kilo Jr. were out doing some shopping like old times. "So what did Kilo say when he found out he had a baby boy?" Ivonne asked, pushing Kilo Jr. through the mall in his stroller. "He was a little skeptical until he seen the baby. After he seen him, all doubts vanished," Kenya said. After Kilo talked to Kenya about being friends, Kenya felt bad about cheating and realized she lost the best thing that's ever happened to her. "But I don't think he'll ever take me back because of what I did," Kenya said. Ivonne told Kenya that if it's meant for them to be together, then Kilo would come back around. "Don't live down on your mistake, Ken. Learn from it. We all make mistakes. Nobody's perfect." Slim was at the house passed out on the couch when Ivonne got back in from shopping with Kenya. "He musta been tired," Ivonne said, pulling Slim's shoes off. Slim woke up around nine that night to the smell of Ivonne's cooking. "What's up, boo? Where you been at?" Slim said, sneaking up behind Ivonne, wrapping his arms around her. Ivonne was in the kitchen— frying some chicken, singing Mariah Carey's "Don't Forget about Us" song—when Slim walked in. "Hey, baby! I've been with Kenya and the baby all day. You were knocked out when I got in," Ivonne said, sitting the spatula down. "Tell Kenya I said don't be tryin' to keep my nephew from me. I still haven't seen that lil nigga," Slim said, picking up a piece of chicken and biting into it. "She said Kilo been by a couple times to see him. They look just alike. The only difference is Big Kilo has dreads and Lil Kilo don't," Ivonne said, smiling, thinking about how cute Lil Kilo was. That night Slim and Ivonne had sex and reproduced a life in the process unknowingly. The next day Slim was riding with Kilo on their way to pick up the ten bricks Pedro had shipped to them the day before. "A lot of shit's about to change now fool," Kilo was saying, pulling up to the drop spot. "We're about to get some real money now. And as you know, with money comes power but problems also. You gotta watch the game from all angles and keep your grass cut low," Kilo told Slim. "I move with caution anyway 'cause I already know how the game go. I know niggas and bitches are alike, both sack chasers." Kilo got and split the ten bricks evenly among Quick, Fresh, Slim, and himself. Feeling like he needed himself a house of his own after staying in the hotel room since he had been out, Kilo went and purchased a two-bedroom condo in a secluded part of Columbus. The condo was so isolated from the rest of the town that without directions one might get lost trying to find it unless they followed him there. Sitting inside the empty condo, Kilo thought about his next move. After spending $70,000 thousand dollars to get the condo completely furnished, Kilo then paid a house designer sixty five hundred more dollars to come and adorn the place since he didn't have an old lady to do it for him. *'This place is still missin something,'* Kilo thought to himself, going from room to room admiring how the house designer had everything arranged. Kilo left his house and drove to the Fish Tank to handle some business he had lined up with Heavy. Sitting in Kilo's Magnum, passing a blunt back and forth, Kilo and Heavy talked business. "I know the prices still fucked up out here," Kilo said then took a pull from the blunt. "Man, these muthafucken price's outrageous out here! These niggas talking thirty-seven to thirty-eight apiece no matter how many you buy," Heavy said. Kilo heard that and grinned. "I can get them to ya for twenty-eight, but that's between me and you." "If you got them for twenty-eight, I want five of them right now!" Heavy said, ready to call Lil Jimmy and have him drop the bread off. "Aite, well, look, I'ma call your phone in thirty minutes, and we'll meet up," Kilo told Heavy. After hollering at Heavy, Kilo went inside the Fish Tank and chopped it up with Benjamen and Cutt for a second before leaving out. "I wonder how much shit about to change around town now that Kilo's back home," Cutt said after Kilo left. "You heard what that nigga said about that drought being over, didn't ya? That should let you know shit's 'bout to change 'round here," Benjamen told Cutt. "Do you think that nigga gone take the Fish Tank back over or let Slim keep it?" Cutt asked. "I'on know fool and don't care as long as the prices drop back down and we can eat again," Benjamen said. Little did they know, Kilo told Slim that he could have the Fish Tank when he first got locked up. "I'on plan on doing nothing else with the Fish Tank or Juice Box once I get out so make the best out of them. They're yours now" Was Kilo's words to Slim. Waiting in line to get himself something to eat, Fresh was talking on his phone in a whole another world, listening to Mikayla talk about being pregnant. "I don't want you to feel that I'm trying to put this on you because I'm not," Mikayla said. "So you telling me you got pregnant the last time we had sex?" Fresh said, not knowing what else to say because he knew Mikayla wasn't the type of female to lie about something like this. "The doctor said that I was fourteen weeks. And if you go back fourteen weeks, that's the same day you was over here and the cable man showed up, remember?" Mikayla said, trying to get Fresh to remember the time. Fresh gazed in the air, thinking back to the day Mikayla was talking about. "Yeah, I do remember beatin' that thang up that day. Hold on right quick, boo," Fresh told Mikayla so he could order his food. "Lemme get a number four supersized with white meat," Fresh ordered then picked his phone back up. "Hello." "What are you eating without asking me am I hungry?" Mikayla said after listening to Fresh order a number four from somewhere. "My bad, boo. I forgot you're a fat gurl now," Fresh joked. "I'm at the Chicken Shack, tho. You want something before I leave?" "So I'm a fat girl, huh? Well, if it wasn't for 'somebody,' I'll still be as thick as I want to be. Now!" Mikayla shot back at Fresh in a joking way, sounding like she was rolling her neck. Mikayla asked Fresh to bring her the same thing he ordered for himself by the house for her if he didn't mind. "I got you, boo," Fresh told Mikayla before he hung up. On his way to Mikayla's house to drop her food off, Fresh was pulled over. "Man, these muthafuckers always fuckin' with a nigga," Fresh said, ready to slick talk the officer just because he knew he didn't have anything on him. As the police officer got up on his truck, Fresh realized who the officer was. *'Ms. Coolwaters? I forgot all about this bitch,'* Fresh thought, dropping his window. "Licenses and registration please," Ms. Coolwaters said. "You know all my shit legit. What's up with you pullin' me over?" Fresh said, giving Ms. Coolwaters his licenses. "What you got in here that I need to know about, Mr. Morgan?" Ms. Coolwaters asked Fresh, bending down to see if anybody was in the passenger seat. "I ain't got nothin' on me this time, baby gurl. Nothing but some chicken and not the kind them dope boys be whippin'," Fresh said and smiled. "Well, I'm going to have to find out for myself." Ms. Coolwaters pulled Fresh out his truck, hoping that she would find something illegal when she searched it so she could charge Fresh lights out for it. Ms. Coolwaters was down, and Fresh peeped it. *'Damn, she searching my shit hard as hell like she tryna find something. She must be broke and in need of some money,'* Fresh thought, watching Ms. Coolwaters search his truck thoroughly, even looking under his floor mats. "Ain't nothing in there, baby gurl. I learned my lesson the first time I was pulled over," Fresh said. Ms. Coolwaters smiled to hide her disappointment then said, "I'm glad that you learned your lesson, Mr. Morgan." Fresh hopped back in his truck and shut the door. "So you gone give me my licenses back, or you wonna hold them to remember me?" Fresh said, hanging out the truck a little bit. "I almost forgot about your licenses. Here you go," Ms. Coolwaters said, pulling them out her back pocket, then walked closer to the truck to hand Fresh his licenses. "Look, I got a thousand dollars right now," Fresh said, grabbing his licenses. "A thousand dollars for what?" Ms. Coolwaters asked like she didn't know what Fresh was talking 'bout. Fresh hit Ms. Coolwaters with a stale face that said, "Quit playin'. You know what I want!" Ms. Coolwaters told Fresh to call her whenever he was ready to put his money where his mouth was. "Keep your phone on then, I might call you tonight," Fresh said, watching Ms. Coolwaters walk back to her cop car. *'Damn! That bitch super thick.'* Fresh pulled up at Mikayla's house twenty minutes later, chicken colder than ever. "I apologize, boo. I had a run-in with the law. We can go and get something else to eat from your favorite restaurant if you want to," Fresh told Mikayla then rubbed her stomach. Mikayla thought that Fresh was going to go about her pregnancy differently, but she knew once she told him and he didn't get smart calling her out her name saying the baby wasn't his that he was going to accept her baby. "Don't be rubbing my stomach trying to pass off your looks to my baby. Lord knows my baby will be picked on in school looking like you," Mikayla said, laughing at her own joke. Fresh liked Mikayla not only because of her looks and the way she put it down in the bedroom but because she had a good personality, a sense of humor and she was down to earth. "Come on now, Kay, you and I both know who we don't want the baby lookin' like." After spending some time out with Mikayla, Fresh got to know her personal side that she kept boggled up and away from him because she knew what type of person Fresh was. Fresh dropped Mikayla off at home and told her that he would be back later on. But later on turned into the next day after Fresh got a phone call from Ms. Coolwaters. "I know ya'll member that police bitch I was tellin ya'll 'bout, don't ya?" Fresh said, ready to brag about fucking a cop to his niggas after it happened. "What police bitch you talkin' 'bout, fool?' Quick questioned. Kilo had Fresh, Slim, and Quick come to his condo to check the spot out now that everything was laid out how he wanted it. "You remember a lil second ago I got pulled over, and the lil police bitch found my pistol and charged a nigga to look the other way," Fresh said. Kilo remembered exactly what Fresh was talking about. "Yeah, I remember who you talkin' 'bout, fool. That's the same bitch that took me to jail. What's up with her?" Kilo asked. "All man you know she pulled a nigga over again, hoping that she would find something. I peeped that she was searching my shit like her life depended on finding something," Fresh said then told them how he figured she was broke and how he offered to pay for the pussy, not saying the price. "That bitch called me the same night and let me act a fool all off inside that pussy. And she got that head on her!" Fresh said, thinking about how Ms. Coolwaters swallowed his kids. Kilo heard that and saw an opportunity. "Call that bitch back and see if she wants to make some more money," Kilo said, thinking ten steps ahead. Fresh called Ms. Coolwaters and asked her if she was trying to make some more money. Ms. Coolwaters was down with it until Fresh told her that it was his nigga trying to knock her socks off. "Nawl . . . it ain't even that type of party," Ms. Coolwaters told Fresh. "I thought you was tryin' to make some more money. My nigga said he'll give you whatever you want," Fresh said back. The phone got quiet, which let Fresh know that Ms. Coolwaters was thinking about what he said. "Tell him I said give me $1,500 and we probably can do something," Ms. Coolwaters said, charging Kilo $500 more. Ms. Coolwaters told Fresh that she got off work at eight o'clock and to have Kilo call her anytime after that if he wanted to get down. "Aite baby gurl. Don't be tryin' to hold out on my nigga eitha. He just got out so make sure you welcome him home properly," Fresh said then hung up. "What she talkin' 'bout, fool?" Kilo asked. "Everything's a go. She get off at eight, so she said call her anytime after that," Fresh told Kilo. "I gotta job for her ass," Kilo said. Quick told Kilo that he was about to bounce and that he would holler at him later. "I gotta move to make." Not too long after Quick left Slim and Fresh left also. "Don't forget to call and get you some of that cop cat, fool," Fresh told Kilo before he left. After everyone left, Kilo felt like seeing his lil nigga, so he called Kenya and asked if it was okay for him to stop by there for a while. Kenya told Kilo that he didn't have to ask to see his son. "You can just stop by anytime you want to see him. You still have your key, don't you?" Kenya asked. "Yeah, I still got it, but you know I—" "But nothing! Don't nobody be here but me and him," Kenya said, cutting Kilo off, knowing that he was about to say something that she didn't want to hear. "Excuse me, Ms. Kenya, my bad. Give me thirty minutes, and I'll be there." Kilo hung up and thought about just how much he still loved Kenya. *'It's gone be hard to shake these feelings,'* Kilo said to himself, grabbing his keys off the kitchen counter. Kilo chilled over Kenya's house playing with his son and kicking the shit with Kenya until his son fell asleep, sucking milk from Kenya's nipple. Kenya laid Kilo Jr. on the other couch and asked Kilo if he was thirsty. "Nawl, boo, I'm straight. I'm funa bust a move. Call me if you need something," Kilo said, then stood up to stretch, then made his way toward the door. "Where the keys to my motorcycle, boo?" Kilo asked Kenya. Kenya walked to the back and came back with the key to Kilo's motorcycle. "Here you go," Kenya said, handing Kilo the key. "Be careful on that thing," Kenya said. Kilo hugged Kenya and squeezed her ass with both hands before he left. Hopping on his motorcycle, Kilo zipped through the streets, not really trying to be seen. Later on that night around nine, Kilo called Ms. Coolwaters and talked with her a few minutes before they both decided to meet up at a hotel in Cincinnati. Kilo got there before Ms. Coolwaters, so he called and gave her the room number and smoked a blunt, waiting on her. After about fifteen minutes of waiting, Ms. Coolwaters was knocking on the door. Kilo opened the door with the blunt still burning. "What up?" Kilo said. Ms. Coolwaters looked at Kilo, trying to remember where she knew him from. "Don't look like that. I ain't here to hurt you. I'm here to help," Kilo said. "I'm trying to remember where I've seen you. I'm not worried about being hurt," Ms. Coolwaters said, patting her purse, letting Kilo know she had her protection with her. "You probably remember taking me to jail a lil over a year ago for a gun you found under my seat," Kilo said after Ms. Coolwaters came in and sat down. Ms. Coolwaters remembered Kilo now that he said where she should remember him from. "That's where I remember you from," Ms. Coolwaters said, feeling a little uncomfortable being in the same hotel room with a person she took to jail. Kilo could sense that she was uncomfortable, so he reassured her that he wasn't on anything dumb. "I'm just tryin' to help you make you some money. A whole lot of it!" Kilo said, dumping the ashes from the blunt. "One thousand five hundred dollars isn't a whole lot of money. My paychecks are bigger than that, so let's do what we got to do so I can get out of here," Ms. Coolwaters said, pulling her jacket off. Kilo told Ms. Coolwaters that he didn't want to fuck her. "Well, what you want me to do, suck your dick?" Ms. Coolwaters asked Kilo. "Nawl boo, it's bigger than that. I'm tryin' to make you more money in a month than you make in a year," Kilo said. "If you thinking about pimping, macking, or anything close to those things, you got the wrong person. I ain't—" Ms. Coolwaters was about to let Kilo have it. "Whoa! Chill, boo. It ain't nothing like that. Calm down," Kilo said then explained what he was trying to do, which was put her on his payroll and pay her for information leads, tips, or anything else the police had on him. "I'll give you $5,000 a week or $20,000 a month. However you want it." It didn't take Ms. Coolwaters long to think about the offer Kilo made her. "Five thousand a week sounds good, but how do I know you're serious?" Ms. Coolwaters asked. Kilo told her that every Friday starting this week, she could pick the money up or he would drop it off personally. "Whatever's best for you," Kilo said. Ms. Coolwaters decided to have the money dropped off. "I'll see how serious you are Friday then," Ms. Coolwaters said, putting her jacket back on, getting up to leave. Before Ms. Coolwaters got to the door, Kilo stopped her and said, "Loose lips sank ships. Keep this between you and I." A few days later, Kilo got a call from Pedro, telling him that the hundred bricks of cocaine were being delivered and should be at their drop spot in a couple of hours. "I'll have my peoples call you when they get there," Pedro told Kilo. Kilo called Slim and told him to shut the Fish Tank down for a lil while. "We need some where to get shit situated. I just got the call that we've been waitin' on," Kilo told Slim. Kilo then called and had Quick ride with him to pick the dope up from the drop spot and had Fresh and Slim trail behind them strapped just in case anything went wrong. Once they made it to the Fish Tank, they counted the dope to make sure everything was there. "One hundred bricks on the dot," Kilo said, stacking the last ten. "Man, I ain't never seen this much dope! This some shit you only see in the movies," Fresh said. "I wonder what that symbol stood for that was stamped in the middle of each brick," Quick said, picking one of the bricks up and looking at the fish and the Roman numeral 12 stamp. "That's how they know which Cartel the dope belongs to. Ain't no telling what the symbol means, tho," Slim said. Jose never mentioned anything to Kilo about the trademark of his Cartel's stamp, so he didn't know either. "The stamp ain't what's important right now. Getting these thangs off and getting rich is what's important to me," Kilo said, thinking about all the money they were about to make. After Kilo said that, they all did a little celebrating talking shit. "But in the midst of all the money we about to get, I want ya'll niggas to remember one thing, and that's where we came from. So don't ever let this shit come between us!" Kilo said seriously. And from that day forward, there wasn't no turning back for them. They were now officially plugged into the El Dorado's Cartel, and the only way out was death. With a hundred kilos of cocaine that they could've broken down and turned into 125 kilos and still have had the strongest dope around, they locked their city down in not even a month. They ran through the dope in less than the two months that Pedro gave them, and everything was looking up for them until Slim got word from Tila one day that some niggas from the block were talking about robbing them. "I heard them niggas say your name personally. They were talkin' about you and Kilo," Tila told Slim. "Aite, good-looking lil nigga. You straight?" "Yeah, I'm good," Tila told Slim over the phone. Slim no longer sold weed but still bought some just to keep Tila supplied now, giving him fifty pounds at a time. Slim called and told Kilo what Tila told him, and twenty minutes later, Kilo and Slim were on the block, getting shit straight. "So ya'll niggas plottin' on robbin' me, huh?" Kilo said, staring at a crowd of niggas. "Well, shit, here I am do what you gone do to me." Didn't nobody say nothing. "I guess ya'll niggas got cold feet now," Kilo said, facing a crowd of about six niggas. "What you talkin' 'bout Kilo ain't nobody plottin' on robbin' you. Shit, I didn't even know you was home," One of the niggas said. "Quit lyin', bitch-ass nigga! I heard you and Pooh talkin' earlier," Tila said, crossing the street from where his weed was stashed. "Don't get scared now, nigga. Tell 'em what you said you was gone do," Tila told the dude that spoke up. "What the fuck you talkin' 'bout, Tila? I ain't said nothin' like that. Kilo, man, that lil nigga don't know what he's talkin' 'bout. I swear I ain't said nothin' like that," The dude was saying. "My lil nigga ain't got no reason to lie," Slim said, pulling his gun from his waist, causing the crowd to move back. Slim walked up on Pooh the other nigga that supposedly had something to do with wanting to rob them and stuck his gun in his face. "What you got to say about this?" "Man . . . I . . . I . . . I . . ." *Smack!* Slim slapped Pooh across the face with his pistol. "Nigga, spit that shit out!" Slim said with his pistol pointed at Pooh. Pooh confessed and got him and his partner pistol whipped. "That's enuff, fool. Don't kill him. Let this send a message," Kilo said, stopping Slim from crushing Pooh's skull. "Next time it ain't gone be no next time. 'Cause next time I'ma drop some cheese on your head like you're a Packers fan!" Kilo said before he and Slim pulled off. Kilo and Slim didn't have any more problems out of the either of the niggas ever again. Over the next few months, Kilo started to network in other cities and states, which caused him to run through the dope a whole lot quicker. "I think it's 'bout time we start expanding our reach. We've locked down the entire state of Ohio. Everything that come through here it's coming from us. It's a lot of money to be made out there, and I feel that we've been put limitations on just how much by not networkin' in other states," Kilo said. He, Fresh, Slim and Quick were all chilling at the Spot, a two story-house Kilo bought and had decked out for him and his niggas to chill at. There was no drug dealing going on at the Spot. They came there just to chill. So if the police ever kicked the door in, the only thing they would find is a few pounds of kush and some money. "I been fuckin' 'round in Kentucky a lil bit. I know a few niggas down there who be hustling. They buyin' them things for $28,000 all day," Quick said. "The prices are fucked up everywhere, and it's been like that ever since that one president left the office. It ain't to many niggas out here that's still connected so take and maximize what we got now because don't nothin last forever," Kilo said, grabbing a blunt from Fresh. "You right, my nigga. That's why I've been stackin'. I've been getting so much money it's hard to keep count of this shit," Slim said. "Keep count? Nigga, I been getting so much mufucken money that I lost count. I'm doing like Fab and putting everything in $20,000 stacks and just throwing it in the bag!" Fresh said. Fresh was actually being more responsible with his money than Kilo thought he would be. *'Maybe it's because he know how serious it is or maybe it's his baby that's on the way that opened his eyes a little,'* Kilo thought. "I thought about doin' a lil celebrating and throw one of the biggest parties Ohio has ever seen and have a bad bitch contest where the baddest bitch there get $5,000 and then have a rock the mic contest where the hardest rapper get $5,000," Kilo said. "What you tryna do nigga, find you a love and an artist all in one night?" Slim said, making everybody laugh. "Nawl, I ain't tryna find love in a club, nigga," Kilo said, laughing himself. "I'm just doin' that to bring the bitches out and find me a rap artist that I can put some of this drug money behind and laundry some of this shit," Kilo said. "That ain't a bad idea. When you tryna do that?" Quick asked Kilo. "I was thinking about the middle of next month. That way, the promoters will have time to promote and get the word out there. I might pay

Jeezy for a walk-through just for the publicity," And just like Kilo expected, the word spread like wildfire around town once he paid a promoter. Everybody in Ohio knew about this event and planned on being there to either be a contestant or to see Jeezy. Even Kenya and Ivonne planned on coming out to show their support. "Gurl, don't tell me you trying to win that $5,000," Ivonne told Kenya once she got in the car with her. Kenya had her hair, nails, and makeup done and was dressed in a solid black dress with a red Prada belt wrapped around her waist and some black-and-red Prada slippers on her feet. "Dressed like this? Girl, quit playing. I just made sure I was matching in something simple. But you, let me find out you've been in desperate need of some money is the only reason you're coming out," Kenya cracked on Ivonne. Ivonne was wearing a white-and-gold Fendi outfit with matching heels, earrings, rings, and a necklace. "I wouldn't mind winning that lil money, girl. Now say you wouldn't and watch how fast I come across this seat." By the time, Kenya and Ivonne got to the club, which was kind of earlier so they wouldn't have to wait to get in, they thought about turning around and going home. "Look at the line, waiting to get in the club!" Ivonne said before Kenya even parked. "Gurl, ain't no way I'm standing in that line," Ivonne said. "I ain't either, girl. Let me call Kilo and see if he can get us in 'cause that line is ridiculous," Kenya said, finding a parking spot as close to the door as she could. Kilo answered and told Kenya and Ivonne to come to the front of the line and he'll be there to let them in. As Kenya and Ivonne made their way to the front of the line, all types of "Who do they think they are?" "They need to get their ass at the back of the line and wait their turn!" "I been here since seven waiting to get in." "I hope they don't think their ugly ass funa win no money." comments could be heard. Once the front door was opened and Kenya and Ivonne were let in without being searched, that made the females even more jealous. Sitting in the top of the club with the owner, Kilo, Slim, Quick, and Fresh were looking like real rappers with the expensive clothing and all the jewelry they had on. Kilo was dressed in an all-black Gucci outfit with Gucci loafers to match and a five-row diamond chain and a bracelet. Slim was also dressed in Gucci, and so were Fresh and Quick. Fresh, being the show-off he was, dressed in an all-white Gucci outfit with the all-white Gucci loafers and belt to match with three diamond chains hanging from around his neck. As if that wasn't enough ice, Fresh had on his diamond-studded bracelet and watch. *'I'ma teach 'em how to stunt,'* Fresh said to himself while he was getting dressed. The owner of the club was telling Kilo that he didn't think the club was big enough to hold all the people that were outside trying to get in. "One thousand people is the club's capacity level, and I know it's at least 2,500 or more out there trying to get in," The club owner said. "Well, let a thousand and one in then. That one person might be the one that I'm looking for," Kilo said sitting up at the top of the club with the owner watching the crowd get bigger and bigger with the ratio of wannabe models and rappers equaling out to about the same. Quick and Slim were all out in the club, giving daps and hugs to damn near everybody in there, while Fresh was at the picture booth flexing with two half-dressed females and two bottles of Moet, one in each hand. "Ya'll came to rip the run way and win that five grand tonight, right?" Fresh said after the last picture was snapped. "I know I'ma win! Ain't a bitch badda than me in here," One of the half-dressed females said. "That makes two of us then 'cus I feel the same way. If I don't win, the judge must be blind!" The other one said. Both of them sounding real sure of themselves. "If ya'll don't win, I got twenty-five hundred to dust both of ya'll tonight," Fresh told the girls then walked off. About an hour or so later, Fresh was onstage hosting the bad-bitch contest after telling the original host to be his co-host. Kilo, Slim, and Quick were watching the contest from the owner's office that had a glass window overlooking the entire club. "Aite, check this out," Fresh spoke into the microphone. "This how we gone do this. Every time I pull a broad onstage, depending on the crowd's reaction will determine who's the baddest bitch in here," Fresh said, making everybody shout out different names, clap, and yell. "Check Fresh out down there hosting the party," Slim said, tripping off Fresh. "You know if a bitch is involved Fresh is involved," Quick said. Kilo, Slim, and Quick sipped Moet and passed a blunt back and forth, watching the show Fresh was putting on. "Aite, will our first contestant please step on the stage and pop lock and drop it, strut, or do whatever you think you need to do to win?" Fresh was having a ball on the stage judging the women, and so was the crowd. "Man, I'on know if it's the drink that got me feeling like all them bitches was bad or what, but it's gone be hard judging that one," Kilo said from the sky box.

"It is some cool lil bitches in here tonight, but only about five outta the whole bunch are really bad bitches. The others are put-togethers," Slim said. "I don't think none of them hoes showed their natural beauty," Quick said, going back to sit down. "I think I'ma let Fresh decide on the winner since he saw them up close and personal," Kilo said. It didn't take Fresh no time to pick the winner(s) after he found out he got to choose who won. "Aite, ya'll we got a tie," Fresh said then called the same two chicks that were at the picture booth with him back onto the stage. *That's free pussy for tonight!'* Fresh thought. "Aite, aite, aite, now that we've found the two hottest broads in the club, let's see if we can find the hottest nigga with a mic in his hand besides me." Fresh gave each MC thirty seconds to do their thing to which ever beat the DJ dropped. "Aite, we got one more MC left to do his thang, but before we let him do his thang, give it up for my man's Pay one more time who said his block got cells like a body. Whoa! That was a mean metaphor right there, son!" Fresh said, giving props to the MC that had the whole club rocking. "Now we are down to the last MC of the night and if he can't rock the mic and get the crowd hype, then I think the judges already have their minds made up. DJ, bring that beat back," Fresh said, telling the DJ to play the beat so the last contestant could do his thing. "Hold up, Fresh," The DJ said. "I'm havin' a lil technical difficulties with the turntables right now. Give me a second." The crowd booed the DJ, and Fresh tried to take the attention off him by asking the MC questions. "So where you from?" "Cashville, Tennessee, born and raised. 615 stand up!" The next MC said into the mic. "You from Nashville, huh? What's yo name?" Fresh asked, stalling so the DJ could fix his equipment. "I'm Streetz." After a few minutes of waiting on the DJ, Streetz told Fresh that he didn't need any beat. "Check this out," Streetz said into the mic. "I'm hot dude and I don't need a beat to tell you dat/ I made my own name in the streets when I was slangin' packs/ Den I copped me a drop on Ashanti's and painted it candy black/ ridin' like a boss but these pussy niggas they hated dat/ But fuck 'em! I earned mine and it ain't no takin dat/ try me if you wonna lil buddy I bet cha pay for dat/ I pull up on the scene dreads hangin' like I'ma a Hatican Cat/ in my navy blue ol skool coupe matchin' my Yankees hat/ It's Streetz, bitch! Real nigga and ain't no changing dat/ Martha Stewart shit in the kitchen I brought tha aprons back/ Nigga

I been one of the best when it comes to manufacturing crack/ the way I whip the white you would've thought that I as a racist cat/ Plus I keep them pills in mo colors than a Jamaican hat/ slow down, homie! Hell nawl, I ain't got no brakes attached/ it's family over everything and money over the rest of dat/ and I ain't taking no shorts lil nigga give me the rest of that!" After Streetz finished spitting, he dropped the mic and walked off the stage. The crowd was going crazy, chanting Streetz's name. "That nigga sick with them words. He's just what I came here looking for," Kilo said after watching Streetz perform from the top of the stairway. While Fresh was onstage, getting the crowd's opinion on the best MC, Kilo was headed down the stairs to find Streetz and found him by the bar with a few other niggas. Kilo introduced himself as the president of Bankroll Records and told Streetz that he was trying to put some money behind him. "I like your flow, and I think you have the potential to take it to the top with the right label pushing you." Kilo didn't even have a studio yet but knew getting one wouldn't take long. "I'on know about signing no deals. I done seen to many niggas sign a deal and don't make a dollar after they sign it," Streetz said, eyeing Kilo's ice. Kilo told Streetz that he could go over a contract (that wasn't even typed) with his lawyer before he made any decisions. Kilo was just making shit sound good right now but had intentions on doing everything he was telling Streetz. Kilo gave Streetz his number. "Call and let me know what you think about the $75,000 signing bonus that's in the contract," Kilo said then told the bartender that the drinks were on the house for Streetz and his partners before he left. Making his way through the crowd, Kilo stopped at Kenya and Ivonne's table and joked with them before they left the club. Kilo was passing the bathrooms on his way back up the stairs when he caught eyes with a set of eyes that he hadn't seen in a long time and even though he only had seen them once he remembered the exact same day he had seen them. It felt as if everything around him became still, and it was just him and the set of eyes in the club. Kilo didn't blink or bat an eye walking to the table where the set of eyes sat. "Harmony, right?" Kilo said once he was face-to-face with the set of eyes.

Chapter 14

Harmony was surprised when Kilo called her by her name because she didn't know his but remember just as well as Kilo did the day she first laid eyes on him. "Yes, you're right, but how do you know?" Harmony asked. *'I know it's been almost two years since I've seen him, so how could he know my name and we didn't converse?'* Harmony asked herself. Kilo told Harmony that he'd been looking for her since the first time he had seen her at Susan's. "You have a good memory. That was how many years ago?" Harmony was sitting at the table with another female whom she introduced as her friend. "It's hard to forget a gorgeous face like yours. I wanted to say something when I first seen you, but I was kinda rushin'," Kilo said, remembering trying to get out of Susan's shop because of the sack chasers that were in there. Kilo and Harmony made small talk, getting to know the basics of each other that night, which would lead to them becoming an idol. Six months after doing the go together, Kilo asked Harmony to move in with him. At first, Harmony was a little reluctant to move in with Kilo because she felt she would lose a sense of her independence and "Never depend on a man for anything!" Was something her daddy always taught her. But Harmony felt like Kilo was worth her taking a chance on. "The very first time you hurt me in any kind of way, I'm leaving Keon, and I mean it!" Harmony told Kilo before she moved into his condo with him. By this time, Kilo had already had the studio built, spending close to a half of a million dollars on it, turning the studio into the new spot for him and his niggas to hang out at. Kilo didn't want Harmony caught up in any of his doings, so he kept his street life in the streets. When he came home, it was to get away from the outside world. Harmony knew about Kilo's son and fell in love with him the first time Kilo brought him home. "He's so handsome! Look at him with his little fat self! Awww . . ." Kilo didn't think Harmony would take a liking to his son the way she did since the baby wasn't hers, but the way she volunteered Kilo to bring his son home every chance he got said otherwise. "I'm taking me a trip to Florida to see how them niggas getting it down there. It done got borin' 'round here," Fresh was telling Quick over the phone. Fresh was sitting in TGI Fridays by himself, eating a full rack of ribs and two fully loaded baked potatoes. "When you leavin'?" Quick asked on his way to meet up with Slim. "I'm thinking 'bout leaving now. I ain't got nothing better to do, so I might as well catch me a flight. What's up you tryna go?" Fresh asked Quick. "Nawl, I ain't fucking with it. I got too much shit tied up right now. How long you stayin' down there? I might shoot down there this weekend," Quick said. "I'on know it just depends on how I'm liking it when I get there," Fresh said. Quick hung up from with Fresh and pulled into Slim's driveway and got out and went inside. Slim and Ivonne moved from their old house into a bigger one, so Slim used their old one for his stash spot. "I just got off the phone with Fresh. That fool talking 'bout he's on his way to Florida," Quick told Slim after Slim let him in. "Shit, I don't blame him. Ain't no sense in sittin' 'round here when you don't have to. But have you talked to yo peoples?" Slim asked. Quick knew somebody that was trying to sell an old building, and Slim was tryin to buy it. "Yeah, I hollered at him the same day you asked me to. He said that the building is old and not in good shape to be trying to open a bizniz. But if you still wanted to buy it, he'll sell it to you for a little under fifty grand," Quick said. Slim wasn't worried about the foundation of the building because he was going to knock it down and build a new one anyway. He just liked the location the building was at. "Tell him I'll give him fifty-five for it right now," Slim told Quick after they both sat down. "What the hell is you going to do with that bullshitty-ass building anyway, nigga? That building been there since we was kids running round here." Quick said, wondering what Slim's plans were. "I'ma knock it down and build a new one," Slim said. "And do what with the new building?" Quick wanted to know. "I'ma open a soul-food restaurant and let my momma run it," Slim said. "Ms. Cook's Cooking." "I can hear niggas and bitches old and young talkin' 'bout, 'Man, you ain't been to Ms. Cook's?' or 'Shit, I'm funa hit Ms. Cook's to get me a plate,'" Slim said, imagining the amount of customers his mother would have from her cooking. "Mom's can cook a mean meal. I can see her restaurant doing good. Have you told her about it?" Quick asked. "Nawl, not yet. I'ma surprise her with it. I'm tryna have it up by November 15. That's her birthday," Slim said. "You ain't got that much time then, fool. November right around the corner," Quick said, grabbing a cigarette off the table. "That's why I need you to be hollerin' at yo people, lettin' him know what's up." "I got you, fool. Matta fact, I'm funa call him now and let you talk to him," Quick said then called and gave Slim the phone. It took Slim maybe ten minutes to negotiate a deal with Quick's people to buy the vacant building. "I told him I got $50,000 in cash, and he ran with it," Slim said after he hung up. "Money talks. Bullshit walks a thousand miles!" Quick said. Slim met up with Quick's people that same day and bought the building. "Use this building at your own risk now, son. It's kind of old," Quick's people told Slim. "I'll have a contractor out here by next week, knocking this thing down and building a new one," Slim told the old man. It took the contractors Slim hired for the job two and a half days to knock the building down and almost four months to build the new one. *'Perfect timing. There's still a month and a half left until November gets here,'* Slim thought to himself one day while watching the men transform the building. November came and left just as fast. Ms. Cook thought she was dreaming when Slim showed her the restaurant that had Ms. Cook's Cooking in huge letters across the top of the building. "Oh, thank you, baby! This is the best birthday of all my years!" Ms. Cook said, hugging Slim, crying tears of joy. Ms. Cook's became the place to chat while you chew in Youngstown. Everybody and their momma ate there. Ms. Cooks Cooking became so popular around Youngstown that it caught the media's attention, and they ran an ad in the newspaper about the restaurant, which made the business for Ms. Cook quadruple. People from all over the state of Ohio came by Ms. Cook's to sample food and loved it. "I knew your mother would make a lot of money in this business the first time I tasted her food," Ivonne told Slim one day while they were there eating. Ivonne was a few months away from having twins—a boy and a girl—and her favorite place to eat was Ms. Cook's Cooking. She helped Ms. Cook run the cash register and at the same time ate everything in sight. Fresh's baby momma Mikayla was due to have their baby this month, and Fresh spent as much time as he could at the hospital with her. Everybody was having babies but Quick. "Shit

THE LONGEST DROUGHT EVER

I move too much to be thinking 'bout kids. Plus I haven't met anybody worthy enuff to have my baby. I've fucked a lot of bitches, but I don't think none of them are worthy. I think most of them fucked a nigga because of my name," Quick was telling Kilo when Kilo asked him when he planned to have some kids. Kilo and lil Kilo who was about to turn one stayed together. Kilo kept his son with him every chance he got. Sometimes he kept him for days at a time. Kenya knew about the relationship Kilo had with Harmony, but that didn't change the way she felt about him. She knew that it was her who held the key to his heart, so she played her position because she also knew that it was her fault that they weren't together anymore. Kenya knew what she did while Kilo was locked up was wrong, so now she's living with the consequences, hoping that Kilo would forgive her and give her another chance. One day while Kenya and Ivonne were sitting in Kenya's living room, Ivonne asked Kenya if she planned on finding herself a new man, and Kenya's response was "Nope, I'm staying celibate until Kilo gives me another chance to prove myself!" "Well, you're doing better than most because normally when a woman loses her man, she let that be the reason for not wanting to take care of herself anymore. But I see you're using that as motivation to keep yourself up and do better," Ivonne said to Kenya who was still going to the gym faithfully to keep her body tight, something Ivonne planned to do after she had her babies. And she did after she gave birth to Isaac Jr., a.k.a. Lil Slim, and Zanola who was born one minute apart with Zanola coming out first. For their first birthday, Ivonne and Kenya took Lil Slim, Zanola, and Lil Kilo, who was now three to the state fair. They were followed the whole time by Pooh and the other nigga Kilo and Slim pistol whipped on the block a lil while back. "I hope them niggas didn't think this shit was over," Pooh said following behind Ivonne's red BMW 328C 3-series Slim bought her as a graduation present. "They should have known better than to pistol whip a nigga and let him live. Where in the fuck do they do that at? And then have the nerve to have their bitches out flossin' in a car that cost more money than I've seen in my entire life," The other nigga said from the passenger side. "This what we gone do. We gone follow them until they pull over, and then we gone block them off and kidnap their kids. Once they see our guns, we shouldn't have a problem," Pooh told his partner then said, "Make sure we get Kilo's son so we can put a ransom price outta this world on him!" Ivonne and Kenya were too busy singing alone with Melanie Fiona to have noticed the black Explorer following them. "Look at all these people trying to get into the fair. They must have something special going on," Ivonne said, pulling into the parking lot. "It's too many people out here to try anything right now, so we might have to wait until they're done having their fun so we can have ours," Pooh told his partner, parking a row over from where Ivonne parked. After watching the kids ride almost every ride and play every game the fair had more than once and eat entirely too much junk food, Ivonne and Kenya were ready to go. "We've been here almost five hours, and ya'll have done everything there is to do more times than I can remember. It's time to go before it gets dark," Ivonne told the kids who all whined, saying that they weren't ready to leave yet. "Can we ride the bumper cars just one more time before we leave, Momma? Pleazze!" Lil Slim begged, and so did Lil Kilo and Zanola. Seeing her babies ask to ride one more ride, Ivonne couldn't help but say yes. "Okay, and this is the last ride and I mean it!" That one ride turned into three more and a funnel cake for everybody. Pooh saw Ivonne, Kenya, and the kids coming out the gate, leaving the fair. "It's about time these muthafuckers are leaving! I was starting to think they noticed us following them and took another way out," Pooh said to his nigga. Ivonne and Kenya put the kids in the car and left the fair, heading back to Ivonne's house where Kilo was waiting to pick Lil Kilo up. Checking her mirrors before getting on the interstate, Ivonne noticed a black truck one car behind her getting on the interstate. It looked a little suspicious to her, so she kept her eyes on it. Ivonne didn't want to scare Kenya by telling her, so she switched lanes to see if the black truck would switch lanes with her, and it did, but the truck was still one car behind her. *'I might just be paranoid,'* Ivonne thought until she switched lanes to get off at the next exit, and the truck did the same thing. "I think we're being followed," Ivonne told Kenya, trying not to let the kids hear her. Kenya gave Ivonne a look that said, "Are you serious?" Ivonne nodded at the passenger-side mirror, telling Kenya to look. "We got their ass now! At the next stop light, I'ma cut their ass off," Pooh said. "Take a detour and see what they do," Kenya told Ivonne after watching the truck make every turn they made. Ivonne turned up and down streets to see what the truck would do, and just like she thought, the truck did the same thing. "Call Slim and tell him that we are being followed!" Ivonne said, driving a little faster. "I think they know we're on to them. She's driving like she's tryin' to lose us!" Pooh said, pressing the gas pedal down a little harder to keep up with Ivonne. "Slim, this is Kenya. We just left the fair with the kids, and now there's a black truck following behind us! Every turn we make, they make!" Kenya told Slim. "Where are ya'll at now?" Slim said, hopping out his seat. "We're like five minutes away from ya'll's house. They're still behind us. What do you want us to do?" A nervous Kenya asked Slim. Slim told them to come straight to the house and "Do not make a complete stop at any stop-signs or lights." Slim hung up with Kenya, and he and Kilo stood outside their house strapped with two MAC-11s. Pooh noticed that Ivonne was not making complete stops anymore and decided to ram the back of the BMW she was driving but couldn't get close enough. "Shoot the tires off their car, man. They are getting away!" Pooh told his partner who dropped his window and shot all seventeen shots out his 9mm, missing the tires, hitting the trunk of the car and the back window. Ivonne heard the bullets hitting her car and screamed. "Nigga, what the fuck are you shooting at? You didn't hit neither one of the tires! Here take this and try again!" Pooh said, trying to keep up with the BMW's V8. Pooh's partner hung out the window again with Pooh's gun and let off shots at Ivonne's and missed again. Slim and Kilo could hear the shots being fired, so they knew Ivonne and Kenya were close. Ivonne turned on their street, and the truck kept going. "They tried to set us up. I know somebody's down that street waiting on us. Why would they turn on a dead end street if it wasn't?" Pooh said then gave his partner some funky talk for not hitting the tires. Ivonne pulled into their driveway where Kilo and Slim were waiting. Slim and Kilo rushed to the car to make sure everybody was okay, and what Slim saw when he opened the back door caused him to blank out. Zanola was lying on the floor in a puddle of her own blood. Kilo pulled Lil Kilo and Lil Slim out the car and told Kenya to take them in the house. Ivonne broke down crying once she saw her little girl, lying there lifeless. Slim tried his best to console Ivonne while trying to stay strong himself. "It's going to be okay, baby," Slim was telling Ivonne while they waited on the ambulance to come. "Whoever's behind this, I'm killin' their whole fuckin' family!" Slim said to Kilo that night while they were sitting downstairs in Slim's den, talking. "I got my peoples with their ears to the streets to see what's what and who's behind this. I think it was a kidnapping that the pussies was trying to carry out," Kilo told Slim. "Yeah, but who in the fuck got the balls to play with my family like that? It ain't like we beefin'," Slim said then turned up the bottle of Remy he was drinking out of. "Nawl, we ain't beefin' with nobody that we know of," Kilo said. "What you mean that we know of? We'll know if we're beefin' or not." Slim didn't understand what Kilo was saying. "What I'm saying is once you start to get money and I'm talkin' 'bout serious money like we're getting, you make enemies without even touchin' them. Most of the time it be niggas that you've never heard of. They just heard about you," Kilo told Slim. Ivonne and Kenya were upstairs, having a similar conversation, when Kilo and Slim came up. Kilo hugged and kissed Ivonne on the forehead and told her that he was sorry for what happened. Before he left, he told Kenya to start looking for somewhere else to live. "I can't risk the chance of them knowin' where you and my son lay ya'll's heads so get on that ASAP! I don't care what the expenses is. I'ma take care of that. I want you moved out by tomorrow night!" The next day, while Slim and Kilo were out trying to find out who was behind Slim's daughter being killed, Ivonne was at the house with Lil Slim, trying to explain as best as she could to him why he'll never see his sister again. "When is Nola coming home, Momma?" Lil Slim wanted to know. It took everything in Ivonne not to break down crying. "Nola is with Jesus now, baby," Ivonne told Lil Slim. "How long do she gota stay wit Geeus for she come home? I want to play wither," Lil Slim said. Ivonne could tell Lil Slim missed his twin by the way he was acting about playing by himself this morning. "Nola and Jesus are watching over me, you, and your daddy to make sure we are okay. She's not coming back. She will always be in your heart and up above, watching over us." Ivonne was trying her best not to cry and to be happy for Zanola. "Why didn't Geeus take me with him to watch over you and daddy 'cus I'm a boy and she's a girl?" The questions from Lil Slim went on and on until Ivonne asked him if he wanted to go play with Lil Kilo. Slim and Kilo were riding around in Slim's truck, hoping to come up with any type of clue that would lead them to who they were looking for. "Swing by Big Ed's spot so I can grab us something to smoke on, cuz," Kilo told Slim who was in deep thought. Slim pulled up to Big Ed's spot, and they both went inside. Kilo bought them a sack of kush and asked Big Ed, "Have you heard anything yet?" Big Ed told Slim that he was sorry to hear about what happened to his daughter and that he still hadn't heard anything. "You know the streets talk tho, so once the right person catch wind that you got $5,000 just for a name it's guaranteed that they'll tell," Big Ed said. Slim and Kilo left Big Ed's spot and stopped at the corner store to get some cigars to roll up with. Sitting in front of the corner store in Slim's truck rolling a blunt, Kilo thought about how Slim must feel losing his twin two-year-old daughter, knowing that it's his fault. Kilo looked at Slim who was staring out the front window of the truck in another world. "I can only imagine how you feel, my nigga. You gotta stay strong for Lil Slim and Ivonne, tho. They need you right now. Zanola's in a better place now," Kilo told Slim who let a single tear drop fall from his right eye. Slim pulled off from the store once the blunt was fired up and swung by the block to scoop Tila up to see if he had heard anything yet. "I ain't heard nothin'! I'm startin to believe that whoever done this ain't from 'round here because don't nobody know nothin'. At least that's what they're sayin'," Tila said from the back of the truck. "Do you think this could link back to that shit that happened in Detroit?" Slim asked Kilo. Kilo thought about it for a second. "Nawl, I don't think this has nothin' to do with that. And the only reason I say that is because you sent Jaz back up there, didn't you?" Kilo asked, grabbing the blunt from Tila. "Yeah, Jaz went back up there a few months later." Slim, Tila, and Kilo rode around, destination-less. Quick called Slim's phone to see if he heard anything yet. "Same ol shit. Ain't nobody talkin'," Slim told him. Quick told Slim to spread the word that it was now $10,000 for a name on who done this. "I got five more grand to put with your five," Quick said before he hung up. The $10,000 reward for a name spread around town faster than a New York's minute. The following week, Zanola's funeral was held for family members and friends only. After the funeral, Slim and Ivonne invited everyone who attended Zanola's funeral over to their house where Ms. Cook had a big meal prepared. After everyone was done eating and left, Slim tucked Lil Slim in his bed. "Daddy, Mommy said Nola's with Geeus watching over us now!" Lil Slim said after Slim kissed him on the forehead. Slim sat and talked to Lil Slim about his sister and where she was until he fell asleep. Ivonne watched from the doorway and let tears fall freely from her eyes, listening to Slim tell his son the truth. The next day Fresh called Slim with the information he was waiting on. "I got names for you, homie," Fresh said. "Where did you get them?" Slim asked, sitting up on his couch. "From a lil broad I been fuckin' she heard about the ten g's and told everything she knew," Fresh said, flicking a cigarette butt out his window. "And who she say?" Slim asked, walking into the bedroom out of earshot from Ivonne. "She said she overheard Pooh and somebody name Zed talkin' about it." Slim heard the names Fresh said and snapped. "How in the fuck did I not think about them bitch-ass niggas?" Slim hung up the phone from with Fresh and called Kilo and told him who's behind this. "I would have never guessed that them niggas would do some shit like this after all this time. Consider them dead men walking, tho. I'll have them floatin' before nightfall," Kilo told Slim, but Slim told Kilo that he wouldn't be satisfied letting somebody else take care of this. "I'ma handle these niggas myself!" Slim said. Kilo told Slim that he was riding with him. "I'll be at your spot in twenty," Kilo said, then hung up, and changed clothes. Kilo pulled up at Slim's house strapped with two Glock 9s and a small MP-5 that held a hundred rounds. Slim came out the house dressed in all black strapped with a baby chopper with a one-hundred-round drum clipped in the bottom of it and a 40 Glock for backup. "You ready?" Kilo asked Slim once he got in the car. "Let's do it?" Was all Slim said. Slim got word from Tila that Pooh and Zed had been showing their face on the block the last couple of days but wouldn't stay long. "Aite well, the next time they pop up and leave follow them and see where they been hangin' at," Slim told Tila. Tila told Slim that he thought they had been hanging over in the duplex. "Why you say that?" Slim asked Tila. "Pooh was tellin' Mannie's lil brother that they come buy their dope from the block and sell it in the duplex's. So that's where Kilo and Slim were headed. It was a little past seven, so the sun was just starting to go down. Turning into the duplex, Slim spotted Pooh standing by a streetlight pole, catching a sell. "There go Pooh bitch ass right there!" Slim said, ready to hop out the car and gun him down. "I see him, but where is his partner Zed at?" Kilo said, cursing threw the duplex's in one of his low-lows with dark tints. Pooh had seen the car passing and tried to look inside to see who was driving but couldn't see past the tint. "Who the fuck is that with them dark-ass tints?" Pooh said. "I don't know but serve me and let me go before the police pull up!" The sell told Pooh. Kilo drove all the way to the back of the duplex and turned around. "I still don't see his bitch-ass partner out here, so we gone hop out and lay Pooh down and make him tell us," Kilo said, coming back around the curve. Kilo and Slim pulled down the ski masks Kilo brought right before they hopped out on Pooh. "What tha fuck!" Pooh yelled, pulling his pistol out from his pants and dumping a couple shots at Kilo and Slim, causing them to duck behind a car, which gave him time to run between two duplex buildings. Slim raised up and pointed the baby chopper he was touting in Pooh's direction and let off about twenty shots. "Go that way, and I'ma go this way," Kilo told Slim, moving around the back of the car they ducked behind. Pooh who was stuck in between the buildings saw the two masked men split up and come at him in two different directions. *'I'ma take one of these muthafuckers with me,'* Pooh thought to himself, pulling out a .38 special he had on him also. Kilo was the first to get up on the building and let his MP-5 spit rapidly, causing fire to jump out of it. Kilo let off close to forty shots and knew that Pooh couldn't still be standing, so he walked in to make sure and caught a bullet to the chest. *'Boom, boom, boom, boom, boom!'* Was all that could be heard. Pooh was lying on the ground while Kilo was shooting and didn't get hit. "Agh, fuck! I'm hit, fool!" Kilo yelled. While Pooh was shooting, Slim saw which direction the fire was jumping out his gun and aimed his chopper in that direction and squeezed the trigger, walking toward Pooh shooting. Slim didn't stop shooting until he got right up on Pooh. "Turn yo bitch ass over, nigga!" Slim said then kicked Pooh in the side. "Aggg, shit, man, who the fuck are you and what tha fuck—" Pooh tried to say before Slim kicked him in the face. "Shut the fuck up, nigga! I didn't ask you to speak." Slim hit Pooh four times with the chopper while he was walking up on him shooting. Two of those bullets went through Pooh's chest and stomach, hitting his spine and paralyzed him from the neck down. Slim pulled his Ski mask off so Pooh would know who he was. "Now we can do this the hard way, or we can do it the easy way. The choice is yours!" Slim said then pointed the baby AK-47 in Pooh's face. Pooh knew that he was about to die once he saw Slim's face. "Nigga, fuck you. Ain't shit easy. I wish it was you I killed instead of yo daughter, ol bitch ass" Was Pooh's last words. Slim shot every bullet that remained in his clip into Pooh's body and was still pulling the trigger even though the gun was clicking. "Come on, fool, let's get outta here before the law get here," Kilo said, pulling Slim back toward their car. "You aite, fool. I thought you was hit," Slim said. "This vest stopped the bullet," Kilo said before they heard another gun go off. *'Boom, boom, boom, boom!'* Kilo and Slim looked up to see Zed standing on a porch across the street from them, shooting. Kilo pushed Slim out the way and aimed his MP-5 at Zed and fired. The MP-5 was so light and accurate that Kilo hit Zed twice in the shoulder, causing him to fall and drop his gun. Kilo ran up on Zed and finished the job. "Playtime's over!" *'Boom, boom, boom!'*

Chapter 15

Slim took Ivonne to Hawaii to try to get her to take her mind off everything that's been going on over the last couple of weeks. Sitting in front of their beach resort Slim rented, Ivonne stared out at the water, letting her mind and body unwind and relax. Feeling a million miles away from the rest of the world, Ivonne sat there and thought about life and the crazy obstacles it threw at you. *'I've been going through a lot of changes the last couple of years. Some good and some bad,'* Ivonne thought to herself. Ivonne believed that all of life's events happen for a reason and that there's always a lesson to be learned from the events, but she couldn't quite figure out what was the lesson to be learned behind her baby being killed. "What's on your mind, boo?" Slim asked, walking up on Ivonne and sitting down next to her. Slim could tell that Ivonne had not been taking the death of their child too well, so he did all he could to comfort her and still give her some space at the same time. "Oh, nothing, just thinking about life and the changes that come with it," Ivonne told Slim who was pouring them a shot of the champagne sitting on the table that was in between them. Slim walked Ivonne down to the shore of the beach where the water was shallow and had a long heart-to-heart conversation with her, letting her know that he will always be there for her. Afterward, they sat in the sand and enjoyed the beautiful view of the sun setting, making the water look a reddish-yellow color. "It's so peaceful here," Ivonne was saying. "I could stay here for the rest of my life." "What about your family and friends back home? You just gone up and leave them?" Slim asked. "I will leave their ass in a heartbeat to wake up to this every day!" Ivonne said, then looked at Slim in the eyes, and asked if he planned to be with her for the rest of her life. "Of course I do, boo! What kind of question is that? You complete me." Slim took Ivonne then pulled her to his lap. "Why you ask?" "I was just wondering," Ivonne said. Slim peeped that Ivonne really wanted to say something else but didn't. "Why would you wonder something you should know?" Slim asked. "Umm . . . I just wanted to hear you say it I guess," Ivonne said. Slim wasn't trying to hear that and pressed on Ivonne until she told him what she was really thinking about. "Okay, okay, I'll tell you but only if you promise not to laugh," Ivonne said, sticking her pinky finger out to make Slim pinky promise. "I promise," Slim said, locking pinkies with Ivonne. "Okay and you bet not to laugh or I'm going to punch you. I was going to ask you, will you marry me? There, I said it." That caught Slim off guard. "Why would I laugh at something like that, boo? That's serious," Slim said. "Because normally it's the male asking the question, but I didn't think you would ever ask, so I asked," Ivonne said. Ivonne was right. Slim probably wouldn't have asked her to marry him anytime soon, but that doesn't mean that he didn't plan to be with her. Slim told Ivonne that he would marry her under one condition. "And what's that condition?" Ivonne asked. "We get married while we're here." That night Slim and Ivonne made love on the beach and then in their resort until the wee hours of the morning. Before they left Hawaii, they said their I dos, and Ivonne became a Cook. Back at home, Kilo had been up all night, counting money, and was just about to pass out and take a nap when Harmony walked into the living room where he was. "Baby! I figured you would have been finished counting by now," Harmony said, flopping down on the couch next to Kilo. Harmony started out helping Kilo count the money last night but fell asleep around $300,000. "I just now finished right before you walked in. I would've finished last night if I wasn't counting by hand," Kilo said. "So you haven't been to sleep?" Harmony asked. "Nawl, but I'm on my way now," Kilo said, yawning. "I bet you are. How much money was it? I think I passed out around $270,000," Harmony said, rubbing Kilo's chest. "It's 1.8 and some change," Kilo said, standing up to stretch with a weary look all over his face. "One million eight hundred thousand dollars?" Harmony asked the dollar amount like she couldn't believe it. "And some change," Kilo said and headed to the bedroom. Kilo woke up six hours later, feeling like something was missing. Not able to figure out why he was feeling this way, Kilo ignored his intuition and headed to the studio where he was sure to find his niggas chilling. Kilo had the studio built from the ground up right outside of

Youngstown. The studio was top of the line, and so was everything in it. Kilo had surveillance cameras surrounding the building so he could sit in the back office or the room where the booth was and see everything that went on outside. After a while, the studio began to turn a profit of its own. Some of the biggest names in the music industry recorded songs at Kilo's studio, and some even featured on songs with Streetz. Kilo walked into the studio, and just like always, the studio was in full effect. Even though the studio was soundproof, voices could be heard from the front door. *'They back there havin' a party, ain't they?'* Kilo thought, locking the door behind him. Walking down the hall to where the booth was, Kilo let himself in and saw what looked like a scene from a strip club. "Ya'll got a private party goin' on in here, don't ya?" Kilo said, watching two big booty girls bounce their ass to a song that Streetz just finished recording. Fresh, Quick, and Kellz the engineer Kilo hired to produce and make music for Streetz, was enjoying the show the two females were putting on. "Man, Streetz just dropped another hit, fool! Listen to him on there," Fresh said, bobbing his head. Streetz came out the booth just as Kellz replayed the track. "Tell me what you think about this one,' Slim told Kilo. "I did one for all this freakin' I've been doing!" Streetz told Kilo. The beat dropped, and Kilo's head started to bob as he listened to the song. "Yeah, I like that one 'cause my nigga I freaks good," Kilo said after the song went off, singing the hook to the song. Streetz told Kilo that his mixtape was almost finished, and Kilo told him to keep dropping that gangster shit because that's what the streets wanted to hear. Kilo went to the office in the back of the studio and sat behind his desk and rolled him a blunt. Sitting in the office with the lights dimmed low, smoking Kilo meditated on his next move. Kilo thought about sending a few niggas he had selling dope for him up to Boston, Massachusetts, to get some of their cocaine money. He had a cousin that lived in Orchard Park housing projects in Roxbury that's been telling him how he could make a killing up there right now because when the drought hit the only thing that could be found was heroin. "As long as yo niggas don't come here tryin' to take over the whole town, they would be all right. These niggas up here ain't havin' that. One more thing, tell yo niggas these niggas up here are crazy about their bitches, so don't come up here fucking any and everything," Kilo's cousin told him a few weeks ago. Kilo decided to make the move and send four niggas he felt could go up there and handle business properly. Kilo called his cousin and told him that he would have some of his niggas up there before the week was out. Reaching for the ashtray to dump the ashes from his blunt, Kilo incidentally hit a button on the monitor screen that was built onto the desktop that surveyed the perimeter of the studio and changed the camera to the one in the booth. Kilo looked at the screen and shook his head. Fresh had one of the females bent over the couch, blowing her back out, while Quick recorded it on the camcorder. *That nigga gone fuck his life away.* Kilo chuckled, watching Fresh perform, while he finished his blunt. Kilo left the studio and thought about going over to Kenya's new house but knew that his son was probably sleep, so he didn't. The last time Kilo had seen Kenya he noticed that she was still prettier than ever and that she'd been working on her body by the toneness of it. Even though Kilo hadn't had sex with Kenya since he's been out of jail, he's had the urge more than once but knew that he couldn't. He even told Kenya that a few times, which let Kenya know that he still loved and thought about her, and that inspired her to hold on to what they shared in the past, hoping that Kilo would come back home. Kilo knew that the connection between him and Kenya was much stronger than the connection he shared with Harmony even after all this time. Truth is Kilo was still in love and cared for Kenya. *Why did she have to do a nigga like that?* Kilo would ask himself when he was thinking about Kenya. Slim and Ivonne came off their vacation and picked Lil Slim up from Kenya's house. Slim sat in the car while Ivonne ran in to get him. "So how was your trip, girl?" Kenya asked Ivonne. "Hawaii is soo beautiful! The atmosphere is so peaceful and relaxing. I didn't want to come back!" Ivonne said. Kenya noticed that Ivonne seemed to be a whole lot more cheerful than she was before she left. "Is that a wedding ring I see on your finger?" Kenya asked Ivonne. "Yes, girl, it is! We got married while we was down there. I'm officially a Cook now!" Ivonne said, showing Kenya her ring. Slim was on the phone talking to Kilo when Ivonne got back in the car with Lil Slim. "What's up, Daddy?" Lil Slim said. "I had fun playing with Lil Kilo. Auntie Kenya let us eat all the cookies we want." "She did?" Slim asked his son, pulling out Kenya's driveway. "Yep! She let us stay up all night long!" Lil Slim said, telling on Kenya. Slim dropped Ivonne and his son off at home, then called Kilo back, and met up with him at the studio. Slim pulled up at the studio and saw a white Maserati outside and wondered which rap star was inside the studio recording. "Whose Maserati parked outside?" Slim asked Kilo. "That's my new toy. I got tired of the old one. It wasn't fit for a boss," Kilo said, giving Slim some dap. "What's good tho, nigga? How was your trip?" Slim let Kilo know that his trip to Hawaii was the best he's ever taken. "I ain't seen nothing like Hawaii. It's even better than what they say. Me and Ivonne even got married while we was down there," Slim said, showing Kilo his wedding band. "Married? You went down there and put a ring on it? Congratulations, homie! What type of celebration ceremony ya'll throwin' since didn't nobody get to attend the wedding?" Kilo asked. "Ion know. Ivonne was sayin' something about that on our way back, but I fell asleep listenin'. You know how them plane rides is. What's up with this move you 'bout to make, tho?" Slim said, following Kilo to the back office. Once they were in the room, Kilo explained in detail what he was about to do. "So who you gone send up there?" Slim asked. "I gotta few nigga from Columbus I be fuckin with that I'ma send up there. I was thinkin' about sending Benjamen and Cutt up there, but them niggas ain't gone do right," Kilo said. "I wouldn't send them niggas up there. They might get up there and get their self killed," Slim said. "But when did you cop that white thang sitting out front? That bitch wet! Now I gotta go and cop me something foreign," Slim said, checking out Kilo's new whip. "I bought that car like three days ago. I know some Arabs that own a car lot with nothing but foreigns on it. So let me know when you tryna cop you something," Kilo told Slim. "I'm tryna cop me something now! I want a Aston Martin," Slim said. Kilo pulled out his cell phone and made a call to the Arab's car dealership. "They got two Aston Martins left but said that he could have one shipped to you if you didn't like the ones they got on their lot," Kilo told Slim after he hung up. "As long as that bitch can do the dash in less than sixty seconds, I want it," Slim said. Kilo took Slim to the car lot, and with no thoughts needed Slim to decided that he wanted the black Aston Martin with tan-colored leather seats that was on the lot. "What's the price tag on this Aston? I gotta have this baby!" Slim told the frail-looking Arab. "The retail price is $92,000 thousand but I give it to you my friend for $80," The Arab said then named all the features the car had. "They can put a stash spot in that bitch for another three g's, fool. You know how you like to ride," Kilo said. "I had them put one in for me, and they're deoxygenated compartments so them punk-ass dogs can't sniff nothin'!" Kilo added. Slim bought the car and told the Arab that he wanted one of those compartments built into it and the Arab told him that the car would be ready in two and a half hours. Once Fresh saw Kilo's and Slim's new whips, the first thing he said was "So ya'll gone roll through and piss on me like that? Ya'll done started something now!" The next day Fresh pulled up in a black Mercedes-Benz coupe with the top peeled off. "Ya'll ain't the only niggas 'round this bitch getting money. That's a hunnet grand on wheels right there, nigga! I got forty on my wrist, I can't even tell the time on this bitch!" Fresh said, hopping out on Slim and Kilo at the studio, stunting. Kilo and Slim couldn't do anything but laugh because they knew when it came to stunting, Fresh couldn't be fucked with. Kilo loved to hear his nigga talk shit, so he added some gas to the fire. "Nigga, I spend that shit you got on your wrist in bills every month! Nigga, I spend that shit every time the seasons change on Lil Kilo's wardrobe," Slim already knew what Kilo was doing, so he added his two cents. "Yeah nigga, I spent that shit plus some on my bitch wedding ring! Nigga, I'll spend forty thou in the club makin' it rain and that ain't including my bar tab!" Fresh, being the king at shit talking, let Kilo and Slim have it at the same time. "Ya'll niggas talkin' like I ain't been ballin' like a muthafucker! That lil shit ya'll talkin' 'bout ain't nothin'! My pussy bill probably more than that shit combined, nigga. I spent $10,000 on Gucci boxers, socks, and wife beaters just last week, nigga. Ya'll oughta see my closet. I never wear the same thing twice!" Fresh said all worked up. Kilo knew he had Fresh on the edge, so he kept pushing. "You ain't getting no real money, nigga! Like Wayne said, "You ain't did it till you done it in five states." "I ain't funa let you drive me, nigga. 'Cause I see now that's what you tryna do, fool. What's up, tho?" Fresh said, catching on to what Kilo and Slim were trying to do. Kilo and Slim busted out laughing once Fresh said that. "Man, ain't nobody tryna drive you fool," Kilo said, still chuckling. "I was just sayin'." "Tell that lie to a fly, nigga. I know you like my mouthpiece, but ya'll niggas ain't gone keep stealing my swag. This shit you can't buy with money." Fresh, Slim and Kilo sat outside the studio clowning one another, passing a blunt of kush back and forth until they saw a police cruiser turn the corner. "What the hell is the police doing in this part of town?" Slim said, cuffing the blunt behind his back. "One of these crazy-ass white dudes probably done kicked the shit out of his ol lady," Fresh said, watching the police car creep down the street and stop in front of the studio. "What the fuck is Ms. Coolwaters doing?" Kilo said. Ms. Coolwaters rolled down the window and told Kilo to come to here. "Mr. Campbell, can I speak with you for a minute?" Kilo walked up on the car, wondering what the hell she wanted when he just paid her Friday and it was just now Tuesday. "What up, sexy?" Kilo said, standing about a foot away from the car. Ms. Coolwaters told Kilo that she was about to get promoted to a detective and that if he still wanted her eyes and ears working for him, then she would need ten thousand instead of the five thousand dollars that he's been paying her. "Ten thou a week? You playin', right? I mean the five I give you every week is already too much. I've been giving you $20,000 a month for almost a year now, and the only piece of information you gave me that was valuable was when you told me the police was about to kick the door to one of my spots. Other than that, I've just been paying you for nothing," Kilo said. Kilo told Ms. Coolwaters that he would give her two extra thousand a week and Ms. Coolwaters agreed. "That bitch just extorted me for an extra two g's a week!" Kilo said, walking back to where Fresh and Slim were. "How she do that, fool?" Slim asked. "She talkin' 'bout since she's a detective now she wants more money 'cause now she will be able to get me a lot more information that she wasn't able to get workin' as an officer," Kilo said. "That bitch is gone be a problem. I can see that now," Fresh said, firing a cigarette up. Kilo thought about cutting Ms. Coolwaters off, but she knew too much and he didn't want to piss her off and have her blackmailing and extorting him for real. "I'll get rid of her ass before I let her become a problem!" Kilo said, then hopped in his Maserati and peeled off. Leaving out of Designers, a clothing store that sold nothing but the best, Kilo bumped into somebody that he hadn't seen or heard from in a while, Fonzi. Kilo and Fonzi sat out in front of the clothing store, catching up on each other. "I see you've found what you've been lookin' for," Fonzi told Kilo. "And what's that?" Kilo asked, already knowing what Fonzi was talking about. "Whatever it is that got you looking like new money," Fonzi said, eyeing Kilo. "Aw, man, cut that out!" Kilo said, laughing a little. "I'm just tryin' to make it that's all. I ain't doin' nothin' that haven't been done already." "Trying to make it? It looks to me like you've made it already and that's the thing. See, a lot of niggas get that confused. They don't know the difference between trying to make it and made it. They keep trying to make it instead of switching their grind up to do something that's legal and make their money work for them. That's what I done. Now I'll never have to work another day of my life, and I'll never have to worry about going to jail either because everything I do is legit," Fonzi said. Kilo took in everything Fonzi said about making it and made it. *'I've made well over $2 million dollars in the short time that I've been out of jail, so I know I've made it,'* Kilo thought to himself then thought about his connection to the El Dorado's cartel. "I gotta run but think about what I said and keep in touch, nigga! My number ain't changed," Fonzi told Kilo before he left. After seeing and talking to Fonzi again, Kilo drove home contemplating Fonzi's words. Kilo knew that he wouldn't be able to be fully go legit because of his connection with the El Dorado's, but that didn't stop him from opening up as many businesses as he could. Kilo opened up business after business from restaurants to construction companies. Anything that he thought to be lucrative, he invested in it. Slim asked him one day after they passed at least five of Kilo's businesses just riding around smoking why he was opening up so many businesses when he didn't need the money. "For a money trail. I'm covering my own ass just in case the alphabet boys start wondering how in the hell am I shining like this," Kilo told him. Over the years, Kilo's business grew, and so did the shipment of cocaine they were getting from Pedro. They went from getting one hundred kilos of cocaine a month to moving five hundred and sometimes six hundred kilos a month. They were selling so much cocaine for the cartel that Pedro considered them his best suppliers and dropped the price on the cocaine for them to $10,000 a brick. Kilo and his crew flooded cocaine not only in Ohio but in twelve other states also. They even went back down to Texas and took over El Paso, the same part of town Ricardo ran before they killed him for Jose. "I got some people down in New Orleans who be moving hella dope. They said it's dry down there. We could go down there and take that bitch over too!" Quick told Kilo while they were at the studio chilling one day.

"I'll send some niggas down there to do their thang, but I ain't going myself. Them niggas too petty down there. They might fuck with a nigga for a second then turn around and murder you the next," Kilo told him. Quick went down there anyway and took over. It was hard for other niggas to compete with the prices of Kilo and his boys had, and that made it that much easier for them to come to any city and take over. They would sometimes have to lay their murder game down because in some states a lot of niggas wouldn't allow out-of-towners to sell dope in their city no matter how cheap the dope was.

Chapter 16

"Keon, we need to talk," Harmony told Kilo as he walked in the house. Kilo was feeling good after leaving from one of his stash houses, running more than $7 million through a money machine. "What's up, baby?" Kilo said, hugging and kissing Harmony who was sitting on their couch, watching nothing on the TV. "Keon, I want you to know that I know what's been going on. I'm not stupid," Harmony said, looking Kilo in the eyes. "What are you talking about, Harmony? You know about what?" Kilo asked. "I know about you and your dealings in the streets. I mean who don't? Everywhere I go, I hear people talking about you," Harmony said, pulling away from Kilo. "Just because you hear my name in the streets doesn't mean I'm in the streets," Kilo said, pointing at himself. "I'm a businessman. I own more property than anybody 'round here, so of course you're going to hear my name," Kilo said, wondering how much Harmony knew about him being in the streets. "Keon, I might not be from the hood, but that doesn't mean that I'm green to the hood. My daddy was in the streets, remember? So I know what type of buzz comes from a person that sell drugs," Harmony said, letting Kilo know that she wasn't green. "So what you saying, Harmony?" Kilo asked. Harmony told Kilo that she just wanted to know truth. Kilo couldn't understand what difference it made. "I've been hustling since we've first met. I get you everything you want, so what difference does it make?" Kilo wanted to say. "Where is all this heading? If I am, then what?" Kilo asked. "If you are, then I'm going to give you the opportunity to either leave the streets alone or leave me alone," Harmony said, turning her back towards Kilo so he wouldn't see the tears in her eyes. "What type of choice is that Harmony, huh? You telling me to choose between shit that's irrelevant! What am I 'pose to do, choose you over makin' money and go broke? Then what we gone do?" Kilo said. Kilo knew that he had more than enough money to leave the game alone and if he could, he would just to start a new life with Harmony and make things right, but he couldn't. He would have to forever sell drugs for Jose and his brother Pedro unless he was ready to meet death. "Keon, you don't have to sell drugs anymore. You have enough money saved and enough businesses opened to never have to work another day of your life," Harmony said. "So why would you continue to play with fire knowing that you will eventually burn yourself?" Harmony asked with tears running down her face. "I lost my daddy to the streets for fifteen years, and I'll be damned if I lose my man! Before I lose you to the system, I rather become friends now so I don't have to worry about it later." Kilo could feel where Harmony was coming from after losing her daddy for fifteen years to the prison system and not wanting to lose him. But there was a lot that she didn't know and probably wouldn't understand if Kilo explained to her that this was something that he *had* to do and not something he wanted to do. Kilo explained to Harmony the best way he could without letting her know that he was plugged into a Cartel and the only way out was death. "So you're going to choose the streets over our relationship? Is that what you're telling me, Keon? You're telling me all this time we've been together has been for nothing!" Harmony said, feeling like Kilo wasn't thinking about anybody but himself. "This time that we've been together hasn't been for nothing, Harmony. I love you and want to spend the rest of my life with you, but some things I have no control over," Kilo said, taking Harmony in his arms, letting her cry on his chest. "Listen boo, I hate that it comes down to this because I thought you and I would be together forever. I'm not going to be the one to make the decision to leave you and what we have. That's something you'll have to do 'cause like I've told you if I could just up and leave the game I would, but I can't. It's not that easy," Kilo told Harmony, holding her tight. Over the years, Kilo and Harmony grew a bond with each other that made them inseparable. Every event that Kilo attended, Harmony was right by his side and vice versa. Kilo was there for Harmony whenever she needed him. After Harmony had a miscarriage with Kilo's child a year ago, that seemed to have brought them closer. Now Harmony was thinking about what Kilo was telling her about not being able to leave the game and couldn't see why he couldn't when he was the boss of everything he did. Harmony still felt like Kilo was telling her that just because he wanted to continue making money off the drugs he sold. Harmony told Kilo that she would leave him if he didn't cut all ties to the drug game within the next two days. "I'm serious, Keon. If you don't tell me that you've gave the game up by Thursday, I'm gone," Harmony said. Kilo became agitated with Harmony's misunderstanding of him getting out the game and shot off on her, telling her that she might as well leave now then. "I've tried my best to explain to you that I can't just up and quit the game. This shit bigger than me. So if you gone leave Harmony, gone head and leave now because that's one thing that's not going to change." Harmony looked at Kilo with hurt in her eyes. "I wish you understood the situation, Harmony. I really do," Kilo said. "But I can see that you don't, so I want you to do whatever you feel is best for you." Just as all good things must come to an end one way or another, Harmony left. Kilo knew what type of girl Harmony was and knew his lifestyle wasn't the type of lifestyle she wanted for her man, so he didn't try to make her stay. Instead, Kilo told Harmony that he understood her reasons for not wanting to be in a relationship with somebody that's in the streets because anything could happen. "You will always be mine. You know that, right?" Kilo told Harmony before she left. Harmony looked at Kilo and smiled. "Always and forever . . ." Kilo and Harmony remained close friends after they split up. Harmony still came by to chill with Kilo from time to time, and Kilo chilled at Harmony's condo that he purchased for her across town. Kilo spent more than $30,000 furnishing the condo for Harmony and told her that she didn't have to pay her bills for as long as he lived. But Harmony didn't want to become dependent on Kilo taking care of her so she chose to pay her own bills. "What would I have to do with my life if I let you pay all my bills, Keon?" Harmony asked Kilo when he told her not to worry about her bills. "You can do whatever you want to do, but all you would 'have' to do is wake up in the morning," Kilo told her while they were sitting on the couch eating a meal that Harmony prepared. "I know you love me but dang, Mr. Kilo! We're not together anymore, and you want to take care of me still. And don't let me find out that you're afraid to stay at home now that I'm not there to protect you anymore," Harmony said. "I'm just saying doe you be at my crib more than you be at yours, nigga. What's up with that?" Harmony added, trying her best to sound project. "So you gone clown me like that, huh?" Kilo said, laughing at Harmony's joke because now that he thought about it, he stayed over her house like it's his. "If you wouldn't have left me, then we wouldn't have this problem, would we?" Kilo said. Harmony hated it when Kilo said things like that because she didn't leave him, he left her. Or at least that's how she felt. "What's up, Slim? Put a nigga on. I'm out here starvin'," One of the niggas said from the block as Slim pulled up to get Tila. "I'ma holla at you when I pull back up. I'm on something right now," Slim told him, unlocking the door for Tila. "Man, I'ma get me one of these soon as I get my money right. Watch!" Tila said, talking about Slim's Aston Martin. "You can get you two of these as long as you stay focused out here. But what's up? What you need to holla at me about?" Slim asked Tila, pulling off the block. Tila called Slim almost an hour ago and told him that he needed to holler at him when he got a chance. "I think it's 'bout time I switch my hustle up. I've been sellin' weed for a long time now. The money is cool, but I want some real money now. I want some fast money. This weed money is slow money," Tila told Slim. Slim listened to Tila and thought about how he and his niggas went from selling weed to selling cocaine. "Switchin' hustles will put you in a whole nother lane. You want the fast money, but fast money ain't always the best money. Sometimes it's best to stick with your same hustle because when a nigga get greedy that's when a nigga get popped!" Slim said. "I ain't getting greedy tho, Slim. I just think it's time for me to elevate to the next level of the game. I ain't tryna be sellin' weed all my life. I'm tryna stack me up some bread and leave the game alone one day," Tila said. "And I can't do that with this weed money. I mean fifty to sixty thou is cool, but it ain't enuff money to consider leaving the game with," Tila added. "Aite well, look, I'ma let you work out of one of my spots, so you won't have to do no block hustling," Slim told Tila, then pulled out his cell phone and called Benjamen and told him the business about putting Tila in the spot with him and Cutt. Benjamen said he was cool with that because now he could take some days off to blow some of the money he's made. "Aite, I'm on my way over there now," Slim said into the phone before he hung up. "I'm funa take you by the spot and let you meet Benjamen and Cutt, the niggas I got running it," Slim said. "You talkin' 'bout them same niggas you had working at the Fish Tank?" Tila asked, remembering

Benjamen's and Cutt's name but couldn't place their faces. Slim shut the Fish Tank down like a year ago when Ms. Coolwaters told Kilo that the police was onto that spot and opened another spot on the other side of town. "Yeah, it's them same niggas. You met them already?" Slim asked, grabbing the blunt that was in the ashtray, and handed it to Tila. "Fire that up." "I met them a few times a lil minute ago," Tila said, firing the blunt up. It took Slim maybe fifteen minutes to get to his new spot on the other part of town, and when they pulled up and went inside, Tila couldn't believe they were selling dope out the house. "Man, ya'll sellin' dope out of here? This spot looks better than the crib I'm livin' in," Tila said, looking around the house at all the expensive shit Slim had in there. "All this shit is just a throw off for the landlord and in case them boys in blue run up in here," Slim said. Tila thought that Slim was taking him to a spot where the junkies knocked on the door, came in, got served, and left. But from the type of neighborhood they were in, it didn't look like the type of neighborhood where junkies roamed. Benjamen and Cutt were sitting on a round leather sectional couch in the living room, playing Madden on the PlayStation 4. "What up, Tila?" Cutt said, sitting the PlayStation controller down. "What up, nigga?" Tila said back, giving Cutt some dap. "So you ready to get this money or what?" Cutt said. "Yeah, I'm tired of playin'. Why stall when I can ball with the big dogs." And ball with the big dogs was what Tila did. Slim made it to where all Tila had to do was answer the phone and weigh dope up. Tila was making more money in a day than he did in a week selling weed. After two months of working in the spot with Benjamen and Cutt, Tila went and paid cash for a Dodge Challenger that was super charged and gave one of his homeboys his Grand Marquis. "That's from me to you," Tila told him. Slim taught Tila everything he knew about cocaine. He taught him how to cut and cook it even though they didn't sell crack, only cocaine. "Ain't no tellin' when you might need to cook up some coke. I still cook from time to time," Slim told Tila, sticking a Pyrex jar in the boiling hot water on the stove. Slim made turning cocaine to crack look easy. "It's all in ya wrist. Like Jeezy said, you want the real bread it's all about yo whip game." It took Tila a few times of messing up over the stove before he got it right and once he did, he was like Chef Boy RD in the kitchen. Tila would cook a nine piece and bring back eleven zips then front the dope to his homeboy who sold dope on the block rock for rock. The way Tila moved reminded Slim of himself when he first started to come up selling dope. Slim looked at Tila as his lil brother and treated him like a brother too. Slim made Tila finish school and go get his licenses a long time ago. "I can't have no dummy riding 'round wreckless with me," Slim told Tila a few years back. "Baby, I'll be back later on. Me and Kenya is about to go do a little shopping before the boys get home from school," Ivonne told Slim who was lying on the couch, daydreaming. "Aite boo, be careful." After Ivonne left, Slim called Kilo to see what he was doing. "I ain't doing shit just chilling, rolling me one up getting ready to watch this game. What's up?" Kilo asked Slim. "Not shit bored to death. Who playin'?" "The Steelers and the Broncos. You know we 'bout to stomp that ass out," Kilo said. Kilo wasn't a sports fanatic, but anytime the Steelers was playing, he was sitting right in front of somebody's TV, watching them play. "Ion know about that one, fool. Ya'll secondary ain't lookin' too good. Everybody hurt," Slim said. Slim was just the opposite of Kilo when it came to sports. Slim loved sports and sounded like a commentator once he got to talking about which team did what and who's who. "I got a light grand we come out on top at the end of the fourth quarter," Kilo said. "They playin' in Denver, right? Shid bet! That's easy money. Matter fact, I got ten g's to yo five that we come out on top," Slim said, challenging Kilo. "You must think them Steelers pussy or sumthing talkin' 'bout you got ten g's to my five we lose. Nigga bet!" Kilo said, firing his blunt up. "Where you at, fool? I'm funa come watch the game with you so I can see the look on yo face at the end of the fourth quarter," Slim said, getting off the couch and sliding his shirt back on. "I'm at the crib. Bring yo ass on over here and stop and holler at Big Ed on yo way. That nigga still owe me a zip of kush anyway," Kilo told Slim before he hung up. After getting the weed from Big Ed, Slim had to call Kilo back to see which crib he was at because Kilo owned a house on every part of town. After stopping to get some gas, Slim pulled up to Kilo's six-bedroom mini mansion that had everything from a pool in the backyard to a movie theater and was let into the gate by a push of a button that Kilo pushed from the inside of the house. "What up, fool? You get that sack from Big Ed?" Kilo asked Slim as he let him in the house. "Yeah, I got it. That nigga told me to tell you that he 'preciate what you done for him. And that he got some OG kush on the way from Cali. Said he gone call you soon as he get it," Slim said, walking into the house. "Some OG kush? So what we been smokin', some baby loc Kush?" Kilo said, chuckling. "Come check out this ceiling I had installed in the den, fool. This bitch hard!" Kilo bragged. Kilo had a transparent ceiling built in the den so he could look up and see everything that was going on in the living room. The first thing Slim said when he looked up and saw the ceiling was "Man, this shit looks like something you see in a movie. What's that I'm looking at the living room?" Slim asked, wondering how much Kilo spent on the transparent ceiling. "Yeah, that's the living you lookin' at from the den, my nigga! What you know 'bout that?" Kilo said, looking up through the ceiling. "I can't lie you killed it with the see-through ceiling, but I gotta know what's the reason for it?" Slim asked. "I did that so I can look up and make sure ain't no stealing going on while my money getting counted. I had them bitches up there last week. You should have see all the ass and titties bouncing!" Kilo laughed. "Man, you crazy! You had some hoes up there naked for real?" "Hell yeah! Just because them hoes naked don't mean they can't roll up $10,000 and stuff it up their pussy. I don't trust nothin'!" Kilo said seriously. "The game is on tho, nigga. I ain't tryna do no mo rappin' 'bout no bitch countin money 'cause I'm about to be countin' yours, my nigga!" Kilo and Slim sat and watched the first half of the game, smoking and talking shit with Kilo talking the most shit because of the Steelers being up 24–10. "You know it's over, right?" Kilo said. "Nawl, it ain't over yet, my nigga. We still got another half left fool," Slim said. "What you got to eat in this, bitch? I'm starvin'." "It's all type of shit in there but you gone have to help yoself ain't no maids over here," Kilo said to Slim who was halfway out the den, heading to the kitchen. Slim came back into the den, holding a plate with two turkey sandwiches with everything from lettuce to tomatoes on them and in the other hand, he was holding a two-liter Dr Pepper and a big bag of sour cream onion chips with his teeth. "You made you a real snack, didn't you?" Kilo chuckled, seeing Slim carrying all that food. "I told you I was hungry, fool. I started to stick some of that meat that's in the freezer on that George Foreman grill you got up there, but it wasn't unthawed," Slim said, letting the big bag of chips fall on the couch from out his mouth. "Lemme get a piece of one of them sandwiches. You got them looking to good!" Kilo told Slim, breaking a piece of Slim's turkey sandwich. At the end of the third quarter, the Steelers was up 35–21 and had the ball on the twenty-yard line with another chance to score. "A Slim, do me a favor and have that ten thou in singles for me so I can make it rain this weekend," Kilo said after the Steelers scored a touchdown, making the score 42–21. "Shit, it ain't over with yet, my nigga. It's still seven minutes and some change left on the clock. That's too much time to give Denver. Watch. They funa turn all the way up!" Slim said. And they did too. The Steelers kicked the ball off, and Denver ran it back for a touchdown, then turned around and got the ball back with an onside kick and scored again, making the score 42–35. "I told you it wasn't over yet, nigga! A Kilo, do me a favor and have them five g's in fives so I can pass them out to the kids on the block," Slim said, mimicking Kilo, laughing. "Nigga, this shit's over with. We funa answer to all that lucky-ass shit ya'll just pulled." Kilo said, slick hot at the Steelers for letting Denver come back like that. The game winded up going into overtime with the score 42–42. "May the best team win," Slim said. "And we just won!" Kilo said after the Steelers won the toss. "Pay me my money," Kilo yelled, clapping his hands as the Steelers drove the ball down the field. First and ten, the Steelers went for the in zone and threw an interception and the Broncos took and drove the ball all the way back up the field and kicked a field goal to win the game. "I told you, boy! Them Broncos ain't to be fucked with, nigga! I won. Give me my money," Slim said, sounding like Smokey on Friday. "Man, that's some bullshit! This nigga threw an interception at the end of the game. What type of shit is that?" Kilo snapped. "I told you ya'll wasn't ready for them but you wanna be hardheaded. Now cough them chips up, nigga! I don't wanna hear all that whining you doing, my nigga." Slim chilled at Kilo's house for another hour or so before he left and headed over to his mother's restaurant and bumped into Jazmine on his way in. "What's up, Ms. Jaz? Long time no see or speak. Where you been at?" Slim said, giving Jazmine a hug. Jazmine still took on hits for Kilo and them whenever they needed her to, but when she wasn't on a mission for them, she was out of town somewhere on a vacation. "Heey, Slim!" Jazmine said, excited to see Slim. "I just came back from Kansas City, visiting my aunt. How have you been?" Jazmine asked Slim, sitting back down. Kilo and Slim still took care of

Jazmine even when they didn't have a job for her. "I'm good just tryna stay a step ahead at all times. You know me," Slim said. Slim sat and talked with Jazmine for a little while then hollered at his momma before he headed home. The next morning Quick and Kilo were knocking at Slim's door, telling him that Fresh was in the hospital laid up from some gunshot wounds. "Some gunshot wounds? When this happen?" Slim said, letting Kilo and Quick in. "I'm thinking sometime last night or either this morning. His baby mama called and told me about it this morning," Kilo said. "Where was he at?" Slim asked, standing in the living room in nothing but some Gucci pajama pants and house shoes on. "Somewhere in Tennessee. He told me that he was 'pose to be hooking up with some niggas from Nashville to serve them some work last week, so I'm guessing he took that trip," Kilo said, pulling out his cell phone to call Mikayla, Fresh's baby mama, back. "We 'bout to fly down there. You going?" Quick asked Slim. "What time does the flight leave? Do I have enuff time to take a ten-minute shower right quick?" Slim asked, hoping that Fresh was okay. "The next flight leaves in an hour, so hurry up!" Quick said. After Slim showered and got dressed, they all hopped in Quick's Cadillac truck and made their way to the airport. "Man, I hope this nigga aite," Slim said again once the plane landed in Nashville. "I talked to Mikayla. She said that he got hit six times, but he's doin' okay," Kilo said once they got to Vanderbilt Hospital where Fresh was. They caught the elevator to the fourth floor and then did a complete circle, looking for room 1716. "Excuse me, Miss. We're lookin for room 1716. Could you point us in the right direction please?" Kilo said, stopping a nurse that was headed in the opposite direction. "You're on the wrong floor, baby. Room 1716 is on the fifth floor," The nurse said. They rode the elevator up one more floor and found the room at the end of the hallway and knocked on the door. Mikayla opened the door, looking like she just got done crying. "What's up, Mikayla? You don't look like you're doing too good. You aite?" Kilo asked. "Yes, I'm fine. I just haven't gotten much rest, but he's in there, resting now. The nurse said that he would have to be here another week before they are able to release him," Mikayla said, opening the door farther so they were able to get in. "Everything's gone be aite, Mikayla." Slim said, giving her a hug. "God got him." Seeing Fresh laid up in the hospital bed with tubes pumping fluids into his body angered Kilo. As they stood over Fresh, watching him breath in and out, no words were needed from Kilo, Quick, or Slim to describe the feelings they were feeling. "How long has he been sleep?" Kilo asked Mikayla who was sitting in a chair off to the side. "He fell asleep right after I got off the phone with you. He should be ready to wake up. The nurse will be in here in a little while to check his vital signs and all that other stuff they do," Mikayla said, holding back tears. The nurse came in and checked on Fresh and said that everything was looking just fine then left right back out. Fresh opened his eyes and cracked a dry smile not too long after the nurse left. "How long ya'll been here?" Fresh asked slowly and in a voice that was scratchy. "A few hours. You sound bad. You want some water?" Kilo asked Fresh who was trying to sit up. Fresh nodded, and Mikayla left out to go get the water for Fresh then came back, gave it to him and left back out so they could have some privacy. "What's up, Fresh? How you feeling, fool?" Quick asked. "I'm blessed. Them niggas tried to kill me. Four to the chest and two in the stomach," Fresh said, wincing from the pain." Who is them niggas?" Kilo asked, ready to make bloodshed all over the streets in Nashville. Fresh told them that he knew who the niggas were but didn't want to say any names until he was able to leave the hospital. "I wouldn't feel right letting ya'll kill them niggas without me being there," Fresh said, laying back on the hospital bed. Slim told Fresh that he didn't have to lift a finger. "All you have to do is say a name and they're dead." Fresh wasn't trying to hear that. He was determined to be there when the niggas that put him in the hospital got what they had coming to them. "Puttin' them niggas six feet under is the only thing that will relax me. They tried to kill me over some crumbs. Thirty-six zips of soft," Fresh said then took another sip of water. "What the fuck is you doing way down there serving a nigga a brick of cocaine anyway?" Kilo asked. Fresh then explained to them that he was down there dropping off more than one brick and got greedy. "I got some niggas on the west side buying twenty of them, and before I got to them, I bumped into some other nigga talking 'bout he trying to buy two bricks. So I go to the room cut and stretch the twenty bricks to get two more to serve the nigga I met, and he winded up robbin' and shootin' a nigga." They all sat perfectly still, listening to Fresh telling them what happened. "If you just met the nigga, how do you know him?" Slim asked. Fresh leaned up and looked toward the door to make sure Mikayla wasn't in the room then told them that he had a broad with him that he was fucking down here that knew the niggas. Fresh was discharged from the hospital in a wheelchair four days after the shooting and was ready to murder something that night, but Kilo wouldn't let him. "You at least gotta give yo wounds a few days to heal," Kilo told him. Fresh and Mikayla laid up in a hotel room for two days exactly before Fresh who was limping badly told Kilo that tonight he was riding out with or without them. "Them niggas gone die tonight! I ain't waiting no longer. I got shit to do. I ain't funa be lyin' 'round here, tryin' to fully recuperate from slugs. Shit, I'm well enuff to pull a trigga!" Fresh told Kilo, Slim and Quick who were all in his hotel room. "Well, tonight is the night then," Kilo said. And that night was the night Fresh called the broad he was fucking that lived in Nashville and got the 411 on the niggas that robbed and shot him. Kilo, Quick and Slim flew to Nashville and rocked the niggas to sleep then flew back to Ohio like nothing ever happened. It took Fresh over seven months to get back to normal, and the whole time he was recovering, Mikayla was right there by his side showing him that she cared. Kilo, Slim and Quick would stop by from time to time to smoke and kick the shit with him since he was on bed rest and wasn't moving around like he used to. "Don't tell me you let those six shots knock the fight outta you, fool," Kilo said one day while he was chilling with Fresh over Mikayla's house. "Nawl, ain't no bullets stopping me. I'ma die hard like Bruce Willis," Fresh told Kilo.

Chapter 17: Four Years Later

After counting out more than $20 million in cash, Slim felt content with what he had gained from the dope game and was ready to do something different with his life. Slim would sit up all times of the night, talking to Ivonne about the things he wanted to do. "I know it's easier said than done, but why don't you just quit what you're doing and follow your dreams, baby?" Ivonne would ask Slim, and Slim would give her the same answer every time, which was "I'on know." One summer, while Slim and Kilo were sitting in Kilo's private jet, heading to Los Angeles to the BET Awards, Slim bought up the subject of leaving the game alone to see how Kilo felt about it. "As bad as I want to leave the game Slim, I know I can't. José wasn't playing when he said the only way out was death. And you know like I know that you can only run for so long from a Cartel," Kilo told him. "You thinking 'bout given it up or something?" Slim let out a breath of air. "Yeah, man. I've been thinking about it. I mean there's got to be more to life than this. True enuff, we got the power and money to do whatever we want, but I just feel like something's missing," Slim said, staring out the window of the private jet. "I feel what you saying homie, because I've laid in bed plenty of nights asking myself, *'What's next?'* I got everything I could ever dream of. I mean what else could I ask for? I counted out $40 million last year, and that's not including the money from my business. That was all dope money," Kilo said. "I been thinking about getting away from all this bullshit. I'm starting to feel as if I'm living a fairy-tale life or something. Like money is the only reason I'm living for. For the last six or seven years, I've woke up with the same agenda. Now I'm feeling like I want something different. I'm tired of killing my people. I was thinking about moving to the Motherland, somewhere like Kenya. To help my people instead of hurting them," Slim said, speaking his true feelings. Kilo felt where Slim was coming from after going through everything he's been through because of the dope game and told Slim that he will always support him in whatever he did. "But before you just up and leave the game, holla at Pedro first and let him know what's up. He shouldn't trip since it's only you that's tryna make an exit." After their flight to and from the BET Awards, Kilo stopped by Kenya's house to see his son and was so tired from the jet ride that he winded up falling asleep over there that night. Kilo and Kenya sat up all night talking about their relationship and getting back together. Kenya told Kilo how sorry she was and that she promised not to let anything like that happen again. "Please give me another chance, Kilo. I need you, and so does your son. I know I've made a mistake, and I'm dealing with the consequences every day I wake up without you in my life," Kenya told Kilo. Kenya haven't had sex since Justice, and that was over seven years ago. She told herself that if it wasn't Kilo she was having sex with, then she would go without. "Give me some time to think about it, boo," Kilo told Kenya. Kenya leaned in and gave Kilo a kiss on the lips and one thing led to another and before Kilo realized what was going on, Kenya was on top of him in his favorite position, riding the shit out of him. That's how he really winded up falling asleep over there. Kilo woke up to his son hitting him on the chest. "Daddy, Daddy, Daddy! Are you living with me and Mommy again?" Lil Kilo asked, happy to see his daddy lying in the bed with his momma. Kilo opened his eyes and looked around. *'Damn, I thought I was dreaming,'* Kilo thought then sat up. Not wanting to answer his son's question, Kilo said, "Where's Mommy at?" "Her in the kitchen, making breakfast," Lil Kilo said, pointing behind him. Kilo got out the bed and slid his socks, pants, and shoes on. "Go get Daddy's shirt off the couch," Kilo told his son who flew out the room full speed to get his daddy's shirt and could be heard all the way down the hall yelling, "Mommy, my daddy up, my daddy up!" Kilo walked into Kenya's bathroom that was connected to her room to take a piss and washed his face. After flushing the toilet, Kilo opened the bathroom closet to get a rag and was surprised at what he saw. On all the shelves in the closet besides the ones on the side, Kenya had pictures of him and her in frames. Kilo stood there for a few minutes, looking at the pictures, reminiscing on the times he shared with Kenya. Hearing his son run back into the room, Kilo grabbed a face cloth and an extra toothbrush from off one of the side shelves and shut the closet back. "Here go your shirt, Daddy!" Lil Kilo said, holding Kilo's shirt out. "Set it on Mommy's bed for me while I brush my teeth and wash my face." Lil Kilo flew out the bathroom and set the shirt down then came right back in the bathroom, asking all types of questions. After Kilo finished brushing his teeth and answering questions, he and Lil Kilo made their way downstairs to the kitchen where Kenya was humming Mary J's "25/8" song and cooking Kilo's favorite. "I see you haven't forgot how to whip my favorite breakfast," Kilo said, sneaking up on Kenya who seemed to be happier than ever. "How could I when ya'll two knuckleheads have the same taste buds? Everything you ate, he eats," Kenya said, cracking an egg open. "This house is bigger than I thought. I didn't know you had a bathroom connected to your room," Kilo said, trying to give Kenya a hint that he had seen the pictures of them she had in the closet. But Kenya was still gloating from last night, so she didn't catch on. "You bought it and inspected it before we moved in, so you should remember how big it is. I asked you what was me and Keon supposed to do with a four-bedroom house before you bought it," Kenya said. "Now go have a seat at the table the food is done." After eating and playing with his son for a little while, Kilo told Kenya that he was about to leave. "I got some bizniz to handle. I'll call and check on ya'll later on," Kilo said, grabbing his cell phone off the table. "Okay baby, we love you!" Kenya said. "I love ya'll too," Kilo said, hugging Lil Kilo then stood up and hugged and kissed Kenya. On his way home, Kilo called Quick and asked him if he had been by the spot to see if Pedro's shipment of cocaine came this morning. "Yeah, I went by there this morning. I've been tryin' to call you, but you ain't been answering. You aite?" Quick asked. "Yeah, I'm straight. So is everything a go with the bizniz?" Kilo said, asking Quick if the shipment was there. "Yeah, everything's there. I did the inventory myself," Quick said. "Aite well, check this out. I'm 'bout to swing by my crib right quick to wash my ass, so give me an hour then meet me at the spot. Cool?" Kilo said, getting off the interstate. "Aite bet! Just hit me when you're ready," Quick said then hung up. Quick was on his way to meet Maria at a five-star restaurant for lunch when Kilo called, so he continued on his way, hoping that Kilo wouldn't call until after he and Maria were done eating. After Quick and Maria finished eating, Quick walked Maria to her car. "What time are you getting off tonight?" Quick said, leaning against Maria's car hugging her. "Probably around seven. Why?" Maria asked. "Just asking. I didn't think lawyers worked so late. What you putting in over time or something?" Quick asked Maria. It took some time, but Quick finally got Maria to put her guard down around him and show him her affectionate side. "I'm not a lawyer. I'm a paralegal. There's a difference. I've told you that once!" "I know. I just like hearing you say, 'I'm not a lawyer. I'm a paralegal,'" Quick said, trying to mock Maria's Pueto Rican accent. "I told you about making fun of me," Maria said, punching Quick playfully in the chest. "Now move before you make me late for work!" Maria tried to move Quick out the way so she could get in her car, but she wasn't strong enough. Quick looked at his watch and said, "You still got fifteen minutes before you have to clock back in, and your office building ain't but two minutes away, so come again!" "Well," Maria started to say. "Well what?" Quick cut her off. "I tell you what, give me a kiss and I'll move," Quick said. Maria stood on her tiptoes and tongued Quick down. Quick was stunned. "Was that enough to move you?" Maria said, smiling. That was the first time Maria used her tongue to kiss Quick. Normally, it's a peck on the lips. "Why you looking so shocked?" Maria questioned. "Because I am. Where did that come from? You ain't never kissed me like that," Quick said, feeling his phone vibrate in his pocket. "There's a first time for everything. Call me tonight, and there will be a first time for something else," Maria said, getting into her car and pulling off. "Hello," Quick said, picking up his phone. "Meet me at the spot." It was Kilo on the other end of his phone. "I'm on my way now," Quick said, pulling out the parking lot of the five-star restaurant. It took Quick maybe fifteen minutes to get to the spot from the restaurant, and when he was pulling up, Kilo was also pulling up. "Perfect timing," Kilo said, giving Quick some dap. "What's up with you and all this smiling tho, my nigga?" Kilo asked Quick. "Man, I ain't gone lie. A kiss got me smilin' like this," Quick said as Kilo was unlocking the door to the spot. "A kiss? Nigga, you talkin' 'bout a kiss kiss, or is that a code word for something else?" Kilo said, opening the door. Quick laughed. "Yeah, nigga, a kiss!" "Who you kiss, Beyonce or somebody fool? 'Cause the way you smiling, it showl seem like it," Kilo said. Quick told Kilo who it was that had him feeling himself and Kilo couldn't believe it.

"What! If she got you smilin' from ear to ear over a kiss, I wonder how you be after ya'll get through fuckin'," Kilo said, clowning Quick. "That's the thing. I still haven't fucked her yet. She was on that boogee shit at first, but it's going down tonight, nigga!" Quick said, imagining what Maria looked like naked. "I thought you would've been hit that as long as ya'll been talkin'. But forget all that. Let's handle our biz so we can get outta here. This my last time being around all these bricks too. A thousand kilos of pure uncut, shid the judge gone put a nigga under the jail!" Kilo said. "I was thinkin' that the last shipment. This what them niggas get paid to do," Quick said. While Kilo and Quick were handling their business, Kilo asked Quick the same thing Slim asked him about leaving the game. "What made you ask me that?" Quick asked Kilo. "Me and Slim had this conversation a few days ago, and I was just seeing how you felt about it," Kilo said. "Like I said homie, I don't plan to leave the game anytime soon. I think I'ma sell drugs for as long as I live, fool. But you know, to each his own. I'ma hustle till I can't hustle no mo!" Kilo could feel where Quick was coming from. But he also felt where Slim was coming from to because even though he loved to hustle, he knew there was more to life than the streets. "I feel you, fool. Now let's get outta here. Everything's here," Kilo said. After leaving the spot, Kilo called Fresh. "What's up, nigga? Where you at?" "I'm leaving Ms. Cook's. Why what's up?" Fresh, said getting into his Benz coupe. "I wanna holla at you about something. Where you headed?" Kilo asked. "Over Mikayla's house to drop these plates off. What's up? Everything aite, ain't it?" Fresh asked. "Yeah, everything's good. I'm just tryna see where yo head at about something, that's all. I'ma meet you over Mikayla's house, so if you get there before me, wait on me," Kilo said then hung up. Kilo pulled up over Mikayla's house and hollered at Fresh about the same thing he talked to Slim and Quick about. Leaving the game. "So what you think about it?" Kilo asked him. "I don't plan on giving the game up. Shid for what? The game's been good to me. I counted out over $10 million and probably spent that times ten since I've been hustling. So why would I quit?" Fresh said without putting too much thought into his answer, which made Kilo wonder if Fresh would try to leave the game once he heard that Slim was trying to get out. After talking to Fresh, Kilo swung by the studio to see what Streetz had going on. "I ain't smoked nothin' all day! What ya'll smokin' on up in here?" Kilo asked Kellz who was sitting behind the computer, mixing a song Streetz just dropped. "It's a zip of dro sitting on that stool in the booth where Streetz at. Tell that nigga hand it to ya," Kellz said. Kilo grabbed the weed from out the booth, then sat on the couch behind Kellz and rolled one up, listening to Streetz spit punch line after punch line. "That nigga 'bout ready to drop a album, ain't he?" Kilo said, firing his blunt up. "Streetz said he was working on another mixtape to drop with DJ Drama," Kellz told Kilo. Streetz had the streets on lock with the rap game. Every show sold out no matter what city he performed in. "Yeah, a Gangsta Grillz would have the streets going crazy," Kilo said, then got up and went into his office in the back of the studio. Sitting behind his desk, Kilo zoned out, thinking about Slim and everything he said about getting out the game. Kilo thought about how Pedro might take it and what Jose would have to say about it because they both told them the outcome of getting out the game before they started. Kilo replayed the conversations he had with Jose while he was in prison over and over in his head. "The only way out is death," Kilo kept hearing Jose say. All Kilo could do was hope that Jose and Pedro showed Slim some type of mercy on getting out the game because if they took Slim's life, then they would have to take his as well because Kilo made a vow to himself that if Jose and Pedro took his homeboy life, then he would surely come at them with his guns blazing—no questions asked.

Chapter 18

Zipping Ivonne's Fendi suitcase with $10 million in cash in it, Slim kissed Ivonne on the forehead and told her that he would be back. "Okay, baby, I'll be here when you get back," Ivonne told Slim. Slim was on his way to talk to Pedro about getting out the game so that he and Ivonne could start their lives over. Ivonne had everything set and ready to go for them. All they had to do was board the plane in the morning and the rest is history. Ivonne bought them a house in Kenya, so once they got there they wouldn't have to go looking for a place to stay or in a hotel until they found one. Slim called Kilo on his way to talk to Pedro to let him know that it was all or nothing for him. "I'm on my way to holla at P now to let him know what's up," Slim told Kilo. "Where ya'll meetin' at? Is he in town?" Kilo asked. "Yeah, he in town. We meetin' at the Hyatt downtown," Slim said, putting his phone on speakerphone so he could fire a cigarette up. "Do you want me to meet you there for just-in-case purposes?" Kilo asked. "Nawl, I'm straight fool. I gotta good feelin' he gone fuck with a nigga since it's just me and not the squad that's tryin' to leave," Slim said. "Aite, but where is you and Ivonne headed to afterwards? I know ya'll ain't staying here starting ya'll life over," Kilo said, wanting to know where Slim was moving to. "Nawl, we moving to Kenya. We gone open up a nonprofit organization to help the poor families that's in need of a lil assistance. You feel me?" Slim said. "Yeah, I feel ya, homie. That's real nigga shit. You gotta heart of gold. Most niggas don't think that deep. They're not thinkin' about their people that's suffering in other parts of the world. I respect everything you're doin'. If you ever need me for anything, I'm here." Slim hung up with Kilo and pulled up to the Hyatt Hotel where he was meeting Pedro. *'Here it is. All or nothing,'* Slim thought to himself, then got out his car and grabbed the suitcase out the trunk, and made his way into the lobby then up to the top floor to room 399. Sitting the suitcase down, Slim knocked on the door and was let in by one of Pedro's henchmen. After Slim was searched, he was then led into the room where Pedro was sitting at a table with two more of his men standing on either side of him. "Slim, come in my friend," Pedro said, looking at the suitcase Slim brought in suspiciously. "Would you like something to drink?" Pedro asked Slim. "Nawl, I'm good. 'Preciate it tho. I came to discuss more important matters," Slim said then sat down at the table across from Pedro. Pedro's next words surprised Slim. "I know why you came, my friend. Trust me. Now have a drink with me and tell me why," Pedro said, pouring Slim some liquor in one of the two glasses that were sitting on the table. Slim looked at Pedro as if to say, "Are you sure you know why I came?" While Slim was meeting with Pedro, Quick was on his way to Cincinnati to holler at some of his people who were trying to cop some work but were cut off and blocked in getting off the interstate. Two black vans with black tinted windows blocked him in, and two men wearing masks holding AK-47s hopped out each van. "What the fuck!" Was all Quick could say as the masked men pulled him out his car. "This ain't got nothing to do with trying to get more cocaine, Pedro. It's the opposite," Slim told Pedro. "Slim, my friend, don't worry I know everything. I just want to know why," Pedro said, taking a sip of liquor from his shot glass. Fresh was leaving the jewelry store, spending a little over eighty grand on a new chain he had custom made, when he got picked up by two masked men holding assault rifles. Slim sat there for a second, trying to figure out just how much Pedro knew. For some reason, Slim felt that Pedro already knew the reason he was there so instead of playing with Pedro's intelligence, Slim didn't cut any corners in telling Pedro what he was trying to do. "I don't know how you know about this already Pedro, but you seem to, so I'ma keep it real with you," Slim said then downed the rest of the liquor that was in his glass. "I want to get out the game. I don't have the passion for this shit like I did seven years ago when we first started moving kilos for the Cartel. I'm tryna do something different with my life. I feel it's more to life than this, so I'm coming to you as a man telling you that I'm done with the game. It's just me that's leaving. Kilo and them will still be doing their thang for you, but I'm out. I bought you $10 million in cash to show you my apperception," Slim said, opening his suitcase, showing Pedro the money. Pedro's phone started ringing.

"Give me a minute," Pedro said. Pedro answered the phone and said something in Spanish that Slim didn't understand. Pedro hung up and nodded at the same henchman that opened the door for Slim, and the henchman went into the other room to do something. "So what's up, Pedro? Let me know something," Slim said, leaning forward putting his arms on the table while Pedro was explaining to Slim that he would have to talk things over with Jose before he could okay anything. Kilo was getting hog tied and threw into a van in the airport parking lot. "When do you think you'll be able to holla at him 'cause me and my family plan to take off tomorrow?" Slim said before he was snatched up from behind and forced to the ground by two of Pedro's henchman. "What the fuck is this about, Pedro?" Slim said before his mouth was taped shut and his hands and feet were tied up. A half hour later, Kilo, Quick and Fresh were dragged into the room with blindfolds over their eyes, their mouths taped, and their hands and feet tied. Nobody knowing where they were but Slim. Kilo thought about that dream he had a few years ago and felt that he was experiencing some type of déjà vu. After he was tossed against something hard and sat there for almost an hour, all types of stuff ran through Kilo's head. The only thing he kept thinking was Ms. Coolwaters setting him up since he cut her off from the team last week for not providing him with information that he didn't already know. Everything Ms. Coolwaters told Kilo he knew already, which made her of no value to him. *'I'm gone kill that bitch,'* Kilo thought to himself. Fresh and Quick had no earthly idea what or who was behind this. All they knew was they got kidnapped. Pedro signaled for his henchmen to lift the blindfolds from their eyes. Kilo's blindfold was the last to be lifted, and since he was blindfolded for longer than two hours, it took a minute for his pupils to dilate to the bright lights in the room and when they did, Kilo knew it was over.

To Be Continued